Lucy King spent ~~glamorous and e~~ when she really ~~attention to her~~ dream world for ever, she ~~ever~~ degree in languages and an eclectic collection of jobs. After a decade in southwest Spain, Lucy now lives with her young family in Wiltshire, England. When not writing, or trying to think up new and innovative things to do with mince, she spends her time reading, failing to finish cryptic crosswords and dreaming of the golden beaches of Andalusia.

Jackie Ashenden writes dark, emotional stories, with alpha heroes who've just got the world to their liking only to have it blown wide apart by their kick-ass heroines. She lives in Auckland, New Zealand, with her husband—the inimitable Dr Jax—two kids and two rats. When she's not torturing alpha males and their gutsy heroines she can be found drinking chocolate martinis, reading anything she can lay her hands on, wasting time on social media or being forced to go mountain biking with her husband. To keep up to date with Jackie's new releases and other news sign up to her newsletter at jackieashenden.com.

Also by Lucy King

Stranded with My Forbidden Billionaire

Passionately Ever After... collection

Undone by Her Ultra-Rich Boss

Heirs to a Greek Empire miniseries

Virgin's Night with the Greek

Also by Jackie Ashenden

The Maid the Greek Married

Three Ruthless Kings miniseries

Wed for Their Royal Heir
Her Vow to Be His Desert Queen
Pregnant with Her Royal Boss's Baby

Discover more at millsandboon.co.uk.

A CHRISTMAS CONSEQUENCE FOR THE GREEK

LUCY KING

HIS INNOCENT UNWRAPPED IN ICELAND

JACKIE ASHENDEN

MILLS & BOON

All rights reserved including the right of reproduction in whole or in part in any form. This edition is published by arrangement with Harlequin Enterprises ULC.

This is a work of fiction. Names, characters, places, locations and incidents are purely fictional and bear no relationship to any real life individuals, living or dead, or to any actual places, business establishments, locations, events or incidents. Any resemblance is entirely coincidental.

This book is sold subject to the condition that it shall not, by way of trade or otherwise, be lent, resold, hired out or otherwise circulated without the prior consent of the publisher in any form of binding or cover other than that in which it is published and without a similar condition including this condition being imposed on the subsequent purchaser.

® and TM are trademarks owned and used by the trademark owner and/or its licensee. Trademarks marked with ® are registered with the United Kingdom Patent Office and/or the Office for Harmonisation in the Internal Market and in other countries.

First published in Great Britain 2023
by Mills & Boon, an imprint of HarperCollins*Publishers* Ltd,
1 London Bridge Street, London, SE1 9GF

www.harpercollins.co.uk

HarperCollins*Publishers*, Macken House, 39/40 Mayor Street Upper,
Dublin 1, D01 C9W8, Ireland

A Christmas Consequence for the Greek © 2023 Lucy King

His Innocent Unwrapped in Iceland © 2023 Jackie Ashenden

ISBN: 978-0-263-30703-0

11/23

MIX
Paper | Supporting
responsible forestry
FSC™ C007454

This book is produced from independently certified FSC™ paper
to ensure responsible forest management.
For more information visit: www.harpercollins.co.uk/green.

Printed and Bound in the UK using 100% Renewable Electricity
at CPI Group (UK) Ltd, Croydon, CR0 4YY

A CHRISTMAS CONSEQUENCE FOR THE GREEK

LUCY KING

MILLS & BOON

CHAPTER ONE

'I KNOW YOU have an aversion to mixing business with pleasure,' Zander Stanhope murmured into Mia Halliday's ear as she handed him a coupe glass filled with raspberry and champagne posset and resisted the ever-present urge to climb him like a tree, 'because you've mentioned it countless times over the last four months. But as of two a.m. tonight, when this club closes and the party's over, you no longer work for me. Just a thought.'

With a smouldering smile, his eyes glinting wickedly, Zander straightened and turned to stride off, all towering height, broad shoulders and athletic grace. Mia just stood there and stared at his retreating figure, struck dumb by his observation and frozen to the spot between a ball-juggling clown and an impossibly bendy fire-eater.

Her mind raced as she watched him sink onto a purple velvet banquette between two of his siblings and begin to make quick work of the dessert. Her heart pounded and her blood heated as his words and their implication sank in.

Just a thought.

The man was a menace, she reflected, pulling herself together to navigate the obstacle course of scantily clad dancers atop podiums, magicians, acrobats, feathers and bubbles that led from louche sensuality to the welcome clinical soullessness of the kitchen. A tall, dark, gorgeous menace.

They'd met back in June, shortly after he'd contacted her to request her catering services at the party he was throwing to celebrate his thirty-fifth birthday.

Initially, she'd thought the call some kind of bizarre prank because why would a half-Greek, half-British shipping and banking tycoon who regularly graced the pages of both the financial and tabloid press be calling *her*? Halliday Catering was growing and gaining a reputation for being fresh and innovative, certainly, but it did not yet cater to members of the elite world in which he operated.

Once she'd got over her shock and disbelief, she'd been ridiculously flattered when he'd told her that he'd read an article about her in a magazine and had instantly determined that no one else would do. She'd fizzled with excitement at the realisation that his influence might lead to a stampede of his well-heeled friends and acquaintances to her door, thereby securing the future of her business.

Because she tended to liaise with clients remotely in the early stages of planning an event, she never imagined that two days later he'd turn up at her premises on an industrial estate in east London to discuss the menu *in person*. At no point had she considered that, having done so, he'd bowl her over so thoroughly with his devastating looks and powerful presence that, from that point on, all she'd be able to think about when it came to him was sex.

Inconveniently, however, that was precisely what had happened.

Without so much as a text to inform her of his intentions, he'd strolled into her unit that afternoon and every one of her senses had switched to high alert. She'd instinctively looked up and then shot to her feet, as if her computer had given her an electric shock. She'd placed her hand in his and gazed dazedly into eyes the colour of cocoa while he'd introduced himself in deep faintly accented tones that oozed through her like warm golden syrup, and she'd been immediately gripped by an attraction that had turned out to be fierce and unrelenting.

In the weeks that followed, whenever an email dropped into her inbox, her heart skipped a beat. At the sight of his name flashing up on her phone her mouth dried and her head swam. In preparation for each of their three working lunches, she'd taken extra care with her clothes and make-up, even as she'd berated herself for her vanity.

It hadn't helped that he'd made no secret of his attraction to her, which she really couldn't fathom when he'd dated virtually every supermodel and socialite on the planet. However, he spoke to her as if she were the only woman in existence and ran his gaze over her body as if mentally undressing her. The intensity of his attention left her dazed and breathless and increasingly on the brink of doing the job for him.

But despite the charm he wielded like a weapon and the slow sexy smile he deployed to dazzling effect, with superhuman effort, Mia had held out. She'd refused his invitation to dinner, even saying no to a drink, and become immune to the teasing gleam in his eye. She'd ignored the knowing air that suggested he enjoyed testing her willpower by subtly laying siege to her defences and had convinced herself that the flare of emotion she'd caught in his expression when she'd turned him down must have been disbelief because in a player like him it couldn't possibly have been hurt.

She would not jeopardise this opportunity to get her name out there by caving in to base desires and fanciful sentimentality and potentially messing up such an important job. She needed to stay focused and on track if she wanted her company to become number one in its field. To achieve the financial and environmental security she'd lacked as a child—a child who'd regularly missed school to care for her increasingly sick mother, a child who'd kept secrets and lived in fear of being ripped away by social services from everything she'd ever known—she had to remain strong.

And she had.

Until he'd murmured those words in her ear just now and sent her into a spin.

Because he had a point.

She'd been so busy pouring her efforts into making the food at this party new and exciting, perfect and memorable, it hadn't occurred to her that, once the event was over, the business she had with him would be concluded, and she'd be free to act on the desire that had clawed away at her for so long. Put there by a man who tormented her day and night, a man she wanted beyond reason and could, in theory, soon have. It was the only thought in her head.

So what was she going to do about it? she wondered, heart thumping as she removed a crate of chocolate truffles from the fridge and handed it to Hattie, her friend, her second-in-command and her only directly employed member of staff, who was charged with the task of arranging them on platters. Was that even a question that needed debate?

No.

She'd never experienced attraction like it and couldn't remember the last time she'd let her hair down. Her last disaster of a relationship, which in hindsight had been more hard work than anything else, had ended two years ago and since then she'd been so focused on the business and achieving the goals she'd had for ever, she hadn't been on so much as a date.

Besides, it wasn't as if she was after a relationship with him, which would have given her pause for thought. She knew what he was. She read the papers and had witnessed in person the skill with which he fielded the myriad personal phone calls he received.

His cavalier attitude towards women—wholly incompatible with her longing for a solid relationship that would provide the security and love she craved as a result of her emotionally tumultuous upbringing—was well-documented. But while he possessed an infamous reputation as a ruthless heartbreaker, he would never break *her* heart. She wouldn't give him the chance. She had no desire to change him. She wasn't stupid. Once upon a time she'd had an unfortunate tendency to expect more from the men she dated than they were willing to give, but not any longer.

And yes, she'd sensed a barely leashed energy in him and had occasionally caught a bleakness in his gaze when it wasn't gleaming wickedly, which suggested that beneath the super cool playboy exterior troubled waters flowed, but of what relevance was that? She wouldn't be swimming in them for long. Even if they *had* shared more than just chemistry, Christmas was coming and she'd soon be busier than ever.

She'd worried that Zander had the ability to derail her ambitions. She'd feared messing this job up if she weakened and wasted the opportunity to strengthen her reputation and expand her company. But from a catering point of view, the event had been a triumph. Her food had been devoured. She'd handed out so many business cards she'd have to order more.

So what was stopping her from celebrating her success with one night of the hot sex she and Zander had both wanted for months?

Absolutely nothing.

From his sprawled position on the plush padded banquette, Zander toyed with a glass of vintage champagne and tracked Mia through narrowed eyes as she expertly weaved a path through guests and performers, distributing after-dinner confectionery.

If he'd known how tough a nut she was going to be to crack, he'd have turned the page on the article that had caught his attention when he'd been idly flicking through the magazine he'd encountered on the jet that had been flying him from San Francisco to Tokyo. He would never have lingered on the accompanying image and carelessly indulged the spike of interest he'd experienced at the arresting combination of red-gold hair and light blue eyes. He'd have gone with the club's own catering team instead of paying them a hefty sum to step aside for hers and saved himself a whole lot of trouble.

Four months of burning, unassuaged need he'd suffered. Four months of rejection both overt and implied, of fitful sleep and frustration unlike anything he'd ever known. Had Mia been a business partner or rival, a sister, an acquaintance or pretty much anyone else, he would have admired her unshakeable resolve. Because she was someone he'd badly wanted to take to bed for weeks, he could not.

'Why are you scowling at the caterer?'

In response to Thalia's question, dryly delivered in Greek, Zander instantly cleared his expression. He pasted on a languid smile instead and swung his attention to his younger sister. 'The risotto was on the gritty side, didn't you think?' he drawled, annoyed that he'd let his irritation show. 'And how original a flavour, really, is pea and mint?'

Thalia rolled her eyes and batted him on the arm. 'All the food was excellent, as you well know. I heard amazing things about the salmon, and the chicken katsu curry was the best I've ever tasted. Little bowls of heaven,' she said on a contented sigh. 'Those circus-themed canapés were exquisite and don't get me started on the dessert. This is an awesome party, even if I did nearly get taken out by a trapeze. Everyone's having a great time. Apart from you.' She stopped and frowned, then leaned in to study him a fraction more intently. 'Why the face of thunder, Zan? Selene's not here to cause a scene, and it can't seriously be the caterer, so what's really up? Is it the business? Are you ill? What?'

Ostensibly, it *was* the caterer. He wasn't ill and Stanhope Kallis, the family banking and shipping empire of which he'd been CEO since his elder brother Leo had resigned from the post six years ago, was going from strength to strength under his leadership. He couldn't care less that Selene—his scandalous, self-absorbed mother—hadn't even responded to the invitation he'd sent her, let alone shown up tonight. When had she ever been interested in him or what he was doing, unless it directly related to the dividends she lived off? Sure, the ease with which his five siblings and their various other halves interacted, something he'd never been able to either understand or emulate, roiled his stomach but that was nothing new.

Mia's attitude towards him was the superficial cause of his brooding tension but as for what was *really* up, he hadn't a clue. Why did her obstinacy bother him so much that he felt the constant urge to challenge it? Why couldn't he accept that she didn't want to act on the obvious chemistry they shared, and move on? Why had he felt so driven to hire her in the first place and why hadn't he taken a step back from the arrangements the minute he'd realised he was fighting a battle he likely wouldn't win?

The unanswerable nature of these questions, which had recently started taking up so much space in his head, set him on edge. His legendary focus was shot. He was unusually plagued by doubt. The suspicion that she could somehow see through his armour into the pit where his many flaws lurked crawled beneath his skin. Worse, somewhere deep inside, he could feel the unacceptable stir of emotions that he'd kept under lock and key for almost three decades.

He hadn't been so hurled off-balance by a woman since his one and only attempt at a relationship at the age of nineteen, which had been a never-to-be-repeated fiasco, and frankly, he'd had enough. Of all of it.

He was done with obsessing over Mia's refusal to have dinner with him. She'd said no and that was fine. He didn't know why it bothered him so much. Because it had never happened before? Because he might have mis-read the signs and could therefore be losing his touch? Whatever was going on, he was sick of the inexplicable, unsettling effect she had on him. She wasn't *that* attrac-tive. He could think of a hundred women more beautiful and intriguing than her. This unrequited…hankering… he had for her was ridiculous. It was a complete waste of his time and, now he thought about it, wholly unac-ceptable.

How could he have forgotten the lessons he'd learned from his parents as a kid—that wanting things he couldn't have never went well and that indulging senti-ment only led to pain and confusion? Since when had he been so weak? And so what if he *had* crashed and burned? It happened. Apparently.

Mia might not want him, but there were plenty of women who did. Some of them were here, in fact. He could find the physical release he craved with any one of them. They wouldn't resist him. They'd be delighted with an invitation to dinner or drinks or something else entirely. Wasn't that why they stayed in touch?

'You know what?' he said to Thalia, firmly shov-ing Mia out of his mind once and for all, the way he should have done weeks ago, before sweeping his gaze around the room to identify potential bedmates and firing smouldering smiles at them scattergun.

'What?'

'You're right.'

'I am?'

As half a dozen women peeled themselves away from the throng and began to sidle over, Zander drained his glass and signalled for more drinks. 'Let's get this party started.'

CHAPTER TWO

BY ONE-FIFTY IN the morning, Mia had sent Hattie and the team home in the van and returned to the kitchen.

Earlier in the evening she'd assumed that round about this time of night she'd be spending a few moments alone, communing with an empty and peaceful space and reflecting on a job well done. She'd imagined excitedly counting down the minutes until two and at that point going in search of Zander, telling him exactly what she wanted and heading off with him for a magical night of hot, steamy sex.

Now, however, while she was certainly watching the clock, she would not be tracking him down any time soon. She would not be telling him anything and the only place she'd be heading was home. Alone.

Too agitated to even think about reflecting on tonight's event with tranquillity and satisfaction, Mia paced the room and battled the urge to bang things together. Pans. Spoons. Her head against the wall.

She'd been such a fool, she inwardly railed as she ran out of space and spun on her heel to retrace her steps. And to think that not so long ago she'd been priding herself on her lack of stupidity. She was the absolute definition of it.

How could she ever have thought that sleeping with Zander would be a good idea?

She must have been out of her tiny little mind.

Because despite his coolly delivered observation when she'd handed him his dessert, the one that had upended her evening and made her feel somehow *special*, it had become blindingly obvious in the interim that she wasn't. Remotely. He didn't want *her*. He just wanted someone to take to bed tonight, someone to extend his birthday celebrations with, most probably. And evidently he didn't mind who.

Mia had nearly dropped the platter of truffles she'd been passing round when she'd caught him shooting come-hither smiles at certain female guests, a metaphorical crooking of his finger to which they'd instantly responded. What was going on? she'd wondered in a fluster of shock and confusion while just about managing to keep the professional smile pinned to her face. What had happened to two a.m.? Had he changed his mind? Was he playing some kind of game with her?

Well. She still had no answers to those questions, which had rocketed around her head for a good hour before she'd finally got a grip, but that was now fine because she was done with him. She was no one's toy. Zander could take his pick of the floozies he'd surrounded himself with, every single one of whom had spent the latter part of the evening vying for his attention, which he clearly hadn't minded *at all* because he'd hardly been fending them off. In fact, he could have the lot of them.

That his rejection stung was ridiculous. Hadn't she spent the last four months *not* wanting his attention? Yes, she'd changed her mind at the last minute, but she was clearly too late and what else had she expected? He was a man driven solely by carnality, so of course he'd move on. And now she thought about it, why *wouldn't* he have pursued her in the time they'd been planning this party? She was, after all, a female with a pulse. No wonder he'd kept throwing her suggestive looks and seductive smiles. His urge to flirt was instinctive. Innate. He simply couldn't help it.

But that was over. Once her invoice was settled, she need have nothing more to do with him. She would draw a line under everything and move on too. There was zero point wishing she'd accepted his invitation to dinner and slept with him when she'd had the chance and to hell with the consequences. Regret was a phenomenal waste of time. Tomorrow, work would return to normal, her own base desires would once again be back under her control, and she wouldn't miss any of it, not the flirting, not the attention, nothing.

The clock struck the hour, heralding the end of their contract. Filled with grim resolve, Mia stalked out of the kitchen, down a service corridor and across the deserted lobby. She pushed open the door to the cloakroom that was bigger than her entire flat and far more lavishly appointed and strode into the softly lit space, only to come to a dead stop at the sight of Zander shrugging on his jacket.

'What are you still doing here?' she said tetchily because he was still the sexiest man she'd ever seen and she still wanted him with every fibre of her being, and despite the extremely stern talking-to she'd just given herself, she *ached* with disappointment.

'I've just seen off the last of my guests,' he said, his

deep, gravelly tones irritatingly fluttering her stomach. 'How about you?'

'Finishing up in the kitchen.'

'Thank you for your services this evening.'

She flashed him a tight smile and headed for the one remaining item on the gleaming brass rails—her coat. 'No problem.'

'The food was excellent.'

'I'm pleased you enjoyed it.'

Blisteringly aware of his gaze tracking her every move, which was ironic when earlier he'd been so busy with his groupies he hadn't so much as *glanced* in her direction, Mia wrenched the garment off the hanger and pulled it on. She wrapped one side tight over the other and with a sharp yank tied the belt.

'Is something the matter?'

Annoyingly, she couldn't help snapping her gaze to him, even though she knew her cheeks were tellingly flushed and if looks could kill he'd likely be dead, which wasn't very professional, but professional was the last thing she was feeling right now. 'Why would anything be the matter?'

'I don't know,' he said coolly, reaching inside the sleeves of his jacket for the cuffs of his shirt and tugging them down. 'But you seem…upset.'

Upset was far too anodyne a word for the tangle of emotions that she was struggling to contain. 'I'm fine,' she said with another stiff smile. 'Just tired.'

'How are you getting home?'

At one stage this evening she'd thought she'd be going home with him. God, she was a fool. 'I'll catch a cab.'

'At this time on a Saturday night in central London?'

'I'm prepared to wait if I have to.'

'I'll take you.'

What? No? Absolutely not. Why prolong the agony? And anyway, surely he hadn't seen off *all* his guests. 'I'd have thought you'd have other…commitments.'

'What are you talking about?'

'Your…harem.'

His eyebrows shot up. 'My *what*?'

'All those women you summoned to your side,' she said crisply as she slipped her scarf off the hanger and looped it around her neck. 'The ones who then draped themselves over you, fawning and simpering, as if desperate to tend to your every need. I'm surprised you weren't sick after the number of truffles they fed you. But I must say, you did look very content with their company.'

'You sound jealous.'

She was. Hugely. And hurt. Which was absurd. 'Was that your intention?'

'No.'

'Well, I couldn't be less jealous,' she said with a casual shrug to prove it. 'It was just a bit nauseating to have to witness something like that in this day and age, that's all. You can sleep with whoever you choose. All of them at the same time if that's what floats your boat. It's none of my concern.'

'Then why do I get the feeling it is?'

'I have no idea. Why would I care what you do?'

'Beats me,' he drawled. 'You've made it very clear you're not interested in me, which I might not like but I do respect. I can see no reason at all why you would begrudge me seeking entertainment elsewhere.'

It was the thought of him doing exactly that, of showing some other woman the pleasure that should—and could—have been hers that made Mia snap. Without warning, the powerful mix of crushing disappointment, devastating hopelessness and the excoriating jealousy she'd just denied broke free, surging through her to steal her wits and her control.

'I'll tell you why,' she said hotly, her feet propelling her across the thick pale grey carpet until she was a metre away from him, in his space, closer than she'd ever dared to get before. 'I begrudge it because you could not be more wrong about me not being interested in you. I've wanted you for *months*. Every time we've talked, every time we've messaged, whenever we've met up, all I've been able to think of is sex. With you. I've never been so attracted to anyone. I dream of your mouth. Of your hands on me and mine on you. I've taken more cold showers than I can count, not that they've worked.

'And before you tell me that I could have had you at any time,' she continued, unable to stop the roll she was on even if she'd wanted to, 'I couldn't. As you so astutely pointed out earlier this evening, I never let anything get in the way of business. There's just too much at stake for me. I want the financial security that success brings and I have every intention of getting it. So I've had to remain focused and keep you—my *client*—at arm's length. But that doesn't mean I haven't wanted to get up close and personal with you every minute of every day.'

She took a step towards him so he could not miss how very *upset* she was, even though his gaze was intent on her face already. 'You have no idea how hard it's been to resist you,' she said heatedly. 'How many times I've been on the verge of giving in. And then, when I was about to do exactly that, tonight, now, at two a.m., after *four months* of denial, which has been unbelievably tough to deal with, you decide to suddenly *abandon* the cat-and-mouse game you've been playing. You casually leave me high and dry and turn the spotlight elsewhere. It's just. Not. Fair.'

Finally running out of steam, Mia stopped, breathing hard, her head throbbing. Zander was staring down at her, utterly still. His eyes were dark and his jaw was rigid and his expression was so unreadable she didn't have a hope of working out what he might be thinking.

The silence thundered. The air between them crackled as if they'd whipped up their own little storm. For several long seconds neither of them moved.

But then, quite unexpectedly, he spun on his heel and stalked to the door, and she could have stamped her foot and screamed in frustration because was he really going to walk out? After everything she'd just confessed? What was wrong with him? With *her*?

But he didn't leave. He closed the door and turned the key and the air whooshed from Mia's lungs. As he slowly wheeled round to retrace his steps, her heart gave a great crash against her ribs and then began to hammer.

He moved with the sleek languid stealth of a stalking panther. His heat-filled gaze locked onto hers like a laser and pinned her to the spot. Her mouth dried. The frustration and pique evaporated in a flash, and she realised with an electrifying thrill that ran the entire length of her body that he'd heard her. He'd taken on board everything she'd said and was shining his spotlight wholly on her and it was as glorious and exciting as she'd hoped.

'You want me to play fair?' he murmured thickly as he splayed his hands on her waist and backed her up against a wall, his voice so low and rough it vibrated in the marrow of her bones.

'I do,' she breathed, going willingly, giddily overwhelmed by his heat, his intoxicating scent, the sheer size and strength of him. 'I really do.'

The smile he gave her was faint but the heat in his gaze was fierce. His grip on her was light but she felt it like a brand. Need clawed at her stomach. Reason fled. He lowered his head and she closed her eyes and the last thing she heard before his mouth claimed hers in a kiss that short-circuited her brain was a soft, gruff, 'Then let's play.'

For someone with a supposedly super-agile brain, it had taken Zander a shockingly long time to reconcile his cool, efficient caterer with the smouldering siren whose passionate words had rendered him speechless and destroyed his reason. Then he'd had to process her astonishing confession and his immediate and dramatic response to it, which had made a complete mockery of both his belief that he'd finally put her from his mind and his assumption that any substitute would do, and that had taken some effort too.

Once he'd emerged from his stupor and recovered a grain of sanity, however, he'd briefly toyed with the option of telling her she was too late, but what on earth would be the point of that when he was so hard he hurt? Instead, he'd decided to punish her for putting him through such agony and riddling him with doubt these last few months, by slowly driving her to the brink of oblivion and keeping her there until she was panting and sobbing and begging him for mercy.

But it had been so long and he still wanted her so much that the minute his mouth landed on hers the need for torture and revenge evaporated. All hope of steely control and cool finesse vanished. The kiss that Mia instantly returned with wild abandon ignited a fire in the pit of his stomach that shot flames along his veins, and when she moaned low in her throat and wrapped her arms tightly around his waist his restraint snapped.

Pressing her to the wall with his hips, Zander thrust his hands in her hair and angled her head to deepen the kiss. Desire pounded through him. Her scent addled what remained of his brain. How many times had he contemplated the plump softness of her lips? The smooth silk of her hair? The satiny texture of her skin? The reality easily surpassed anything he'd imagined.

When she pushed her hands beneath his shirt and planted them on his back, waves of heat radiated into every cell of his body. His muscles jumped and his skin sizzled, and though he'd thought he was as hard as he could be, she whimpered and writhed against him and proved him wrong.

Deeply relieved that he wasn't losing his touch, that she hadn't seen something in him that she didn't like but simply possessed an abundance of drive and ambition and a stubborn streak that rivalled his, needing to get closer, Zander broke off the kiss, breathing hard, and put just enough space between them to be able to untie the belt of her coat.

She looked charmingly dazed, he noted with satisfaction as he worked the knot free. Her blue eyes were glazed and her cheeks were flushed and she was breathing even more raggedly than he was. But then she blinked and put a staying hand on his and said urgently, 'Wait,' and he froze.

'What's wrong?' he rasped, thinking with his one remaining functioning brain cell that he might explode if they had to stop this now.

'Those women.'

He frowned. Reeled. Who? What the hell was she talking about? 'What women?'

'The moths to your flame.'

Ah. Right. Them. 'An attempt at distraction,' he muttered, rather regretting the move but at least understanding now why none of them had appealed. 'Which proved to be futile. So I sent them home. I've wanted you since the minute I laid eyes on you, Mia. Even after you turned down my invitation to dinner and drinks. You have no idea of the things I've imagined doing with you. You're not the only one who's been taking cold showers. Who's been going out of their mind. And, to add insult to injury, it would appear you've ruined me for anyone else.'

Her hands fell away from his, her head dropped back and a faint smile curved her gorgeous mouth. 'God, you're good,' she breathed as her gaze softened.

'I am,' he agreed, although, unusually, none of it was a line. He'd meant every word, which he did not want to analyse right now—or ever, for that matter, since navel-gazing was not his thing, unless literally. 'But know that you have no reason to be bothered by anyone.'

Clearly something in his tone or his expression reassured her because she said, 'We're wasting time,' and knocked his hands off her belt to take care of it herself.

His heart pounding, his need for her rushing back and hitting an almost unbearable high, Zander reached into his back pocket for his wallet. He shoved his trousers and shorts down and, with gritted teeth, rolled on protection. Mia slipped off her underwear and yanked up her dress and then, with hands that were strangely trembling, he gripped her thighs and lifted her up. She locked her legs around his waist and her arms around his neck and, unable to hold back a moment longer, he thrust into her warm, wet heat on a rough shuddery groan.

He cut off her cry with a kiss that was desperate and fierce and, powerless to wait, he began to move. He clasped her hips and she clutched at his hair and he tried to maintain control, but it had been four months and she felt like heaven. She was urging him on, panting and begging with increasing excitement, and he was fast unravelling.

Her legs tightened around his waist. Her inner muscles clenched around him as if she didn't want to ever let him go. Desperate for air, he wrenched his mouth from hers. As he slid it along her jaw, he could feel her ragged breath hot against his face. The exquisite tension in his muscles was building. His head was swimming and a wave of pleasure was beginning to ripple up from the base of his spine and he couldn't hold back any longer.

With a primitive growl, he nipped her earlobe and adjusted the angle of her hips and thrust hard, lodging so deep in her smooth, tight heat he saw stars. While she came apart, convulsing and trembling and pressing her mouth to his neck to muffle her cry, he shattered, pulsating into her relentlessly and burying his face in the crook of her neck as white-hot ecstasy crashed through him.

How long they stayed there locked together, hearts pounding against each other, slowing as they began to recover, he couldn't have said. It was only once the adrenalin had drained from his body, turning his muscles to mush and rendering his legs so weak they could barely hold him up, that he lifted his head from her neck, gently eased from her and set her down.

'So that was good,' Mia murmured hoarsely, blinking as if stunned, still plastered to the wall as if moving away from it might land her in a boneless heap on the floor.

Zander turned away to deal with the condom and thought that good was an understatement. Never before had lights actually flashed behind his eyelids. Never before had undoing one gorgeous yet stubborn woman given him such satisfaction.

'You really do live up to your reputation.'

'I've barely even started,' he muttered, briefly wondering whether the fact that he'd never surrendered control to such mindlessness before either was a concern or merely the consequence of four months of abstinence. 'We have months to make up for and I have plans for your scarf.'

'Well, we can't stay here,' she observed with breathless excitement and a glance at the door that wouldn't remain locked for ever.

She was right. They couldn't. So, the only question that remained was, 'Your place or mine?'

CHAPTER THREE

Seven weeks later

'STILL NO REPLY?'

With a scowl, Mia shoved her frustratingly silent phone into the back pocket of her jeans and reached for a giant colander. 'Nothing,' she said, dumping it in the sink and heading to the fridge.

Hattie, who was blitzing a pile of parsley and thyme with a gleaming ten-inch knife, grimaced. 'What's the tally now?'

'Twelve calls, fifteen messages and seven emails in total.'

'Maybe he's somewhere that doesn't have a mobile signal or Wi-Fi.'

'For forty-eight hours?'

'Yeah, I guess that is pretty unlikely,' came the dry response. 'Your emails now go straight into his junk mail folder, then. He's deleted you from his contacts and doesn't answer calls from unknown numbers.'

Retrieving the mussels—the main course for tonight's dinner party for twenty—Mia had to admit that that explanation for Zander's lack of response to her attempts at communication wasn't beyond the realms of possibility. The morning after the incredible night they'd spent incinerating her sheets, when she'd woken up to find him gone, no note, no nothing, she'd neatly excised him from her life too, although luckily, given recent developments, she did at least archive past clients' correspondence details.

'Even so,' she said, slicing open the netted bag and pouring its contents into the colander, 'you'd think that a text saying, I'M PREGNANT, CALL ME!—in caps— might have generated *some* sort of response. I mean, as messages go, it's not exactly ambiguous.'

'Perhaps he really is as heartless as his reputation suggests.'

Physically he wasn't, of course. Many times that night Mia had felt it thundering beneath her palm as they hurtled again and again into blissful oblivion.

His morning-after etiquette, however, left a lot to be desired, she reflected as she switched on the tap and swirled the colander around beneath it.

Not that she was still smarting over the way he'd disappeared or anything. Well aware of his reputation, she hadn't expected him to linger over breakfast and then suggest a romantic walk in the park. A 'thanks for a fun time' and a goodbye might have been nice, but she'd never had a one-night stand before—it had never struck her as the best way of achieving the commitment she was after—so who knew? Presumably, rendering women boneless with pleasure and then sneakily creeping from their bed while they recovered was his modus operandi.

'I accept that he may have forgotten me,' she said, wincing at the unflattering thought, made worse by the fact that, despite her every effort, she had not forgotten him. 'But even a "who is this?" would be better than complete radio silence.'

'Could he have blocked you?'

'How would I know?'

'Try my phone.'

Mia put down the mussels and switched off the tap, then took the device Hattie was holding out. She entered the number that was now etched into her memory, hit the button to dial it and braced herself for the impact of Zander's deep, spine-tingling voice pouring into her ear. But, as she'd expected, it rang a couple of times and went to an automated voicemail, and there didn't seem much point in leaving yet another message.

'This doesn't work either,' she said, handing the phone back with a tut of irritation.

'So what will you do next?'

It was an excellent question, and right now Mia was all out of answers. She was weak from having thrown up for seven mornings in a row. She was still in shock from discovering two days ago that she was pregnant and not, as she'd initially wondered, suffering from either a bug or food poisoning. Hattie, to whom she'd had to confess almost everything after gagging violently at the sight of some undressed squid, was doing her best to be helpful, but her failure to contact the father of her baby was only adding to her stress, and she was exhausted.

'Quite honestly, I'd like to go and lie down in a dark room and stay there for a month,' she said, heaving the colander out of the sink and setting it on the side.

'You can't,' said Hattie, aghast.

'I know.'

However tempting, running away and hiding wasn't an option. Not only did she not do that any more, but also Christmas was Halliday Catering's busiest time of the year. Bookings were pretty much back to back for the next five weeks, and she would not let anyone down.

Nor would she give up on Zander until she'd turned over every stone in her efforts to speak to him. He had the right to know she was pregnant with his child. How involved he wanted to be, if at all, was his choice to make and she would not deprive him of that.

She'd never known her own father. She too was the product of a one-night stand, the irony of which did not escape her. But at least she knew the father of *her* baby's name. Her mother had not. In fact, her mother had known very little about the stranger she'd met in a nightclub thirty-one years ago, which had made tracking him down to inform him of his impending fatherhood impossible.

Growing up, Mia had felt his absence keenly. No amount of daydreaming about who and where he might be and what he might be doing had filled the yawning gap inside her. Reason and fortitude had been no match for the rejection and the longing she'd experienced.

If her father had been around when her mother had fallen ill with dementia, she might have had an easier time of it. She might have felt less shamefully resentful and angry at the situation that was no one's fault. As she'd matured, she'd come to terms with living with the empty space that her father should have occupied but she would never willingly or deliberately foist that aching sense of loss and abandonment on any child of hers.

And then there was the paralysing fear that if something happened to her, her child would be left on its own, with no one to care for them and no one to rely on. Tests had shown that she didn't carry the gene that had caused her mother's illness, so her risk of young-onset dementia was no greater than anyone else's, but plenty of other things could befall her. She could be run over by a bus or get sick with some other disease, and in the event of her untimely demise there was no one else. Apart from Zander.

'So?'

Pulling herself together and returning to the present, Mia snapped on a pair of latex gloves. 'I'm going to have to carry on looking for him until I find him.'

'How are you going to do that?'

Wasn't that the million-dollar question? 'I have absolutely no idea.'

Alone in the boardroom after a three-hour meeting to which he'd paid unusually scant attention, Zander surged to his feet and snatched his coat off a peg. The glass walls were closing in on him. His chest was tight and his head pounded. He needed to move. He needed some air.

The restlessness that had set in over the last month was getting worse, he thought grimly as he strode to the lift and jabbed at the button. The niggling sense of dissatisfaction and the strange ennui, which he just couldn't seem to shake, no matter how busy he kept himself both professionally and socially, were becoming increasingly intolerable.

Maybe he was burning out.

Or perhaps turning thirty-five had triggered a mid-life crisis.

The lift arrived and in he stepped.

Could he be getting old?

No. He was in his prime. At the height of success with a lifestyle that he knew many envied.

The flurry of invitations to weddings and christenings he'd received recently suggested that the people around him were moving on, but he was fine exactly where he was. He wanted a wife and kids like a hole in the head. Even if he *had* possessed the necessary skill set to maintain a relationship, which he did not, why anyone would willingly put their emotions out there to be dismissed at best and destroyed at worst was completely beyond him.

Only once had he made the mistake of letting someone get too close. He'd met Valentina at a party on Zakynthos at the age of nineteen, and had instantly been dazzled. They'd dated for six months, during which he'd tried to give her what she wanted and to form the kind of attachment others seemed to have no trouble achieving, even introducing her to his siblings. But ultimately he'd failed because, as she'd told him when she'd been breaking up with him, he was emotionally void, in possession of a heart of stone and incapable of giving anything of himself to anyone, other than his body.

That experience had left him feeling wounded and bewildered. It had dredged up memories of his youth and stirred feelings of inadequacy that he'd believed he'd conquered long before. Determined to never have to go through anything like that again, hating the weakness and pain it had caused, he'd vowed to remain alone and untouchable, strong and safe. And by keeping his emotions buried and his defences up, he had. Successfully. For years.

So meaningless one-night stands that scratched an itch but never probed any deeper? Great. Love and commitment? Very much not.

Most probably it was the time of year that was making him feel so unsettled, he figured, shrugging on his coat as the lift began its smooth, silent descent. He'd never liked Christmas with its emphasis on festivity and family. He couldn't remember a time the members of his had celebrated it all together. His mother had always jetted off in early December in search of winter sun and unencumbered fun, and still did. His father, before his fatal heart attack eighteen years ago, had believed that children should be seen and not heard and had therefore spent as little time as possible in their company—with the exception of Leo, the heir to the family business—even on Christmas Day. Zander had invariably spent the holidays kicking around the mansion in Athens with the five siblings he increasingly failed to understand and the two nannies, stuffing his face with *kourabiedes* and wondering where the jollity was.

The lift came to a sibilant stop at the ground floor, putting the brakes on his turbulent thoughts not a moment too soon. The doors opened and he was immediately hit by the not unpleasant scent of a wintry forest, courtesy of the thirty-metre Nordic spruce being craned into place in the centre of the lobby, and a faintly desperate female voice coming from the reception area which stopped him in his tracks and froze him to the spot.

'He *has* to be here. I read there was a board meeting today. Where else would he be?'

His pulse leapt. His breath caught. He recognised that voice. The last time he'd heard it, it had been panting in his ear, begging him to go harder, faster, deeper. He recognised the red-gold hair too, rippling out from beneath a navy bobble hat. He could still recall the silky feel of it tangled around his fingers and sweeping over his skin.

Mia.

A woman who irritatingly refused to remain in the past and continued to haunt his dreams.

What was she doing here?

Why was she looking for him?

Catching his eye, the receptionist gave a subtle nod in the direction of the security guard and raised her eyebrows in silent question. Zander shook his head because avoidance might have been his parents' style but it certainly wasn't his, and already Mia was attracting attention.

He strode across the white marble floor towards the woman who'd turned out to be infinitely more disturbing than he'd ever envisaged. In response to the receptionist's gesture, she spun on her heel and, as her gaze collided with his, it occurred to him belatedly that he should have spent those few frozen moments bracing himself for her impact. While he vividly recalled every detail of what they'd once done to each other, he'd forgotten how breathtaking she was in the flesh.

'Aha!' she said, flashing him a dazzling smile that struck him like a blow to the gut. 'Finally! You're a hard man to track down, Zander Stanhope. Did you block my number?'

He had. He'd had to. The night they'd spent together had rocked his world. So much so that he'd forced himself to leave before she woke up and tempted him to stay for a week, a month, for ever.

Not that that had put an end to his bizarre fixation with her. He'd lost count of the times he'd considered calling her up and inviting her over for more. On one particularly alarming occasion his finger had hovered over her name for several seconds before a warning signal had sounded in his brain, reminding him of his once-only policy, and snapped him out of it. Deleting her details hadn't been enough. He couldn't risk her contacting him, weakening, and all those buried emotions and bizarre doubts stirring again. He'd had to go nuclear.

'It was nothing personal,' he said, directing her behind a wall of greenery that would afford them a small degree of privacy.

'So *you* think.'

'I apologise.'

'I don't believe you mean that,' she said with disconcerting perception. 'Do you get personal with any of the women you sleep with?'

'No.' Not these days.

'Too many of them to bother with?'

Quite the opposite. In fact, he hadn't taken anyone to bed since Mia. Over a month ago. Which, come to think of it, perhaps explained his restlessness. 'Something like that.'

'So you block them,' she said with a rueful shake of her beautiful head. 'Harsh. Nevertheless, I wish you'd kept me in your phone. I've been trying to contact you since Thursday. I've sent you countless emails and texts and left numerous voicemails. You haven't made it easy.'

That had been the plan.

But why had she wanted to contact him? And why since Thursday? Had she been as affected by what they'd done as he had? Could she not stand the frustration any longer? He ignored the quick surge of his pulse at the thought of it and refocused.

'I'll admit the night we spent together was good,' he said, blocking the hot, distracting memories that were trying to barge their way into his head. 'Very good, in fact.' The best he'd ever had, even. 'But it was still just one night.'

'Well, that was certainly the *intention*.'

'What do you mean?'

'We need to talk.'

On the contrary, they did not need to talk. He'd already spent far too long on this unexpected conversation, and he didn't appreciate the effect she was having on him, even after all this time. He should never have indulged his curiosity in the first place by talking to her. What on earth had he been thinking?

'No, we don't,' he said, beginning to regret that he hadn't left her to Security after all.

'It won't take long,' she said, with irritating disregard for his objection. 'Can we go somewhere a bit more private?'

Absolutely not. He didn't want to be alone with her when she put him so on edge. He didn't want to be anywhere with her full stop, and if he had to be brutal to reinforce that point, then so be it.

'I'm not after a relationship, Mia,' he said, his voice low so as not to be overheard through the bamboo. 'I never have been. I thought that was clear.'

'It was,' she replied, leaning towards him, equally discreet. 'It was crystal clear. And neither am I. At least, not with you. That's *not* why I'm here.'

Good. That was a relief. So why was he suddenly wondering, why not him? What was wrong with *him*? It was an absurd and unnecessary thought—he knew exactly what was wrong with him—so he shoved it aside and focused.

'Then why *are* you here?' he said, ignoring her dizzying proximity and the scent he apparently hadn't forgotten. 'Is there a problem with the payment of your invoice?'

'No.'

'Do you have some other business involving my company?'

'No.'

'Are you in trouble?'

'Not exactly.'

'I don't have time for riddles,' he said, his surging frustration at the way she was addling his brain *finally* igniting some strength of character. 'And I fail to see anything else we might have to discuss, so if you'll excuse me, I have somewhere else to be.'

Wrenching himself away from her compelling gaze before he drowned in it, Zander turned on his heel, intending to round the screen and head for the exit, practically tasting fresh air and freedom, only to come to an abrupt stop when she spoke, the words flying through the space and landing on him like darts.

'I'm pregnant.'

CHAPTER FOUR

AT MIA'S ANNOUNCEMENT, every cell of Zander's body froze. His head emptied and he went numb. Beyond the bamboo, people moved. Outside on the street, traffic flowed. The world continued turning, even if here, behind the plants, it had shuddered to a halt.

Slowly, warily, his pulse thudding so loudly he could hear it in his ears, he turned back to face her. 'What did you say?'

'I'm pregnant,' she repeated, chin up, shoulders squared as if ready for battle. 'And the baby's yours.'

He gave his head one sharp shake of denial. That couldn't be right. 'No.'

'Yes, as a matter of fact. I did a test a week ago. Well, four, actually. Just in case. All were positive and it was later confirmed by my doctor. You're the father, Zander. You're the only person I've slept with in two years.'

White noise. That was all he could hear beyond her words. A loud rushing nothingness that obliterated everything in its path. 'How is that possible?'

She flushed. 'I've been focusing on my career,' she said defensively. 'And not everyone has a different person in their bed each week.'

Her barb bounced straight off him. As if his sex life,

or lack of it, was of any significance right now. 'I was talking about protection,' he said, struggling to claw back some of the trademark languor that was rapidly deserting him. 'Which we used.'

'No contraception is one hundred percent foolproof,' she said, wrapping her coat around herself more tightly, as if warding off a chill. 'And we put it to the test a lot.'

They had. Once they'd got to her flat, they'd tested it on the console table in her hall. Her shower, her sofa and her bed, over and over again.

So much heat…

So much pleasure…

So irrelevant right now.

'It's a shock,' she said, her voice muffled by the shrieking chaos swirling around inside him. 'I get that. It was to me too when I found out. I thought I had food poisoning or a bug or something. Even when I'd worked out the dates, I didn't want to believe it. It still doesn't seem real, to be honest. I don't expect anything from you, Zander. I just thought you should know, that's all. If you want to be involved in this child's life, that would be great. I never knew my own father and I wish I had. So I'd like us to do this together, however that works. I'm aware it wouldn't be easy. Our lives are very different. There'd be compromises and sacrifices, which I'm willing to make.'

She paused, presumably to give him the opportunity to respond, but he had nothing. Absolutely nothing. He was sinking into quicksand, already up to his neck, and there was no rope to hand to pull himself free.

'However, if none of that appeals,' she continued after a moment, 'then fine. It's my choice to have this baby.

The circumstances aren't ideal, I admit, but I've always wanted children. I'm thirty and single and this might be my only chance. However, I'm perfectly capable of doing it on my own. I believe that having you around would be best for our child, but I don't *need* you. You're under no obligation from me to do anything. You could walk away right now, and that would be fine. Whatever you decide, Zander, it's entirely up to you.'

It was unfortunate that the degree of his involvement in this was entirely up to him because right now he was utterly incapable of making a decision. He could barely think straight. He felt light-headed. He couldn't breathe. His chest was tingling and his stomach was churning and all the blood in his body was rushing to his feet.

He needed a minute. He needed a drink. But the nearest bottle of industrial strength liquor was in his office, which was far too far away, so he had to make do with focusing on his breathing, in and out, deep and slow, until the threat of keeling over receded.

Theos.

How the hell could this have happened? He'd always been so careful. He didn't want a kid. He never had. He wasn't equipped to be a father. He'd be useless. He couldn't even keep a houseplant alive. What hope would he have of successfully raising an actual human being?

It wasn't as if he'd had a good role model. His own father had been cold and distant, so intolerant of tears and emotion of any kind that Zander had swiftly learned to suppress both. Support, interest, praise, affection—he'd had none of that, although there'd been plenty of criticism and discipline. His mother had been no better.

Every time she'd looked at him, it was as if she were surprised to see him there, as if she'd forgotten he existed.

He knew nothing of emotional connection and communication, so what if *his* son or daughter needed something from him that he was simply unable to provide? Would the patterns of the past repeat themselves? Might no father be better than a bad one? Wouldn't Mia ably fill both roles? Shouldn't he take the escape route she'd given him, declare he wanted to have nothing do with them and leave them both better off?

On the other hand, Leo, his older brother, seemed to be doing all right with *his* family. As the heir to the Stanhope Kallis empire, he'd received the lion's share of their father's attention growing up, but it hadn't been warm, and their mother had been just as negligent with him. However, Leo was soppy as hell over his two daughters and madly in love with his wife.

What if he—Zander—decided he couldn't turn his back on his child and subject him or her to the neglect and rejection he'd experienced as a youth and, against all the odds, the same thing happened to him? Not the loving a wife part—no one would ever get close enough for that because, if they did, the gaping lack of a soul they'd find would send them running for the hills—but the sentimentality over a child.

What if he decided to try and do better than his pathetic excuse for parents, learning from those of his siblings with offspring, perhaps, became invested in the pregnancy and the baby and then did something to mess it all up? If, in the course of their co-parenting, Mia decided he just wasn't good enough—after all, as she'd pointed out, she didn't *need* him—she could cut him out completely, and where would that leave him then?

No. He would not allow that to happen. Such vulnerability was unacceptable. He couldn't abandon this child of his—that wasn't the man he was or wanted to be—and he could hardly do a worse job than either of his parents had. Therefore, he had to secure his position. Lock this thing down on his terms. As he did day in, day out, at work. So that when he did screw things up, as he undoubtedly would, Mia couldn't just take off with their child, leaving him broken, alone, with nothing for company but emptiness.

Quashing the doubts and thinking purely of his position, Zander set his jaw. He pulled himself up to his full height, looked directly at the woman who'd just tossed a grenade into his life and altered it for good, and said, 'We'd better get married.'

Blurting out her news in the middle of the busy lunchtime lobby, even from behind a dense wall of foliage, had not been Mia's intention when she'd decided to ambush Zander at his office. However, he hadn't given her a choice. She'd spent *days* trying to get hold of him— she'd even contemplated hiring a private investigator if today's efforts had proven fruitless—and it had been beyond stressful, so she had not been about to let him push her aside and stalk off without knowing the truth.

Understandably, he'd been stunned by her news. He'd inhaled as if winded and gone so white she'd feared he was about to faint. Once she'd finished explaining, she'd wondered whether she could have rendered him permanently speechless. But then he'd responded, with a proposal no less, and now it was her turn to be shocked.

What planet was he on? Marriage for the sake of a baby? In *this* day and age? Even she, with all her concerns about what might or might not happen in the future, didn't think that necessary. Besides, he was the ultimate no-strings-attached wonder. Why on earth would he even *want* to get married?

'I don't think there's any need to be quite so dramatic,' she said, once she'd unglued her tongue from the roof of her mouth.

'I would like to guarantee my rights.'

Her heart gave a little leap of hope. 'So you want to be involved?'

He nodded. 'At every stage.'

Oh, thank God for that. 'Well, that's good,' she said with what had to be the understatement of the century when he'd just allayed her greatest fear by indicating that if something happened to her he'd step up. 'But marriage is unnecessary. I would never prevent you from being part of anything. I grew up without knowing my father and I would never deliberately do that to my child. You have my word.'

'I don't know if I can count on your word,' he said curtly. 'Not on this.'

Ouch. 'You can count on the law.'

'That's not enough.'

Zander folded his arms across his broad, solid chest, which she'd once explored at length, his expression implacable, his dark gaze steely, and it occurred to her suddenly that the delicious wickedness she'd always associated with him was no longer there. In fact, she could see no hint of the playboy she'd become acquainted with while planning his party. Or the towering inferno she'd taken to bed. In front of her, pinning her to the spot from a deliberate position of dominance, was an altogether more dangerous sort of man, a man with a reputation for ruthlessness as well as seduction, who got what he wanted, whatever the cost, a force to be reckoned with.

But she would not be intimidated. Or distracted, no matter how unexpectedly thrilling she found this particular version of him. Thanks to her tough adolescence, she was no pushover either and she certainly wasn't going to agree to something neither of them had had time to consider. Plenty of people had children out of wedlock. It was hardly taboo these days.

And anyway, when she got married it would be for love. She wanted a husband who adored her, and a genuine partnership based on friendship and respect. She hadn't just dreamed of creating a successful business and gaining financial security all these years. She also, perhaps even more desperately, yearned for a family. She'd been on her own for so long, and in the quiet early hours of the morning, when she hadn't been able to sleep and sometimes still couldn't, she ached with loneliness that grew by the day.

Admittedly, she hadn't had much luck on that front. When it came to relationships, she knew she came across as clingy and needy, pushing for too much too soon, because she'd been told so by her last boyfriend while he'd been breaking up with her. And in the aftermath, during which she'd forced herself to revisit and analyse her two relationships before that one, she'd discovered a pattern that, with hindsight, was pretty self-destructive.

She'd vowed to do things differently next time, to remove the pressure and let things play out at their own speed, but 'differently' did not mean blindly tying herself to a man she barely knew simply because she was pregnant and he didn't trust her.

'Well, it'll have to be enough for now,' she said firmly, refusing to indulge his posturing and needing to escape both the unsettling intensity with which he was looking at her and the bizarre desire to step in closer. 'It's far too early to be talking about that sort of commitment. Or any sort of commitment, for that matter. The first trimester can be precarious and, according to the doctor, I'm only a couple of months into it. Anything could happen in the next few weeks. So let's just see how things go.'

As CEO of one of the world's largest privately owned companies, 'seeing how things went' was not Zander's preferred way of doing things and if Mia hadn't shot off before he'd had the time and the head space to process the stunning realisation that she'd challenged him, he'd have informed her of that fact.

But in the days that followed he repeatedly revisited their conversation and eventually concluded that in this situation the unilateral decision-making and expecting everyone to go along with it that he was used to was probably not going to work. Mia wasn't one of his employees or a potential business partner. She was the mother of his child, with opinions of her own.

However, he wasn't unduly worried. There was plenty of time to persuade her to see things his way. Everyone did, in the end, and he remained ever more convinced that marriage was the only way to guarantee the outcome he desired. His request for her birth certificate so he could begin the paperwork had so far gone unanswered, but if that situation persisted he'd simply request a copy of the public document for himself.

He had plenty of time too to get a grip on the idea of impending fatherhood. Having unblocked Mia's number and reinstated her as a contact, he'd read her messages and listened to her voicemails, and the news was sinking in. Gradually.

At some point he'd find a way through the chaos in his head, he was certain. He wouldn't be riding this weird, frustratingly irrepressible roller coaster of panic and confusion, pride and elation for ever and he'd soon tire of imagining what the kid he'd created with Mia might look like.

Unwelcome thoughts of his own parents and his relationship with them kept popping up to plague him, which was annoying when that bore no relevance to anything, but with effort he was just about managing to suppress at least those. His entire life had been turned upside down. It was only natural for his thoughts to be in disarray and his focus to be off.

'Are you listening to a word I've been saying?'

From behind his desk, Zander stifled a sigh and returned his attention to his one surviving parent, his mother, who'd waltzed into his office ten minutes ago without an appointment, swathed in caramel cashmere and indignation. 'Your dividends are down this year because we've invested heavily in the Kallis side of the business,' he said. 'We bought a fleet of cruise ships and overhauled six of the shipyards. It was all in the share-holders' report. Did you read it?'

Selene pouted. 'No.'

There was a surprise. 'Your income will be back to seven figures next year.'

'What am I meant to do in the meantime?'

With the several hundreds of thousands of euros she'd still receive? Quite honestly, he didn't care. 'You could try economising.'

'I don't even know what that means,' she said petulantly. 'You're more of a disappointment than Leo was when he sat behind that desk. I never thought *you* would spoil my fun too. I do miss your father.'

Selene's criticism ricocheted off his armour without making so much as a dent, but miss his father? That was a joke. Not only had the ink barely had time to dry on the marriage certificate before she'd embarked on a string of affairs that she'd made little attempt to hide, but also the only person she had any sort of feeling for was herself. Edward Stanhope had been so busy merging his banking empire with Selene's shipping one, which he'd acquired on their marriage, he'd turned a blind eye to his wife's scandalous behaviour and her profligacy, and it was that that she missed.

'You'll survive.'

'I don't know how. You'll be tossing me out of the house and onto the streets next.'

Zander gritted his teeth and resisted the urge to tell his mother to grow up because that approach had never worked. 'Was there anything else?' he asked instead. Such as, say, an enquiry into how he was. What plans he might have for Christmas. Whether he had any major news to impart.

'No,' she said, rising elegantly from the chair and throwing one end of her scarf over her shoulder. 'I'm late for my flight as it is, and I don't suppose they'll hold it for me. Really, this is a very inconvenient time of year for the jet to have a technical fault. It's eleven hours to the Maldives. It's going to be ghastly, even in first class.'

From habit, Zander got up too, and was about to stride to the door to open it to let his mother and her eternal disappointment in him out when his phone rang. He glanced down at the screen and, on seeing who it was, stopped in his tracks.

'Excuse me,' he muttered with a frown. 'I need to take this. You can see yourself out.'

With a huff and a pointed comment about manners, his mother flounced from his office, but all Zander was interested in now was why Mia was calling him after four days' silence. Could she have considered his proposal and concluded it was for the best? Was that why his pulse had spiked? Because he'd won?

'Mia.'

'Hi,' she said. 'Are you busy?'

Always. He had a series of meetings this Monday afternoon and the delightful interlude with his mother had already set him back half an hour. But something in her voice concerned him. He thought he could detect a note of desperation behind her words and a certain raggedness to her breathing, and he didn't like any of it.

'No,' he said. 'I'm not. What's going on?'

'I'm bleeding, Zander, and I'm cramping. It hurts. A lot. I think I may be miscarrying.'

His blood froze. His heart stopped. The ground rocked beneath his feet and his stomach went into freefall, which meant that he had to ignore the sudden crushing pressure in his chest and switch to the practical. 'Where are you?'

'On my way to hospital,' she said with a sharp intake of breath that turned into a shuddery sort of a sob.

'Text me the details,' he said, already at the lift that would zoom him down to the garage, with his coat, his wallet, his keys. 'I'll be there as soon as I can.'

CHAPTER FIVE

MIA EMERGED FROM the clinic a lot less terrified than she'd been when she'd gone in. She'd never felt fear like it and hoped never to again.

It had all happened so suddenly. One minute she'd been deboning a chicken while humming along to the radio, in an effort to not think about Zander's arrogant presumption in emailing his request for her birth certificate, as if her feelings on the subject of marriage were so immaterial they could simply be bulldozed to bits, the next a shooting pain had sliced across her abdomen and a wet warmth had seeped between her legs.

Stunned, devastated, she'd dropped the knife and doubled over, clutching at her midriff, tears springing to her eyes, a voice in her head screaming *No, no, no!*

With trembling hands, her chest aching as if her heart had been yanked out, she'd called her doctor, who'd advised her to go straight to hospital, and then she'd rung Zander. She had no idea why. It wasn't as if she didn't have friends and, for all she knew, her number might still be blocked. But it wasn't. He must have meant what he'd said about intending to be involved at every stage and reinstated it.

When he'd turned up at the hospital ten minutes after

her, however, taking charge and demanding answers, she'd never been so glad to see anyone in her life. She really hadn't wanted to go through whatever she was going through alone, and why *wouldn't* she have called him when anything to do with the pregnancy and their baby was his business too? He'd dealt with the estimated eight-hour wait by whisking her off to a private clinic where she'd been seen immediately, and she was now even more convinced she'd made the right decision in contacting him.

Still shaky and raw, despite the positive outcome of the appointment, Mia pushed through the door that opened into the lobby, her gaze landing on the man pacing up and down in front of the reception desk. In his beautiful charcoal grey coat that probably cost more than she turned over in a month, he looked far more at home here among the wood panelling and cream carpet than the chaos of Accident and Emergency.

'Well?' he said, striding over to her, his jaw tight as he raked his gaze over her.

'Everything's fine.'

He came to an abrupt stop and his brows snapped together. Shadows lurked in the depths of his eyes and his thick dark hair was dishevelled. 'Fine?' he demanded. 'What do you mean, fine? You look as if you've been crying.'

That was because she had. But not with grief. 'The baby's OK,' she hastened to assure him with a stab at a watery smile. 'We're both OK.'

'Are you certain?'

'So I've been told.'

'You're not miscarrying?'

'No. I had an ultrasound. I heard the heartbeat. It sounded a bit like galloping horses. It was kind of mind-blowing.'

And the relief when the quick, strong, rhythmic pulses had filled the room... God, the *relief.* She'd wept with it and only just refrained from hugging the sonographer when he'd told her everything was all right.

'They gave me two pictures of the baby,' she said, swallowing down the hot, tight lump in her throat and blinking back the fresh sting of tears. 'Here. This one's for you.'

As she handed him the tiny black and white photo his fingers touched hers and an unexpected sizzle of heat rushed through her. He stared at the grainy image, thankfully too absorbed in it to notice the tiny gasp she gave in both shock and horror, because here and now was neither the time nor the place for that sort of thing, and muttered something in Greek before falling silent.

Determinedly ignoring the memories of the steamy night they'd spent together, which were now inappropriately trying to muscle their way in to her head, Mia sought to fill the oddly intimate quiet.

'I feel a bit foolish, actually,' she said, shifting her weight from one foot to the other, her cheeks heating when she recalled how overwrought she'd been when she'd called him. 'There was pain and blood, and I automatically assumed the worst. But apparently it's not that uncommon at this stage of pregnancy. I'm so sorry to have dragged you away from work for nothing.'

'Forget it.'

That was unlikely. She didn't think she'd *ever* forget

the terror and the desolation she'd felt. 'Thank you for your help.'

'Any time,' he muttered as he tucked the photo into the top inside pocket of his coat. 'So is that it?' He lifted his dark gaze to hers, his expression oddly inscrutable. 'No treatment? You don't need to stay here for observation?'

'No, that's it,' she said. 'Well, I was advised to rest for a week or two,' she amended with a faint frown, 'but that's not likely to happen. I mean it's December and I'm a caterer. It's my busiest time of year. Tonight, for example, I have a drinks party for a hundred.'

His eyebrows shot up. 'A hundred?'

'Yes.'

'Tonight?'

'Yes.'

'Cancel it. In fact, cancel everything.'

She blinked up at him in shock. 'What? No. I can't possibly do that. It'll destroy my business.'

There was a second of stunned silence before he spoke. 'Are you *serious*?'

'It's all right for you and your three-hundred-year-old billion-euro company,' she said, bristling in response to his incredulous arrogance. 'Mine is at a crucial stage, both reputationally and financially. I can't just cancel events that have been months in the planning. I promise I'll take it easy. I'll make sure I sit down when I can and drink lots of water.'

'And risk this happening again? Only for real?'

That sobered her up. The dizzying relief and the adrenalin rushing through her system evaporated in an instant and her chest tightened as a cold sweat broke out all over her skin.

Because Zander had a point.

How could she possibly continue as planned, as if this afternoon had been nothing more than a minor inconvenience? Even though she'd been assured there was no reason to suspect it *would* happen again, every minute of every day and night she'd be worried. And rightly so, because she'd even told him that the first three months could be precarious.

This pregnancy wasn't some sort of abstract idea, as it had felt up until now. The baby growing inside her had a shape and a heartbeat and already she loved it fiercely. Currently, it was dependent entirely on her for its well-being, so she had to stop thinking solely of herself. Even Zander wasn't doing that. By putting the baby first, not only was he proving that he'd fully step in if something happened to her, thank God, but also he was behaving in the way she supposed most fathers-to-be would, although what would she know when she hadn't had one of her own?

In fact, her child was enviably lucky to have two present and engaged parents. She wanted to make that work, so perhaps now was the time for one of the sacrifices she'd told him in the lobby of his building that she'd be willing to make.

'You're right,' she conceded, swiftly working through the practicable options while trying and failing to process both the enormous reality of her situation and her complicated feelings about fathers. 'Of course you're right.'

'Stanhope Kallis has a corporate entertainment department,' said Zander, a fraction calmer than a moment ago although, judging by the set of his jaw, no less determined to get his way. 'I can parachute in a substitute events organiser right now.'

'That won't be necessary.'

'Why not?'

'Because *I* have someone who can temporarily take over,' she said without hesitation, while nevertheless inwardly wincing at the thought of giving up control of the company to which she'd dedicated the last six years of her life, however briefly. 'Hattie. Harriet. My number two. She's been with me since the beginning and I trust her implicitly. All the menus for December have been finalised and the food is on order. It's just a question of logistics now and she's more than capable of handling those. I can get in more staff to help her, if needs be, and I'll be on the end of the phone.'

After a moment's consideration, he gave a short nod. 'That would be acceptable.'

Was it now. 'I'm delighted you think so,' she said dryly.

Planting a hand on her lower back, which bizarrely she could feel, despite the thick layers of clothing she was wearing, Zander steered her with care in the direction of the exit.

What was she going to *do* for a fortnight? she wondered as she tried to ignore both his disconcerting proximity and the touch that felt almost protective. She hadn't had so much time off in years. Maybe she could work on some new recipes. Or tweak her five-year forecast. She could even put up those shelves that had been propped up against the living room wall for months.

And when the inevitable boredom set in?

Well, surely an *occasional* trip to the unit to see how things were going wouldn't hurt. She would, of course, leave any heavy lifting to others, but she could easily peel a potato. Rinsing a lettuce or whipping up a quick *beurre blanc* didn't exactly require much in the way of effort.

And if she found herself just happening to pass by a venue at which an event she'd organised was taking place, it would be only natural to drop in for a moment. The client would be expecting it. In fact, wouldn't it actually be *good* for her and the baby if she checked in from time to time? Wouldn't the stress of worrying about how her business was faring in her absence be worse?

'One more thing,' Zander said as he released her to reach for the door.

'What?'

'You're moving in with me.'

Mia froze in the process of pulling on her gloves and shot him a startled glance. What? No. How would she be able to keep an eye on things if he was keeping an eye on her? And did she really want him witnessing the unpleasantness of morning sickness, even if it did seem to be easing? She did not.

'Oh, there's no need for that,' she said with an airy wave and a reassuring smile. 'I have a perfectly good flat of my own. It has central heating and running water and everything. You should know. You've been there.'

For a split second she thought she saw a flicker of heat light the dark depths of his eyes, as if he were re-membering not only being there but everything they'd done within its four walls. But a moment later it was gone and he was pulling open the door and standing to one side and she figured she must have been mistaken.

'If you think I'm going to let you out of my sight for even a second,' he said, giving her a level look that was disturbingly knowing in an altogether different kind of way, 'you can think again.'

'That's a ridiculous overreaction.' Mia stepped past him, out into the cold, and shivered as the freezing air hit her cheeks. 'Anyone would think you don't trust me.'

'I don't. At least, not to put your feet up and rest.'

'Why not?'

'Because you're as ambitious, driven and dedicated as I am,' he said. 'In your situation, I might start wondering what the fuss had been about and be planning a quick trip to the office to make sure that everything was all right.'

Despite the cold, her entire body heated. The man was annoyingly perceptive. 'The idea never crossed my mind.'

'Didn't it?'

'I care as much as you obviously do about the health of this baby, Zander. I'm not going to do anything stupid.'

'I hope not,' he said, stamping his feet and blowing on his hands. 'Which is why you'll agree to move in with me.'

'That *would* be stupid.'

'Who will look after you if you go home alone?'

'I don't need looking after. I can rest on my own. I'll be fine.'

'I disagree.'

He took her elbow, as if he feared she might slip perhaps, but she wasn't geriatric and his touch did odd things to her equilibrium so she shook herself free. With a barely concealed huff of exasperation, Zander set off for the car and she followed, her breath condensing into little puffs of clouds as she trotted along beside him.

'What makes you think you would be the best person for the job anyway?' she said, nevertheless rather glad when he adjusted his long stride to match her shorter one. 'Do you have any caring experience?'

'None at all. But is there anyone else?'

No. But that was beside the point. 'Wouldn't you have work to do?'

'I will work from home,' he said, as if it were a fait accompli, which it most certainly was *not*. 'And when I cannot, I will delegate.'

'Would you be ready to curtail your social life too?'

'What makes you think it needs curtailing?'

'You've been out practically every night since we—' she broke off, flushing at the memory of exactly what they'd done together, then finished '—created this situation.'

'How do you know that?'

'I've seen the photos.'

The gleam that flashed in his eyes did all sorts of things it shouldn't to her insides. 'Have you been checking up on me?'

Maybe. Because frustratingly, despite removing him from her phone, despite *knowing* that what they'd had had been one night only, she hadn't been able to get him out of her head. She'd succumbed to temptation irritatingly quickly but googling his name and then being confronted with dozens of images of him at parties and dinners and events, invariably with a beautiful woman hanging off his arm, hadn't done her any favours so she'd forced herself to stop.

'Not at all,' she lied smoothly. 'The reports of your comings and goings are hard to avoid, that's all.'

'*I* manage to avoid them,' he observed dryly as the car lit up like a Christmas tree at their approach.

'So much for me ruining you for anyone else,' she said, not that she'd ever believed she had because she wasn't a complete idiot. 'But I tell you what *would* ruin you. Or at least your reputation. A flatmate, pregnant with your baby.'

'Let me worry about that.'

Mia watched Zander stride around the car towards the passenger seat door, and thought, hah. As if. When had she ever let someone else worry about anything? For as long as she could remember the worry had been all hers. Her mother's rapidly deteriorating health. The threat of social services turning up and taking her away. Money, food, school. Her business, her future, her *life*. She couldn't imagine having nothing to worry about at all.

'How would you see it playing out?' she asked, not that she was particularly interested or anything.

'The baby is my responsibility,' he said, opening the door and standing to one side. 'I will do everything in my power to keep it safe. And therefore you too. I'll get the world's top obstetrician on speed dial. You'll be waited on hand and foot. You won't have to lift a finger. You can avail yourself of my library and my cinema. Your comfort will be my only concern. Anything you want, anything you need, tell me and I will arrange it. Your wish will be my command.'

He stopped and in the ensuing silence Mia thought with a sigh of longing that actually that did all sound really rather heavenly. When was the last time she'd been taken care of? She couldn't remember. The first signs of her mother's dementia had begun the summer after she'd turned eleven, even though they hadn't had a formal diagnosis until much later, and from that moment on, for the next five years, their roles had slowly reversed.

Mia was the one who'd kept everything together while her mother became increasingly incapable. She'd done the shopping, the cleaning, the washing and the cooking. She'd got rid of nosy neighbours and come up with endless plausible excuses for not being at school. She'd done whatever it had taken to keep up the pretence that everything was all right because she'd been terrified of having to confront the unknowns and uncertainties of reality. And as if that hadn't been enough, she'd done it all while struggling to work out what was happening to the mother she adored, who sometimes adored her back and sometimes didn't, who was sometimes lucid and sometimes wasn't, which had been bewildering and scary and heartbreaking.

So why was she resisting Zander's proposal when being cared for and not having to worry about a thing had once been the stuff of her dreams?

Because it was more of a command than a suggestion and she was used to being in control of her life? Because of the annoying way she still responded to him? Because after nearly two decades of fending for herself she suspected she might actually find the attention a bit stifling?

Well, she should probably get used to occasionally relinquishing control if they were going to parent together, and her reaction to him needn't be an issue. She'd spent the four months prior to his party ignoring it. She could do so for another couple of weeks. No doubt the searing attraction she still felt was down to rampaging hormones anyway, but all she had to do if it did become a problem was remind herself that he'd once blocked her phone, a sure sign if ever there was one that he was absolutely not interested in a repeat of the night they'd spent together.

They were going to be connected for years. They needed to get to know each other, and wouldn't that be easier if they were in the same vicinity? Wouldn't a short period of cohabitation provide an excellent opportunity to discuss the future? He could hardly move in with her. She only had the one bedroom. If she did feel a bit smothered, she could find ways to sneak out, she was sure. Presumably he wouldn't be there *all* the time. And the library and cinema did sound intriguing.

'How many bedrooms do you have?' she asked because if she was going to do this it seemed prudent to check the sleeping arrangements.

'There are three guest suites, of which you can take your pick.'

Excellent. 'What's your kitchen like?'

'Pristine. Enormous. State-of-the-art and very well equipped.'

'May I use it?'

'It would be all yours.'

'All right, then,' she said, and got in the car.

CHAPTER SIX

HAVING INSTRUCTED HIS assistants to cancel his plans for the rest of the week, Zander moved Mia and her luggage into his central London penthouse apartment that evening. He wasn't taking any chances. In the six months since they'd met, he hadn't known her to sit still or stop moving once. He'd detected a certain shiftiness in her demeanour outside the clinic, which suggested that, left to her own devices, she might make unwise decisions. Besides, the sooner she was safely installed in one of his guest rooms, he'd figured, the sooner he could start changing her mind about marriage.

With hindsight, however, he should have given some thought to what happened beyond that short-term goal because now he'd got her here, for the first time since he could remember, he was at a loss as to how to proceed.

Generally, the women in his life fell into one of three categories—family member, colleague or business acquaintance, object of his desire—and generally, he had no trouble adapting his behaviour to suit the occasion. When it came to his sisters, he rolled with the punches. At work, he treated everyone with equal decisiveness and respect. His seduction technique was second to none and he could operate the app that controlled the lights in this apartment, which had no fewer than nine settings that mostly ranged from low to off, with his eyes closed.

Mia, however, was in a category all of her own, for which there were no guidelines, and he had the suspicion that this experience was going to be like stumbling around uncharted territory in the dark with neither a compass nor a torch.

'Is there anything in particular you need?' he asked, setting down her one suitcase and her overnight bag just inside the guest room door.

'No, this looks amazingly comfortable,' she said as she swept her gaze around the space and then headed to one of the floor-to-ceiling triple-glazed windows. 'Very soothing, all these neutrals. Great views in the daylight, I imagine.'

The views were indeed excellent. This bedroom overlooked Hyde Park on one side and on another Green Park and beyond, all the way to the City. At a push, on a very clear day, you could even see the sixty-storey Stanhope Kallis tower in Canary Wharf, where she'd changed his life for ever.

However, Zander wasn't remotely interested in the views. Every drop of willpower he possessed was engaged in keeping his attention off the enormous bed that dominated the space and resisting the onslaught of the hot, vivid memories that brought to mind what had happened the last time he and Mia had been in such proximity to one.

Sex was *not* what this arrangement was about, he reminded himself sternly as he willed his pulse to slow and the fire scorching through him to ease. It was about keeping Mia and his baby safe and securing the future.

A purely practical plan, the only kind he knew how to make, the kind he excelled at.

So he would not think about the electrifying heat of her mouth, the dazzling strength of her desire for him and the way he'd repeatedly lost his mind in her arms. He would not dwell on the irritating way the details kept haunting his dreams by night and derailing his thoughts by day, or the knee-buckling attraction that inconveniently still burned as brightly as it ever had.

Nor would he allow himself to revisit the events of this afternoon and his utterly unfathomable response to her panicked phone call. What that suffocating pressure in his chest and the hollowing out of his stomach had been about he had no idea. He hadn't felt anything like it in decades. But it required no analysis. In the general scheme of things, it was unimportant.

What *was* important was coming up with another of those purely practical plans pretty damn quickly, because how was he going to get through the next two weeks if every time he looked at her he was struck by the overwhelming urge to flatten her against the nearest suitable surface and keep her there until his hunger was satisfied and she couldn't move? He'd go mad. It had to stop.

Thanks to his once-only rule, Mia could no longer be the object of his desire and she certainly wasn't a family member, so perhaps the way forward was to treat her like a business acquaintance.

Respect.

Casual interest.

Charm.

Could that be the right approach? Absolutely. Because there was no other. And who knew? She might even welcome it. She gave no indication that she was similarly tormented by an ongoing attraction, but if she was and her reluctance to move in had not been about a loss of independence at all, then proceeding in this way would be win-win.

There'd have to be conversation, of course. His apartment was large but ensuring her comfort and their baby's safety would naturally necessitate interaction and he liked silence as much as he liked being on his own, in other words, not at all. In the absence of company and activity, his thoughts tended to circle round his faults and his worth—or obvious lack thereof—and he preferred to dwell on neither. Small talk generally made him want to grind his teeth because it was such a waste of time, but here and now it might be exactly the thing.

'What would you like for supper?' he said, practically sagging with relief at having found a way to handle his unexpected and very disturbing house guest.

'I'll eat anything,' she said with a quick smile that for a second made him think of the bed before he told himself sternly, *Business acquaintance...business acquaintance*. 'Although all the good stuff like blue cheese and shellfish is off the menu for a while.'

He obliterated the impulse to take several forward and took a decisive step back instead. 'Right. I'll leave you to settle in,' he said with a nod.

'Thank you.'

'Come down when you're ready.'

It took Mia more time to shower and change than it did to unpack. She hadn't brought much because she wouldn't be staying long. Once her clothes were stowed in the walk-in wardrobe and her toiletries lined up in the limestone-tiled shower room, she called Hattie for the fourth time since leaving the clinic for assurance that everything was on track for the party this evening, then ventured back down the wide floating staircase.

Unsurprisingly, the vast living space of Zander's penthouse apartment, which occupied the three top floors of London's most exclusive residential address, was very masculine—all moody colours, bold lines and a stark absence of daintiness, much like the man himself.

It was also, clearly, a party pad.

At one end of the room, above a granite fireplace that looked as if it was rarely used, hung the largest TV she'd ever seen. In front of the grate, three steel and leather sofas were arranged around a glass coffee table, together with a pair of armchairs that suggested style trumped comfort. In the middle of the space stood a full-size pool table, its petrol blue baize the only shot of colour in a palette of dark, sensuous neutrals, and at the other end was a bar area that stretched along the entire length of the wall, where dozens of bottles lined up on the softly lit shelves behind a counter large enough to accommodate half a dozen stools.

Arriving at the bottom of the stairs, Mia assessed the brown and gold colour scheme and the natural but hard surfaces, similar in style to upstairs, although way more intense, and decided that the décor wasn't to her taste at all. She preferred brighter colours and a wider variety of them. She liked a curtain and a cushion or two and favoured easy comfort over sophisticated style. The only softness to be found here was in the thick cream rugs that covered the dark wood floor. The pictures on the walls were large and abstract. The books on the coffee table were hardbacked showpieces. Even the lamps dotted around the room had a sculptural air about them.

And where were the photos, the evidence of the people in his life? Admittedly, she only had one—of her and her mother, taken at the Herschel Museum of Astronomy that they'd visited the summer before she'd become ill—but Zander had five siblings and a mother, a smattering of in-laws and a clutch of nieces and nephews. If she'd been lucky enough to have a family the size of his, her bookcases would be buckling beneath the number and weight of the frames.

However, what her host chose to surround himself with was none of her concern. *She* didn't have to live in this lavish yet strangely soulless apartment. She was just a temporary guest. And presumably not the first, although how many women he'd entertained here and in what way wasn't any of her business either. No. She couldn't care less about what he'd got up to in the days since their one-night stand. So what if he *had* slept with all the women he'd been pictured with? The future was what was important, not the past.

After a quick look in first the study—no photos in there either—and then the dining room that could seat twenty, Mia eventually found Zander in the kitchen where, beyond the mile-long island, he was transferring silver-cloche-covered dishes from a trolley onto a round marble table encircled by four brass-framed and black velvet-covered chairs.

'How are you feeling?' he said, glancing up with those

darkly compelling eyes of his that never failed to make her tingle in places she shouldn't.

'Fine.'

'Any pain? Any twinges?'

'No.' At least, not of the kind he was referring to, thank goodness. Plenty of throbbing in other places though. He'd swapped his suit for faded jeans and a white shirt, which emphasised his Greek heritage, and looked even more gorgeous than he had in full billionaire businessman mode, striding around the hospital demanding answers.

'Let me know immediately if that changes.'

'I will.'

'Take a seat.'

Doing as he suggested at one of the laid places in order not to ogle him, Mia surveyed the space with a professional eye. Along one wall, a two-plate oven-microwave combination was built into a bank of sleek graphite units. To her right, a full height wine fridge held what had to amount to three dozen bottles. There was ample storage and on the stainless-steel island only a gleaming hob and a sparkling sink broke up the acres of worktop. As he'd assured her earlier, it was state-of-the-art and pristine, and clearly not a lot of cooking went on in here.

'Something smells amazing,' she said, her mouth watering as he lifted off the cloches to reveal a platter of what looked like roast cod with sides of crisp French beans and buttery baby new potatoes.

'The restaurant downstairs is the best in the city,' he said, dispensing with the silverware and then languidly folding himself into the seat opposite her. 'Help yourself.'

Mia picked up a fish slice and transferred a portion of cod from the platter to her plate. 'Do you ever cook?'

'Coffee and toast and that's about it,' he said, sitting back and watching her lazily. 'I'm out a lot of the time. When I'm here I order in.'

'How are you not the size of a house?'

'There's a gym and a pool in the basement.'

'You must be incredibly disciplined.'

'I am.'

And hadn't she reaped the benefit of it, she reflected as she added some beans and potatoes to the fish. From what she could recall of the night they'd spent together— and she could recall every single minute as if it were yesterday—his muscles really were something else: hard and defined, as if he'd been sculpted from warm marble.

And his strength, his power... That first time, in the nightclub cloakroom, he'd picked her up as if she'd weighed nothing and then held her against the wall with only his hands and the thrust of his hips. Once at her flat, there'd been sweat and breathlessness aplenty, but not from the effort of moving her into and keeping her in the positions they'd achieved.

His stamina had been impressive. His mouth a deliciously wicked thing that had instantly turned her into a puddle of need every time he put it on her. And she just had to *look* at his hands to remember them slowly and sensuously sliding over her skin.

The faultlessness of her memory was why she'd babbled on about the views from her room earlier, which she couldn't even see because it was dark. All she'd been able to think about was the enormous bed and the magical things he'd once done to her in hers. She'd had to move to the window before she'd forgotten she was only here because of the scare they'd had this afternoon, lost control and given in to the tidal wave of need that had rushed through her.

Even now, with him leaning forward to help himself, which sent a wave of his scent in her direction, it was a struggle to focus. In her mind's eye, she could see him pushing aside the crockery. Slowly getting to his feet and drawing her up and onto the table, where he'd gently push her back and feast on her until she was trembling all over and crying out and—

'What would you like to drink?'

His question shattered the silence like a shot and she jumped. She went hot. Her gaze flew up and collided with his, but his expression gave no indication that he knew what she'd been thinking, which was a relief because if he did she'd be mortified.

'Some sparkling water would be great,' she said, thinking that the next couple of weeks were going to be a lot tougher than she'd imagined if she couldn't get a handle on her response to him.

Zander got up and headed to the fridge. Mia flapped out her napkin to cool herself down, then laid it across her lap and took the opportunity to remind herself that the only context in which she should be thinking of her host was as the father of her child.

When he returned to the table, she took a much-needed sip of water and turned her attention to the food. The beautifully cooked cod flaked beneath the barest pressure of her knife. The beans were as bright green as they had been on the vine. Someone downstairs definitely knew what they were doing.

'What do you think of the food?' he asked, and as the heat whipping around inside her dissipated Mia sent up a little prayer of thanks to the god of conversation.

'Delicious,' she said, using her fork to prod a potato that was neither too soft nor too hard but just perfect. 'The combination of chicory and seaweed with the cod is an interesting one. I might see if I can add something similar to the menus I offer. I'm always looking for new dishes.'

'You're exceptionally good at what you do.'

A ripple of pride shimmered through her. 'Thank you.'

'How did you get into it?'

'I left school at sixteen and went to catering college,' she said, figuring there was no time like the present for getting to know one another and they had to talk about *something*. 'I was there for two years and then took up an apprenticeship as a *chef de partie*. Six years ago, with eight years' training and experience under my belt, I set up my own business, which has gone from strength to strength ever since.'

He arched one dark eyebrow. 'That simple?'

If only. 'It's been anything but simple,' she said wryly. 'It's taken a lot of blood, sweat and tears to get where I am. It can be a brutal industry. The hours are horrendous and some of the chefs I worked for wouldn't last five minutes in an office. But I started cooking properly at the age of twelve and it's all I've wanted to do ever since.'

'Twelve is young.'

'My mother fell ill,' she said. 'She ended up needing a lot of care and because it was always just the two of us, it all fell on me. Cooking was my happy place when I didn't know what was going on but was terrified nonetheless.'

Zander twirled the stem of his wine glass between his fingers, the picture of casual interest. 'What happened?'

Abandoning her plate for a moment, Mia braced herself since it was still so difficult to talk about. 'The first sign that something was wrong was when she sent me into school on a Saturday, convinced it was a Friday,' she said with a sigh. 'Soon after that, her memory started failing and she couldn't find the words she wanted. She lost her job and once nearly set fire to the kitchen. I took over the cooking after that. I took over everything so that social services wouldn't find out about the situation and take me into care.'

'That must have been tough.'

'It was. Massively. Every day was a worry. I missed so much school. Money was impossibly tight. But the worst of it was seeing the mother I adored, who'd always fought my corner, disappear. We were so intense. It was always us against the world. And then it wasn't. As time went on, more often than not it became her against me and that was so devastating. Her mood swings were unpredictable and merciless. Some of the things she said cut through me like a knife and I was too young to fully understand what was going on.'

'Didn't anybody else?'

She shook her head. 'I got very good at lying and hiding to keep us together. I didn't want to be taken into care. Anyway. She was eventually diagnosed with rapid onset dementia. Whether the progression of the disease could have been slowed if she had had help is something I'll never know. I've learned to live with the guilt of that, but it was hard for a while.'

'You talk about her in the past.'

Mia swallowed hard. 'She went into hospital after falling and breaking her arm and caught a superbug which turned into sepsis. She never came home. I was sixteen when she died.'

'I'm so sorry.'

'So am I,' she said, her heart aching at the loss, even now after fourteen years. 'But I'd grieved for her long before that.'

'I can see why financial security would be so important to you.'

'Security in general is important to me.'

'Marry me and you'll have it,' he said, his dark, mesmerising gaze intent on hers but his expression otherwise blank. 'Marry me, Mia, and you'll never have to worry about anything ever again.'

CHAPTER SEVEN

THAT ZANDER HAD chosen that particular moment to push his agenda should not have stung quite as much as it did, Mia thought, stamping out the strange sense of hurt and disappointment and determinedly pulling herself together.

She should have known he wouldn't let the subject of marriage lie. Hadn't she already seen how tenacious and unyielding he could be when he wanted something? Didn't he have a reputation for ruthlessness? Why wouldn't he take advantage of her rare moment of vulnerability? It was probably her fault in the first place, for carelessly revealing such personal details and furnishing him with ammunition that he hadn't hesitated to use.

'We've already discussed this,' she said coolly, reminding herself to keep her wits about her before she was lulled into another false sense of security and quite possibly found herself at the altar.

'Not to my satisfaction.'

'My position on the subject remains unchanged.'

'So does mine.'

'Yes, I got that from the demand for my birth certificate.'

'Which you still haven't provided.'

Appetite gone, Mia pushed her plate to one side. 'You really do have a problem with trust, don't you?' she said, deciding that it was now his turn to talk. He might even reveal a vulnerability of his own that she could exploit. 'Is that why you're still single?'

Zander half got up, leaned over and reached for her plate. 'What makes you think that?'

'You're handsome, successful and rich, and you're thirty-five,' she replied, steeling herself against the temptation to close her eyes and breathe him in. 'Evolutionarily, you should have been snapped up years ago. There has to be some reason you aren't.'

'Perhaps I simply haven't wanted to be snapped up.'

'Ah, yes,' she said dryly. 'Too many women, too little time, I seem to recall.'

He gave a shrug and flashed her a smile filled with self-deprecation that she didn't believe for a moment. 'Your words, not mine.'

'Yet you're willing to be hitched to me.'

'That's different,' he said, removing their plates to the trolley and returning with a beautiful blueberry tart. 'Our marriage will be purely one of convenience. A legality. Nothing more.'

'How romantic.'

'I'm not interested in romance.'

'What about love?'

He sat back down, frowning in obvious confusion, as if she were speaking Swahili. 'Love?'

'You know. The heart-thumping, giddy feeling that's generally considered to be the basis of a long-term union.'

'I can't think of anything worse,' he said with a tiny yet visible shudder as he picked up a cake slice.

'Why not?'

'What is there to admire about vulnerability and exposure and losing control?'

Mia didn't know quite how to respond to that. She'd never thought of it in those terms. Who would?

'That's quite an indictment,' she said after a moment, as taken aback by his cynical view on the subject as she was intrigued. 'Are you speaking from experience?'

'It's merely an observation,' he said, interestingly avoiding the question as he deftly cut the tart into eighths.

'In that case, love could just as easily be joy and contentment and finding strength and support in sharing the highs as well as the lows.'

'Only if you believe in fairy tales.'

'I do.'

'Why?'

'Because my mother's illness made life really hard and love got lost amongst all the fear and resentment and worry and confusion,' she said, deciding to pause her embargo on the disclosure of personal information in order to get her point across once and for all. 'At times, her cruelty and her dependency made me hate her, which I still feel sickeningly guilty about even though I know that none of what happened was anyone's fault. But the trauma of those five years means that now I crave love. I want to find my soulmate, someone to share my life with, to not feel lonely any more. Even more than I want success and financial security, in fact. And that's why I won't marry you simply for the sake of our child.'

'You're putting your needs first.'

She nodded. 'I am.' And there was nothing wrong with that.

'Finding your soulmate will be hard once the baby comes along and you're parenting with me,' he observed. 'We're going to be in each other's lives for years.'

'I know,' she agreed with a flurry of emotion that seemed to be an odd concoction of excitement, panic, exhilaration and terror. 'I realise that the obstacles littering my path to a happy ending are significant. But other people manage it and I refuse to give up hope.'

'You'll eventually come round to my way of thinking.'

'I won't.'

Zander waved aside Mia's offer of help with the clearing up and merely nodded when she coolly thanked him for supper, claimed exhaustion and bade him goodnight.

Having sent the dishes back downstairs, he poured himself a drink and took it into his study with the intention of catching up on work. After half an hour, however, he had to admit defeat because all he could think about was the meal they'd just shared and the complete and utter failure of his plan to consider her nothing more than a business acquaintance.

Firstly, he couldn't fathom ever understanding anyone who had such a delusional attitude to romantic relationships. He got why Mia might think she wanted one after the childhood experiences she'd had, and it was clear she found his opinion on the subject incomprehensible, but couldn't she see how risky it was to indulge emotion and potentially wind up exposed to immense torment and pain? How could she be so naïve? So trusting in something so fickle? It was a mystery, and she was a fool.

Secondly, it had become apparent as soon as they'd started talking that his interest in her was anything but casual. In response to the revelations about her upbringing he'd been gripped with the desire to know more. Shockingly, he'd felt a certain kinship with her on account of sharing the experience of having parents who were—or had been—physically or emotionally absent and feeling bewilderingly isolated despite existing in the company of others.

His curiosity did not need indulging, he'd had to remind himself sternly when it had been on the tip of his tongue to point the similarities out. There was no need whatsoever to compare and contrast the ways in which they'd grown up or to wish things could have been easier for her. Neither how she still felt about it nor her loneliness was any of his concern.

Developing that sort of a connection was not what was required here, which was a relief because his experience with Valentina had proved that, for some reason he'd never been able to work out, he had zero ability to maintain such a thing anyway.

All that *was* required was a practical relationship based on the needs of their child, as he'd mentioned once he'd finally got a grip on the appalling, petrifying urge to share with her some stories of his own.

There was no earthly reason to confess that the reason he was so disciplined about food and exercise was because as a kid he'd eaten anything he could lay his hands on, which had had an inevitable effect, until he'd figured that a better, healthier way of dealing with his parents' lack of interest in him was to simply shut him self off from anything that hurt so nothing could ever bother him again.

Mia did not need to know that when *he* was twelve he'd spent most of his time trying to find out where his mother was, failing to comprehend why his father preferred to spend more time with his older brother than him and attempting to understand his siblings.

Perhaps it had been callous of him to bring marriage up so soon after she'd revealed so much that was so personal. Judging by the way she'd cooled in response, she'd certainly thought so. But the alternative—caving in to temptation and allowing her a glimpse into the emptiness of his soul—was infinitely worse.

Finally, and most worryingly, it had become increasingly obvious over the past couple of hours that although Mia could not be the object of his desire, given that he'd already slept with her, she still was.

Sitting across the table from her had been torture. Keeping his mind out of the gutter and his hands to himself had proved far harder than he'd envisaged. His attention had been repeatedly drawn to her mouth, which had conjured up uncomfortable memories of other things she could do with it. If he hadn't suddenly recalled his plan to engage in small talk and asked her if she wanted a drink, he might well have acted on the insistent desire drumming through him and carted her off to bed.

None of these discoveries were good, he thought darkly as he poured himself another generous measure of Metaxa. His rampant curiosity about her, the unexpected fragility of his guard, even his bizarre enjoyment of her defiance, were concerning. His one-night-only rule felt unacceptably under threat. The usual louche detachment with which he liked to approach life was deserting him.

So what was he going to do about it?

Despite his original intention to keep a very close eye on her, it seemed wise to temporarily put some distance between them until he'd got used to the situation and had his continuing desire for her under control.

But how was he to achieve that?

Simply holing up in his study here wouldn't work. She'd still be in the vicinity, moving around in his space, filling the air with her scent and tempting him to throw caution to the wind. How long would he last before the defences that had served him so well over the years crumbled beneath the weight of his need for her?

He'd have to go into the office instead. There he'd get the breathing space he needed. Workwise, that would be the right move too. Despite his assurances earlier that he could work from home and delegate if necessary, the thought of spending too long away from his desk made him jumpy. The shipping side of the company was launching a new cruise line and the plans were at a crucial stage. Decisions would be made far more efficiently if he were there.

He could still ensure Mia's comfort and monitor her well-being, of course. She would still be fed and watered and want for nothing. He'd simply outsource her care instead of seeing to it himself. It mattered not one jot who kept an eye on her as long as she was safe, and he'd put every resource he had—with the exception of himself—at her disposal.

He wouldn't be gone for long. He'd soon get everything under control and be back on track. In fact, if she *was* suffering from the attraction in the way he was, she might even welcome his absence and some breathing space of her own.

It was another excellent plan, he thought with satisfaction as he stared out at the twinkling Christmas lights of Knightsbridge and drained his glass. And this time it would work.

Contrary to his assumption, Mia did not welcome Zander's absence.

Once again, she'd gone to sleep in his vicinity and woken up late to an empty apartment but, unlike before, he'd left a note.

She discovered it on the island in the kitchen, into which she'd ventured after recovering from the lingering nausea, showering and dressing. Apparently, an urgent meeting had called him into the office, but the concierge would help with anything she needed, the restaurant downstairs would send lunch up at one and his driver would take her wherever she wanted to go. Zander would be in touch later, but in the meantime she was to put her feet up and relax.

Mia frowned down at the note, not a little put out. Last night as she'd been getting ready for bed, not only had she vowed to ignore the clearly one-sided attraction but also she'd decided to be less sensitive and more pragmatic about the situation. To adopt *his* approach, in fact. To that end, she'd been looking forward to quizzing him about himself over breakfast. She wanted to know more about his family, his work, and explore his fascinating opinions about love.

That, now, would not be happening. However, she was not going to let it overly bother her. Presumably, being CEO of a giant global company meant that delegating took time and she imagined that not all meetings could be done virtually. No doubt he'd had to leave early and hadn't wanted to wake her. At some point today he'd be back, surely, and as it was less than twenty-four hours since the scare that had landed her here, she probably ought to take this opportunity to consider their baby and do as he suggested.

So, after a cup of green tea and some crackers, magicked up by Tony, the obliging concierge at the front desk, Mia spent an hour analysing her spreadsheets. She then called Hattie to check that everything was on track for the dinner party this evening and answered some emails.

At eleven, she wrapped up warm and took a walk. At one, she had lunch—a melt-in-the-mouth quiche followed by a creamy lemon mousse that exploded her taste buds and had her taking notes. Following a brief nap, she headed downstairs to check out the well-stocked library and fourteen-seat cinema, then googled how to play pool and put what she'd learned into practice.

By six in the evening, however, having run out of things to do and heard not a word from Zander, despite the declaration that he'd be in touch, Mia frowned into the empty fridge as she contemplated dinner, and wondered if she should message him.

Would an enquiry into his plans come across as needy? A bit on the clingy side? She'd faced that accusation a number of times before and had pledged to be more circumspect when it came to relationships, but no, this was an entirely different situation. They were equals and she had every right to want to know what the father of her child was up to, especially when she was here at his insistence. Besides, communication was going to be key in the future and she might as well start now, so she closed the fridge door and fished out her phone to text him.

Hope all's going well. Will you be back in time for supper? I could cook.

His reply came a few minutes later.

Back late. Don't wait up.

At the bald words—and the message they conveyed—Mia's eyebrows shot up. Well. That was an unexpected development. Hadn't he made a very firm point about not trusting her to rest and therefore needing to keep watch over her at all times?

But perhaps something unavoidable had come up, something that trumped his lack of trust, like the sinking of a ship or a scandal at the bank. Or maybe delegating and arranging to work from home was proving easier said than done. Whatever it was, she wasn't going to stress about it. She could ask him in the morning, along with all the other questions she had piling up.

In the meantime, she thought as she exited the kitchen and headed for the stairs, since she was exhausted, despite having achieved very little and not at all hungry after lunch, she was going to take his advice and get an early night.

* * *

Unfortunately for Mia's plans to find out what lay behind Zander's absence that day and get to know him better over breakfast, the next forty-eight hours followed a similar pattern to the first twenty-four.

During that time, she saw neither hide nor hair of him. Did he even return to the apartment at night? There was no evidence to suggest he did. They communicated entirely by text, she with increasing irritation and confusion, he with a frustrating lack of urgency and brevity. How long did it take to sort out working from home? she wondered with growing resentment as she tried to keep herself occupied without losing her mind. What was keeping him so busy? Was it *just* work, as he claimed?

She took endless walks. She made the mistake of visiting the department store down the road, which, two weeks before Christmas, had been a bunfight. She read two books and watched five films. By the afternoon of day three, however, having organised into alphabetical order the bottles on the shelves behind the bar—a new low—she'd had enough.

The situation had become wholly unacceptable, she thought, tight-jawed, as she read yet another obfuscating message and her patience, stretched to its absolute limit, finally snapped.

What on earth was going on?

She frequently didn't hear from him for hours. She hadn't seen him in days. What had happened to his alleged concern for the welfare of her and their baby? That had been the whole point of moving her in, and he'd been so resolute, yet almost immediately it seemed to have fallen off his radar. Had she been wrong about his paternal instincts? Mistaken about his ability to step up should something happen to her? And what about seeing to her every need?

How were they supposed to get to know each other and discuss the future if he wasn't around? What the hell had been the point of installing her here in the first place if he'd been intending to abandon her all along? What was he *thinking*?

None of these questions she could answer—and she point blank refused to entertain thoughts about where he was at night, what he got up to and who he did it with because that only tied her in ridiculously jealous knots—but as her frustration and resentment mounted, of one thing she was certain: she was done with sitting here twiddling her thumbs until he finally deigned to grace her with his presence. She was climbing the walls. She couldn't stand being so unproductive. She needed to keep busy, to constantly move forward, not stagnate like this, passive and idle.

Why were the sacrifices all hers? Why should he get to work and she not? At this very minute Hattie and the team were arranging canapés on trays in readiness for a private view at a cutting-edge art gallery. The client was new and influential. Her reputation was on the line, and she'd been twitching all day about not being there in person.

These past few days, she'd managed to control her anxiety about staying away from her business in order to play her part in their arrangement but now she was thinking—if Zander was going to renege on his side of the deal, then why on earth should she continue to bother with hers? She felt absolutely fine. She'd experienced no more pain, no more spotting. The gallery was only a ten-minute walk from here and when they'd swung by her flat to pick up a bag the afternoon she'd moved in, she'd packed her black dress, just in case. There was nothing stopping her from dropping in to make sure things were going smoothly. She could be there and back in a couple of hours. And not that it mattered in the slightest, but Zander would never even know.

CHAPTER EIGHT

'SHE'S DOING *WHAT*?'

In response to Tony the concierge's bombshell, Zander nearly dropped his phone.

'Miss Halliday just left,' Tony repeated slowly and loudly, as if Zander's hearing was somehow impaired rather than merely succumbing to outrage and shock. 'And when I asked her where she was going, as per your instructions, she mentioned popping to a gallery around the corner. I understand that her company is catering an event there. A private viewing, she said. We had a very interesting conversation about modern art and the food she designed to accompany it.'

Zander didn't give a toss about modern art. Or designer food. He did, however, object greatly to Mia taking advantage of his absence to do what they'd agreed she wouldn't.

'Many thanks for the update, Tony,' he muttered, then hung up and leapt to his feet.

What the hell was she playing at? he wondered as he grabbed his coat and strode to the lift. Did she have no concern at all for the safety of the child she was carrying? Short walks and a brief trip to the shops were one thing. Defying his orders to go to work and most likely overdoing it—because why wouldn't she give an event she'd planned anything less than one hundred percent?—was quite another. How could she be so selfish?

With every step he took his anger climbed, but it wasn't solely directed at her. Much as he'd like not to, he had to accept part of the blame for what had happened, which only added fuel to the fire.

He shouldn't have stayed away so long. He hadn't planned to. He'd assumed a day would be more than enough to get a grip on his unruly reaction to her, but then she'd texted him, offering to cook, and with the previous meal's struggles fresh in his mind, he'd thought it wise to maintain his distance a little while longer. A little while stretched into a longer while, with regular updates from Tony assuring him she was fine, but once again the plan that had seemed such a solid one at the time had *not* worked out as he'd hoped.

So much for out of sight, out of mind, he thought darkly as he stalked to his car. Despite his hopes to the contrary, Mia occupied his thoughts all the damn time. At night, while he tossed and turned in the bedroom suite that connected to his office, she invaded his dreams and destroyed his peace. By day, thoughts of what she was doing and how she was derailed his focus so severely it was a miracle he hadn't seriously screwed up.

As he fired up the powerful engine and steered the low-slung convertible out of the car park, he tried, and failed, to work out what it was about her that was so all-consuming, so distracting. Yes, she was beautiful and sexy, but so were many women and he'd met a lot of them. Could it be the fact that she was carrying his baby, which was sparking in him some primitive instinct to defend and protect, even though he wasn't doing a very good job of it at the moment? Or was it simply down to the unsettling novelty of never having had a guest who'd stayed longer than one night?

Whatever it was, spending the last three days at his desk and away from her had not suppressed anything. He had not got his desire for her under control at all. His defences felt as rocky as ever and he was more on edge than he could remember.

The tiny voice in his head, the one which a moment ago had prompted a rare reflection on his role in this debacle, was now urging him to exercise extreme caution. He was in a febrile state. He wasn't thinking clearly. But it was far too late for that. The decision to go home and confront her had been sealed the minute he'd heard what she was up to. Wild horses wouldn't drag him from it now, because Mia had some serious explaining to do.

Two hours after she'd left, Mia let herself back into the apartment. She toed off her shoes with a sigh of relief and headed for the stairs, adrenalin still whooshing around her system like wildfire.

What a night.

What an event.

Celebrities had abounded. Champagne had flowed and canapés had been devoured. Within half an hour every piece that hung on the walls had had a little red dot on its label.

Quite frankly, she hadn't understood the art at all and had liked it even less, but if someone wanted to spend a cool two million on a blue circle with a red line through it, that was up to them. She was hardly going to complain. The enormous amounts of money that moved around this city financed the catering and gave her a job she loved.

She didn't regret dropping in for a moment. Hattie had been faintly put out to see her, true, and she was tired and her feet hurt, but she'd felt so *alive*, so full of purpose. The event had been a resounding success. The effusive gallery owner had said she'd be recommending Halliday Catering to everyone she knew. Tomorrow, there was a lunch in the Docklands for which her company was supplying the food and she'd be going to that too.

'Good evening.'

At the low rumbling voice that came from the depths of the living space, Mia froze for a second then spun round to see Zander behind the bar, in the shadows, fixing himself a drink.

Her head emptied. Her heart lurched and then began to pound. Heat poured through her and her cheeks flamed, as if she'd been caught in the act. But she had nothing whatsoever to feel guilty about. If anyone did, it was him for having got her here under false pretences and then abandoning her. So she took a deep breath and willed herself to calm down.

'Goodness, you gave me a fright,' she said, nevertheless needing a moment to gather her wits and stamp out the inconvenient surge of desire that the sight of him always provoked, even now when she was so annoyed with him.

'My apologies.'

'What are you doing here?' How ironic that he should show up the very evening she'd gone out.

He pulled off the top of a bottle that contained an amber liquid, a shot of which he poured into a tumbler. 'I live here, if I remember correctly.'

'You could have fooled me.'

The only indication that her jibe had hit its mark was a minute clenching of his jaw. He slowly and pointedly ran his dark gaze over her, taking in the dress she wore and the file she carried, obviously putting two and two together, and she flushed—ridiculously—all over again.

'You've been to work.'

In response to his accusation, she bristled and lifted her chin. 'And?'

'You said you'd stay away from your business.'

That was rich, coming from him. 'Yes, well, *you* said you'd work from home,' she countered, padding to the bar because, for her at least, this conversation had been brewing for days and she wanted to be able to see every single reaction.

'Is that what this was, then? A tit-for-tat?'

'Of course not. I'm not that petty. This was me having had enough of being treated so shabbily, of being the only one around here making any sacrifices at all and doing something to stop myself going completely out of my mind with boredom.'

A flicker of what she hoped was guilt flared in the dark depths of his eyes, but all too soon his expression reverted to uncompromising.

'Was it worth taking a risk on the safety of our baby?'

What? That was a bit much. 'I wasn't risking anything.'

'Only a few days ago you thought you were miscarrying,' he said, the simmering anger she could now feel emanating from him tightening his voice. 'On the advice of the doctor, you are supposed to be resting.'

'And I have been resting,' she said, her own temper stirring in response to his wholly outrageous ire. 'For *days*. But I'm not used to lounging around and doing nothing. I'm not an invalid. I feel absolutely fine. And I'm not going to sit here gathering dust while you waltz off to do whatever it is you've been doing. I have no clue why you'd vanish at the first available opportunity when you were so adamant about not letting me out of your sight, and you can work from dawn until dusk and then party the night away with whoever you like, for all I care. What I will say, however, is that your recent behaviour certainly won't make me more amenable to marriage. And if this is the way things are going to be from now on, then what's the point of me being here at all?'

A tiny muscle twitched in his cheek. 'The point,' he said stonily, 'is that with you here at least *someone* will be looking out for your welfare and that of our child.'

'Who?' she challenged. 'Because it obviously won't be you.'

'I've had someone keeping an eye on you.'

At that Mia reeled. What? The only person she'd interacted with at all had been the concierge.

'Tony?' she said, thinking of the many conversations they'd had and feeling absurdly betrayed. 'He's your informant?'

Zander, whose presence here this evening, she now realised, was clearly no coincidence, didn't like the implication that he'd been spying on her. She could tell by the way his jaw set and his eyes narrowed, but she didn't much like his underhand tactics so that was just too bad.

'It was important to me to know that you and the baby were all right,' he said tightly.

'But not important enough to take care of it yourself.'

'My absence was unavoidable.'

'For *three days*?'

'Why? Did you miss me?'

Yes. Bizarrely, she *had* missed him. She *hated* the thought of him partying the night away with who knew who. The days—and the nights—had been so long, so frustrating. But that wasn't the point.

'Your implication that I'm irresponsible is disgraceful,' she said hotly. 'The best person to decide how I am is me. It's certainly not you, either in person or by proxy. And know this, Zander Stanhope. I'm not going to languish in this bachelor pad of yours just because you demand it. And how would you keep me here anyway? By handcuffing me to the bed?'

His eyes glinted. A flash of colour flared across his cheekbones. 'It's an idea.'

Time seemed to slam to a halt. The image that flew into her head dried her mouth and sent shivers racing up and down her spine. Her temperature rocketed and her lungs collapsed and the fiery antagonism that was swirling between them morphed into something more sensuous, something darker, something entirely more thrilling.

'And what would you do with me then?' she asked, heart pounding, chin up, shoulders back, a lot more breathless than she'd have wished.

'What would you want me to do with you?' he said, his voice appearing to have dropped an octave.

'I'd want you to hand me the key so I could unlock myself and then get out of the room.'

'Would you?'

No. She'd want him to spread her out and have his wicked way with her until she was boneless and trembling. She'd want him to do to her everything she dreamed of at night, despite his recent shoddy behaviour. But she would not succumb. Seduction came as naturally to him as breathing, and she'd already fallen for it once. Besides, she was still furious with him. 'Absolutely.'

'So why do I get the feeling you're lying?'

'I have no idea,' she shot back. 'But I can assure you I'm not.'

Without warning, he banged his glass down with enough force to make her jump and planted his hands wide apart on the bar. 'Do you want to know why I've really stayed away from you for so long?' he practically growled, his eyes locking with hers, the intensity of their connection pinning her to the stool.

'You said it was work,' she managed, her entire body on fire in response to both his intoxicating proximity and the unexpected passion of his outburst.

'It wasn't work.'

'No?'

'It was because I can't get you out of my head.'

At his gritted confession, she stared at him for one frozen moment, her eyes wide, her mouth forming a little O of shock. 'What?'

'You've been in there since the moment we met,' he said, eyes blazing. 'I assumed taking you to bed would cure me of my fixation. That normally scratches the itch. But not in your case. You refuse to leave. Every time I look at you, I'm gripped with the urge to pull you into my arms and kiss you senseless. Every time I think of you, I develop an erection that *hurts*. The last three days—which, for your information, I have spent either at my desk or in the bedroom suite attached to my office and *not* partying—have been torture. Even now, when I'm furious with you, all I can think about is stripping that dress off you and doing to you what I did the last time I saw you wearing it.'

He stopped. Mia closed her mouth and released a breath before her lungs exploded.

'You want me?' she said, struggling to process the realisation that the attraction was not just on her side.

'I have never not wanted you,' he grated. 'You're driving me to distraction. Right now, I'm so hard it's possible I may suffer a permanent injury.'

'That's quite a line.'

'I very much wish it was.'

His obvious frustration implied that this wasn't a casual attempt to seduce. He wanted her against his will. Which was fascinating, but something to be analysed later because if he wanted her as much as she wanted him, stayed away because he didn't trust *himself* instead of not trusting *her*, then that changed everything.

'Yes, well, I can empathise,' she replied dazedly, her head spinning as she raked her gaze over the navy suit that emphasised his broad shoulders and lean physique and the white shirt open at the neck, which contrasted devastatingly with his olive skin and dark hair and eyes. 'I feel the same way about you. I can't forget the night we spent together either and, believe me, I've tried. At dinner the other evening I kept imagining you sweeping everything off the table and devouring me instead. Even though you left me here to moulder and I've been so annoyed and frustrated with you, I haven't been able to stop thinking about you. The nights are the worst.'

'It's unacceptable,' he said, a muscle clenching in his cheek.

'It's certainly uncomfortable,' she agreed, the desire pummelling through her robbing her of every thought except one. 'But there is an alternative solution to fleeing to the office and hiding out there whenever it gets too much to bear.'

'And what is that?'

'We could just have sex again.'

Complete silence followed that. For a moment or two Zander simply stared at her as if she'd sprouted horns. Then his brows snapped together and he gave his head a shake, clearly unable to believe what he was hearing. 'Are you mad?'

'I'm heading that way, hence the suggestion.'

'It's ridiculous.'

Quite possibly. Their situation was complicated enough as it was. However, it had become apparent that things couldn't go on as they were. Neither of them would survive. The tension had to be defused somehow. And what was his problem? Wasn't he all about no-strings-attached sex? If anyone was to have had an issue with it, it should have been her. But she didn't. She was all for some unencumbered action. Anything to release the pressure she'd been feeling for days. She'd handled one night with him with equanimity. Why not two?

'I disagree,' she said, refusing to be intimidated by his incredulous intransigence. 'Unless we do something about this wild attraction, it's always going to be between us. It's going to make life even more difficult than it already is. It's only been three days and look at us. I'm not sure distance will provide much in the way of relief. We can't avoid each other for ever. In my opinion, it needs addressing, and sooner rather than later.'

'No,' he countered, jaw set in rebuttal, his dark eyes unusually stormy.

'Why not?'

'I won't allow it.'

'Because?'

'I have a once-only rule.'

Her eyebrows shot up. 'A what?'

'I only sleep with a woman once.'

'Seriously?'

'I don't want a relationship.'

He'd told her that before and she hadn't questioned it at the time, but now she was temporarily lost for words.

'Are you saying that you're so irresistible that two nights or more with you and a woman might get the wrong idea?' she asked, taken aback by the sheer arrogance of that because, though he'd demonstrated instances of that particular character trait before, this took it to a whole new level.

'I prefer not to put it to the test.'

'Since when?'

'Long enough to know it's a policy that serves me well.'

'What are you afraid of?'

'Nothing.'

Rubbish. He appeared to be afraid of clingy women at the very least, and she knew all about those because she, with her previous tendency to start picking out curtains a mere week into a relationship, used to be one of them. But while that definitely merited further investigation, now was not the time. Now was the time to get him to see things her way and satisfy the longing that throbbed inside her.

'Our situation is unique,' she said, holding his gaze, leaning a little into his space. 'I'm not one of your casual hook-ups. At least, not any longer. So the usual rules don't apply. I certainly wouldn't read anything into another night of sex with you. I'm not going to get the wrong idea. It would be a physical release, nothing more, and one which you obviously need as much as I do.'

'It's too dangerous.'

'Not from a medical point of view. The doctor said it would be fine.' She tilted her head and regarded him thoughtfully. 'Or is it me that's dangerous?'

'Don't be absurd,' he said through gritted teeth, looking as if he was resisting the urge to reach for her.

'I'm not the one being absurd,' she said in exasperation, disappointed, thwarted, but knowing that there was a fine line between persuading him to see sense and harassment. 'But OK. Stick your head in the sand if you want. I'm going up to bed. You know where to find me when you realise I'm right.'

Fists clenched, muscles so tight he feared they might snap, Zander watched Mia saunter off to the stairs, her shoes dangling from her fingers and her hips swinging in pure temptation, and thought that she was wrong. Dead wrong. The chemistry that burned between them would fizzle out. It had to. Even if he didn't have the rule by which he'd lived almost his entire adult life, sleeping with her again was a terrible idea. She might not read anything into it, but what if he did?

If he was being brutally honest with himself—a rare event, he'd be the first to admit—she'd never been a casual hook-up. That had certainly been the intention when he'd initially decided to hire her catering services, but it had swiftly turned into something different. Why else would he have pursued her when it had become apparent that the odds of success were zero?

It hadn't just been a reluctance to fail. Over the months, he'd come to admire her brain, her ambition and her drive to succeed as much as he was dazzled by her looks. The snippets of information about her that he hadn't sought but had acquired nonetheless—favourite colour yellow, go to comfort food spaghetti carbonara— had piqued his interest before he'd belatedly reminded himself that his interest had no business being piqued.

He was less enamoured with her levels of perceptiveness, however. Especially now, with the way that the question *But could she be right?* was pushing out everything else from his head. He didn't want to contemplate the implications of that. The notion that his reluctance to act on his desire for her could drive them apart and ruin his plans to bind her and their child to him permanently tightened his chest like a vice. Where would such an outcome leave him? Wandering alone through the wasteland that was the moral high ground, that was where, most probably.

He didn't appreciate the niggling suspicion that he hadn't really thought she'd put their baby in danger this evening but had subconsciously been waiting for an excuse to return to her. He didn't like the fact that he wanted her so much he hadn't been able to stop himself confessing it when he should have been remonstrating with her regardless.

But apparently she wanted him equally fiercely and, quite frankly, he didn't know how much more he could take. Why was he putting himself through the wringer like this? It was true that he never went back, but this was different. *She* was different.

So what on earth was he doing? It wasn't as if he was going to fall under her spell. He was far too disciplined for that. But his strategy for dealing with his desire for her clearly wasn't working, so what did he have to lose from testing hers? His life was hardly going to implode if he surrendered to one more night. Unless he completely lost his mind, which he wouldn't, it would still be just sex.

Ignoring his conscience, which was commanding him to stop the insanity *this instant*, to stick to the plan that had served him so well for nearly two decades because it suspected she could turn out to be very dangerous indeed, every cell of his body now taut with purpose and anticipation, Zander pushed himself off the counter, stalked round the bar and barked, 'Wait.'

CHAPTER NINE

ZANDER'S VOICE CRACKED through the silence like a whip and halfway up the stairs Mia froze. She turned to see him striding towards her with steely purpose and thrilling intensity. He took the stairs two at a time and stopped on the step one down from her and once she'd recovered from her shock she nearly passed out with excitement, because surely this could only mean one thing.

'You've realised I'm right,' she breathed, her heart leaping about her chest and shivers racing through her.

'I'm prepared to consider the possibility,' he said, his voice very rough, very low, smouldering energy pouring off him in great buffeting waves.

'What took you so long?'

'You've almost completely destroyed my brain's processing power.'

'What about your rule?'

'A temporary hiatus will do no harm.'

'You're going to break it for me,' she said giddily. 'And you were so adamant.'

'Don't overthink it,' he muttered, his gaze fixed to her mouth. 'I don't intend to.'

And she didn't want to. She didn't need to. How, or

why, he'd changed his mind was none of her concern. She just wanted whatever came next.

'Here's to living in the moment.'

'I couldn't agree more.'

Eyes blazing, he grabbed her hand and before she could catch her breath he'd led her up the stairs and into his room. He kicked the door shut and pulled her into his arms and their mouths met in a desperate clash of heat and desire.

With a harsh groan that skated over her nerve-endings and set them on fire, Zander tightened his hold on her, exploring her mouth with such skill and intent that her limbs went weak. Lost to sensation, dizzy with his scent and revelling in the hard power of his body pressed up against hers, Mia wound her arms round his shoulders before her legs could give way and kissed him back with equal passion.

One large, warm hand found its way to the back of her neck. The other moved to the base of her spine to clamp her in place. Eventually, the hot, wild, desperate kiss slid into ones that were slower, less feverish, but somehow all the hotter for it. She felt them everywhere, in her toes, in her fingers, even in her ears. The blood flowing through her veins heated and thickened. Her stomach liquefied.

With a soft moan, she twitched her hips so that his hardness pressed into the place where she so desperately ached for him. He slid the hand at the small of her back lower, over the curve of her bottom, and ground her against him, and that kicked everything up a gear.

The sparks of electricity that shot through her nearly took out her knees. Her heart began to pound even harder and desire poured through her like warm honey. She broke the kisses in order to gulp in some much-needed air and he took immediate advantage of the move by shifting his attention to her jaw, her ear, and then slowly, hotly, down her neck.

Instinctively, she dropped her head back to give him better access to wherever he wanted to go, her swollen, achy, tingling breasts desperate for his touch, but the high neckline of her dress was in the way and quite suddenly she needed both of them, her and him, naked, *now*.

Zander clearly shared her thoughts, or perhaps he sensed her urgency, because the devastating kisses stopped abruptly and his hands went from caressing to searching.

'Where's the zip on this thing?' he muttered after a moment of thorough searching that she hadn't minded one bit.

'At the side,' she said, her voice so thick and raspy she barely recognised it.

Having found the tab, he slowly slid it down and she shivered, though the room was warm. He reached down and slipped his hands beneath the hem at her knees to push her dress up, over her head and off.

His smouldering gaze roamed over her, taking in the black lace bra that these days barely contained her breasts and matching knickers. It lingered on her abdomen for a moment, and her heart fluttered, but she didn't want to think about the baby right now, about what this was and wasn't, so she stepped forwards, lost herself in the intensity of his expression and eased off his jacket.

'You're overdressed,' she murmured, her breath hitching as she unbuttoned his shirt and pushed that off him too and thought that God, she'd forgotten how magnificent his chest was. All those muscles. The solidity, the strength.

The night of his party, she hadn't had nearly enough time to fully explore the expanse of it or to properly savour the feel of his hair-roughened skin beneath her palms. Tonight, she planned to rectify that, so she put her hands on him and, emboldened by the shudder that ripped through him, slowly trailed her fingertips over the ridges and dips. Her mouth watered at the thought of tasting him, and she leaned in closer, closer, shutting her eyes and breathing him in, but it seemed that he had other plans because he suddenly swept her up in his arms, carried her across the room and deposited her on the bed.

While she lay against the pile of pillows, catching her breath and recovering from the surprise move, Zander stripped off the rest of his clothes with impressive speed and efficiency and, although she'd seen it all before, it was as if she was looking at him for the first time.

She'd assumed her dreams had embellished his assets, but no. In the soft glowing light, she could see that his shoulders were just as broad as she remembered, his thighs just as powerful. And in between them, jutting up, long, thick and hard, the massive erection that had driven her to heights of pleasure she'd never experienced before.

Her heart thudded wildly as he joined her on the bed. He shifted onto his side, then half rolled on top of her, and her entire body trembled.

'Are you sure it's medically safe to do this?' he said, smoothing back a rogue lock of hair from her cheek.

'Definitely,' she said with a shiver at the unexpected nature of his touch. 'The doctor recommended leaving it for forty-eight hours, but it's been longer than that so we're good.'

His dark eyes glinted. 'We are better than good. We are exceptional.'

And Mia knew that he was an ace seducer, that these smooth lines might be practised even if some weren't, that making women swoon was his thing, but nevertheless, she did exactly that. He lowered his head to hers, their mouths meeting again for a slow, hot kiss that sent flames flickering along her veins and dissolved her stomach, and her head actually spun.

Needing to touch him, she lifted her hands to his shoulders and ran them over his hard muscles and into his hair, and he moved his beneath her to unclip her bra. He tossed it aside and then slid a hand from her waist up, and when he cupped one breast with it, she moaned at the palpitations that jolted through her. She was so sensitive. She had goosebumps all over and quivered everywhere. His thumb brushed over her nipple and she almost came on the spot.

Had she felt this level of desperation before? she wondered with the one brain cell that was still functioning. She couldn't remember. She could barely recall her own name, especially when he replaced his hand with his mouth and she saw stars.

He lavished exquisite attention on her, taking his time, in no hurry to move on until, almost inside out with desire, she whimpered, 'I need more,' and he obligingly inched his way down her body, singeing her skin with his kisses, before finally stopping at the molten spot where she burned.

His hot, ragged breath on her made her quake with need. He removed her knickers, then put his hands on her knees and parted them. He draped her thighs over his shoulders and curled his arms around them. Then he put his mouth on her, where she so desperately throbbed for his touch and ached for his possession, and she had to bite her lip to stop herself from crying out, even though there was no one around to hear her except him.

Within seconds she was struggling for breath. He was going to blow the top of her head off. And soon. Her muscles were tightening and she was impossibly hot. Her heart was pounding. She was clutching at the sheet. The exquisite pleasure was building. A familiar tingling was beginning in her toes and then it was rolling up through her in a giant unstoppable wave until it tipped her over the edge, and she shattered.

Liquid heat rushed from her pelvis into every cell of her being. White lights flashed behind her eyes, while the contractions she felt vibrating through her went on and on, rendering her dazed and limp.

She gradually came to, to find Zander had moved and was once more gazing down at her from above.

'That was fast,' he said, his voice so low and rough it was almost feral.

Fast and intense and incredible. 'Hormones,' she said, still breathless, still dizzy. 'They've gone a bit mad.'

'This *is* going to be fun.'

A gleam lit the dark depths of his eyes and, incredibly, a fresh wave of desire washed over her. But she wanted to make him fall apart as she'd just done, for him to be putty in *her* hands, so she pushed him onto his back, arranged herself so she straddled him, and said, with a slow wicked smile, 'It certainly is.'

Zander woke late the following morning to an empty half of the bed, which would have been a cause for annoyance and alarm were it not for the mouth-watering smells that presumably came from the kitchen and meant that while Mia wasn't around to help him out with his mammoth erection she wasn't far away.

What a night, he thought with a yawn and a stretch. Her response to him had been as stunning as that first night they'd spent together. Over and over again she'd shattered in his arms, and she'd blown his mind more times than he could count. How his bed had survived it, he had no idea. Why he'd ever had reservations about sleeping with her again he couldn't imagine. What on earth had he been thinking? Together, like that, they truly were extraordinary.

After reassuring her that he'd *always* practised safe sex and that there hadn't been anyone since her anyway, for the first time in his life he hadn't used protection and it had been a revelation. She'd felt like warm, wet velvet and the heightened friction, the exquisite sensitivity and the unexpected intimacy had rocked his world.

Rubbing his eyes, Zander reached for his watch, which sat on the bedside table, and squinted at the dial. It was ten o'clock. And a Friday. He ought to have been at his desk over two hours ago, and under normal circumstances he would have been. Yet this morning, after that night, work didn't remotely appeal. What *did* appeal was firstly food and secondly returning Mia to his bed and keeping her there to explore further ways in which they could be exceptional.

He'd built up a very capable team in the six years since he'd taken over from Leo as CEO of Stanhope Kallis, he reminded himself as he tossed aside the covers. The three-hundred-year-old company, which employed thousands across the globe and had a several-billion-euro turnover, wouldn't collapse if he didn't go in today. Unable to find his shirt, he located his shorts and trousers and pulled them on. Then, lured by the distinctive scent of frying bacon, he headed downstairs.

Mia was at the stove with her back to him, humming along to the Christmassy sounding music emanating from her phone. No wonder he hadn't been able to find his shirt. She was wearing it. And not a lot else, it appeared.

For a moment, he leaned against the door frame and simply drank in the view. The long bare legs. The glimpses of her bottom which the tails of his shirt didn't quite cover. All that red-gold soft, silky hair. And as the seconds ticked by, he was filled with the clamouring urge to walk up to her, wrap his arms around her from behind, push her hair to one side and kiss her neck until she was breathless. Instead, because he did still possess *some* self-control and that somehow felt important, he pushed himself off the door frame and walked into the room.

'Good morning,' he said, thinking it was a very good morning indeed.

'Good morning,' she replied, looking charmingly sexy and dishevelled and disconcertingly at home at his stove.

Aware that what little self-control he'd prided himself on retaining was in danger of slipping away in response to the evident curve of her breasts and the hard points of her nipples beneath the crumpled white cotton, Zander slid his gaze to the pots and pans and food beyond her. 'You're cooking breakfast.'

'I am,' she said, casting her eyes over his torso for one long, lingering moment before abruptly turning back to the stove and flipping the bacon with the deftness of someone who'd done it many times before. 'I've made pancakes and French toast. The tomatoes are under the grill and the sausages are keeping warm in the oven with everything else.'

For both their sakes, Zander gave her a deliberately wide berth as he walked around the island to the other side and pulled out a stool. 'You don't need to cook for me.'

'I know. But I enjoy it and we need to eat. Are you hungry?'

'Ravenous.'

'Grab a plate.'

'Where did all this come from?' he asked, waving a hand at the dishes on the counter and those she was removing from various appliances that before this morning had never been used.

'The food hall down the road. I was going to go shopping myself, but Tony insisted on taking my list and having everything delivered instead.'

'I'm not surprised he went out of his way to be helpful if you were dressed like that.'

'It was the first thing that came to hand and he was in an apologetic frame of mind.'

A dart of guilt stabbed him in the chest. Roping Tony in to ease his conscience while he'd been hiding out at the office hadn't been his finest moment, although he had done his best to make up for it in the bath he and Mia had taken some time around midnight. 'It looks better on you than it does on me.'

'I don't know about that,' she murmured, her gaze drifting over his chest once again, leaving fresh scorch marks in its wake. 'You could wear a paper bag and still look gorgeous. But if it makes you feel better, I threw on some leggings and a coat.'

That did make him feel marginally better. He didn't know why. Tony was sixty-five and happily married, with three children and ten grandchildren, and jealousy had never been his thing.

'You could have just ordered something in,' he said, choosing to ignore the unfathomable twist of his gut and reaching for a perfectly warm plate.

'You can't survive on restaurant food for ever.'

'I'm living proof you can.'

'Do you mind I took over your kitchen?'

After considering her question for a moment, Zander decided he did. He found both the sensual domesticity of the scene and the fact that he couldn't remember the last time anyone had cooked for him unnerving. But he couldn't tell her that. Only a few days ago he'd used it as bait to entice her to move in, so instead he gave her a smile that had been described as devastating on more than one occasion and said, 'Not at all.'

'I would have asked, but I didn't want to wake you.'

'That I wouldn't have minded either,' he said, dropping three rashers of bacon on his plate and thinking of all the very pleasurable and not at all domesticated ways in which she could have done so. 'Remember that next time.'

Her gaze dipped to his mouth and darkened, as if she was imagining kissing him, and her breath caught. 'So there *is* going to be a next time?'

Of course there was going to be a next time. His hunger for her hadn't abated one bit.

'Sooner than you might think if you keep looking at me like that,' he said, adding eggs, tomatoes and sausages to the bacon and noting the wild fluttering of the pulse at the base of her neck.

The faintest of smiles tugged at her lips. 'We can't have that after all the effort I've been to.'

'Then save the smouldering for later.'

'Would that be wise?'

'You're the one who pointed out the wisdom of it in the first place,' he said, needing her to see things his way because he didn't want to contemplate not having sex with her again. 'We've slept together on two separate occasions and, from my point of view, the world hasn't imploded. How's it looking from yours?'

'Still intact.'

That was a relief. And yet the tiny frown that appeared between her eyebrows was a concern. 'Are you having second thoughts?'

'No,' she said, 'but I am wondering how long we give it.'

He had no idea. He didn't have a template for this totally unprecedented situation. All he had was logic and the points she'd so effectively made last night. 'I suggest we continue until the attraction disappears and we can co-exist in peace.'

'What if it doesn't disappear?'

'It will,' he said, as much to assure himself as her. 'In my experience, which, as you know, is extensive, it always does. Generally after one night, admittedly, but even the longest lasting, most spectacular firework burns out eventually.'

Mia didn't look convinced as she took the seat opposite him and loaded her plate with French toast and tomatoes. 'I'll have to take your word for it.'

'You do that. And while you're doing that, think of the fun we're going to have in the meantime. I know I am.'

Her breath caught and her cheeks flushed and for one electrifying moment he thought she was going to suggest abandoning breakfast after all. But a second later, disappointingly, she'd given herself a visible shake and pulled herself together. 'That can wait.'

Could it? That was a shame. Unless she'd somehow thought of a better plan. 'What do you have in mind instead?'

'Something I've been wanting to do for the last three days,' she said with an enticing stretch for some cutlery.

That did sound interesting. 'Which is?'

'Regardless of how you feel about relationships, it's looking increasingly likely that we're going to be having one of *some* kind. So I think we should get to know each other better. I'd like to find out more about the father of my child. We've already talked quite a bit about me. So, while we eat, I'd like to talk about you.'

CHAPTER TEN

OUTWARDLY, ZANDER SWALLOWED down the eggs he'd just put in his mouth and carefully returned his fork to his plate with barely a sound. Inwardly, however, all thoughts of fun had vanished, and alarm was now rushing into every millimetre of his body, coating his skin in a film of cold sweat and threatening a reappearance of the coffee he'd drunk.

Talk about himself?

He'd never heard a more preposterous, more petrifying proposal in his life. It went against his number one principle when it came to women—not getting personal and staying safe.

The exposure…

The vulnerability…

Even the thought of knowingly putting himself in such a position made his blood chill and his insides shrivel. Wasn't that yet another reason he'd stayed away from her this week? Because deep down he'd feared that all too soon small talk would not suffice.

Well, he'd been right.

He did not want to talk about himself. At all. But what choice did he have? Given the circumstances, Mia's suggestion wasn't outrageous and she wouldn't let him get away with suddenly remembering a meeting. If he stonewalled too much, she might start to wonder what his problem was. She might figure it had to be bad and decide she didn't want him around their baby. The likelihood of getting her to agree to marry him would become even more remote than it already was.

And even if that *didn't* happen, her point about them being connected for years to come was a salient one. He'd even told her the same thing at dinner the night she'd moved in, just before he'd offered her a slice of blueberry tart. In six months or so, all being well, they'd be bringing up a child. Together. Which would presumably require communication of some sort on a regular basis.

So perhaps he ought to practise. He didn't have to reveal anything particularly deep. Much of his life was already in the public domain. He had decades of experience in deflection and obfuscation, when it came to others as well as himself. But on a superficial level he could give her elements of what she wanted, surely. If he prevaricated, she'd only push harder and with his inexperience he'd likely lose control of the narrative, which was not an appealing prospect.

So he cleared his throat, sat back and braced himself. 'What do you want to know?' he said, ignoring the sliver of unease and deliberately relaxing his shoulders, as if this conversation really was no big deal.

Mia took a sip of orange juice, thought for a moment, then said, 'Do you like your life?'

Zander's eyebrows shot up. That was what she was opening with? Existentialism? He didn't know how he felt about his life. He didn't often analyse it. Or ever, in fact. So he went for a smouldering smile and a pleasingly ambiguous, 'Who wouldn't?'

'Well, a baby, I would imagine.'

'I see no reason for anything to change,' he said, largely because he hadn't been to a party in a fortnight and he hadn't slept with anyone other than her in the last six months, so it already had.

She frowned. 'So you're not planning on being that involved, then.'

He shot her a wolfish grin. 'I'm very good at multitasking, I think you'll agree.'

'Because I need to know that if anything happens to me, you'll be there.'

Ah. The grin slid from his face and he shifted on his seat. 'What do you think is going to happen to you?' he said, his gut clenching in the oddest way at the idea of anything happening to her at all.

'Probably nothing. I mean, I don't carry the gene that caused my mother's disease, so that's not a worry, but there is only me. And I don't ever want a child of mine to face the prospect of growing up alone.'

'I'll always be there,' he said, for once deadly serious. 'And if for some reason I'm not, I have a lot of siblings and in-laws. Whatever happens, our child will never be alone. You have my word.'

'Do you trust them?'

'Yes.'

'Do you get on well with them?'

'Sure.'

At least, he didn't get on *badly* with them. En masse, they could be a challenge, what with the instinctive, natural way they interacted, which confounded and unnerved him in equal measure. He found the marriages unfathomable and he'd never get used to the displays of affection between those who'd coupled up, which was why he'd be avoiding the annual Christmas get-together this evening. But on a one-to-one basis they were easier. Under those circumstances he got on with each of them in different ways.

'So why don't you have any photos of them?'

Why on earth would he? If he had photos of them then they'd want ones of him and that wasn't happening when who knew what could be captured in an unguarded moment. 'I'm not one for photos.'

'If I were you, I'd have albums of the things. I so envy you your siblings,' she said with a sigh. 'I used to imagine I had four. Two older, two younger. Two boys, two girls. We'd get up to all sorts of things. Japes and escapades and jam sandwiches. We never argued. It was always perfect. Too much Enid Blyton from the library, probably. And then something would happen to burst the bubble and I'd land back in reality, which was pretty bloody awful most of the time and somehow even worse after one of my idyllic daydreams.'

'At least you had a mother who loved you,' he said, not much liking the shadows that clouded the clear blue of her irises, which set off an odd twang in his chest.

'Didn't yours?'

'The only person my mother truly loves is herself. She isn't, and never has been, around all that much.'

'Not even when you were young?'

'Especially not then.'

'What about your father?'

'He had a fatal heart attack eighteen years ago,' he

said. 'He was the stiff upper lip type. Aristocratic, stern and obsessed with building an empire. He didn't have much time for us either. Or rather, none of us but Leo, who he was grooming to inherit the company.'

'That must have hurt.'

He gave a shrug, as if it hadn't cut him to the bone before he'd decided to deal with it by simply shutting his emotions down. 'I didn't know any differently.'

'So what was growing up with but without them like?'

Pretty bloody awful, to steal her phrase, but this conversation had turned out to be deeper than he'd anticipated. It was one thing her voicing her fears, but he couldn't afford to do the same. He wouldn't even know how. In his desire to erase the wistfulness from her expression he'd already revealed too much and he really didn't need the sympathy that was radiating in his direction.

'It was fine,' he said with a dismissive wave of his hand. 'We had excellent nannies.'

'That's no substitute.'

'We survived.' He shot her his wickedest smile. 'Some of them were stunning.'

'Of course they were,' she said dryly. 'I hope I get a chance to meet them.'

'Who?' Not the nannies, surely.

'Your brothers and sisters.'

Well, *that* was never going to happen. He hadn't introduced anyone to his family since Valentina, who'd convinced him such a thing was normal and whom he'd been trying to please, and what a waste of time that had turned out to be.

These days, his conquests were never around long

enough to even enquire into his family and none of them, before Mia, had ever meant anything anyway. Not that she meant something, of course. It was just... well, he didn't know what it was.

But as his pulse slowed and his lungs began to function again, it occurred to him that he'd have to explain her and the pregnancy to his siblings at some point, preferably before the press got wind of it, so why not at the party this evening? He'd declined the invitation, not needing the peculiar tension and roiling stomach that meeting up with them always provoked in him, but that was easily fixable. He could handle any tricky questions that came his way. He'd simply smile lazily and bat them away as he usually did. The addition of Mia to the proceedings would certainly be novel.

'If you're feeling up to it,' he said, stuffing the unacceptably stirring emotions back into the locked box where they belonged, 'you can meet some of them tonight.'

The Stanhope family's dinner was being held in a small private room at an exclusive central London members' club that was housed in a building which dated back to 1774.

Climbing the sweeping marble staircase with Zander at her side, Mia was glad she'd had the opportunity earlier to pick up a suitable outfit from her flat. As unassuming as the exterior of the club was, it was not the sort of establishment that would look favourably on the comfy jeans and baggy sweatshirts she'd packed for her stay with him. Nor did she want to wear her black dress and feel like one of the staff. More importantly, however, there was no way she was going to meet members of his ultra-glamorous family in anything other than her best cocktail dress and highest heels.

She could scarcely believe she was here in the first place, if she was being honest. She'd only suggested meeting them because her curiosity over his upbringing had got the better of her. How could his childhood possibly have been fine when it sounded as if he and his siblings had largely been neglected by the two people who should have done the opposite? What effect would that have on a boy, and the man he'd become?

At least *she'd* had eleven years of love and affection and a photo to prove it. Even though she couldn't remember much about that period of her life, eclipsed as it had been by time and the illness that had destroyed her mother and robbed her of her adolescence, she knew she'd been adored and nurtured in the beginning, that there had been shared hopes and dreams, and there was comfort in that.

'Are you all right? You're very quiet.'

Zander's murmured concern cut into her musings about how he was so much more complex than she could ever have imagined, and she switched her attention to the evening ahead.

'Just nervous.'

'Don't be.'

'That's easy for you to say,' she said as up and round they went, her stomach fluttering more wildly with every step she took. 'They're your relatives. You've known them all your life. Do they know about me?'

'They're about to.'

'Are you planning on telling them about the baby?'

'It would be the ideal opportunity. Would you mind?'

'I don't know,' she confessed with a faint frown. 'What if they hate me? What if they think I'm a gold-digger who's deliberately trapped you or something?'

'They won't,' he said, glancing across at her, clearly bemused. 'Why would they?'

'I don't know that either. I've never done anything like this before.' She took a deep breath and let it out slowly, but it didn't do much to ease her jitters. 'I can't believe I thought it was a good idea.'

'You've never done this before?' he asked, one dark eyebrow arched in surprise.

'I'm not very good at relationships. I've only had three and none of them reached the meet-the-family stage. Not that that's what this is exactly, I know.'

'What about the fairy tale?'

'It's remained elusive.'

'Why?'

'I've been told I have a tendency to cling,' she said with a wince. 'It's a fair assessment. I so badly want to be part of something bigger than just me, it sometimes skews my judgement.'

'That's understandable.'

Now the surprise was all hers. 'Is it?'

'Given your upbringing, I would say so.'

'That's quite some insight.'

'It's logic, nothing more.'

She supposed it was. It didn't require a degree in psychology to look at the past to see how it influenced the present. She'd spent so many hours doing precisely that she was practically an expert.

'Would it be logical to assume this is a first for you, too?' she said.

'Why would you assume that?'

'Because presumably the women you sleep with—just the once, naturally—would get even more of the wrong idea if they were introduced to your family.'

'Now *that's* insight,' he said, neither confirming nor denying her point, which she would have found interesting had she not been reminding herself that *she* wouldn't be making that mistake, of course.

There was nothing to read into this evening, so she would *not* be thinking about how if she did marry him she'd be instantly part of the something bigger she'd always longed for. The in-laws. The nieces and nephews. The birthdays, the Christmases, the belonging.

She was only here because she was carrying his child. None of it was real and there was no point in wishing it was. Which she didn't. Because that would be a one-way ride to despair, as she'd reminded herself this morning while she'd lain beside him, staring up at the ceiling in the half-light, wondering where they went from there.

Did they view last night as a one-off and hope it had done the trick? she'd asked herself, the questions tumbling around in her head like clothes in the wash. Or did they carry on indulging the off-the-charts chemistry and cross their fingers that it wouldn't cause problems down the line? Neither course of action had seemed like a solid one but with desire stirring and thoughts of waking him up *extremely* nicely to be checked, option two had felt infinitely preferable.

As long as she heeded her own advice and kept in mind that what existed between them was purely physical, she'd assured herself, her heart would be safe. That he hadn't slept with anyone else since her was irrelevant and didn't require analysis, even if it had come as a surprise. Chemistry was simply one set of pheromones responding to another. She wouldn't fall in love with him because fundamentally they wanted different things, so he was not and never would be the man of her dreams, and she wouldn't be marrying him anyway.

'This way,' he said when they reached the landing. 'Showtime.'

Zander planted a hand on her back to propel her in the direction of a purple panelled door. Banking the nerves and resisting the urge to cling to him for support, Mia braced herself for a situation that was filled with the unknown and went on in.

Great swathes of raspberry-coloured velvet hung at the multi-paned sash windows. The walls were lined with striped silk of a similar but paler hue and the woodwork was painted a fresh light green. The comfortable furnishings and abstract art were a clever combination of modern and traditional. With elaborate cornicing, gilt moulding and tassels dangling from the spectacular chandelier, sumptuous the room was, minimalist it was not.

But, beyond that, she barely noticed the décor. The warm pressure of his hand on her back vanished. All she saw was a bunch of impossibly beautiful, achingly sophisticated people, chattering animatedly in both Greek and English, clearly at ease and enjoying themselves, and all she felt now was a wave of longing so strong it nearly took out her knees.

'Zan!' said a stunning brunette, catching sight of them

and heading over, her smile so bright it was blinding. 'What are you doing here? We didn't think you were coming.'

She reached up and planted a kiss on Zander's cheek, and while he returned it Mia grappled for control because she had to remember that this family was not and never would be hers.

'Change of plan.'

'And with a *date*,' said the woman, her brown eyes sparkling as they took in Mia with rampant curiosity. 'It has to have been *years* since that last happened. What was her name?' She appeared to think for a moment and then said, 'Aha! Valentina. That was it, wasn't it?'

At her side, Mia felt Zander tense but his smile stayed in place and he continued to radiate nonchalance, which was a *very* interesting paradox.

'I don't recall,' he said languidly while Mia thought, not so languidly, Valentina? Who was *she*? 'Mia, this is my sister, Thalia. Thalia, this is Mia Halliday.'

Thalia held out her hand. 'It's a pleasure to meet you.'

Parking the intriguing Valentina for now, Mia shook it and returned his sister's megawatt smile with an attempt at one of her own. 'Likewise.'

'Great dress.'

'Thank you.'

Zander had certainly approved of it, she recalled, a hot flush rolling through her body from her feet up. Earlier this evening, she'd emerged from her bedroom in the gold fringed knee-length affair that she liked because it was easy to wear and shimmied when she moved, only to be hustled straight back into it. 'Liquid sunshine' was how he'd described it, while whipping it off her before tumbling her to the bed, messing up her hair and make-up and making them very late indeed.

'You look familiar,' said Thalia with an assessing tilt of her head and a slight frown. 'Have we met before?'

'I catered Zander's birthday party back in October,' said Mia, batting away the steamy memories of earlier in order to be able to concentrate on the conversation happening now. 'You may have seen me there.'

'Ah, yes, that's right. I remember. Zander was scowling at you.'

'I was not.'

'My mistake,' his sister said, a recognisably wicked glint dancing in her eyes. 'If I recall correctly, it was the risotto that was the source of your displeasure.'

Oh? 'The risotto?' said Mia, her eyes narrowing as she slid her gaze in his direction. 'What was wrong with it?'

'Nothing,' he said, sounding supremely unperturbed but looking as though he'd quite like to throttle his sister.

Thalia was evidently unaware of the danger she was in. 'He thought the flavours unoriginal,' she said blithely. 'Which they were very much not.'

Unoriginal? Seriously? 'Did you?'

With a tut of exasperation, he leaned in close and bent his head. 'I wanted you,' he murmured, the admission for her ears only. 'You didn't want me. It was frustrating. But I wasn't going to tell Thalia that. She'd never have let it go. Your risotto was perfect.'

'Oh,' she breathed softly, her pique melting clean away. 'Well, that's all right then.'

'I'll make it up to you later.'

Why later? she thought giddily. She wanted him to

make it up to her now. Because in response to his proximity, his warm breath that caressed her skin, the spicy scent that scrambled her senses, her pulse was drumming in her ears and even though they'd spent all day in bed, the desire that was sweeping through her was as fresh and hot and wild as ever. But, unfortunately, they were in public, so she got a grip and murmured, 'I'll hold you to that.'

'I'll make sure you do.'

Straightening slowly, almost reluctantly, she sensed, Zander cleared his throat, shoved his hands in his pocket and switched his attention back to his sister. 'Where's Santi?'

'Phone call,' said Thalia, fanning her face with her hand. 'He'll be back in a minute. So are you two an item?'

'When am I ever an item?'

'What's the deal, then? Because I nearly got singed just now—and don't take this the wrong way, Zan—but Mia isn't your usual type.'

'I know she isn't,' he said, enviably cool while Mia still burned. 'She is, however, pregnant, and the baby's mine.'

CHAPTER ELEVEN

WHY ZANDER HAD chosen that particular moment to impart their news, he had no idea. All he knew was that the words had bizarrely been piling up on his tongue from the moment they'd walked into the room and had spilled out before he could stop them.

Perhaps he'd been thrown by the unusual intensity of the unpleasantness that had slithered into the pit of his stomach in an all too familiar way on seeing his siblings chatting away with each other so naturally.

How did they do it? he'd wondered queasily as he'd watched his younger brother Atticus laugh at something Thalia had said. They were twins, so that had always given them a special bond, he assumed, but what excuse was there for Leo to instinctively lean into Willow, his wife, when she touched him lightly on the arm? More bafflingly, *why* did they do it? Didn't they care about exposing their emotions to each other and risk being destroyed? Didn't they realise how vulnerable they were making themselves?

These were questions he'd never been able to answer so, as usual, he'd buried them deep, profoundly relieved that he was so practised at hiding and dissembling that no one would have had the slightest idea what was going on, which meant that a far more likely explanation for blurting out that Mia was pregnant was that he'd been shaken to the core by his response to the heated moment they'd shared in the aftermath of Thalia's unforgivably good memory.

For several long, heart-thumping seconds it had felt to him as though they were the only two people in existence. Overwhelmed with excoriating need, he'd been a hair's breadth from kissing the life out of her in front of an audience, which had never been his thing, and he thanked God he'd come to his senses in time.

Either way, the news was now out, suspended in the ether, immobilising every animate thing. There was a stunned frozen silence, which lasted several thudding beats of his pulse and a full revolution of his stomach, then the room erupted into a flurry of excited activity.

'Congratulations,' said Leo, striding forwards, smiling broadly and clapping Zander on the back before introducing himself to Mia and kissing her warmly on both cheeks.

'Will you be getting married?' asked Atticus, to which Mia replied 'No' at the same time as Zander said 'Yes'.

Then it was the turn of Willow, an artist with piercings and multicoloured hair, who shouldn't have suited his tightly controlled older brother but somehow did. 'How are you feeling?' she said, addressing Mia, who was looking a little shellshocked by the hugs and kisses that were coming her way.

'Anything I can do to help,' added Zoe, another sister-in-law, Atticus' wife, mother of one, soon to be two, 'let me know.'

Zander accepted the congratulations automatically,

waiting with his breath stuck in his throat for the incredulity, the doubts, the ribbing, because surely at least one of them would point out how unsuited to the role of father he was. But no one said anything. The subject of his perceived lifestyle—wholly incompatible with a baby, as Mia herself had pointed out—didn't come up once. Of his self-centredness and lack of depth, not a word. Instead, to his astonishment, Leo insisted on a toast, of all things.

When they sat down to eat, two glasses of champagne and five minutes later, Zander was still waiting on tenterhooks for the other shoe to drop but, staggeringly, it didn't. Conversation flowed from the children to the company to Daphne and Olympia—his two youngest sisters, who weren't in attendance—and then moved on to their mother.

'Have you heard the latest from Selene?' said Thalia as she helped herself to some potatoes.

On easier to understand ground now, but nevertheless thinking that couldn't possibly be it, Zander sat back and raised his eyebrows. 'No. Why? What's she been up to?'

'She's been arrested for cavorting topless on a beach. Not the done thing in the Maldives, apparently.'

'Just what I need when we're about to launch the new cruise line arm of the business,' he said dryly. 'Her timing is impeccable, as always.'

'Don't worry,' said Atticus, head of the company's legal department. 'I'm on it. Any damage will be limited.'

'You'd think a full-size nude portrait would be enough to satisfy even the most determined exhibitionist,' Leo mused, topping up Mia's water glass. 'Although I suppose that *was* six years ago.'

'I still haven't got over it,' Zander said with a wince and a shudder. 'Talk about mortifying.'

'Hey, that's one of the finest pieces of work I've ever produced,' protested Willow without rancour. 'It launched my career.'

'I went to one of your exhibitions,' said Mia, who up to that point had hardly said a word, which was odd when she was not usually backward in coming forward. 'In London. Three years ago. It was amazing. You're incredibly talented.'

Willow beamed. 'Thank you. I'd love to paint you if you're up for it. I know I'm hardly one to talk, but the colour of your hair is highly unusual. Your skin is incredible. You'd look great in pastels. What do you think?'

By the look of things, Mia didn't know what to think. Wide-eyed and pink-cheeked, she appeared to be struck dumb. She opened her mouth. Then closed it. When she did manage to formulate an answer, it was an unexpectedly tremulous, 'I don't know what to say.'

'Say yes,' prompted Willow.

Mia blinked. Then nodded. 'OK,' she said a fraction more firmly, with a small yet blinding smile. 'Yes.'

'Great! Maybe you could persuade Zander to pose too. That bone structure and that smile… The delicious hint of wickedness… I've been trying to get him to sit for me for years, but to no avail.'

At the thought of it a shudder ran through him. 'I have a global multi-billion-euro company to run,' he said, hiding his recoil of horror behind an apologetic grin and a what-can-I-do? sort of a shrug. 'I hate to disappoint you, but my spare time is limited.'

'I'll make it happen one day.'

No, she wouldn't. Because Willow liked to get to know her subjects by delving deep. Apparently, it added a certain depth and luminosity to her work. But if she dug around in his psyche, she'd find nothing luminous, nothing good, and the sense of worthlessness that lurked inside him was *not* for public display.

'Don't hold your breath.'

To his relief, the conversation then moved on to other less troublesome topics, but for some reason he couldn't stop thinking about Mia's smile when she'd agreed to sit for his sister-in-law. Something about it had felt important. He couldn't put his finger on what.

As the evening progressed, he continued to ponder the conundrum as they ate and drank and he watched her from afar. At first she'd preferred to observe the proceedings rather than participate in them. But gradually she seemed to relax and the balance shifted in the other direction. Before long, she and his siblings were chatting away as if they'd known each other for years instead of hours.

He largely listened and learned. Atticus and Zoe had recently been to a restaurant that served its customers in the dark, which prompted a discussion about the importance of senses when dining and gimmickry. Santi was buying an island off the Brazilian coast. Mia's dream holiday destination was Lapland, to see the aurora borealis.

One part of him ached with envy over her ability to fit in so easily and tried desperately to work out how she was doing it. Another was dazzled by the way she somehow shone, in a way that had nothing to do with the sexy gold sparkly dress she had on.

A third, however, was noting that she was avidly drinking everything in, wholly wrapped up in the banter and the affection, and quite suddenly, just as coffee and chocolates were being served, he had an epiphany.

He knew exactly what he'd seen in that smile.

Longing.

This was what she'd always dreamed of, he realised with a rush to the head, stunned that he hadn't figured it out sooner. To be part of a family. To belong. And while he would never be able to offer her the love she wanted when he abhorred emotion, especially of the sentimental kind, and simply wasn't capable of it anyway, it was within his power to give *this* to her.

Marriage was no longer as remote a possibility as it had felt last night, he thought with a surge of satisfaction. Securing his position in case, unlike his siblings, she recognised his lack of depth and selfishness and took against it and decided she'd had enough, was once again at the top of his agenda. Because now, after days of wondering what the hell he was going to do about it, he had the leverage to get it.

What an absolutely fascinating evening, Mia reflected, kicking off her shoes back at the apartment and padding after Zander into the kitchen. And to think she'd been so nervous. His announcement had come completely without warning, but she hadn't had time to panic over how all those beautiful people were going to take the news of her pregnancy because, to her utter amazement and relief, she'd been enveloped in warmth and any concerns she'd had had simply disappeared.

There'd been no sly comments, no judgement, just delight and support to an extent that she'd never have expected. She hadn't met any of them before—they moved in *very* different circles—but that hadn't dimmed their effusiveness or acceptance of her and their nephew-or niece-to-be one bit, and for a while she'd been so overwhelmed, her throat so tight, that she'd hardly been able to speak.

But at least she hadn't fallen into the trap of thinking any of it was real. Every time she *had* caught herself drifting off into dangerous little daydreams in which Zander was interested in her welfare for her sake and not just their baby's and they were all one big happy family, she remembered him telling Thalia—most emphatically—they were not an item and hauled herself back on track.

Instead, she'd eaten supper without really tasting it—a rarity—and observed the dynamics like a kid with their face pressed up against the window of a sweetshop, only allowing herself to be drawn into the conversation once she'd strengthened her defences.

And hadn't those dynamics been intriguing.

Zander's exchange with Willow on the subject of his reluctance to sit for a portrait had been particularly interesting. She didn't buy his 'not enough time' excuse. Everyone else had managed to make time. Their portraits all hung in the exhibition she'd been to. But not his. Behind the smile and the careless shrug, she thought she'd caught a flicker of irritation in his eyes. And something else. Something that had looked a bit like fear. Which was odd, because while she could understand the irritation if he genuinely didn't want to be painted, what on earth would he have to fear?

And that wasn't the only perplexing aspect of the evening. Forget Valentina for a moment, whoever she might be. Of far greater interest had been the other undercurrents she'd sensed swirling around him. It had been clear that everyone there was very fond of him and that the dinner had been a happy, relaxed occasion, but for some reason he'd seemed on edge. Sort of removed from the proceedings. He hid it well, but once or twice she'd even caught him looking at his siblings as if they were a different species, which was bizarre.

And what was the lazy smile, the lounging and the insouciant drawl all about? That wasn't the real him. She'd glimpsed the man behind the mask and he was far more layered than he was making out. The conversation they'd had on the way up was an example of that. Yet the minute they'd walked in, it was as if he'd flicked a switch and become a completely different person and she didn't think it was a one-off because no one called him out on it.

Why did he feel the need to put on a show, especially for his nearest and dearest? What was going on beneath the handsome, laid-back and very assured surface? And if she asked, would he ever tell her?

Having furnished Mia with a cup of the green tea she favoured, Zander made himself the thick black coffee he preferred and then joined her at the breakfast bar end of the island. Now he knew how to get what he wanted, like any deal, he was keen to get it wrapped up. Before he got side-tracked by her dress, her tousled hair and sexily smudged eye make-up and the moment passed. So he pulled out a stool, sat down opposite her and gave her a level look. 'We need to talk.'

'We do indeed,' she agreed with an equally level look of her own. 'You can start by telling me why you were so on edge tonight when it was such a wonderful evening.'

He stilled. His pulse skipped a beat. What the hell?

'I wasn't on edge,' he said, his intentions for the conversation momentarily derailed.

'Not outwardly,' she conceded. 'Outwardly, you were all lazy smiles and devilish charm from the minute we walked into that room. But it felt like some sort of a front, because you seemed watchful and wary. There but not really there. As if you'd landed from another planet. I'd like to know why.'

Well, *that* wasn't happening. He could barely unravel it in his head, let alone articulate it. But how had Mia noticed? What had given him away? What else could she have seen?

He shifted on the stool and adjusted his jacket, his blood chilling at the thought of being so transparent. 'There's nothing to know.'

'I think there is.' She wrapped her hands around the cup and tilted her head, continuing before he could interject. 'I think that behind that gorgeous facade of yours there's a *maelstrom* going on. I mean, how could there not be? You have a mother who sounds as selfish and embarrassing as the tabloid press reports and a father who by your own admission was never around for you. That neglect has to have been painful beyond words. You don't seem at all comfortable around your siblings, and I find myself wondering if Valentina, whoever she is, is the reason you're so sceptical about love, if she's the one who made you feel vulnerable and exposed, out of control and powerless. For some reason I've yet to work out, the idea of sitting for your portrait terrifies you and right now a muscle is pounding in your cheek and your jaw is so tight it looks as if it's about to shatter. I'd like to know what you're feeling. What you're thinking. You never know, I might even be able to help.'

Zander didn't need help. He just needed this unnecessary psychoanalysis to stop, along with her terrifying perceptiveness. The expanding pressure in his chest was crushing the air from his lungs. A swarm of a thousand bees seemed to be buzzing in his head.

So much for dissembling. It was as if she'd drawn back the curtain to his soul and taken a good long look at it. How had she done that? Did she understand what she'd seen? How had he not noticed?

The situation was slipping dangerously out of hand. His very foundations were cracking and he couldn't allow that. He had to contain the emotions trying to break their bonds to surge through him. He had to restore order and regain control and remember why he'd wanted to talk to her in the first place. So he willed his head to clear and concentrated on his breathing until he was cold and numb and back in command of himself. 'That's quite some analysis.'

'You're a fascinating man and it was an illuminating evening.'

'Did you enjoy yourself?'

'Very much. Your siblings and their spouses are great. I can't think why you'd have a problem with them.'

And that was the way things were going to stay. With her not thinking about him. At least, not like that.

'Has it ever occurred to you that if you married me you'd have instant access to them?' he said. 'That you'd immediately become part of the something bigger you want?'

'It has,' she replied with a nod. 'Well, once. Briefly. On our way to the dinner. But we both know such a relationship would be built on sand.'

Did they? For his part, he wasn't sure he knew anything any more. 'What makes you say that?'

'It would never be real. It would never truly give me what I want. What I think I deserve. Unless you're in love with me, of course. Then we might have a chance. Is that the case?'

His heart gave a great lurch. His entire body clenched, every single cell he comprised curling up like a pill bug, and the coffee in his stomach turned acidic. 'No.'

'Might it ever *be* the case?'

'Absolutely not.'

'Ouch,' she said with a wince that he hoped to God didn't mean she *wanted* it to be the case because he'd have no idea how to handle that. 'At least you're honest.'

'You should try it some time.'

Her eyes widened for a moment and then she frowned. 'What do you mean?'

'Admit there'd be advantages to being married to me.'

'Such as?'

'Firstly, your business. With one snap of my fingers—' he gave one snap of his fingers '—I could make Halliday Catering the number one catering company in the country. Even the world.'

'I think I'd rather do it on my own, thanks all the same.'

'And then there's the money,' he continued undeterred, because he was now in control of this conversation. 'Consider the costs of bringing up a child. Childcare. Education. Housing. Is a second floor flat really where you'd want to be lugging a pushchair? I could buy us a house with a garden tomorrow. Employ round-the-clock nannies. You'd never have to worry about money again. You could go back to work as soon as you liked. And if that doesn't sway you, think of the sex. I can't imagine getting bored with that any time soon. Can you?'

Her gaze dipped to his mouth and darkened. 'No.'

'Love is no guarantee of happiness,' he said, resisting the sudden blinding urge to lean over, take her face in his hands and kiss the daylights out of her because, for what had to be the first time ever for him, that wasn't important. 'I like you. I admire everything you've achieved. Lots of marriages are built on less. Think of the bigger picture. Think of the aunts and uncles our child would have on tap. The cousins to play with. The grandmother, although I admit that might not be such a draw. We'd be a family, a unit, and one that could even expand. You'd no longer be alone. You'd have all the things you've always wanted, except one. Wouldn't that be something?'

For a while Mia didn't say anything. She just sat there, barely moving, as if somehow winded. The seconds ticked by. He could practically see her working through what he'd said, and he waited, his breath stuck in his lungs, for her response, which came a moment later.

She gave herself a shake, cleared her throat and swallowed hard. 'I tell you what,' she said with a tiny jut of her chin. 'You address the points I just made and I'll promise to think about it. How does that sound?'

What? No. Out of the question. Why on earth would he lay out all his flaws for her inspection? He had been reckless on many occasions, but he wasn't completely out of his mind. And what did she think she was doing, turning the tables on him? Wasn't the leverage supposed to be his?

'That sounds like blackmail,' he said, flabbergasted.

'Call it what you like,' she said with unbelievable cool, 'but you're asking a lot of me. You're asking me to give up on a major dream of mine, a dream I've had for years. I've already conceded so much. I agreed to move in here temporarily. I took a step back from my business. I spent three days *resting*, which was the hardest thing I've done in a long time. What sacrifices have you made? None, as far as I can see. In what areas are *you* compromising? We each owe it to our child to be as baggage free as possible by the time he or she comes along. It's taken me years, but I've dealt with mine. Can you say the same for yours?'

Well, no. He couldn't. He was aware he had a lot but he'd never addressed any of it. He'd always preferred not to analyse his behaviour or the reasons for it, but to simply live with his issues, as if fearing a hornet's nest that he might not be able to withstand if he prodded it. So he'd never wondered how his past influenced his present in the way she clearly had. He'd never considered how it might affect his future.

And that had been fine when it had affected no one but himself, but he no longer existed in isolation, he realised with an unsettling jolt. Whether he liked it or not, he now had someone else in his life to consider. Mia. And, in approximately six months' time, a baby who would be dependent on him for years.

His days of thinking only about himself were over. If he wanted to be better than his own parents, he had to adapt. He had to at least *try* and become a more complete human being. Because his kid *did* deserve the best version of himself, however inadequate that might be.

Currently, he was not that. He didn't even know what that could look like, although it had to be better than the mess he was at the moment. So perhaps he did need Mia's help. As she'd said, she'd worked through her issues. Could she sort through his?

Even if she couldn't, she'd still have to hold up her end of the bargain, and he didn't have to strip himself bare by telling her *everything*. Some things, such as his reasons for not wanting his portrait painted and the black hole of emptiness that lurked inside him, would never be up for dissection.

But others?

Why not?

It would mean discarding a lifetime of keeping a firm lid on the box that contained everything he didn't want to think about. It would mean exposing to her certain parts of his bleak inner self that had never seen the light of day. But if it got him what he wanted, if it neutralised the possibility of her disappearing with their child when she realised he was damaged beyond repair, it was a price worth paying.

CHAPTER TWELVE

MIA HAD NOT really expected Zander to accept the deal that she'd offered him even though it had felt slightly on the exploitative side, which should have felt like payback, but annoyingly didn't.

In fact, when he *did*, she thought she must have misheard. That wouldn't have been beyond the realms of possibility. She'd been thoroughly distracted by the picture of marriage he'd painted, the silver-tongued devil. She'd been pondering the odd reaction she'd had to his declaration that he would never love her, which was nothing new and should not have come as a blow but had nevertheless caught her off-guard.

But she had to park all that for now. The glimpses of the man beneath the surface that she'd previously had had been accidental, she was certain. Tonight, he'd decided to actively seek her input—he must *really* want her to marry him, although she couldn't see why when surely he'd realised by now that he could trust her, her quick trip to the gallery notwithstanding—and it somehow felt momentous.

He took his time pouring himself the drink he'd muttered he'd need if he was really going to do this. More to deliberate where they should sit, before settling on the library downstairs, a cosy space that had two chairs, both facing a built-in electric fireplace, which meant there was no facing each other.

Mia sat in her chair and sipped her tea, tracking Zander's movements as he set the bottle he'd brought with him down in anticipation of a challenging conversation, he'd said, and sat in the chair next to her. The suspense was killing her, but she would not revert to old bad habits and push. She would sit back and let this play out in its own time. He would start when he was comfortable. To her relief, however, because patience really wasn't her strong point unless she was in the kitchen, she didn't have long to wait.

'So about this evening,' he said eventually, staring into the fire. 'I *was* tense.'

Aha. She knew it. 'Why?'

'I always am when we meet up as a group.' He scowled and knocked back half of his drink. 'I just don't get them. They seem so relaxed with each other. I can't understand how they do it.'

So he *did* feel like an outsider. 'Well, obviously I have no experience of siblings,' she said, reminding herself to rein in her rampant curiosity and tread carefully, 'but I wouldn't have thought it's a conscious thing. Presumably, you spent your childhood together. You must all know each other inside and out. They're relaxed with you too.'

'Only because I make it easy for them.'

That wasn't necessarily true. 'I think you're underestimating yourself. By taking me along to dinner this evening and dropping our baby bombshell you could have made things very difficult for them indeed if they hadn't approved.'

'Possibly.'

Definitely. 'What do you think would happen if you dropped the facade?'

'I'm not sure I ever want to find out,' he said with a shudder that suggested she'd been right about the maelstrom.

'What are you hiding?'

'Nothing in particular.'

She found that hard to believe. At the very least, his super confident exterior had to conceal a chronic lack of self-esteem. She should know. She'd suffered from it herself, and the fundamentals of their circumstances weren't that dissimilar.

'I'm just no good at relationships and I'd like to correct that,' he said gruffly. 'The last thing I want is to turn out like either of my parents.'

'You won't. I won't let you.' And besides, despite the occasionally odd way of showing it, he did have the baby's best interests at heart.

'I might if I don't figure out how to be better.'

'You run one of the largest private companies in the world,' she pointed out. 'You couldn't do that without building and maintaining relationships.'

He frowned and fell silent for a moment, as if he'd never considered that before. 'That's different,' he said eventually. 'That's work.'

'So it's just close personal ones you struggle with.'

'Yes.'

'Then what about Valentina? You must have dated

her more than once. You introduced her to your family. You broke your rule for her.'

'Valentina predated the rule,' he said with a grimace. 'She was the reason for the rule.'

Oh? 'In what way?'

'We met at a party when I was nineteen and went out for six months. To begin with everything was great. But then she wanted more.'

'That's not entirely unreasonable.'

'I know.' He drained his glass and refilled it. 'So I tried to make it work. I *wanted* to make it work. As you said, I even introduced her to my family. But that wasn't enough. Apparently, I was unable to give her what she needed. I couldn't commit to her—' he winced '—emotionally.'

'Was that true?'

'I'm not very good at connecting on a deep personal level,' he admitted, sounding as though he was having to grind out every word.

'Or maybe you just weren't as into her as she was to you.'

'I was. Or at least I wanted to be. But it didn't end well. I didn't understand what I'd done wrong. She made her disappointment in me very clear. I've been careful to avoid a similar situation ever since.'

'That's understandable,' Mia said, intensely disliking this woman whom she'd never met. 'Who'd want to go through that again? Although it *was* sixteen years ago, which is a long time to let something like that dictate your sex life.'

'I don't deny I also like variety,' he said with a faint quirk of his lips.

Hmm. 'Yes, well, it seems to me that your so-called inability to connect on a deeper level isn't all that hard to figure out.'

'Isn't it?' he asked, shooting her a curious glance before returning it to the fire.

'With parents like yours, who by the sounds of things were never around much and therefore didn't engage with you when you were young, how could you ever have learned how to do anything else? Where were your role models?'

'I suppose I didn't really have any,' he conceded after a beat.

'Who supported you? Championed you? Listened to your worries?'

'I dealt with everything on my own.'

As she had done. She'd had no support, no one to celebrate her successes or go to with her worries either, and for years she'd questioned her value.

For her, catering college had turned that around. Surrounded by like-minded people, being kept busy doing something she loved, even though she'd been grieving for the mother she'd lost, she'd slowly made friends and under the guidance of mentors had discovered her sense of self-worth. It had given her the courage to believe in herself and to set up on her own and had got her through some tough times in the beginning.

But who had he had? No one.

'You were neglected,' she said, feeling a sudden hot rush of anger on his behalf, there and gone in a flash. 'You had no one to meet your emotional needs.'

He considered that for a moment then said with a nod, 'I suspect you're right.'

'How on earth did you handle it?'

'I learned not to let it affect me. Like you, there was nothing I could do to change it. I just had to accept it.'

'There's a world of difference between accepting a situation that was nobody's fault and one that was.'

'It's worked for me so far.'

'But it doesn't sound as though it's working for you now and I'm not sure what good leaving these things unaddressed has ever done anyone. So, having said all that, I do believe you can *learn* to connect with other people on an emotional level.'

'Can you?'

'Absolutely,' she confirmed with a nod. 'I'm an example of that. I didn't get what I needed from my parents either. Or, rather, I did, from one of them, but not for long. With no one around to validate your feelings and experiences you find yourself questioning your self-worth. Your self-esteem nosedives. You get used to doing everything on your own. You become so strong that any hint of vulnerability or any request for help feels like weakness. It's hard to let people in. But you have to at some point, because no one is an island. Life is so much better with other people in it.'

'I know that,' he said. 'Deep down, I've always wanted that. I've just never known how to do it.'

Her heart gave a little ache at that but she would not let it distract her. 'I'm not saying it doesn't take time because it does. And it's not easy either. But you can't move forward if you don't understand and make peace with the past. And you can't overcome your faults and your flaws if you don't acknowledge them in the first place.'

Mia finished and took a sip of her tea while that sank in.

'Do you want to know what my greatest flaw is?' he said after a moment, setting down his still full glass and turning to face her, his eyes dark and intent on hers.

Her heart skipped a beat. She wanted to know everything there was to know about the gorgeous, brave, compelling man her child was lucky to have as its father, whatever his faults. 'Sure.'

'Not being able to control my need for you.'

And, as he reached for her, it was clear that Zander was done with this conversation, which filled Mia with as much disappointment as desire.

Zander had had to bring the conversation to a halt that night in the library. He'd been hit by one earth-shattering revelation after another and his bruised and battered brain simply hadn't been able to take any more. He'd had to take refuge in sex. By that point it was all he'd understood.

He hadn't liked Mia's point about his experience with Valentina overshadowing the last sixteen years. Her spin on it made him sound weak. Nor had he appreciated her implication that his so-called inability to connect on a deeper level was all in his head. It wasn't. It was a very real, very deep-rooted part of him. But at least she hadn't pushed him on what he was hiding. At least she hadn't had a chance to quiz him on why he would never sit for his portrait.

The rest of their conversation, though, which had shone a spotlight on his upbringing, had made a whole lot of sense. Of course he'd been neglected. Of course he'd never learned how to communicate properly. He *hadn't* had anyone to observe and emulate. The nannies had been great, but they hadn't exactly set an example to follow. So how could he ever have known what to do?

And as for his siblings' ability to forge and maintain relationships, which had always bothered him because, after all, they'd all grown up in the same house, it occurred to him as he lay awake in the early hours of Saturday morning, the conversation looping around his head, that emotional neglect and having self-absorbed parents might affect different people in different ways. He'd overeaten. Leo had crashed a boat. Olympia had spent a year in rehab. Atticus and Thalia were twins, they'd had each other, which presumably had made things easier. And Daphne had certainly suffered. She'd been diagnosed with acute myeloid leukaemia at the age of thirteen and although she'd been in remission for nearly a decade, she'd spent most of her adolescence in and out of hospital. How had she coped with their parents' approach to parenting?

Discovering and accepting that his problem with close personal relationships wasn't his fault, but rather a by-product of his less than ideal upbringing, was something of a game changer. It suggested he had no fundamental flaws, as he'd feared, and that he might not be as worthless as he'd always assumed, courtesy of the belief that if even his own parents weren't interested in him then it had to mean that there was nothing about him to be interested in.

Over the next forty-eight hours, the bleak emptiness that had existed inside him for so long like a living, breathing thing seemed to ease. Far from feeling raw and exposed in the aftermath of their conversation, as he'd expected, he was aware of an odd sense of lightness and liberation.

He found he wasn't even that bothered about pushing Mia to comply with her side of their deal any more. Marriage was no longer the pressing necessity it once had been. She'd seen into the deepest parts of him and hadn't run a mile. And why would she? Apparently, there wasn't anything there to run a mile from. So she had no reason whatsoever to deny him access to their child.

In fact, he was now really rather relieved she'd resisted. Marriage for the sake of their child would only have complicated the situation. They could easily co-parent apart. Many thousands of other people did.

He had further work to do on his journey to becoming a fully functioning human being, of course. The thought of large family gatherings was still going to make him uncomfortable for a while. He obviously had *some* flaws.

But he'd taken those first tentative steps and they hadn't been a disaster, and he was keen to take more because building a sustainable relationship with Mia and their child didn't now feel as impossible as it once had. The more he'd talked to her and shared with her, the more he'd learned and the less insurmountable the challenges he faced seemed.

She even had the ability to soothe his agitation on the rare occasion it arose. This morning, for example, he'd run his hand down her body and when he'd felt the very faint curve of her abdomen he, a man of thirty-five who'd stared down countless rivals in the boardroom and possessed more power and influence than the leaders of some small countries, had started to shake.

'Are you all right?' she'd murmured, but he hadn't been able to reply because he hadn't been all right at all. His pulse had been racing and the walls had been closing in on him and he'd genuinely thought he'd been going to faint even though he'd been horizontal at the time.

But then she'd put her hand over his and the dizziness had faded enough for him to start breathing in and out, deeply and slowly, to be able to push down hard on everything that was demanding to be let in until it had all gone away.

'I'm fine.'

'I know you have concerns about your ability to be a father,' she'd then said, 'but you *will* be good at it. You're instinctively protective, you want the best and you care. That's quite a start.'

Was that really what she thought of him? he'd wondered as the chaos raging inside calmed. Did she genuinely believe he'd succeed at this? Astonishingly, it had sounded as though she did.

'Well, when you put it like that,' he'd said, the doubt beginning to slink off in the face of her certainty, 'maybe it is.'

Attempting a deeper, more personal connection between them was nothing to fear, nothing to avoid. It might even be something to look forward to. Contrary to what he'd been led to believe, he wasn't a disappointment. He didn't lack depth or value. He was fine. And that he now knew it was all down to Mia who, if catering didn't work out, could retrain as a psychotherapist. Whose insight and self-awareness were to be envied.

Who'd told him how much she'd admired the way he'd thrown himself into something he'd clearly found a challenge and made him feel ten feet tall.

She hadn't given up on him. She'd fixed him. Or some parts at least. And for that she deserved a thank you.

Mia had never received much in the way of presents. Her mother had left school to have her and had then got a job as a part-time shop assistant when Mia had started at nursery, but there'd been little money for toys. And then, later on, she hadn't had anyone to exchange them with anyway.

So when Zander had told her he was giving her an early Christmas present, once she'd got over the urge to dance around the room and smother him in kisses—a ridiculous overreaction—she hadn't been able to think what that might be. A diamond necklace? Something for the baby? A brand-new spatula? She hadn't a clue.

Never in a million years would she have imagined being driven to her flat first thing on Monday morning to pack a bag of warm clothes and find her passport. Less still could she have envisaged him then whisking her to the airport, where his private jet was sitting on the tarmac, sleek and white and sparkling in the frosty December sunshine.

'Where are we going?' she said in something of a daze as she handed her bag to a member of the crew and then walked with him towards the plane.

Zander grinned, clearly extremely pleased with himself, which for some reason made her head spin and her heart melt like a snowflake in the sun. 'It's a surprise.'

That was a phrase no planner of anything ever liked to hear.

'I'm not sure I like surprises.'

'You'll like this one.'

'How enigmatic.'

'Not any more,' he said, taking her hand as they went up the steps. 'Thanks to you, I'm an open book.'

Burning up with curiosity and nervous excitement, Mia entered the cabin ahead of him and thought that he certainly was that. He'd confessed that he'd shut the conversation down that night in the library because it had been too much to handle, but they'd talked a lot over the weekend. They'd compared childhoods. Shared stories and experiences. Discussed such wide-ranging topics as politics, books and culinary loves and hates. She'd wanted to discover as much as she could about the father of her child and she'd done exactly that.

Of the future there'd been less discussion but there was plenty of time. They had months. The important thing was that they were communicating, on a number of different levels, and things were looking rosy.

Her book, however, was slightly less open, of course. But if he knew that she was not only thinking about his marriage proposal but actually considering it, *in his favour*, he'd be unbearable. She could hardly believe she was entertaining the idea of it herself. She'd always been so resolute about only marrying for love, so convinced that that would give her everything she'd ever wanted.

But over the weekend she'd begun to wonder, would it?

What if she never fell in love? Or what if she did and it all went wrong? Could Zander be right? Was what they already had enough? She found him fascinating. They got on well. They were on the same parenting page, trusted each other enough to reveal the bad as well as the good, and the chemistry showed no signs of diminishing.

Dare she imagine that, given the fact that he'd changed his mind about opening up to her, albeit under duress, his opinion on other things might shift too? Like love?

She probably shouldn't, but she did nonetheless. Because evidently he hadn't always been against it. Surely his relationship with Valentina was proof of that. It had been short and he'd been young, but despite Mia's suggestion at the time that perhaps he hadn't been as into it as Valentina had been, in hindsight, he must have loved her for their breakup to have had such a long-lasting effect. And if he'd been capable of it once, perhaps, if he could get over the breakup, he could be so again, in theory, which did possibly throw a different light on the future.

'How long will we be away for?' she said, sitting down in one of the cream leather seats and fastening her seatbelt as she cast a glance over the matching sofas, the thick shortbread-coloured carpet and the polished walnut trim, more akin to a sitting room than an aircraft.

'One night only, so there's no need to panic. We'll be back by tomorrow afternoon.'

He knew her and her need to be near her business too well.

'And the flight time?'

'Three and a half hours.'

Perhaps the destination was Athens. That would be great. She would love to see where he grew up. She might even get to meet his mother, who, following her brush with the Maldivian law, had returned home and

LUCY KING
155

was under strict orders not to leave it. But there didn't
seem much point in asking because she doubted he'd
tell her.

'However are we going to occupy ourselves?'

'There's a cabin at the back with a bed in it,' he said
as he took the seat opposite her and smouldered. 'I'm
sure we'll think of something.'

After take-off, they had breakfast. Over a plate of
pastries, she told him that she used to dream her father was a pilot—or maybe a scientist or a farmer—
and create whole worlds around him. She told him that,
along with the cooking, being able to lose herself in her
imagination had come in handy when things had got a
bit much later on and she'd needed a way to handle the
resentment and anger that developed along with everything else. He downed coffee after coffee and responded
by confessing that he'd dealt with the neglect he'd suffered by comfort eating, in a classically futile attempt
to make himself feel better, which was why he was so
disciplined in hitting the gym.

That reminded Mia of his muscles, as if she needed
a reminder, and they headed to the cabin, where she
joined the mile high club and for a deliciously long while
stopped tormenting herself with the pros and cons of
marrying him and didn't think about the possible engagement of her heart in all this.

She didn't notice that outside the sun was starboard or
that the sky was darkening instead of brightening even
though it was mid-morning. She was aware of nothing
but the wild, all-consuming heat that burned between
them and losing control of her body and mind.

It was only when they touched down, some three

hours and several orgasms later, that Zander finally lifted his head from the crook of her neck and said with a grin that suggested he was thoroughly proud of himself, and not just because he'd repeatedly dissolved her bones, 'Welcome to Lapland.'

CHAPTER THIRTEEN

MIA DID NOT react to his announcement that they'd arrived in Lapland the way Zander had expected. He'd imagined a gasp of surprise and then perhaps a squeal of enthusiastic delight and a pleasing display of gratitude. He'd been so proud of himself that he'd thought of this. He'd never been any good at giving presents. He'd always worried about getting it wrong, as his parents invariably had on the rare occasion they'd remembered a birthday, and figured it would be simpler just to not give anyone anything at all.

But this had felt like a winner. Utterly fail-safe. Lapland was Mia's dream holiday destination. December was an excellent time of year to see the Northern Lights. She'd be thrilled, he'd assured himself as he'd fleshed out the plan and instructed his team of assistants to see to the details. He certainly was. What he was doing was the ultimate proof that he was complete and could operate in the relationship arena just as successfully as everyone else did.

But Mia wasn't thrilled. Her gasp was a sharp one of dismay rather than a breathy one of excited surprise. She wriggled out from beneath him and pulled on her clothes, pale and shaking, so quiet and withdrawn suddenly it was as if someone had switched her off. Shockingly cold after all that heat, buffeted by confusion, Zander was too stunned to do anything but go through the motions as they disembarked the plane and went through Customs.

Now, they were in the car for the twenty-minute journey that would take them to the treehouse cabin where they were to be spending the night. Mia sat turned away from him, staring out of the window, but he could tell she was battling tears—*tears*—and his shock gave way to a surge of emotion that he just couldn't contain.

Why was she so upset? was the question that pounded through his head while he flailed about for an explanation, completely at sea and devastated, the pride, the hope, the relief draining utterly away. Had he got it wrong? How? It didn't seem possible. But he must have done. Why else would she be crying?

Theos, he was *no* good at this. Communication. Relationships. Trying to do something that he thought might make someone else happy. He never had been. Why he'd ever believed he'd be able to change the habits of a lifetime he had no idea. As if one weekend of self-analysis was going to fix anything. His issues stretched back decades. They were imprinted on the very marrow of his bones. This was a disaster. *He* was a disaster.

He knew he ought to ask her what was wrong, to see if there was anything he could do to help, but he didn't dare to in case she confirmed that he'd failed. Again. He didn't think he could bear to know that he'd made no progress at all, in spite of his best efforts, and most likely never would. What would that mean for him? For them? That, he couldn't bring himself to contemplate either.

'Do you want to go back?' was as much of a question as he would risk.

'No.' Her voice was thick, hoarse.

'Are you sure?'

'Yes. Just give me a minute. Please. I'll be fine.'

The nausea churned. He shifted on the seat. But he complied with her request because that, at least, he could do.

Zander had brought her to Lapland. He'd remembered a throwaway comment she'd made at the dinner with his siblings two nights ago when they'd been talking about dream holiday destinations, which in hindsight had been pretty surreal since the globetrotting bunch had all been pretty much everywhere already, and turned it into a reality.

Throat tight, eyes stinging, but not because of the biting cold that had hit her the minute she'd got off the plane, Mia swallowed hard, struggling to contain the tears that were threatening to fall.

She'd been a mess ever since he'd told her with that lethal smile where they were. For three hours he'd wrecked her physically and then he'd destroyed her emotionally. How many times had her cosmos-obsessed mother read her stories in books they'd taken out of the library about the magical place where the sun never set in summer and barely rose in winter? How often had they talked about one day actually making the journey to the Arctic to gasp in awe at the Northern Lights and to wish upon the stars?

It had never happened. There'd never been enough money or time, and once the dementia had sunk in its teeth, no one had been travelling anywhere. But even when her mother had been at her most confused and Mia at her most distressed, in her increasingly rare moments of lucidity she'd talked excitedly about when they would go, how they would get there and what they might do, and just for a while Mia had allowed herself to believe it, a beacon of light in the darkness, a flicker of hope in the desolation.

She missed her mother so much she felt as though her heart had been ripped from her chest. Her emotions had burst through the dam she'd built to contain them and were now rushing through her like a roaring river, so powerful, so strong that they crushed the air from her lungs.

She was filled with a bone-deep sense of loss. She ached with the agony of longing for things she'd never have. Such as this, the experience of a lifetime that she and her mother had dreamed of so often but had never got to share. Such as the maternal support and advice and the unique bond created by a child. The grandparent her child would never get to know.

But she couldn't collapse in a heap on Zander. This trip of his had been a lovely idea. She didn't want to ruin it for either of them, which she could tell she was in danger of doing because he was clearly thrown by her reaction. The tension and bewilderment radiated off him in waves.

So, as the sun emerged for its brief daily dalliance with the horizon, she took a deep breath and fought for control. Determinedly, she buried the grief that still had the power to blindside her when she least expected it and blinked back the tears. She focused on the landscape and let the beauty and serenity of the scenery sweep away the sorrow.

Thick snow lay on the ground and clung to trees that soared into the clear blue sky and cast long shadows. They passed through no villages, encountered no other vehicle, nothing but the dark green and blinding white forest for mile after otherworldly mile and the occasional glimpse of a reindeer.

Zander didn't ask her what was wrong. She supposed he didn't want to invade her privacy. But once she'd composed herself, she swallowed hard and told him anyway because she needed to clear the air.

'I'm sorry about that,' she said, her words sounding loud in the thick, swirling silence of the back seat. 'My mother and I planned this trip. We never got to make it. It threw me a bit. Sometimes I miss her so much it hurts.'

For a moment he said nothing. Then he let out a long, slow breath and his entire body relaxed. 'I had no idea.'

'Why would you?'

He took her hand and gave it a squeeze that she felt from head to toe. 'I know it's not the same,' he said gruffly, 'but you have my family now.'

And then he pulled her into his arms and gave her a kiss that was hot and hard and so full of *feeling* that her eyes started stinging all over again.

The glass and wood cabin at which they soon arrived was built on stilts, halfway up a hillside, nestled high amongst the trees. The driver took their bags up and then departed, leaving them utterly alone in this winter wonderland, but she didn't need anyone else. She just needed him.

However, since daylight in this part of the world at

this time of the year was limited, they decided to save test driving the bed for later and take the snowmobile out for a spin instead.

'Do you know how to drive this thing?' Mia asked, only slightly reassured by the fact that she was so wrapped up in the thick winter clothing provided that if she did fall off at least her baby would be protected.

Zander stepped in close and put a helmet on her head. 'I do,' he murmured, taking his time as he did up the strap, brushing his fingers over what little skin was visible and making her shiver, deliberately, she suspected. 'Back in the day, before I took over the company and had more time, I spent a lot of time in the mountains. Skiing, snowboarding, I was up for anything.'

'Did you mind about having to give that up?'

'Not at all. I always wanted Leo's job. He was never happy in the role but clung onto it out of a misguided sense of duty until he met Willow and saw the light. I'm much better at it than he was.'

That remark, along with the wicked grin that accompanied it, made her heart flip with relief. She hadn't ruined anything. If anything, their connection felt closer and deeper than ever.

Reminding herself that she must not do anything else to spoil things, Mia hopped on the back of the two-person machine and clung on as Zander sped them through the eerily quiet wilderness and into a snowy canyon that featured a huge frozen waterfall so stunningly beautiful she wanted to weep. They had a drink in the fairy light lit restaurant of an ice hotel that was reconstructed every year, then he showed her how to drive the snowmobile and she took them back in the twilight, weaving through ancient pines and past picturesque lakes while he curled his big body around her, making her feel so protected, so safe that she didn't ever want it to stop.

Back at the cabin, they warmed up in front of a roaring fire that cast dancing golden shadows across the rugs. Zander assembled a late lunch while Mia stood at the huge picture window through which warm light spilled out and watched a pair of arctic fox cubs frolicking in the snow.

'Thank you for this,' she said over cheese baked into the shape of a pie and served with cloudberry jam and a bowl of *lohikeitto*, her smile soft, her throat tight, her heart thumping at twice its usual rate. 'And I don't just mean lunch. Today has been amazing.'

'You're very welcome.'

Later, lying in the huge bed next to him as he slept, naked beneath the silk sheets and cashmere blankets, she gazed up through the laser-heated glass roof at the aurora borealis painting the dark starlit sky with great swathes of glowing colours. The sheer scale and awesome majesty of what was going on overhead stole her breath and brought tears to her eyes all over again, and it was only when she thought that her mother would have loved this that she realised she'd stopped thinking about her mother hours ago.

From the moment she'd stepped out of the car all she'd thought about was Zander and this wonderful trip he'd arranged for her. Not for their baby or anyone else. For her. To please her and her alone.

He did care about her, she thought giddily. Possibly even more than that because he'd told her he'd never given anyone a present before, so this had to be special, surely. He was the most thoughtful, most amazing man she'd ever met. Not flawless—who was?—but deep and layered and complex. Her child was so lucky to have him as a father. She couldn't wait to see him caring for and playing with his son or daughter. She'd never had that experience with her own father, but she knew Zander was going to be great.

This was the most perfect Christmas present she could ever have been given, and as a shooting star streaked through the sky she knew that she didn't have to wonder any more about whether or not her heart was engaged. It was—wholly and irrevocably—because she was head over heels in love with him.

He was everything she'd always wanted. He'd talked to her, he trusted her, he valued her. He was the fairy tale. And she was pretty sure he loved her back. It was there in the tenderness of his touch. The warm heat of his smile. The faint trembling she'd felt in him when he'd kissed her in the car.

So what was she going to do about it? Wait to see how things panned out? That had never been her style. And how much of a risk would it really be to tell him how she felt? Surely it had to be minimal. Success, security, happiness, love—you had to reach out and grab them when you could. Because, as she well knew, life could simply be too short not to.

But a little voice in her head was telling her to exercise caution. These were early days still, and they'd been pretty intense ones at that. Only a fortnight ago Zander's life had changed for ever with the news that he, the tabloids' favourite international billionaire playboy, was going to be a father. Over the weekend everything he'd believed for the last thirty years had been tossed in the air and reshaped. It was a lot to contend with.

What if she dived right in and it was too much too soon? She did have form on that. What if, in the single-minded pursuit of her own happiness, she demolished his? If she told him how she felt and he spooked, definitely a possibility, how awkward would that be?

On this occasion, then, perhaps it would be wise to wait. To test the waters first. She had to get it right. Her future, and their baby's, depended on it. She could not afford to screw it up.

Overall, it had been an extremely successful twenty-four hours, Zander thought with satisfaction as he made Mia a cup of green tea the following morning and took it back to her in bed.

Admittedly, the start had been shaky, but she'd explained what had happened and the relief that it hadn't been his fault, that his self-reflection hadn't been for naught, made him feel quite light-headed. The rest of the day had pleasingly played out as he'd envisaged—pure, exhilarating, carefree fun of the kind he hadn't had in a long time.

Zipping through the trees on the snowmobile first with Mia wrapped round him and then with him around her had given him more of a rush than any ski run, and he'd made it down La Chavanette intact, twice. Her delight at the ice hotel had been infectious. Her avid interest in the precise formation of the frozen waterfall another fascinating facet to discover.

He wasn't immune to the impact of the scenery either. More than once his breath had caught at the sheer magnificence of the landscape. Last night, he'd looked up at the canopy of stars and the swirling colours that danced across the sky and was perfectly willing to admit the sight had brought a lump to his throat.

There'd been something unique about making love beneath it. A new dimension to their heat. As if they'd somehow, impossibly, been trying to match up to the glory of nature. Mia's passion had been wild, her desire to please him infinitely more intense than usual. He still hadn't fully recovered.

'Can you believe it's Christmas Day in less than a week?' she said, taking the tea from him and snuggling back against the pillows. 'Scoffing jelly babies and watching old films in my pyjamas is going to be quite an anti-climax after this.'

'Is that what you usually do?'

'Yes.'

He frowned. 'On your own?'

'I know it doesn't sound much fun, but it's fine,' she said with a reassuring grin that strangely didn't reassure him at all. 'Really. I've had invitations over the years, but being part of other people's families only emphasises the fact that I don't have one. It's easier to treat it as just another day and I'm normally exhausted after the manic December rush anyway. There doesn't seem much point in going to a lot of effort when it's just me, and I've had more than enough of food by then. I don't even have the energy to put up a tree, let alone hang any decorations.'

She took a sip of her tea and he recalled her admitting to loneliness, thought about her breakdown yesterday morning, and found himself wishing he could remove her pain the way she'd removed his.

'What about you?' she said, pulling him away from that perplexing and faintly troubling notion and back to the conversation.

'Christmas isn't my favourite time of the year either,' he said. 'Neither of my parents was ever at home. My father was inevitably immersed in work. My mother was always somewhere hot and sunny. There wasn't a lot of festive spirit around. These days I have an open invitation to Leo's place on Santorini.'

'Is that what you're going to do this year?'

It was an idea. He never had before. He'd always felt as if he'd be intruding, so he tended to head to the office and then, when the eerie quiet got to him, which it inevitably did after a couple of hours, he walked the seven miles home and had an uncharacteristically early night. But this year, because of all the personal revelations he'd recently had and the implications of them, he could indeed buy some presents for his nieces and take them to Santorini.

'I'm undecided.'

'Well, I know that, technically, my two weeks will be up by then,' she said, her eyes shimmering as she looked at him from above the rim of her cup, 'but maybe we could spend the day together this year. Maybe we could start making some traditions of our own.'

The back of his neck prickled. His stomach pitched. But where his sudden discomfort came from, he couldn't say. It wasn't an outlandish suggestion because they could well be sharing many Christmases to come.

However, the sparkle in her gaze and the expression

on her face unnerved him. She seemed to be radiating hope, warmth, yearning, and he couldn't work out whether all that was for his body or for something else.

Worse was the way in which his stomach was revolting at the thought of her moving out. Did she want to leave? Why? Wasn't she happy with their arrangement? He'd thought it was working well. He'd been thinking about making it permanent, for the sake of convenience.

But he didn't want to analyse the weird sense of impending doom that was descending and settling over him like a weighted blanket. Or the disturbing feeling that he was suddenly on shaky ground. That could wait until they got back. This morning, as soon as the sun was up, they were heading out on a husky safari. No petrol fumes, no rumbling engines—just Mia and him and the call of the wild—and he wanted to enjoy it.

So he shoved aside the misgivings that he didn't understand, gave her a smile designed to disguise and said, 'Why not?'

It was six in the evening when they landed back in London. Encouraged by the events and conversations of the day, Mia asked Zander if they could take a detour to her flat en route to his apartment.

She could hardly contain her excitement as she riffled through the filing cabinet in the study area of her sitting room while he inspected the books on her shelves. To think that only a few short weeks ago she'd been all alone in this world, plodding along as she had for years, trying to carve out the future she wanted and so very lonely, and now here she was with a child on the way and the most gorgeous man in her life.

The signs that she'd been right about how he felt about her were all there. They were to spend Christmas Day together, the first, she hoped, of many. And the husky safari. What a ride that had been. He'd held her so close, so tightly. As if he never wanted to let her go. He hadn't missed an opportunity to touch her, to kiss her. And his smiles… Every single one of them spread through her like sunshine, warming the parts of her that had been so cold for so long.

If he'd been a fraction quieter on the flight back, a little withdrawn, a faint furrow between his brows, it had to be because he regretted the end of a wonderful two days. She could have stayed there for ever too.

'Aha.'

Having found what she wanted, Mia closed the drawer with a flourish, whirled round and held out a white rectangular envelope. 'Here,' she said, her heart skipping about all over the place, her breath catching in her throat. 'For you.'

He took it and frowned. 'What's this?'

'Open it.'

He did. He took out the document and unfolded it. Scanned it. And went very still. 'It's your birth certificate.'

'That's right,' she said, the adrenalin fizzing through her so powerful it made her head spin. 'The paperwork you requested. So we can get married.'

For a moment he didn't say anything, clearly too overwhelmed to speak, which was understandable because she was on the overwhelmed side too. It was an overwhelming moment.

But then he slowly folded the document back up and

returned it to its envelope. He handed it back to her with a cool, 'Thanks, but no thanks,' and the excitement, the adrenalin, every good thing she'd been feeling instantly vaporised.

'Thanks, but no thanks?' she echoed, stunned, immobile, her breath catching at the sight of his now unreadable expression and a smile that did not spread warmth.

'I no longer see the need.'

What? She opened her mouth, found she had no words so closed it, then eventually managed a bewildered, 'Since when?'

'Since we started talking.'

'What about securing your rights?'

'The law is enough.'

'But you were so adamant.'

He gave a shrug. 'That came from a place of insecurity which, thanks to you, I no longer have.'

Mia didn't know what to say. This was not going the way she'd expected. She'd assumed he'd be delighted and whisk her off to the register office right then and there. It had never occurred to her that he might have changed his mind.

But she was not done. Because she'd been waiting for the right time to tell him how she felt and that time was now. 'What if *I* see the need?' she said, her voice tight, her pulse pounding in her ears. 'What if I *want* to marry you?'

'Do you?'

'Yes.' So much.

'I won't withhold access to my family, if that's what you're worried about. You'll have a generous allowance to use as you see fit. I'll buy you a house with a garden, of any description, wherever you wish. We don't need to marry to make this work. This isn't the nineteenth century.'

Those had been her words once, but not any more. What he was offering wasn't enough. It wasn't even the point. 'I don't want to marry you for the sake of our child,' she said, needing to clarify her desires and make him see what he clearly didn't. 'I want to marry you for no one's sake but *me*.'

'What do you mean?'

'I'm in love with you,' she said, unable to contain the feelings whipping about inside her like a Catherine wheel any longer. 'And you're in love with me.'

CHAPTER FOURTEEN

STANDING THERE IN the centre of Mia's small but cosy sitting room, Zander froze. Outside a car honked and someone shouted. Through the window he could see that the sun was shining and the sky was blue. In here, however, the silence thundered and the thick, heavy air crackled with the electrical charge of an approaching storm.

'That's absurd,' he said, denial slamming into every inch of him.

Mia gasped and recoiled as if winded, but nevertheless pulled her shoulders back and lifted her chin, which was inevitable because she'd never backed down from anything. 'Which bit of it?'

'All of it.' It had to be. How could it be anything else? 'You're doing what you said you wouldn't and reading something into this that simply isn't there. Apart from the baby, rampant lust with a side order of conversation is all we have.'

'You're being reductive.'

'I'm being honest.'

'No, you're not,' she said, her gaze fixing him to the spot. 'You introduced me to your family. You sought my opinion and advice and trusted me enough to share with me your deepest fears. You let me in. You *welcomed* me in. You took me to Lapland.'

Zander's jaw clenched. When she put it like that, he could see why she'd got the wrong idea. Her ridiculous assertion that they were in love with each other was a wholly unintended consequence of his desire to over-come the past in order to look forward to the future. Yes, they'd talked and developed a certain connection, but he'd been building a relationship, a practical arrange-ment that would lead to a smoother future, and that was it. Nothing more.

'As a thank you for helping me overcome my past.'

'You could have just taken me out to dinner.'

'I'd already done that.'

She folded her arms across her chest and arched one elegant red-gold eyebrow. 'So how do you explain the way you kissed me in the car on the way to the cabin?'

'That was merely sympathy.'

'We both know it was more than that,' she said with a sharp shake of her head. 'I felt you trembling.'

'With relief. Because I thought I'd got it wrong. I thought I'd failed. Again.'

'On the husky safari you held me in that sled as if you couldn't bear to let me go.'

'To stop you falling out and our baby coming to harm.'

'I was securely strapped in.'

Zander's words dried up. His head emptied. He had no counter-argument to that. What she said was true. They'd both been strapped in. And as it hit him that her other points were also true, his blood rushed to his feet and the ground surged up to reach him and he had to plant a hand on the bookcase to stop himself from passing out.

He could have taken her out to dinner. What he'd felt when he'd kissed her in the car hadn't just been sympathy and relief. He'd also ached with the need to draw out her pain and absorb it himself.

Which meant what? That he'd been lying to himself? No. He wasn't. He couldn't be. Because that would indicate that she was right and they had something more than he'd assumed, which could not be the case.

He couldn't be in love with her, he thought, a cold sweat breaking out all over his skin. He was incapable of it. He'd got so good at burying his emotions, which had been abhorred by his father and ignored by his mother, and which he'd always considered so very dangerous, that he'd felt nothing deeply at all for years.

Except that ever since he'd met Mia he had.

Hurt, panic, confusion, relief, exhilaration, pride, terror—he'd felt them all, on occasion so profoundly, so volatilely that he'd staggered beneath their weight.

How many times had he tried to suppress them? Many. How often had he succeeded? Rarely.

She did mean something to him, he realised, his chest tight, his lungs constricting, the knuckles of the hand that was clutching the shelf whitening. She meant everything. And because of it, she had the power to destroy him. To trample all over his feelings, these new terrifying feelings that he hadn't even realised he had, and leave him there to bleed out, broken and hurting, a wreck.

But he couldn't have that. Such vulnerability was unacceptable. He would not put himself in a position where he could wind up weak and indecisive and doubting himself. He had to remain strong and steady and not slice himself open and offer her everything. He couldn't go there again and there'd been more than enough opening up already.

But it wasn't too late to retreat and pull up the drawbridge while he figured out how to fix what he'd done. All he had to do was take a deep breath and calm down and find a way through the chaos.

So, deploying the strategies that had worked so well for him so many times before, he shut down the cacophony in his head and switched himself off. A blessed numbness swept through him. Ice now flowed through his veins. And at last he could think clearly.

'Excuse me,' he said, wholly focused on the need to escape to safety and regroup. 'I need to go.'

The slam of her front door rang in her ears for hours, but although gutted that Zander hadn't swept her into his arms while confessing he loved her too, Mia wasn't entirely surprised that he'd hared off as if he had the hounds of hell at his feet. Spooking him with her declaration of love had always been a possibility. It wasn't the first time he'd retreated when feeling under threat. He'd frequently needed a moment or two to process information he'd been presented with.

The important thing was that she'd told him how she felt and made him aware of how she was certain he felt. The ball was now in his court, and with any luck it wouldn't take him too long to work things through and bat it back.

Until that happened she had plenty to occupy herself.

She'd reacquaint herself with her flat, which seemed very small and cramped after eight days in his palatial apartment. She'd hunt around for a spare toothbrush and toothpaste since she'd left hers in her bag in his car. Then she'd work on the plans she'd conceived while staying with him. She'd been thinking of making Hattie a partner in the business. She'd soon need a lot of help and support, not to mention time off, and not only did she trust Hattie implicitly, her friend and colleague had earned it.

Giving him space would be tough and she'd miss him hugely, but she wasn't a teenager, pining by the phone. She could handle one night on her own. Her future and that of their child depended on her giving him space to come to the only conclusion there was, so the one thing she would *not* do was pressurise him.

However, after two days of complete radio silence, an increasingly confused and distressed Mia had to confront the fact that not only did Zander not intend to send anything back in the way of a ball, but also, he quite possibly wasn't even in the game.

What was taking him so long? she wondered worriedly as she deveined some prawns for tonight's drinks party for fifty with a peeling knife. Why did history seem to be repeating itself? Surely it was blindingly obvious how good they could be together.

Unless it wasn't, of course, and he couldn't think of anything worse.

Could that be it?

Had she somehow managed to get completely the wrong idea and pushed him away with her prodding and poking and the attempts she'd kept making to burrow beneath his surface? Had she put him under pressure to give her something he wasn't ready to give?

That had happened before.

Could it have happened again?

Her heart gave a quick lurch at the thought of it, the knife slipped and she nicked her finger. Berating her stupidity on more than one front, Mia abandoned the prawns, grabbed some kitchen towel and went in search of the first aid kit.

Had she really not learned *anything* from her previous relationships? Why had she had to say something? Why hadn't she been content with the status quo, with seeing how things played out, as she'd told herself she would on so many occasions?

But what if he'd *never* be able to give her what she truly wanted, which was him? she wondered, her hands trembling as she opened the box and hunted around for a plaster. What if he didn't love her? What then? She hadn't considered that possibility—one of many, it seemed, that had slipped her by—but now she had to. She had to accept the fact that she might well have taken a risk and lost.

And, God, it was as if that knife had sliced and diced her heart, so much did it hurt. Her eyes stung and a hot lump lodged in her throat.

If that *was* the case, how would she bear it?

What had she done?

And when he met someone else—or many someone elses, as he inevitably would—even if he didn't parade them in front of her and their child, she'd know they were there, and the thought of it was agony.

'The smallest cuts are the worst,' said Hattie, wincing in sympathy as Mia removed the kitchen towel pad and applied the plaster.

'You're absolutely right,' Mia replied, swallowing down that lump and snapping on a glove.

No doubt she was going to suffer a thousand of them. But she had to be strong because she couldn't just draw a line under everything and try to move on. At some point they were going to have to communicate, and if Zander wasn't going to initiate it, then she would.

But for that, she'd have to get her feelings under control so she wouldn't break down in front of him and beg him to forget she'd ever said anything, and that wasn't yet.

Three days after Zander had fled Mia's flat he'd fixed nothing and was no closer to working anything through.

They'd been the longest, most frustrating days of his life.

He couldn't concentrate. His appetite had dropped off a cliff. Unable to sleep at his apartment, which held too many damn memories, he'd taken up residence in the suite at his office, not that that had made any difference.

He didn't know which way was up. He was scratchy and unreasonable. The minute he arrived at the office, his assistants scurried to hide.

And he hated it.

It wasn't him.

He'd had plenty of time to think about everything Mia had said. Certainly enough to admit she was right. He *was* in love with her. He probably had been from the moment he'd laid eyes on her. He'd spent weeks suppressing the memory of it, but when he'd taken her hand in her unit on an east London industrial estate that ordinary afternoon in June, he'd felt as though he'd splintered apart and reformed differently. Even if she hadn't got pregnant, he would have eventually given in and sought her out.

He didn't want to be alone, he now knew, he wanted her, but he just couldn't get past his fears about vulnerability and potential destruction. He didn't know why. He'd tried to analyse it, he'd even googled it, but to no avail.

Currently, Zander was not alone. He was standing at the bar just off the ballroom of one of London's top hotels, the venue for the company's Christmas party— not catered by Halliday Catering, thank God—downing whisky like it was water.

He didn't want to be here. He was not in a party mood. The noise generated by the chatter of five hundred merry people and the thumping of the band was hurting his head. The trouble was, he didn't want to be anywhere else either. Being on his own, a situation in which there'd be no distraction from the utter hopelessness of his thoughts, certainly didn't appeal. In fact, he didn't know what he wanted. Apart from Mia. Who he couldn't have. And freedom from this horrible state of paralysis that meant he hadn't dealt with her belongings and, worse, hadn't been in touch.

Thalia, who was in attendance as head of the company's charitable foundation arm, joined him at the bar and ordered herself a glass of white wine. 'No Mia this evening?' she said, as if able to read his poor tortured mind.

His chest tightened. His head pounded. How much more of this could he take? 'Not tonight.'

'Nothing serious, I hope.'

His sister hoped in vain. And in the past he might have made light of it with a shrug and a smile, but tonight he didn't have the energy to put up a front.

'We're no longer together.'

'I didn't realise you had been in the first place.'

He knocked back the contents of his glass and signalled for another. 'No, well, neither did I.'

'That's a shame.'

'It is.'

'Are you in love with her?'

'What makes you ask that?'

'You couldn't take your eyes off her at dinner last week. I honestly thought the room was going to go up in flames. Even Leo noticed.'

'I'm crazy about her,' he said, seeing little point in denying it when apparently it had been obvious to everyone but him.

'Does she love you?'

'So she says.'

'Then what's going on?'

He hadn't a clue. He hadn't a clue about anything any more. 'It's complicated.'

'You love her. She loves you. There isn't anyone else involved. What's complicated about that?'

If only it *were* that simple. But Thalia didn't fear having her heart ripped out and stamped all over.

'How do you do it?' he muttered, needing help like he'd never needed it before. 'How do you all do it?'

'Do what?'

'Embrace the love. How do you get past the fear of it all going wrong and winding up in pieces?'

Thalia tilted her head in consideration for a moment. 'I guess you just have to weigh up the alternatives and then decide if the risk is worth taking.'

And therein lay the problem. His decision-making ability was history. The risk seemed insurmountable. But what *was* the alternative? A lifetime of misery and regret? Wanting Mia but not having her? Watching her gradually fall out of love with him and into it with someone else, as she inevitably would because she wasn't afraid to go for what she wanted?

Was that any way to live? Was that really the future he could see for himself? On the outside looking in? Letting her go out of cowardice? No. Absolutely not. Many things required a leap into the unknown. Not all of them ended in disaster. And why would she rip his heart out? She loved him. Or at least she had, three days ago.

'She told me she loved me and I walked out on her,' he muttered, sick at the memory of doing such a thing.

'Oh, dear.'

His gut churned with shame and remorse. 'I know.'

'Can you fix it?'

If he wasn't too late. If she hadn't given up on him. If she gave him a second chance. 'I hope so.'

The last thing Mia felt like doing at five in the afternoon was dropping by Zander's apartment in the cold and the dark to pick up the things she'd left behind. It was so final. So heartbreaking. And to make her do it on Christmas Eve? When they'd once planned to spend the following day together? She'd thought him many things, but never cruel.

Well.

She'd do this one last thing and draw a line under the last sorry fortnight. Chalk it up to experience and move on. They'd have to stay in touch, obviously, but not for months and she'd have got over him by then. Already her heart had begun to mend. A bit. Because did she really need someone in her life who scuttled off when the going got tough? No, she did not. Someone had to be the grownup in this relationship of theirs and it clearly wasn't going to be him.

But that was fine. As she'd told him weeks ago, she was perfectly capable of raising their child on her own. She had money. She didn't need Zander to buy her a house. She'd buy or rent one of her own when the time came. Her friends would be her baby's family. And if he still wanted to be involved, well, that was fine too. She could do cool. She could do detached. She'd take lessons from him.

But when she stepped out of the lift and strode into his apartment and saw what he'd done, she skidded to a halt, all her excellent intentions, her composure, her control, the very strength from her limbs just draining clean away.

Strings of fairy lights hung from every available point. Tasteful arrangements of foliage, pinecones and clove-studded oranges sat on almost every horizontal surface. A twelve-foot tree stood in one corner of the living room, swathed in garlands of lights and adorned with glass baubles. A fire crackled in the grate and innumerable flickering cinnamon-scented candles filled the air with the warm, spicy scent of Christmas.

Stunned into immobility, her heart shredded, Mia surveyed the scene, complete with carols softly emanating from somewhere and… Oh, no, she was going to cry again.

But she swallowed down the emotion, dug deep for cool detachment and turned to the man standing just to her left. 'If you could point me in the direction of my things,' she said with a bright, nothing-bothers-me smile that cost her everything she had, 'I'll be out of your hair in a jiffy.'

Zander started. Blinked, as if jolted out of a trance. 'What?'

'My belongings? I'm here to collect them.'

'Is that what you want?' he said, his brows snapping together in a deep frown.

No. Of course it wasn't what she wanted. She wanted him, so much still that she might as well not have bothered armour-plating her defences. He looked terrible, pale and drawn, but it did nothing to diminish his gorgeousness, which really wasn't fair when even though she'd spent hours on her hair, clothes and make-up—of which she was not proud—she still looked a mess. He was wearing a black shirt and faded blue jeans with nothing on his feet, and that wasn't fair either because he knew, because she'd told him, that she found that combination unbearably sexy.

She had to be so careful around this man. So very, very careful. Because if she let him, he could break her, for good this time.

'That's what *you* want.'

'No, it isn't,' he said. 'That was just a ruse to get you here. I didn't think you'd come otherwise, after the last few days.'

Now it was Mia's turn to startle. 'Oh?'

'Why would I do all this if I didn't want you to stay?' he said, sounding a little wild, a little desperate. 'You were the one who mentioned creating new traditions.'

She reeled. Her heart lurched and then began to race. 'You did this for me?'

'Who else would I have done it for?'

'I don't know. Someone you've met in the last few days?'

'For six months, there's only been you, Mia,' he said, his dark eyes so intent on hers she could barely breathe. 'For the rest of my life there will always only be you. You even told me that.'

'At which point you walked out.'

'And I'll regret it for ever.' He took a step towards her and for one giddy moment she thought he was going to touch her, but then he stopped as if unsure whether that would be welcome. 'I'm so sorry about that. I was terrified of the strength of my feelings for you. Of how vulnerable they made me. I've spent years locking up my emotions. It was the only way I could handle my parents' neglect. Life just seemed easier and safer if I just didn't feel anything at all. But then I met you and that strategy went to hell in a handcart. You petrify and thrill me in equal measure, Mia. You could crucify me if you chose to, and that fear's taken a while to dispatch. But there is no one on this planet I would rather spend the rest of my life with. No one. I love you. You are the most magnificent woman I've ever met. I can't wait to meet our child and there is nothing more I'd like than to build a family with you. I want to give you everything. I want to make all your dreams come true.' He stopped, swallowed hard, then took a breath. 'If I didn't think there was a chance you might throw it back in my face,' he said gruffly, 'I'd start by giving you this.'

He dug a hand into the back pocket of his jeans and withdrew a small, square, black velvet box. And when he opened it with ever so slightly shaking hands, to reveal a blinding white diamond solitaire ring, despite all her attempts to remain cool and detached, the floor beneath her feet began to quake, sending shockwaves up through her body and cracking her heart wide open to spill love and joy and relief into every cell of her being.

She had no defence against this man who could crucify her too but wouldn't, because why would they do that to each other when theirs was a love strong enough to withstand whatever life had to throw at them? No defence at all against the tsunami of feeling rushing through her, which made her chest swell with such happiness she thought she would burst.

'I wouldn't throw it back in your face,' she said, perilously close to tears again.

He stilled. A light began to shimmer in those wonderful dark eyes of his. 'No?'

'I'd wear it every day.'

Barely before she'd finished her sentence he stepped forward and yanked her into his arms, kissing her so hard and for so long she saw stars. He tangled his hands in her hair, holding her close, murmuring things in Greek that she didn't technically understand but nevertheless did because they were so passionate they could only be words of love.

'I thought I'd ruined everything,' he muttered when at last he lifted his head, looking dazed, breathing hard.

Mia leaned back in his arms, looked around the room

so thoughtfully, so stunningly transformed and shot him a smile. 'The decorations were a good move.'

'I hoped they would be.'

'And, as proposals go, an engagement ring certainly beats a birth certificate.'

'I thought that too.' He took her left hand and threaded his fingers through hers and brought it up to the gap that separated his heart from hers. 'Would you like to put it on now?'

She looked down at their joined hands, knowing they'd be united for ever, so excited to see what the future would bring, and said softly, 'I can't think of anything I'd like more.'

EPILOGUE

One year later

'A LITTLE TO the left,' said Mia, tilting her head from side to side and narrowing her eyes. 'No. That's too far. A fraction to the right... Perfect.'

Zander, who had been up a ladder, stepped down off it, set it to one side and then returned to the bed, where she lay with their six-month-old son, Toby, who was asleep, starfished across her chest.

The mattress dipped as he sprawled himself beside her and surveyed his handiwork. 'I can see why Willow didn't think it suitable for public display.'

So could Mia. The portrait was of the two of them, fully clothed, arranged on a bench in the garden beneath a blossoming apple tree. There was nothing untoward about the pose, but they were gazing at each other in such adoration, the chemistry between them so strong it was almost tangible, that they might as well have been naked. The only place it could hang was in their bedroom. 'She said she had to switch on the fan in her studio to cool herself down the first few times she worked on it.'

'You look as if you want to devour me.'

'You look as if you just *have* devoured me.'

'I had, if I recall correctly,' he mused with the beginnings of a smile that always meant trouble. 'It's giving me ideas.'

Her heart skipped a beat. Desire stirred. 'Ideas, huh?'

'Hold that thought.'

While Zander gently lifted their son off her and went to settle him in the nursery, Mia held that thought, along with a million others that she had to pinch herself every day to believe.

So much had happened in the last twelve months. They'd married in spring and, after a two-week honeymoon in Tahiti, had moved into this six-bedroomed house with a garden in the leafy London suburb that buzzed with cafés and parks. Hattie had become a partner in the business soon after that and in the summer Toby had been born.

Gone were the shadows and loneliness of the past. Zander now found family gatherings a joy and she had all the love and security she'd ever wanted. He'd promised to give her everything, to make her dreams come true, and he had. He'd given her the fairy tale.

'Now, where were we?' he murmured, strolling back into the bedroom and letting his gaze drift over her so thoroughly, so leisurely that she burned.

'You were having ideas.'

'So I was.'

He lowered himself onto the bed and she welcomed him into her arms and they explored and expanded on his ideas until they collapsed into a breathless heap of thundering hearts and tangled limbs.

And when the clock struck twelve and he murmured, 'Happy Christmas, *agàpi mou*,' Mia knew that it absolutely was.

* * * * *

HIS INNOCENT UNWRAPPED IN ICELAND

JACKIE ASHENDEN

MILLS & BOON

One day I'll write a book with gunfights
and car chases.

But it is not this day and it is not this book. :)

CHAPTER ONE

ISLA KENDRICK, DRAPED in the delicate ivory silk of her wedding gown, stood in the narthex of the ancient abbey where she was about to get married and clutched at her bouquet of delicate pink peonies as if they were a lifeline.

Orion North, the man who for the past year had been angling to take over Kendricks' Family Christmas, the company that had been in David Kendrick's family for generations and provided much of the Christmas-themed products and services around the world, surveyed her dispassionately, his amber gaze cold as it always was.

He'd simply appeared in the narthex as if by magic, and she didn't know what he was doing here. She certainly hadn't invited him to the wedding, and her adoptive father wouldn't have either. She'd met him across the boardroom table, of course, during his negotiations to buy Kendricks' off her father, and also at a few business functions she'd attended. She'd found him cold and distinctly unlikeable.

She liked him even less now.

Her two bridesmaids—her father's two secretaries, since she didn't have any sisters—were fussing with her train, but as soon as Orion had stepped into the narthex they'd stopped and stared at him instead. Unsurprisingly.

He was a man who commanded if not demanded attention, and that was only one of the reasons Isla found him so irritating.

He was six-five and broad-shouldered, built like a warrior rather than the multibillion-dollar businessman he actually was, and he towered over most people like an ancient oak towers over just about every tree in the forest. Then again, he was one of the world's most feared corporate raiders and had the cold, acquisitive gaze to match, so maybe the warrior simile was more apt.

He was also devastatingly attractive, which didn't make her any more well disposed towards him. Taken by themselves, his features were too rough and blunt for handsomeness, but there was something about their arrangement, something to do with the straight black brows and the proud jut of his nose, the curve of his lower lip, and the fact that his eyes were the colour of ancient amber that made people turn and stare.

Isla didn't want to stare. She didn't want her breath to catch every time he entered a room she was in. He was a wolf, a stone-cold predator, and she hated how he made her feel like prey. Not that he'd ever made any move towards her. Sometimes she noticed him staring at her disconcertingly from across the boardroom table, but he never said anything to her, so why he was even here she had no idea.

Just as she had no idea why he'd been circling Kendricks' for so long, not unlike a vulture circling a lion that wasn't quite dead. He hadn't made a move, though, which had made her father jumpy since North had a reputation for a quick kill when it came to acquiring companies.

He glanced at her bridesmaids and nodded towards

the doors that led into the church proper. The unspoken command was clear, so they stopped fussing with Isla's train and went, leaving Isla alone with him.

A shiver of trepidation went through her, a cold feeling settling in her gut.

She'd been full of nerves this morning, wondering if she was doing the right thing in marrying Gianni, one of her father's protégés. Her father had introduced them six months earlier and Isla had known immediately that this was the sign that David thought it was time for her to settle down. Family was important for Kendricks' and most especially for the Kendricks' board. It wouldn't do for the heir to remain single, and since Gianni had been nice enough and was clearly on her father's list of approved suitors, she'd started seeing him.

And when he'd proposed six months later, she'd said yes.

She didn't love him, but that didn't matter. David thought he'd make a good husband and son-in-law and since Isla wanted to do David proud, she'd agreed. She wanted a family of her own, so why not? Except her prewedding jitters hadn't agreed, and now Orion's sudden appearance hadn't helped.

Today, he wore an expertly tailored dove-grey morning suit that made him look even more devastatingly attractive than he already was and that unsettled her even further. She was about to get married. She shouldn't be looking at other men. She shouldn't even be aware of them.

Ignoring the slow creep of ice in her gut, Isla lifted her chin and stared at the man who'd so casually interrupted the proceedings. 'What on earth are you doing here, Mr

North?' She consciously tried to imitate the note of cool command her father used in the boardroom. Cool didn't come naturally to her, but she was trying. 'I'm about to get married in case you hadn't noticed and I don't believe you were invited.'

Orion's harshly carved features betrayed nothing, though there was a strange gleam in his wolf-gold eyes. 'No,' he said calmly. 'I was not.'

'Then why are you here?'

'I hate to be the bearer of bad news, Isla. But your groom isn't coming.'

The words didn't make any sense. 'Not coming?' she repeated blankly. 'What do you mean he's not coming?'

'I mean, he took a private jet out of Stansted early this morning, bound for Rome.' Orion's cold voice was full of harsh edges and deep chasms. 'I advised him not to poach on my territory and offered him a significant amount of money to go away. So he did.'

Isla blinked. His territory? Poaching? What on earth was he talking about? 'Excuse me? You did what?'

Orion didn't move, but that odd, hot light in his eyes glinted again. 'He will not be marrying you, Isla. Not today, not tomorrow and not next week. In fact, I would go so far as to say that he will not be marrying you at all.'

A deafening silence fell in the narthex and yet Isla was conscious of a roaring in her ears. The bouquet of peonies slipped from her nerveless fingers to land in a shower of petals on the stone floor. 'What?' Her voice came out scratchy, a raw scrape of sound. 'I don't understand.'

Orion calmly bent and retrieved her bouquet from the floor just as some footsteps echoed on the stone and a man she didn't recognise came through the front door of the church. Orion murmured a few words to him and the man left again, this time going through into the church proper and closing the doors behind him.

Something was happening. Something wasn't right.

'Mr North,' she said, forcing away the cold clutch of shock. 'I want an explanation. Where is Gianni? Why isn't he here? And what do you mean you paid him to go away?'

A rustling sound was coming from the church and the low buzz of shocked conversation. There were five hundred people out there waiting to see her get married, the cream of London high society, as well as many of her father's business cronies, not to mention Gianni's family. But something was happening there too, because they'd been silent before and they weren't now.

Orion took a step towards her and held the bouquet out to her. 'I just told you why he isn't here. He's on his way to Rome. And I paid him to go away because he should never have asked you to marry him in the first place.'

Shock was creeping through her and she had to fight to force it down. She didn't know what was happening, but going to pieces wouldn't help. Her father had always said that staying calm in a crisis was a valuable skill and one she needed to learn before she took over Kendricks' as CEO. In fact, there were many skills she needed to learn before she took over, and while some of them had been easy, others were more difficult. She had to detach, David had told her. She was too much at the mercy of her emotions.

Isla already knew that—there was a reason her first adoption had fallen through—and so when David had adopted her at twelve, she'd resolved to make sure her temper stayed leashed and she'd be the perfect daughter.

Except keeping her emotions locked down with shock coursing through her veins and a man she didn't like standing in front of her telling her that he'd paid her fiancé to jilt her, her brittle, cool authority was in danger of cracking entirely.

'Why on earth shouldn't he have asked me to marry him?' she demanded.

'Because he doesn't love you,' Orion said without hesitation. 'And you don't love him.'

Isla stared at him in astonishment. This made no sense, none of it. His presence, Gianni's absence, what he was saying to her...

'That...' she said stupidly. 'That's none of your business.'

'It's true, though.' There was a note of certainty in his voice. As if he knew her feelings better than she did herself. 'You're marrying him because David wanted you to.'

Anger stirred inside her, threatening her grip on her detachment. 'Don't be ridiculous. You know nothing about me or Gianni.' She snatched her bouquet from him and straightened, trying to inject some steel into her spine, projecting 'future CEO' and not 'angry orphan'. 'I don't care what you paid him or why. You need to bring him back this instant.'

Orion simply looked at her, the glitter of the wolf in his eyes. 'No,' he said in the same calm tone. 'I will not.'

Her fingers felt cold, and she could hear the buzz of conversation from the assembled guests. It was louder now.

It couldn't be true. It couldn't be happening. Surely

Gianni was already at the altar, waiting for her. Surely he was.

He would have sent someone to see what the delay was about by now.

True. Yet no one had come except that employee of Orion's.

Ice crept through her as reality began to assert itself. Gianni didn't appear and neither did her father, and all she could hear was the conversation of the guests, getting even louder.

While Orion merely stood there looking at her, dressed in his exquisite grey morning suit.

The roaring was back in her ears, the floor feeling as if it had shifted beneath her feet and then unexpectedly, a large, warm hand was beneath her elbow.

Orion. His grip was firm and strong, the solidity of mountains keeping her upright, and for a split second, she almost leaned into his hold, because her knees felt weak.

'I know this is a shock,' he continued in that same steady, implacable tone. 'But I'm not here to hurt you.'

'I don't understand.' She hated how uncertain and weak she sounded. 'Why are you here then?'

His palm beneath her elbow was warm, in stark contrast to the cool of his voice. Yet his amber eyes gleamed with a sudden, dark fire. 'Why do you think? I'm here to marry you instead, Isla.'

Orion watched Isla's pretty blue eyes widen in shock.

He wasn't surprised. It was, after all, a very shocking proposal.

Yet that had been the plan he'd been formulating for the past month, ever since he'd found out that Isla Kendrick was going to marry one of her father's protégés. Orion simply couldn't allow that to happen.

He'd been playing the long game for months now, deciding initially that he'd take the slow, careful approach with her. Then her engagement had been announced, which he hadn't been expecting, and he'd had to rethink his plans.

He wasn't in love with her—love wasn't possible for him these days—but he'd admit to being in the grip of a singular…fascination with her.

It had all started at a business gala held at the National Gallery, where he'd found her standing in a small gallery away from the crowd, in front of a painting, and there had been a rapt look on her face.

He hadn't known who she was, but she'd seemed illuminated, lit from within by something he didn't understand and his interest had been caught. He'd checked the painting to see what it was that held her attention so completely. But it was only Van Gogh's painting of a night sky.

Orion didn't like it when he didn't understand something. His instinct was always to make sense of it, so he'd gone over and asked her what was so interesting about the painting.

She'd smiled, like the sun rising on a midwinter morning, and started talking about the brushstrokes, the layers of the paint, the flowing motion of the painted sky and how they came together to form a beautiful, luminous whole. Her hands had moved as she spoke, as eloquent and graceful as her words, and he'd been…transfixed.

He'd never much appreciated art and the creative impulse was a mystery to him. He was a man who took things apart. He didn't create. He'd tried once, long ago, to build something, but that had left him broken, so now he didn't bother. Satisfaction came from looking at a system that wasn't performing, at identifying why it wasn't and what was broken, and then deciding what to do about it. Rather like a mechanic taking apart an old car and selling some parts for scrap, while reconditioning other parts to make it go better.

He was good at it.

So it was all very mysterious why he'd found looking at this woman while she talked about a bit of paint on a board so fascinating. There was something about her. About the way she came alive that consumed his interest so completely he hadn't been able to do anything but stare.

That was the night he'd decided that he simply had to know more about her.

It hadn't taken him long to discover that she was David Kendrick's adopted daughter, Isla, the apparent heir to Kendrick's underperforming Christmas company. Her adoption thirteen years earlier, at the age of twelve, had been a media sensation—'Childless Christmas company magnate adopts orphan girl at Christmas time!'—and Kendrick had made much of her potential. Having been an orphan himself, Orion was further intrigued to see what kind of businesswoman she'd grown into. Perhaps she came alive when talking about sales projections as well as paintings?

However, that turned out to be not the case which at first he'd found underwhelming. She was quiet, barely saying a word even when asked, and she seemed uncertain of herself. Not at all the hungry go-getter Kendrick had always portrayed her to be and not at all that luminous woman he'd seen in the gallery that night.

Her milkmaid appearance didn't help the CEO image, all spun gold hair, dark blue eyes and peaches and cream complexion. She looked like a porcelain doll—if a porcelain doll had been petite and curvy, all rounded breasts, hips and thighs. The male animal in him had appreciated the feminine in her, and while he certainly found her lovely, she didn't have the same luminosity in the boardroom that she had in the gallery.

It puzzled him and, since he liked a puzzle, he'd arranged more meetings with Kendrick on the pretext of buying his company, but in reality wanting to observe Isla Kendrick more closely and find out just what was so fascinating about her.

She was always very polished and put together, yet he'd noticed that sometimes a lock of blond hair would come loose from its elegant chignon. That her red lipstick was sometimes smudged a little at the side of her pouty mouth. Or that the top button of her white tailored blouses had a tendency to come undone.

And that wasn't all. There were moments in the boardroom on the rare occasions she spoke, where although she seemed poised, he was certain that she wasn't. Where he sensed she was out of her depth. It seemed so at odds with the woman who spoke so knowledgeably and confidently about the painting, that he found himself to be even more intrigued.

On a number of occasions during those meetings, he'd tried having a conversation with her, but it soon became clear that she didn't like him and avoided him. He was used to being disliked. No one warmed to the pirate who boarded their ship and took all their gold, after all, but he found it…annoying when it came to her.

He'd been planning on how to overcome her dislike when news of her engagement had broken. And that's when he'd decided she would be his next takeover.

There had only been a week between her engagement and the date for her wedding, which meant there had been no time for the 'slow and careful' approach. No time for finesse or subtlety. He'd already discovered by then that the marriage had been engineered by Kendrick himself to improve her already poor standing with the company board and hardly the love match portrayed in the press—not that he would have put his plans on hold even if she had been in love—so he had no qualms about making his move on her wedding day.

It was the perfect opportunity to use shock to his advantage in order to get what he wanted, and he wouldn't have been the ruthless businessman he was if he hadn't made the most of his opportunities. He was a man who got what he wanted, when he wanted it, and he wanted her.

He'd gone to Kendrick the night before and told him that he wanted Isla, and that if Kendrick knew what was good for his company, he'd let Orion have her. The old man though hadn't just rolled over. Orion's interest in Kendricks' had unsettled him and he'd known his company was vulnerable to a takeover. So he'd told Orion that if he wanted Isla, not only would he have to buy Kendricks' outright for an extortionate amount, but he'd have to retain Isla as CEO for the optics—a family Christmas company needed a Kendrick to remain in charge and preferably a married Kendrick. Oh, yes, and he'd also insisted that Orion keep the company intact and Isla as CEO and his wife for at least a year, before making a decision about what to do with either.

Orion had no feelings at all about the company—he'd keep it the year Kendrick specified but then he'd likely break it up and sell the more profitable parts—nor did he care whether Isla stayed on as CEO. But he wanted to secure his asset and if he had to marry her to secure her, he would. He didn't mind marrying her. Marriage had always seemed a pointless institution to him and a year should be more than enough time to explore his fascination with her.

Not that a year of marriage was his biggest issue right now.

No, his biggest issue was going to be getting her to agree to go through with it.

Luckily, he had leverage on his side in the form of Kendricks' itself, plus a few well-rehearsed speeches about how it would be a win-win situation for both of them. All he had to do was convince her.

The frothing fall of her veil didn't hide how her dark blue eyes had deepened into indigo with shock or how white she'd gone. Almost as white as her wedding gown.

'Marry you?' Her light, cool voice had gone hoarse. 'Are you mad?'

'No,' he said, smiling slightly. 'Think of it as an opportunity.'

'An opportunity?' A couple more petals from the poor, abused peonies in her hand drifted to the stone floor. 'An opportunity for what?'

He tightened his grip on her elbow a little, hoping the physical touch would jolt her out of her shock response.

Nothing to do with how the warmth of her silken skin under his fingers made his breath catch. It had been a reflexive thing to steady her, but now he was touching her, he couldn't bring himself to let her go.

'An opportunity for you to save Kendricks',' he replied. He preferred not to use threats when it came to business negotiations, but he would if it got him what he wanted. So he let her see the pirate, the ruthless part of him that had driven him from a hand-to-mouth existence as an unwanted orphan, to being CEO of one of the world's most dangerous acquisitions companies. 'I went to your father last night and we had a very interesting discussion. He was quite happy for me to marry you instead of Gianni, as long as I not only bought Kendricks', but kept you as CEO. I did make him a promise to keep the company intact for at least a year, but...' He lifted a shoulder. 'Perhaps I won't. Perhaps I'll break it up and sell it for a healthy profit. Unless of course my wife advises me otherwise.'

Anger sparked suddenly in her blue eyes and a hint of colour washed through her pale cheeks. That was good. She had a bit of backbone it seemed. 'If you expect that I'm going to let you—'

'Think,' he murmured, giving her elbow another squeeze, watching how the reminder of his touch made the colour in her cheeks deepen still further. Interesting. He was well aware that she didn't like him, but that blush indicated that she was affected by his hand on her arm at least, which was pleasing. 'As CEO and my wife, you'll be able to discuss with me any restructures. Perhaps you might advise against them. Perhaps I might listen to you.'

She took a breath and he watched as she visibly forced aside her shock, her pretty features hardening. It was impressive. Was this the potential her father had seen in her? Certainly it was more feeling than he'd ever observed in the boardroom.

'Is that a threat?'

'Not at all. As I said, I'm merely pointing out an opportunity.'

'Or you could just not buy Kendricks' at all,' she said coldly. 'Or not be my stand-in groom. You could just go back to doing what you do best which is destroying things. How's that for an opportunity?'

He allowed himself another smile. Oh, she definitely had more backbone than he'd expected, which was pleasing. However, she didn't know him. She didn't know that he never gave up when he wanted something, never ever. Once, long ago, when he'd still had a conscience and a heart that hadn't completely frozen over, he'd let something go. Something very, very precious to him. But he never would again. The conscience he'd once had was dead and so was his heart, and now nothing could touch him.

'I could,' he said. 'But alas, I wish to marry you more.'

Beyond the big doors of the church's interior, he could hear more rustlings as people shifted in their seats, the hum of conversation now a dull roar.

He needed her to make a decision and to make it quickly.

'I won't require anything of you,' he went on, keeping his voice low and steady. 'It'll be a marriage in name only. We can hash out the details on our honeymoon.'

Isla was white beneath her veil, but he could see her

pretty mouth. The lipstick she had on today was a soft pink, highlighting the lush fullness of her lips. 'A honeymoon? You can't be serious.'

'Of course I'm serious.' He'd already planned it out in the hours before the wedding, because he was nothing if not prepared. 'We will need a honeymoon to let the dust settle here and so we can discuss our arrangement.' And so he could discover his own peculiar fascination with her.

She was staring at him now as if she'd never seen him before in all her life. 'So let me get this straight,' she said slowly. 'If I don't marry you today, now, you'll remove me as CEO and break Kendricks' up?'

'Correct.'

'But that's blackmail.'

He lifted a shoulder. 'I prefer to think of it as an incentive.'

'But you're not giving me a choice.'

'Naturally, you have a choice. You can choose not to marry me. I'm not forcing you into anything.'

Her gaze behind her veil was very dark, her posture stiff, and he could feel the tension in her arm.

Time was passing and they'd been standing there too long, and if he waited any longer, her shock would wear off and she would start thinking clearly and logically, and his window of opportunity would be gone. He couldn't let that happen.

'Come,' he murmured. 'We can't stay here too much longer. People are getting impatient. You can refuse, in which case I'll leave, then take the company anyway, removing you as CEO and your father gets nothing. Or you can agree, in which case your father gets the nice little windfall from the sale of the company he was expecting, you get to remain as CEO and I get to keep the company intact for the year that I promised. You might even convince me to keep it intact longer than a year.'

She was trembling slightly. 'You're a bastard.'

Unperturbed, Orion inclined his head. He'd expected her anger. 'Indeed. Though, I've been called worse.'

'Doesn't it matter to you at all that you paid my fiancé off? That you—'

'Enough with the outrage,' he interrupted mildly. 'You didn't love him, as I already pointed out. You don't love me either, so really, all you're doing is swapping one means to an end with another. It's no big deal.'

The blush in her cheeks burned more intensely, which intrigued him. He'd assumed that her tremble was fear, and though he hadn't wanted to frighten her, he'd accepted that she might be afraid. However, that blush wasn't fear, that was anger.

Good. Anger was better than fear. It was certainly more powerful.

'No big deal?' she hissed. 'Are you mad?'

'Isla,' he murmured. 'Yes or no.'

For a second he thought she might refuse and his muscles tensed in response.

Then she tore her arm from his grip. Yet instead of heading out of the church and escaping, she marched straight over to the big oak double doors that led to the church proper. She stopped in front of them, clutching the remains of her peonies in a white-knuckled grip. 'Come on then,' she said, not looking at him. 'Let's get this over with.'

Orion smiled. She had more spirit than he'd expected, a lot more, in fact. And he liked that. He liked it very much.

So he came over to where she stood, and pushed open the doors, and let the strains of the wedding march fill the church.

CHAPTER TWO

ISLA IGNORED THE stares of the guests as she and Orion stepped through the doors. She ignored her father standing there, and the look of relief on his face.

Anger seethed in the pit of her stomach, and it was only sheer force of will that was preventing her from flinging her bouquet in Orion's stupid, smug face, kicking her father in the shins, then running straight out the doors and never coming back.

But anger wouldn't help, it never did, and she had no choice now but to hold tight to her bouquet and act as though the change of groom had been her idea all along.

Firstly she could barely believe Orion had gone to her father and done this apparent deal for her behind her back, without even a word to her. Secondly, she could barely believe her father had agreed to it.

Then again, maybe it wasn't so difficult to believe. Orion's reputation as a businessman who got what he wanted was well-known, and as for her father, Kendricks' and its legacy was the only thing that mattered to him. That's why he'd adopted her, to take over the helm once he was gone. He certainly hadn't cared who her groom was as long as it was someone. And from a business perspective selling Kendricks' made sense—the board was unhappy and the company had been underperforming for years—and extracting a promise from Orion to keep it intact had been a good move. As had making sure she stayed on as CEO in order to retain the illusion of family control.

Yet she was furious all the same that David hadn't said anything to her, leaving her to have to deal with Orion turning up just before she had to walk down the aisle.

Leaving her to deal with Orion's threats to Kendricks' if he didn't marry her.

Because of course, she couldn't allow that to happen. The whole reason she'd been adopted had been to take over Kendricks' since her father hadn't had any other children. His wife hadn't been able to have them and after she'd died, he hadn't wanted to marry again. Yet Kendricks' was a family company and because he'd wanted to pass it on to a child of his, he'd decided to adopt. And she'd been his choice.

Which also made Orion her problem to fix.

She had no idea why he wanted to marry her, none at all. Apart from that one conversation in the National Gallery where he'd rudely turned around and walked out, he'd never shown her the slightest bit of interest. So for him to turn up here, telling her that he'd paid Gianni off and that he'd take Kendricks' if she didn't marry him… It was baffling.

Regardless of his reasons, that didn't make her any less furious. Furious with him for threatening her into this and furious at herself, because surely, she should have anticipated this. Perhaps not his arrival at her wedding or his paying off Gianni, but surely she should have felt alarm bells at his interest in Kendricks' and wondered why he hadn't moved to acquire it straight away.

David had taught her to be sharp and observant in the boardroom, yet she hadn't noticed Orion betray anything more than his usual cold interest.

And you know why you didn't notice, don't you?

Isla gritted her teeth, keeping her gaze squarely on the altar at the end of the aisle and not on the shocked gazes of the guests.

Yes, she knew. She just hated to admit that the reason she hadn't noticed anything untoward about Orion was that she'd tried very hard not to notice him at all. He unsettled her, he always had, right from the first moment he'd walked into the boardroom a week after their first meeting at the National Gallery a year ago. He'd brought some kind of hissing, crackling electricity with him that had found its way under her skin, making her feel antsy and restless and bothered.

She'd hated it. Emotions had no place in the boardroom, as she well knew. She had to be cool and sharp, and she was learning to be both, but it was something she'd always found difficult. She felt things deeply and passionately, and even the years in the foster system hadn't quite put out the fire that burned in her heart. The fire that Orion's mere presence only stoked, apparently. She'd tried to tune him out whenever he was around, tried to pretend she didn't notice when his gaze rested on her, staying quiet and still in the hope that he'd lose whatever interest in her he had. Except that hadn't worked because if it had, she wouldn't be walking down the aisle with him right now.

She should have paid attention. If she'd put her personal feelings aside and talked to him, discovered what his intentions were with Kendricks' and with her, then perhaps this could have been avoided.

It doesn't help that the board don't want you at the helm.

That was also true. They were dissatisfied with her performance—they hadn't thought she was CEO material—and that made the company vulnerable to someone like Orion, a wolf lying in wait looking for prey to attack and pull apart.

It was a vulnerability she'd been hoping to fix. David had adopted her to be the future of Kendricks' and the marriage to Gianni was supposed to help cement that future with the board. Some of them wouldn't like this new development with Orion, but it was likely the majority would approve—they might even like him better than Gianni, in which case marrying him would achieve the same aim. But only if it looked like her decision rather than a deal done behind her back between Orion and her father, that she had no part in.

So you'd better keep smiling and acting like this was all your idea, hadn't you?

Isla shoved down her anger and bitter self-recriminations as she came to a stop before the altar, forcing herself to smile. There was a murmured exchange between Orion and the vicar, who then launched into the marriage service.

Dead silence fell over the entire church.

It didn't matter that it wasn't the wedding she'd thought she'd have.

It didn't matter that Orion had paid off the man she'd thought she was going to marry and Gianni had… Well, he'd taken the money and run.

You can't have been that important to him. He didn't really want to marry you. He didn't want a wife any more than David had wanted a daughter.

Something ached and burned in her heart, but she was familiar with the sensation, so she ignored it. Instead, she concentrated on saying her vows when prompted, then listening to Orion say his. And when he held out his hand, she gave it to him. He produced a ring from his pocket and slid it onto her finger, and dimly it occurred to her that there were a whole lot of questions she should be asking him. Such as why he was marrying her in the first place and how long had he been planning for it.

People were murmuring, and that was no surprise. They'd all be wondering why the Kendricks' heir was suddenly walking down the aisle with a different man, and what had happened to her original groom.

What must they think of you? What must David think of you? He sold you to one man first, before selling you off to another...

She felt cold, the winter outside penetrating the stone of the church, or maybe it wasn't the winter. Maybe it was just the cold settling down inside her, a slow creeping shock she couldn't shake.

Yet she couldn't allow that to take hold, just as she couldn't keep going back over that late-night phone conversation of her father's that she shouldn't have overheard.

She was standing before the altar, with people staring at her, and she couldn't afford to look weak and uncertain in front of them, not when her suitability as future CEO was already being questioned. She had to look strong and in control, as if this had been her decision all along, not one forced on her.

So she put some steel into her spine as Orion took hold of her veil and lifted it. His gaze wasn't cold now. Instead, it burned with a dark golden flame that made her heart beat inexplicably fast.

She didn't like him. Everything about him made her restless and uneasy, and the way he was looking at her now…

Gianni never looked at you that way.

No, he hadn't. He'd liked her and the kisses they'd shared had been pleasant if undemanding. But he'd never looked at her the way Orion was looking at her. As if he wanted to eat her alive…

Her heartbeat thumped loudly in her head as Orion bent and brushed his mouth over hers. It was the world's most fleeting kiss and even though she'd been expecting it, she hadn't been expecting the static electricity that prickled over her skin the moment their lips met.

It was the same electricity she felt whenever he was around, the one that made her restless and unsettled, that made the fire inside her flicker and leap. Now it was as if that electricity had found its way beneath her skin, shocking her in ways she didn't expect.

You should have just walked out of the church and damn the consequences.

She should have. But it was too late now.

Orion lifted his head, tucking her hand into his elbow, and then they were walking back up the aisle, now husband and wife.

She felt icy yet her lips burned from that brief kiss. Ignoring both sensations, she kept her chin lifted and her spine straight, ignoring the shocked expressions on the faces of the wedding guests.

It was completely her choice to marry the man who'd been going to acquire Kendricks'. A shock move, yes, but as Orion had said, it was an opportunity.

An opportunity to keep Kendricks' safe and stay in control as CEO. Perhaps also an opportunity to learn more about the enemy.

Talk it up all you want. The truth is that all of this is your fault. If you'd been able to realise the potential your father saw in you, then Orion wouldn't have targeted Kendricks' in the first place.

Isla shoved the thought away. She'd fix this. She would.

As they stepped out of the church, it was snowing. David had thought a December wedding would be perfect since the marriage of the Kendricks' heir really should take place at Christmas time, and Isla had agreed.

Except it was cold, the icy breeze whispering over her exposed skin and making her shiver.

Somehow Orion had the thick white shawl she'd bought for this moment and for the photos, and he placed it around her shoulders. 'I will be coming shortly,' he murmured and then someone else in a dark uniform was at her side, ushering her along to the icy path to the church gate.

The tight knot in her chest that had gathered in anticipation of the confrontation that would no doubt occur with her father loosened a little. Clearly there was to be no confrontation with either her guests or her father, or at least, not one that she'd have to deal with.

Still, she felt like a coward as she went through the church gate without a protest and then into the long black car that stood idling at the kerb.

It was warm inside the car, the butter-soft leather of

the seats enveloping her as she was bundled inside, the train of her gown folded in neatly with her.

Then there was silence.

Had it really happened? Had she really married Orion North?

A shudder worked its way down her spine, but Isla pushed the weakness viciously away. It was done now. She'd have to deal with David at some point, not to mention the media fallout, but the main thing was that Kendricks' was safe. That was assuming Orion was a man of his word.

You should have got an assurance of that in writing before *you married him.*

Isla sat back in her seat, still feeling cold, trying to ignore the voice in her head. She hadn't thought of getting an agreement from him in the narthex. She'd been in shock and he'd taken advantage of that mercilessly. And she'd been the one to stamp angrily to the church doors, telling him to 'get this over with'.

She'd been stupid, allowed her anger at his threat to get to her, and had handled this thing badly. But there was no use beating herself up about it. She'd done it now and the only way forward was to protect Kendricks' from Orion any way she could.

'Mrs North?' The driver was holding a phone out to her from the front seat. 'Mr North would like a word.'

Isla blinked. Yes, that's right. She was Mrs North now, wasn't she? She leaned forward and took the phone, raising it to her ear. 'Yes?'

'I'm staying to clear up matters here.' Orion's deep voice was as cool as the snow falling outside. 'Also to have a word with your father. I'll meet you at the airport.'

The airport. They were going to airport. And *he* was going to talk to her father.

'I see,' she said, ignoring the anger that had resumed boiling at the calm way he'd taken charge of everything. 'I'd appreciate it if you informed my father to be clear to the media and the board that this was *my* decision, not some shady backroom deal you two did between yourselves behind my back.'

'Of course,' Orion said smoothly and without a trace of shame. 'After all, it *was* your decision.'

Isla gritted her teeth. 'And the reception? The guests?' There, she could sound as cool and as calm as he did.

'Leave that to me. I'm sure you'd prefer to avoid any awkwardness.'

It was so close to the truth that she was very tempted to open the car door and go running back into the church just to prove him wrong. But that *would* be letting her emotions get the better of her. Perhaps it would look more powerful if she let him explain. After all, this was all his doing.

'Fine,' she said, giving him nothing.

'Good.' He sounded infuriatingly smug. 'My jet will be waiting for you to relax in.'

'Lovely.' She meant the opposite.

'We'll be taking a flight to Iceland where I have a lodge. We can spend some time there talking about where we go from here. Or would you prefer the tropics?'

She and Gianni had planned a week's honeymoon in the Caribbean. She hadn't been looking forward to it, though she hadn't been able to put her finger on why. Probably because she hadn't felt she could take a week off, nothing at all to do with the thought of spending a week in Gianni's company.

'Does it matter?' she asked, feeling suddenly exhausted.

'No,' Orion said. 'Iceland it is.' Then his voice changed, warming fractionally. 'Don't worry, Isla. I'll deal with it all.'

There shouldn't have been any reason for her to like the way he'd said that any better than the way he'd said everything else. Yet for some reason she found his casual reassurance...relieving. Because right now, yes. She wanted someone else to deal with it.

Someone who won't make a mess of everything.

'I should speak to David myself,' she said, ignoring the thought.

'Perhaps later,' Orion said casually. 'I'm talking to him right now. All you need to do is get on the plane.' Then without even saying goodbye, he ended the call.

Isla let out a breath, handed the phone back to the driver, then leaned back in her seat as the car finally pulled away and into the snowy village road.

Her thoughts whirled, but she ignored them all, staring out at the snow falling on the villages they passed. Trying not to feel the slight pressure of her new wedding ring on her finger, or think about the million questions she wanted answers to. Because the man she wanted those answers from wasn't here.

Eventually the car pulled into a private airfield, where a sleek little jet waited on the runway. The driver helped Isla out of the car and up the stairs, and soon she was inside and ensconced in another extremely comfortable soft leather seat.

She took off her veil and folded it neatly, setting it onto the seat beside her, before drawing the shawl more firmly around her shoulders. A stewardess approached with a glass of champagne, which Isla found a little on the nose since there wasn't anything to celebrate from her perspective. But since it seemed churlish to refuse and quite frankly, she could use a drink, she took it.

A short time later, the jet's door opened in a rush of cold air, and Orion strode in.

Snow dusted the shoulders of his morning suit and his coal-black hair, but he didn't look cold or seem bothered by it in the least. In fact, judging from his expression, what he seemed was extremely pleased with himself. Not unlike an ancient Roman emperor about to embark on a triumph down the Appian Way. Isla was almost surprised that he wasn't cloaked in purple and wearing a laurel wreath.

A good thing. It would suit him far too well.

She tried to drag her gaze away from him as he paused to talk to the stewardess, but it was difficult.

He was her husband and the electricity that had slid beneath her skin during their kiss at the altar was again humming and crackling, making her feel restless, unable to sit still.

She hadn't liked it then and she didn't like it now, most especially because she had an idea what it was: physical attraction. She'd hadn't felt it with Gianni and she'd liked him, so why she should feel it for a man who was essentially the enemy, she had no idea. It bothered her, especially when that brief kiss at the altar still burned in her memory.

Forcing her gaze from Orion's mesmerising figure, Isla stared out the window into the swirling snow as the plane taxied down the runway and lifted into the air, trying to think of absolutely nothing. But then, as they reached cruising altitude, she became aware of someone tall and powerful and very definitely male approaching and sitting in the seat opposite her.

Her heart thudded and she tensed.

'Come now, Isla,' Orion said, clearly noticing her tension. 'The hard part is over. Now you can relax.'

Bracing herself, she took her gaze from the window and looked at him.

He was sitting with his elbows on his knees, his hands clasped between them, and his gaze fixed on her with disturbing intensity. He smiled and it was so full of an unexpected, slow-burning heat her breath caught.

He was looking at her as if she was a prize he'd fought for hard and won.

She could feel herself blushing, the electricity under her skin prickling.

Even your own father never looked at you that way, as if you were worth something.

The thought wound through her, a small thread of jagged ice. David had certainly been pleased with her when he'd first adopted her. He'd been satisfied with her excellent marks at school and the reports detailing her potential, as well as her polite manner and how articulate she was. Smart, he'd called her, and she'd been thrilled. She hadn't cared that he was the Christmas magnate and he'd adopted her to be his heir. She'd just been happy someone had wanted her, and she'd been excited to be part of a family again.

She'd thought he wanted a daughter, but it soon became apparent that David had no use for daughters, and what he actually wanted was a business protégé, an employee he could mould into his perfect successor. He found her emotional needs tiresome, frequently telling her that he hadn't adopted her because he wanted hugs and family time. He'd adopted her because her school marks were excellent and she had potential. A potential she knew she hadn't lived up to.

But she didn't want to think about that. The only thing that mattered right now was getting answers from Orion North.

Ignoring the heat in her cheeks and the electricity in her bloodstream, Isla forced herself to hold his gaze. 'So, Mr North,' she said flatly. 'You promised me Kendricks' would remain intact for a year if I married you, and that I would be CEO. So now I have, in fact, married you, I want that promise in writing and I want it now.'

Orion contemplated the new Mrs Isla North with not a little bit of satisfaction.

She looked like a snow maiden, all swathed in white, and yet there were so many delicate colours to her. Colours he'd never noticed before. The angry sapphire of her eyes and her full, pink mouth. The rose petal stain of a blush on her cheeks and the golden curls escaping from her careful bridal up-do and falling down around her ears.

His wife now.

Even though marriage had never been his intention—or at least not until a week earlier—he found the thought of her being his wife very satisfying. He'd promised Kendrick he'd stay married to her for a year, not that he cared overmuch about time frames since it probably wouldn't take all that long to get to the bottom of his fascination with her. And once he had, he'd already decided that they'd lead separate lives until the year was up and then he'd divorce her.

He had no need for a wife and a family was not on his list of things to accomplish. He had no things to accomplish, not since he'd already accomplished everything he'd set out to do. All except one, of course. But that was something that would remain undone.

However, now Isla was his, he could take some time to find out exactly what it was about her that drew him so intensely.

Certainly he'd admired her poise back in the church. She'd been furious, but she'd taken him and his threat seriously and hadn't balked when he'd promised to carry it through if she didn't agree to be his wife. And, of course, a written agreement was exactly what he'd demand if he was in her shoes.

Which was why he'd already had his legal department draw one up.

'Funny you should ask.' He lifted a hand. Obligingly, the stewardess came over with the agreement that she'd just finished printing out and handed it to him.

He took it and held it out to Isla. 'I trust this will suffice.'

The look she gave him was deeply suspicious as she reached for the papers, and became even more so when he didn't let them go.

The colour of her eyes was so very pretty. A deep, endless blue, like a summer sky at midnight. He'd liked it when he'd lifted her veil by the altar and had looked down into them, seeing all those challenging, glittering sparks.

It wasn't the same as when she'd talked to him about that Van Gogh painting and she'd become so luminous he hadn't been able to look away, yet it was similar.

You want her to come alive for you too.

Maybe he did. He certainly didn't need to hold on to

the papers the way he was doing now, but he was and purely to see that hot blue flame burn in her gaze.

'I don't know if it will suffice,' she said. 'Not if you don't let me look at it.'

Really, she was quite delicious like this, all pink and white and furious. If he'd known, he'd have somehow engineered things so he could have married her sooner. Either that or he'd have seduced her. Though, he could still seduce her. He'd told her in the church it would be a marriage in name only, but that had been before he'd got close to her. Before he'd touched her silky skin and kissed that soft pouty mouth in front of the altar.

In fact, he was starting to think that perhaps he might want a wedding night, and perhaps she might agree. After all, she wasn't unaffected by him, not given the way she was blushing now.

Clearly it was time to test that.

'Say please,' he murmured.

She blinked. 'Excuse me?'

'I think you heard.' He smiled. 'Politeness is key to any business negotiation.'

More anger glittered in her eyes and he liked it. He liked it far too much. She'd been so very contained in all those business meetings he'd had with her and her father, and yet he'd had the sense that her control was imperfect. Sometimes her fingers would drum on the desk or she'd tap her foot on the floor. Or she'd shift minutely in her seat, as if she couldn't sit still.

She seemed like a champagne bottle that had been shaken with the cork still in it, all the liquid fizzing and seething inside just waiting for a chance to explode.

Perhaps he might see that explosion now.

The thought made him catch his breath.

'Please,' she said through gritted teeth.

Disappointing. He didn't want her to give in. He wanted her to fight. He wanted her to come alive the way she had in the National Gallery, and he didn't even know why.

That he no longer experienced the passion he'd seen in her face that day perhaps accounted for it. He didn't have room in his life for feelings that intense, not any more. He allowed himself moments of physical pleasure, but beyond that, the only thing that held his interest was the pursuit of underperforming companies. The thrill of the chase.

He hadn't known he'd wanted more than that until he'd seen Isla Kendrick explain to him why *Starry Night* by Vincent Van Gogh was one of her favourite paintings and what made it so transformative.

He hadn't understood what she was talking about when she'd explained, but he'd understood that look on her face. He wanted to see it again.

He wanted to see it for *him*.

'Oh, no,' he chided gently. 'That's no way to drive a bargain. You don't give in straight away. You negotiate. You make a counter offer.'

'This is not a negotiation, Mr North. This is you giving me some papers to look over.'

'Mr North? I'm your husband, Isla. The least you could call me is Orion.'

'I'd much prefer to call you a stone-cold bastard, how does that sound?'

He smiled. 'That's the spirit. How about this then? I'll give you the agreement to look over in return for a kiss.'

She flushed. 'Absolutely not. I don't need to read it that badly.'

'*Au contraire.* If you don't read it, then I can't sign it. And if I don't sign it, you won't get my promise in writing, and Kendricks' will still be at risk.'

Emotions flickered over her face, gone so fast he couldn't read them all. Fury seemed to be her primary emotion, and he couldn't blame her. He had, after all, completely upset her wedding day by paying off her ridiculous excuse for a fiancé, and threatening to get rid of her as CEO and take apart her company if she didn't marry him. That couldn't have been easy for her, yet she'd coped with it all admirably, displaying unexpected backbone.

She was proving to be much more interesting than he'd anticipated and he was intrigued to see where this fury might lead her. Anger could be far more productive and useful if it was properly focused, and it was certainly preferable to her being upset or afraid.

In fact, he didn't like the thought of her being upset or afraid.

Isla gave him a look of disdain from beneath long, feathery golden lashes. 'You've already had one kiss. You don't get another.'

'Then offer me something else,' he countered. 'Something you can give me right now, that's easy and quick and something I want.'

Her blue gaze narrowed. 'What do you want then?'

Orion was a gambler and he never gave anything away. He kept his cards close to his chest, what little emotion he allowed himself under strict control and his desires very firmly hidden. Not that he had any desires. Desiring nothing meant no one had power over you, and if there was one thing he hated, it was anyone having any kind of power over him.

These days, *he* was the one with the power. He held all the cards and he won all the games. Always.

He smiled. 'Guess.'

The explosion he'd been hoping for didn't come. Instead, she let go of the papers and sat back in her seat, regarding him with a cool blue stare. 'You know, I really don't like you. In fact, I've never liked you.'

He only raised a brow. 'That has never been a barrier to people doing business with me.'

'This isn't business.'

'Isn't it? You married me to retain your family's company, Isla. What is that if not business?'

Her jaw hardened, frustration glittering in her eyes. 'Just give me the damn papers.'

'Only if you give me what I want.'

'But you won't tell me what you want.'

'You know already, Snow White. I told you.'

She looked like she wanted to spit something at him, and he was already relishing the fight. Instead, she looked away for a moment and when she glanced back, she was once more cold, all the liquid sapphire in her eyes hardening into glittering gems.

'Fine,' she said. 'Have it your way.' She leaned forward into the space between them and stuck out her chin. 'Come on, here I am. Take your kiss.'

Then she closed her eyes.

Orion stared at her for a long moment, conscious of a certain dark hunger stirring inside him. A hunger he'd thought he'd long since cut out of his soul.

A hunger to show her that he too could come alive if

certain conditions were met, and that he too could make her fascinated with him the way he was fascinated with her.

She didn't like him, she'd been very clear on that. But she didn't need to like him in order to be fascinated with him, and he was tired of that fascination all being one way.

He could show her passion too, and it wasn't in paint or brushstrokes.

Slowly, he reached out and took her rounded little chin between his fingers and held it, watching her tense as he did so. But he didn't kiss her, not yet. He wanted her to look at him first.

Eventually, she let out an impatient breath and sure enough, her eyes opened. 'What are you doing? I thought you were going to take this kiss.'

'I am.' He gazed at her, relishing the soft feel of her skin beneath his fingers. Conscious of the faint, sweet scent of jasmine and vanilla. Pretty. 'Don't rush me.'

'You said you wanted easy and quick and—'

He leaned forward abruptly and covered her mouth with his, silencing whatever else she'd been going to say.

And for a second, he remained very still, aware of the softness of her mouth and her scent, the warmth of her skin where he held her. She'd gone still, too, and he could feel the tension in her. But since she hadn't pulled away, he touched her lips with his tongue, gently exploring, coaxing her to open to him. She was reluctant at first, then a sigh escaped her, and her mouth opened and he deepened the kiss, exploring her slowly. She tasted of mint and a tart sweetness that he found unexpectedly delicious so he chased it, the kiss getting hotter, deeper.

Her eyes had closed again, but this time it wasn't because she was shutting him out. He could feel the resistance bleeding out of her as she leaned into him, her lips moving against his, starting to kiss him back.

Satisfaction hit him like a gut punch. Ah, there it was, that passion, that life. He'd seen it sparking in her eyes and now he could taste it in her kiss. She wasn't at all cool now, was she? And one other thing was also clear: she hadn't loved her fiancé. Because if she had she wouldn't now be kissing him, another man, on her wedding day.

Orion released her chin, allowing his fingers to stroke down the silky warmth of her neck before gently circling her throat, letting his hand rest there so she was aware of it.

She tasted so good and he wanted more, and he could take it, he knew. She'd let him. But he was aware all of a sudden that he was tired of taking things. He wanted something to be given to him for a change. So after a moment, he took his hand away and lifted his mouth from hers.

Her lashes rose, her blue eyes deep as a midsummer night.

'You can have the papers,' he said, his voice rougher than he would have liked. 'But if you want anything more… Well. Let's just say I'm open to negotiations.'

Then he pulled back from her completely, tossed the papers onto the seat beside her, then rose and went down the back of the plane where he could tie up the loose ends that needed tying up without any more distractions from his new wife.

CHAPTER THREE

THE FLIGHT TO ICELAND wasn't long and Isla spent it going over the fine print of the agreement Orion had tossed at her, not to mention trying very hard not to think about the kiss he'd bargained out of her. The kiss she'd given him thinking it was only a kiss, light and fleeting and forgettable. Very much like the kiss he'd given her during their wedding ceremony.

Except it hadn't been either light, or even forgettable.

The print of Orion's agreement blurred in front of her as she remembered again the heat of his mouth and the taste of him, a hot, dark flavour with a spice to it that had taken her utterly by surprise. She hadn't known she'd find the taste of a man delicious. She hadn't known that the stroke of his tongue and the touch of his fingers could make her tremble.

Gianni, of course, had kissed her, but they hadn't slept together and neither of them had been in a hurry to do so. She'd been fine with that. In fact, she'd been relieved that she hadn't felt that same restlessness, that same electricity, around him that she felt when she was around Orion. It was dangerous that electricity. It made her feel out of control, made the flame in her heart burn hot, made her feel…hungry.

She didn't want to feel like that, especially now when she had most of the things she'd once hungered for. A home. A purpose. A future.

Not a family, though. Not someone who cares for you. Not someone to belong to.

She gritted her teeth, ignoring that betraying little thought. This was about Orion and nothing else. Anyway, she'd kissed him because he'd demanded it and because she wasn't going to get into any ridiculous bargaining nonsense. A kiss was nothing and if it meant she'd get the agreement he'd promised her then what of it?

That it hadn't been nothing was immaterial. The less said about it the better and anyway, it wasn't going to happen again. He might be her husband, but it was in name only and that's how it would stay.

Once she'd finished going over the agreement, Isla rose from her seat and went down the back of the plane. Orion was sitting at a table covered in papers, a sleek laptop open, and he was studying the screen with the same intensity of focus that he'd directed at her just before.

She put the agreement down on the table and clutched her shawl more closely around her shoulders. 'I've looked over it,' she said crisply. 'You can send that to Kendricks' legal department for them to study too.'

Orion glanced up from his screen and raised one black brow. 'You don't trust my word that it's fine?'

'No. I wouldn't trust you as far as I could throw you.'

'A wise decision.' He glanced back down at his computer screen in obvious dismissal. 'I'll send it to them.'

'Why did you want to marry me?' she asked abruptly, since it was time he started answering some of her questions and she was tired of being in the dark. 'Because if it was Kendricks' you wanted, you could have just taken it.'

He didn't look up. 'I didn't, because it wasn't Kendricks' I wanted.'

Her. He'd wanted *her*.

A tiny shock arrowed down her spine. 'That's not an answer.'

'Sadly, it's the only one you're getting. I'm extremely busy, Snow White. Why don't you go back to your seat and read a magazine or something.'

Isla gritted her teeth. 'Snow White? Really?'

His gaze remained on the screen and he said nothing, but his mouth quirked. She couldn't help looking at it. His bottom lip was full and beautifully carved. It had felt soft on hers and yet there had been a firmness to it, an insistent demand...

The electricity that hummed beneath her skin turned into a wash of heat, making her breath catch. Why had he wanted her? What was it that had made him promise to buy an entire company just so he could marry her?

'If you're not going to read a magazine,' Orion murmured, 'you're quite welcome to stand there for the rest of the flight looking at my mouth. I don't mind. Though I warn you, I might expect something for the privilege.'

The heat reached her cheeks, making her blush, and she suddenly wanted to shake him in some way, make him as restless and unsettled as he made her. It had been going on for months now and she was tired of it. Except she didn't know how she could. He was one of the most successful corporate raiders in the world, a stone-cold, razor-sharp businessman, while she was only the adopted daughter of the Kendricks' Family Christmas

CEO. The adopted daughter who'd been all potential and nothing else.

David should have returned you. That's what he should have done.

No, she could still realise that potential. Orion had promised she'd be CEO. She could still show David that his decision to adopt her thirteen years ago had been the right one. She just had to stop letting her more…intense feelings get in the way of making decisions that were good for the business. Being sympathetic to unhappy staff working long hours on a minimum wage and wanting to help them was all well and good, but paying more meant more expenses for the company, which the board didn't like. They hadn't been happy either with her informing her father that while the factory that made the Christmas decorations might have been cheap, it also contravened several labour laws and put people's lives in danger, and so they needed to change to a different supplier. Yes, it was more expensive, but could you really put a cost on people's lives?

Apparently you could and they hadn't liked her arguing with them about it.

So now that's what she needed to learn. To put her sympathies aside. To become harder, colder. To become more ruthless.

You could try learning from him.

Now, *that* was a good idea. He was certainly hard and cold, not to mention extremely ruthless. She didn't like the thought of admitting that she needed to learn anything from him, but if she wanted to make her father proud, she had to do something.

She very much wanted to shock Orion in some way

before that, though. He'd been in charge from the moment he'd walked into the church and she was tired of it.

'If you want another kiss,' he murmured without looking up. 'Please don't hesitate to ask. Though, as I said, I'll probably want something more in return for one this time.'

Something more...

Another wash of heat swept through her, her mind reeling at the thought of the 'more' he might want. But no, thinking those things was reckless of her, dangerous even.

To stay in control of herself, she had to take control of the situation, not let him get the upper hand. And well, he was a man who took what he wanted, or so he'd said, so why couldn't she? Why couldn't she take from him? Give him a taste of his own medicine? Had anyone ever done that to him? She was thinking not.

'Orion,' she said softly.

And was gratified when he looked up. In the dim lighting of the plane, his dark golden eyes met hers and they gleamed. As if he knew already what she was about to do.

He didn't, though, she was sure. He was far too satisfied with himself, far too pleased that his little threat had worked. He thought he had her exactly where he wanted her, and well, she'd show him.

Isla reached down and grabbed him by the tie, then she bent and kissed him.

He stiffened in surprise, but didn't pull away. His mouth was firm and warm and within moments she was already half-desperate for the taste of him again. She touched her tongue to his lips the way he had with her not an hour or so ago, wanting entry.

He didn't give it.

Isla made a frustrated sound, because that wasn't fair. All she wanted was another taste; that wasn't so much to ask for was it? She traced his bottom lip with her tongue and then nipped it. She wasn't experienced, and she'd certainly never had this kind of kiss with Gianni, but then, she'd never wanted to. She'd never been as desperate to taste him as she was to taste Orion.

She wasn't expecting it when he opened his mouth slightly, turning the kiss just as hot as it had been before. Yet this time there was a wild element to it. Something raw and burning. It was thrilling and scary, and she wanted to—

Orion pulled back abruptly and she was left clutching empty air.

'Well,' he murmured, his eyes gone a brilliant, lambent gold. 'Aren't you full of surprises?'

She let go of his tie, her hands shaking, her heart beating far too fast and far too loud.

That was a mistake.

Very much so. She'd almost lost herself that time and she couldn't do that. She knew what happened when she let her hunger for what she wanted overcome her control. She ended up losing everything.

She straightened, not letting even a hint of how he'd affected her show. 'Don't get ahead of yourself, Mr North. I only wanted you to know that I can also take what I want, when I want it.'

He smiled, predatory and dangerous and everything in her tightened. 'You didn't love him at all, did you?'

A hot flush of shame washed through her, but not for Gianni's sake. They both knew she didn't love him. No, the shame she felt was for her father and the plans he'd made for her. The plans she'd agreed on that now lay in ruins, and all because of her.

But there hadn't been another choice. Orion hadn't given her one.

Or perhaps there was and you just didn't see it?

She ignored that thought and since there was nothing else she could say to that, she turned her back on him and returned to her seat.

Orion tried to work, tried to put the puzzle of his new wife out of his head, but try as he might, he couldn't.

It was a first not to be able to stop thinking of a woman. Normally, he had no trouble whatsoever. His lovers never impinged on his day-to-day life because he made sure that they didn't. He paid attention to them when he was with them, but when he wasn't, it was out of sight, out of mind.

He didn't want anyone to be important to him, because once someone became important, that's when they had power over you. That's what had happened with Cleo and their baby, and he'd never do it again. Not after that baby was taken from him.

His son. Luke.

Luke would be twenty now and what he was doing, God only knew. Orion didn't and neither did he want to, not after the decision he'd made years earlier. He'd been twenty-six and had already made the first major deal of his career, and finally he'd had the money and the power to take his son back from those who'd kept him.

He'd hired the best lawyers and filled a car full of toys, and he'd arrived at Cleo's chic little Chelsea townhouse. She'd married a tech company CEO and was now living in the manner to which she'd become very much accustomed.

It had been Luke's tenth birthday and a party was being held, with lots of people going in and out. He'd told the lawyer to wait in the car and he'd gone in alone. He'd wanted to confront Cleo personally, tell her he wasn't sixteen any longer, that he had money now, and if she wouldn't give him his son back, Orion would take him.

But he'd come through the light, airy hallway and out into the back garden, and into the cheerful chaos of a kid's birthday party in full swing. Luke was standing at a picnic table, a huge cake in the shape of some superhero or other on the top of it and everyone was singing 'Happy Birthday'. Then he bent to blow out the candles and they all cheered. Cleo's husband leaned down to say something to him and Luke laughed. Cleo's hand was on Luke's shoulder and in amongst the happy kids, he saw Cleo's father also smiling.

God, how he'd hated Cleo's father.

But all that really mattered was Luke, and his son was also smiling. His son was laughing. His son was happy. His son had everything Orion had never had himself and yet had always wanted to give him.

Orion had stood for a moment in the hallway, watching as the boy he hadn't seen since he was a baby, and only in photos since, turned ten years old. Surrounded by his family and his friends. And Orion had known there and then that he couldn't do it.

He couldn't rip his child away from the only home the boy had ever known, to go and live with the father he'd never met. The father he didn't even know he had, since

Cleo had made it very clear that it would be better for Luke if he didn't know of Orion's existence.

Orion couldn't take Luke away from his family and his friends. His mother and his grandparents. The people who'd brought him up, just because he was Orion's son and Orion wanted him.

It wasn't right and he couldn't do it.

So he'd turned around and walked out of that house, and he'd never gone back.

His heart had been ripped out of his chest the day Cleo's father had told him he wasn't to have any contact with Cleo or Luke ever again, and yet some piece of it had still remained inside him.

But in that hallway in Chelsea, he'd cut out that last remaining piece. Luke was happy, that was all that mattered, and as for himself, well, it was easier to pretend he'd never had a son at all.

Luke was the one thing he'd let go of, because he'd had to. But afterwards, he'd decided that there would be no family for him. No more children. No wife. No happy home full of love and laughter. He'd grown up without any of that and he was fine, and besides, love was a power game, and one he'd lost, so now he simply refused to play.

Not that he was in any danger of falling in love with Isla. Marrying her had been part of Kendrick's deal and he'd agreed since it was either that or Kendrick found some other groom for her, and he hadn't been about to let that happen. Once he set his sights on a target he generally acquired it. He didn't like to lose. He'd keep her for the year specified, but then he'd divorce her, no harm done.

Slowly, he pushed shut his laptop and leaned back in his seat.

That kiss she'd given him… She'd taken him by surprise, he had to admit. He hadn't been expecting her to grab his tie, lean down and deliver a kiss just as hot as the one he'd given her. It took a lot to surprise him these days, but she'd managed it and he respected the hell out of her for it.

But she didn't know that in kissing him, she'd issued him with a challenge. A challenge that fired his blood. He was a wolf at heart and he loved the thrill of the chase, the hunt. He loved the fight, too, when he ran his prey down. But people didn't fight him the way they used to, his reputation had ensured that. They mostly just lay down and offered him their throat, which wasn't satisfying in any way.

Isla wouldn't just lie down and offer him her throat, he suspected. She would fight him and he relished the thought of that particular chase very much.

He hadn't planned on anything physical happening between them. All he'd wanted was to get close to her, talk to her, find out why a bit of paint on a board should have illuminated her so completely, and what exactly was the nature of that light inside her. But he wouldn't mind exploring their physical attraction if she was willing. And then once he'd explored that, perhaps this fascination would go away. Because he was tired of her being in his thoughts so continually.

Of course, that all depended on her wanting to stay at his lodge. He could make it difficult for her to leave physically—the lodge was remote and the weather could make transport to and from it tricky—but it would be much more satisfying if she chose to stay.

He could make her choose that. His new wife might

look like a snow maiden, but her kiss was full of heat, and that had set him thinking about her fiancé and whether he'd been able to satisfy her and the answer was potentially not, since she'd been able to kiss another man not once, but twice. Three times if you counted the kiss at the altar.

Perhaps he'd find that out too. It had been a long time since a woman had obsessed him in such a way and now with physical chemistry added to the equation, he wasn't about to let her go anytime soon. Not until he'd exhausted his interest.

Orion spent the rest of the short remaining flight time tying up some loose ends and then making a few plans. He sent off the agreement to the Kendricks' lawyers as promised, and then made a few calls to his PR department. His shock wedding would attract some media attention, but if they stayed in Iceland long enough, the fuss would die down. Not that he particularly cared about it, but Isla might.

Soon enough, the jet began to descend into Reykjavik. Once they'd landed and the formalities were dealt with, they then boarded the helicopter that would take them to the lodge.

It was far to the south and east of the country, the lodge built at the edge of a small lake and surrounded by mountains and woodland that he was in the process of regenerating.

He had a few lodges scattered around the globe, but the one in Iceland was his favourite simply because it was so remote and wild. The ruggedness of the landscape and the changing shape of it due to the constant, churning volcanic activity appealed to him. He appreciated nature's power and how small humanity seemed against it, and ultimately how powerless.

It was a bracing perspective and he liked that.

The flight there was a spectacular one, but since it had darkened into night since they left the UK, there was no view to take in. Isla didn't say a word and kept her gaze on the blackness outside the helicopter window the whole time.

It didn't matter. They'd have plenty of time to talk when they arrived.

Luckily the weather was still and Orion had had the helipad cleared of snow so there were no issues with landing. It was freezing outside, though.

He opened the door and helped her out, the icy air immediately catching them. She gave a little gasp and shuddered, clutching her shawl around her.

It was snowing now, and in the lights coming from the lodge and from the lit stone path that led to the front door he could see snowflakes catching her hair and on her gown, glittering and sparkling.

She looked even more like a snow maiden than ever.

She also looked as if she was freezing to death.

Before he could think better of it, he murmured, 'Come here, Snow White,' and swept her up into his arms. 'I'm supposed to carry you over the threshold.'

'No.' She'd gone stiff as a board. 'I don't want you to carry me.'

'You're freezing and your shoes are going to get wet.' He settled her more firmly against him as he turned towards the lodge. 'Also, I'm cold too and I could use the extra warmth.'

There was a fiercely resistant look on her pretty face,

yet her body slowly relaxed against his. Clearly the cold had overcome her pride. 'Don't take this as a sign I like you,' she said. 'Because I don't.'

'Noted.' The tart note in her voice made him smile as he strode along the lit stone path that led to the huge wooden double front doors of the lodge. 'Tomorrow we can discuss why exactly you don't like me.'

'No, we can't.'

He glanced down at her, amused that despite her grumpy tone, she'd somehow nestled even closer. She was very warm in his arms, the scent of her body sweet in the frigid night air.

'We don't have to discuss anything if you don't want to,' he said, purely to annoy her. 'You can try and take some more kisses from me instead.'

She gave a little snort, but even in the darkness he could see her blush.

He'd had the staff member who managed the property prepare the lodge for their arrival, and the woman was there to open the big wooden double front doors for them. He stepped into the welcome warmth of the flagstone entrance way, the door shutting firmly on the arctic winter night.

He didn't pause, heading straight into the lounge to the right of the front doors. It was a vast area with big floor-to-ceiling double-glazed windows that looked out over the lake. The floor was rustic wood overlaid with thick rugs and a huge fire burned down one end. There were a couple of low sectional couches upholstered in pale leather and a low coffee table that had been rough-hewn out of a piece of pale wood and the top sanded smooth.

He carried Isla over to the couch near the fire and put

her down so she could get warm, then he went to see the property manager to make sure the luggage had been unloaded and everything had been prepared to his liking. Once that had been sorted and the woman had left in the helicopter back to Reykjavik, he went back into the lounge.

Isla had slid off the couch and was sitting on her knees in front of the fire, her hands stretched out towards the blaze. She still had her shawl around her shoulders and the snow that had settled on her and her gown had melted, leaving her hair and the silk of her dress sodden.

His snow maiden melting in the heat.

An unexpected and unwelcome protectiveness rose inside him and before he could stop himself, he said, 'You need to get out of that gown and into a hot shower, and then put on something warm.'

'Love to,' she muttered, not moving. 'But I don't have any clothes with me since I wasn't exactly expecting to be taken to Iceland on my wedding day.'

'Then isn't it a good thing then that I had your luggage put on the jet when we left England?' he said. 'It's upstairs in your room now.'

'Of course you did.' She looked at him, her lush mouth trying very hard to compress itself into a firm line. 'Though I'm not sure my bikinis will be useful what with all the snow.'

He smiled. 'Oh, you'd be surprised. Come. Let me show you upstairs to your room before you freeze to death.'

'I'm quite happy here, thank you.'

'Isla.' He pitched his voice low and with an element of command in it, and was gratified when she blinked and looked at him. 'I know you don't like me, you've made that clear, but this is childish. You're cold.'

Anger flared briefly in her dark blue eyes then she looked away, long golden lashes veiling her expression. 'Fine.' The word was determindedly neutral. 'Show me where my room is then.'

Interesting how she simply shut away her emotions. Interesting too to note that she hadn't shut them away completely, because the stain of annoyance lingered in her cheeks and her shoulders were tense.

He was reminded again of a fizzing champagne bottle imperfectly capped, though that implied light bubbles of joy and she wasn't fizzy like that. She was more like a volcano, with fires burning hot and slow deep inside. A woman of passion. And a woman who had difficulty keeping that passion locked down.

You could let that passion out. You could make it explode.

Oh, he certainly could, and he was starting to think that maybe he would. Her kiss still burned on his tongue, the taste of her as sweet as her scent.

He'd like another, a deeper taste.

He kept all these thoughts from his face as he turned and led her up the rustic wooden stairs to the second floor where the bedrooms were located. He'd made sure she'd been given one of the large rooms at the end of the hall that looked out over the lake.

Inside was a rustic-looking four-poster bed hung with curtains and piled with pillows, and a white faux fur bedspread. There were rugs on the floors, the thick pale curtains pulled across the windows to shut out the freezing night.

His property manager had already unpacked for her

and a delicate white lace nightgown that seemed to be sheer all the way down was laid out on the bed.

A nightgown for a wedding night.

He found himself staring at it. She had been going to wear that for Gianni…

She could wear it for you.

Heat burst through him, so intense he had to grit his teeth as she brushed past him on her way into the room, engulfing him in her sweet scent. Then she, too, stopped, staring at the nightgown. A fierce blush stained her cheeks. She darted forward and snatched the sheer bit of nothing from the bed. 'Obviously I'm not going to wear that,' she muttered.

Orion was conscious that the best thing for both of them was to let her have her shower and get changed. Now that he had her here, there was no rush for anything more quite yet.

Instead, he leaned against the doorframe and said, 'Oh? Why not?'

She didn't look at him, moving over to the bags at the foot of her bed and dumping the nightgown into one of them. 'Because it's for my wedding night and I'd hardly call this an actual wedding night.'

He watched her, swathed in her damp gown, the ends of her shawl trailing, soft golden curls coming down from her wilting up-do. Not at all the polished bride she'd been in the church, but a more rumpled, sexier and altogether more touchable version of her.

'I can give you one, though,' he said, very unwisely. 'If you want one.'

CHAPTER FOUR

ISLA STILLED. HIS VOICE was soft and very dark and not at all cold. Not this time.

Her heartbeat had accelerated and her cheeks felt hot, the embarrassment at having that ridiculous nightgown spread out on the bed so blatantly lingering.

She'd bought it for herself in a fit of optimism, because despite her misgivings, she thought she should have something sexy and beautiful to wear for her wedding night. Something that her new husband would enjoy too, though she'd expected Gianni to be that husband.

Not Orion North.

She was very conscious of him leaning in the doorway, one shoulder hitched against the doorframe, his gaze on hers. She could still feel the hard warmth of his chest as she'd lain against it on the walk from the helicopter into the lodge.

Being carried by him was the last thing she wanted, especially after those kisses, but he hadn't given her a choice. Yet the worst thing had been that once she'd found herself in his arms, she hadn't wanted to leave them. He'd been so very warm and the night had been so cold, and he'd smelled good, that dark, spicy scent of his surrounding her. And all she'd been able to think about was how delicious he'd tasted on the jet and how she wanted more.

You want more than his kiss.

She stared down at the nightgown she'd dropped into the bag at her feet. Her wedding dress felt damp and despite the room's warmth, she was shivering. But it wasn't all due to the cold.

Slowly, she turned to look at him.

He hadn't moved, his tall, powerful figure utterly still. But the glow in his wolf's eyes stole her breath. He'd looked at her that way back in the church and then just as he was about to kiss her in front of the altar.

He wants you.

A shiver stole through her.

'Well?' he prompted softly.

'A wedding night,' she said. 'Is that for me or for yourself?'

His eyes glinted. 'A very astute question. Let's just say I wouldn't be unmoved by it.'

Her mouth felt dry. He was like this in the boardroom meetings she'd been in with him, his posture relaxed, his tone casual. He was a master gambler with a true poker face, never letting a hint of his true thoughts or feelings escape.

A panther lying in wait. A wolf stalking his prey.

He was stalking her now; she could feel it.

That electricity was back as it always was whenever she was near him, humming and crackling over her skin. Maddening, relentless and also wildly exciting.

Why not a wedding night with him? What would you have to lose? Perhaps if you sleep with him, this feeling will finally leave you alone.

A tempting thought and yet so dangerous. Those kisses up in the plane had made the whole world fall away, stoked the flame in her heart, and she was half afraid of what his touch would do to her. Especially when his very presence made her unsettled and angry.

He made her feel volatile and she didn't like that. Being volatile had caused her so many problems in the past. Because David hadn't been the first person who'd wanted to adopt her. There had been another couple. They'd already had a son and now longed for a daughter. She'd been ten and thrilled to be given a home, except their son hadn't been thrilled. He'd hated her from the moment she'd arrived and seemed determined to keep hating her, no matter how friendly she'd been. She hadn't wanted to upset anything and lose her home and her new-found family, so she'd tried her best to fit in and to not make things difficult.

Her new brother never hurt her, but he consistently made life difficult, breaking things and making messes and blaming them on her. She hadn't argued. She hadn't wanted to rock the boat. Yet the unfairness of it burned in her heart. She'd been there six months when one day he scratched his father's prized new car and told his parents that she'd done it. They'd been angry, unable to understand why she kept doing these things when all they'd done was give her a home. And that day she'd had enough. She'd told them that none of it had been her fault, that he'd scratched the car not her, and that he didn't like her and he didn't want her there, and that it wasn't fair. She'd been so angry.

They hadn't believed her and they'd called the social

workers the next day, telling them to halt the adoption process. That it wasn't going to work out.

It had hurt. It had hurt to have the family she'd wanted so much snatched away, but she knew she only had herself to blame. Perhaps if she hadn't said anything, if she'd just kept on accepting the blame it would have been okay. Perhaps that boy would have grown out of taunting her, perhaps he would have grown to like her, but she'd never got the chance to find out, because her anger at the unfairness of it had erupted and turned everything to ashes.

Even now, it still hurt to think of it. The shame of being returned like an unwanted pet, and the frustrated fury at how it had all gone down. Fury at that boy and the adults who hadn't believed her, and most of all at herself for losing her temper. She shouldn't have been so caught up in her own feelings that she lost sight of what was important. A family and a place to belong.

But you don't even have that now though, do you? You never belonged to David or Gianni, and you don't even belong at Kendricks'. You don't belong anywhere.

Isla shoved that thought away and turned to face Orion, her heart thudding hard in her ears. Answers, that's what she needed now, not passion.

'Why did you marry me, Orion?' she asked abruptly. 'What was so important about me that you felt the need to pay off Gianni and buy Kendricks' in order to have me? I need an answer.'

He didn't reply for a long moment, still staring at her, the weight of his gaze driving all the breath from her lungs. 'I saw an opportunity,' he said at last. 'And I took it.' He pushed himself away from the doorframe and took a step into the room. 'Do you remember that function at

the National Gallery? Some fundraiser, I think it was.'
He took another step, full lazy, predatory grace.

Isla stared at him, her heartbeat getting louder, electricity prickling everywhere. Of course she remembered that fundraiser, how could she not?

Sometimes, when she'd been a kid and things had been difficult at whichever foster home she'd been in, she would slip away to a gallery or a museum and spend time looking at beautiful things. It was a cheap way to distract herself, and art especially was her favourite.

She shouldn't have sneaked away that night at the National Gallery, because her attendance had been required. Yet there had been a special Van Gogh exhibition on, and she hadn't been able to resist the temptation of looking at one of her favourite paintings.

'Yes,' she said. 'I remember.'

'I found you looking at *Starry Night*,' he murmured and took another step, getting closer. 'I asked you what you found so interesting about it and you told me.' Another step. He was so tall, she felt dwarfed by him. 'You talked about the paint, and the layers and the brush strokes. You talked about movement and luminosity.' Another step. His eyes had gone from dark amber to brilliant gold. 'But the most luminous thing in the gallery that night was you.' A final step brought him so close she could feel his heat, smell his scent. 'And I want to know why.'

Her heartbeat was frantic now, the electricity between them morphing into a delicious kind of exhilaration. It was such a strange feeling, almost akin to fear, though not fear for her life or that he'd hurt her. More the kind of fear you experienced being on an extremely fast rollercoaster, knowing you couldn't get off and that the only thing you could do was surrender to the moment and the breathless excitement of it all.

The only other time she'd felt that same thrill was standing in front of a particularly beautiful painting. Getting lost in the colour, becoming absorbed by the layers of paint and the brushstrokes and the play of light…

She'd known who he was when he'd entered the small gallery—most people in the business sector know who Orion North was—though they'd never actually met. She'd felt vaguely unsettled by his presence and her instant, electric response to him, and she'd been trying to think of a way to leave without being too offensive, when after a moment's tense silence, he'd asked her about the painting.

It had been the last thing she'd expected and had been so surprised, she'd answered him. She hadn't talked about art to anyone before and so had been hesitant to talk about it with a complete stranger. Yet he'd remained silent, and because she hadn't liked the silence, she'd started to speak. Then, before she knew what she was doing, she'd shared everything she knew about it and that was a lot since she researched all her favourite artists and paintings extensively.

He hadn't said a word the whole time, though she'd felt him watching her. And when she'd finished, all he'd said was, 'Fascinating.' Then he'd turned his back on her and walked out.

She'd felt like an idiot in that moment, as if she'd shown him something precious and he'd crushed it under his foot.

She stared up at him now, remembering that feeling, wanting to step back and put some distance between them, yet also bizarrely wanting to get closer.

'You remembered?' she asked stupidly. 'I thought I'd bored you.'

'You didn't bore me.' He was staring at her with such intentness she could barely breathe. 'Quite the opposite in fact.'

'But…' Her heart was beating even faster now. 'You just…walked away.'

'Of course, I walked away.' He lifted a hand and casually pulled one of the pins in her hair out and dropped it. 'It was either that or demand to know why you were the most luminous thing in the whole damn gallery.' He pulled out another pin. 'I didn't think you'd appreciate that.'

She should stop him. She should tell him to leave her hair alone, that she could take out her own pins, but she couldn't seem to form the words.

He'd thought she was luminous…

No one had ever thought she was that. Too volatile. Too quiet. Too obedient. Lots of potential. But never *luminous…*

'So you married me for…that?' She couldn't keep the raw husk of emotion out of her voice. 'I don't understand.'

'Like I told you.' He calmly took another pin out and then another. 'When I see an opportunity to acquire something I want, I take it.'

'So I'm an acquisition?' Freed from its pins her hair was starting to slip out of the carefully constructed wedding up-do. 'Like a company you target?'

'Yes.' Carefully he lifted both hands and threaded his fingers through her hair, combing through it so her curls tumbled to her shoulders and down her back. A quiver ran through her. 'I take companies and examine them.

Then I dismantle them and figure out what's working and what isn't, what's broken and what's not. What parts to keep and what to get rid of. That's why I told David I wanted to marry you. I'm hoping that once I dismantle my fascination with you, I'll finally be able get rid of it.'

Her breath had gone and all she was aware of was the pull of his fingers in her hair and how much she liked it. How much she liked being a fascination to him too, especially after years of being only a source of disappointment.

'Seems extreme.' She made no move away from him even though she knew she should. 'To pay off my fiancé and do a deal with my father to buy a whole company in exchange for me.'

His mouth curved. 'I'm not a man known for moderation when it comes to business. All or nothing, Snow White.' His fingers curled into her hair, holding her in a gentle grip. It was possessive that grip, and she found it unspeakably erotic. 'I don't regret paying off your fiancé—he accepted my money without protest which only goes to prove he wasn't good enough for you. And since buying Kendricks' was the only way I could get you, I had to buy it. I'm not a man who likes to lose.'

Her heart was beating way too fast. 'It was leverage too, wasn't it? To get me to do what you wanted.'

'Yes. But…perhaps, I regret the threat to Kendricks'.'

She stared up into his amber eyes, part of her angry with him for his sheer arrogance, part of her fascinated. She hadn't known, had barely even dreamt that anyone, let alone a man as powerful as Orion North, would want her so badly he'd do all of that just to have her. 'Do you really regret it?'

His faint smile deepened. 'No.'

She wasn't sure why she liked the combination of that rueful smile and the heat in his eyes. It softened his hard, handsome features, making him seem more approachable, not to mention even more devastatingly attractive. It made her want to smile too, which was odd given he'd threatened her into marriage for nothing more than some strange fascination with her.

She shouldn't smile at him. She shouldn't find his hands in her hair so breathtakingly erotic either, yet she did.

No one had ever found her fascinating. She'd been chosen twice and both times the people who'd chosen her had regretted their choices, first that family, and then David. Orion wasn't disappointed though, not given the way he was looking at her. As if she was the most important discovery he'd ever made.

Give him time.

No, she wasn't going to think about that. There was only this moment and the expression in his eyes and she could enjoy that, couldn't she?

'Well?' he murmured. 'Have you considered my wedding night offer? I should very much like to see you in that nightgown. Seems a waste not to wear it.'

She shouldn't. She barely knew him and she certainly didn't like him, and the thought of sleeping with him filled her with a certain trepidation. Then again, this electricity between them wasn't going away anytime soon and she needed it to, especially when it was affecting what she did in the boardroom. Perhaps spending the night with him would be enough to get rid of it.

It's not just about the electricity. You want him.

She couldn't deny it. She'd never met another man who made her feel the way he did. And she was tired of feeling like a massive disappointment. Tired of trying to fulfil the potential her father saw in her. Tired of trying to be something she suspected she wasn't.

Why couldn't she have something for herself for a change? That was allowed, wasn't it? Just one night. He wanted her and it was thrilling to be wanted. It was thrilling to be able to put that look in his eyes, to fascinate such a powerful, ruthless man.

She'd been starting to think lately that she wasn't good at anything she did, but if she could fascinate Orion North, then maybe she wasn't as bad as she'd thought.

She wasn't just going to give in, though. He'd liked it when she'd taken that kiss from him in the plane; she knew he had. He'd liked that she'd surprised him. She wanted to keep doing that.

'Let me go,' she said quietly, making her decision.

He didn't say anything as he released his hold on her hair, but she could see the flicker of disappointment in his eyes.

Good. Let him be disappointed.

Without a word, she went to the bag where she'd put the nightgown and retrieved it. Then she moved over to the bed and laid the nightgown down on it again. 'You'll need to help me with my zip,' she said and turned around, presenting her back to him.

There was a moment of silence.

He moved so silently she didn't hear him and she only knew he was near when she felt warmth behind her, the dark spice of his scent wrapping around her, and then the tug of his fingers on her zip.

'Are you going to tease me?' His voice was full of heat and gravel. 'Because if so, I should warn you, I like to tease back.' As if to demonstrate, he drew down the zip of her gown with aching slowness, making her very aware of every inch of skin that was revealed as the material parted.

She didn't know what to say in response to that, because her voice had vanished. She felt hot, awareness of him prickling over her, humming and crackling like static.

This was madness, but she wasn't going to stop.

He was right. She'd bought that nightgown for a reason and it hadn't been Gianni she'd been thinking of when she'd bought it. Not that she'd been thinking of Orion specifically, but she'd been thinking of a man. A man who'd take a *lot* of pleasure at seeing her in it and how much that would please her too.

She moved away and allowed the gown to slide down her body and pool at her feet. Then she stepped out of the fabric, wearing only a white lace bra, knickers, stockings and heels. She wasn't quite brave enough to undress while facing him, so she kept her back to him as she kicked off her shoes, eased down her stockings, unclipped her bra and then stepped out of her knickers.

He was utterly silent, though she could feel him watching her. It made her heart race.

She reached for the nightgown. The white silk lace was sheer all the way to the hem and it hid nothing. It was designed purely to enflame.

Isla put it over her head, shivering as the cool material slid down over her skin. She adjusted the straps a little and then paused to gather her courage.

She was going to take what she wanted. And she wanted this. She wanted her wedding night and she wanted it with Orion.

Slowly, she turned around.

Orion had thought it would be easy to wait until his new wife made a decision about his offer of a wedding night. It had no doubt been a mistake to offer it in the first place, but that nightgown had decided him.

It was an opportunity.

He'd known she wanted him. He'd tasted her hunger in her kiss, and that sexy little nightgown had definitely been chosen with passion in mind. Why couldn't she experience some of that passion with him?

So he'd put the offer out there to see what she did with it.

He'd expected her to turn him down immediately and when she hadn't, he couldn't stop himself from stalking over to her. He'd wanted to see what was going on in that pretty head of hers, wanted to see the sparks in her deep blue eyes, and sure enough they'd been there.

Perhaps it had been unwise of him to let her know how much she'd fascinated him that day in the National Gallery, but when she'd asked him directly why he'd married her, he hadn't been able to lie to her.

It wasn't as if he was confessing to a lifelong passion, after all. Merely a fascination that he would soon deal with. A fascination he would take apart to see how it worked and he'd then get rid of it.

He hadn't thought he'd be impatient for an answer to his wedding night offer. He hadn't thought it would matter to him. Yet he'd found himself unable to stop touching her, taking the pins from her hair and running his fingers through all the soft golden curls. Watching her eyes darken as they looked up into his and the pulse at the base of her throat race.

Oh, yes, she wanted him, that was undeniable.

Which had then made her request to stop touching her so very disappointing.

In fact, he'd been surprised by how disappointed he was. She might want him, but he hadn't realised the full extent of his own hunger for her.

He'd told himself it didn't matter, that he didn't care, and then she'd picked up that damn nightgown, gone over to the bed and laid it down. Then she'd turned her back on him and requested help with her zip.

Apparently, she wasn't saying no after all.

Something savage had filled him in that moment, triumph and satisfaction and hunger all mixed into one. The intensity of it had disturbed him since he reserved all his passions for the boardroom not the bedroom.

He enjoyed sex but he never lost himself to it. He couldn't afford to. His control over himself, both emotionally and physically, was vital and he kept himself in hand at all times. Besides, sex simply wasn't important enough to him to be worth the risk of an unwanted pregnancy.

Apparently, though, all of that didn't matter as he slowly undid the zip on Isla's dress and all that smooth, pale porcelain skin came into view. Watching as her wedding dress slipped slowly from her, revealing rounded thighs, generous hips and a small waist.

And all his control was worth nothing because the only thing he could think about was grabbing her by those luscious hips and simply flinging her on the bed.

Covering herself with the nightgown didn't help and when she finally turned around to face him, he knew the battle with himself and his control was lost.

Because he'd never seen anything so delicious in all his life.

The nightgown clung, revealing the gorgeous curves of her breasts and the soft pink of her nipples visible through the lace. The curls between her thighs were visible too and they were as golden as the hair on her head.

Her chin had lifted, her shoulders tensed, and her gaze when it met his was defiant, though what she was defiant about he didn't know, because there was nothing about her that wasn't completely and utterly delicious. And he wanted her to know that, so he let his hunger show in his eyes.

Something ignited in her then, a blaze of heat flushing her cheeks, making her glow, and in that moment, he knew something true: she was his painting. She was his *Starry Night*. All curves and movement and luminous colours. Cream and gold and pink and the deep dark blue of her eyes. She came alive the way she had that night at the gallery as she'd explained that painting to him. Startlingly lovely. Luminous.

He was barely aware of moving, of striding over to her and settling his hands on her hips, feeling the warmth of her skin through her gown. And at the same time, she reached for him, lifting her hands and taking his face between them.

There was no fear in her eyes, only the same hunger that burned in him, and when he bent and took her mouth, it felt like a relief. As if he'd been in the desert dying of thirst and she was his first taste of water.

She leaned into him, kissing him back the way she'd kissed him in the jet, full of an unpractised passion that had the blood surging in his veins. Briefly, it occurred to him to wonder just how experienced she was with men, then her hands fell from his face and she was winding her arms around his neck, her body pressing delicately against his and all thought left him.

He wrenched his mouth from hers, pulled her arms from around his neck and held her away from him.

She stared at him, her mouth full and red, her eyes dark. 'What?' she asked breathlessly. 'Did I do something—?'

'Hush,' he ordered, low and rough. 'And keep still. I want to look at you.'

'Oh…' She let out a breath, her cheeks flushing an even deeper pink as he let his gaze wander over that incredibly sexy nightgown, studying the delicate rose of her hard nipples and how the lace both revealed and hid those beautiful golden curls between her thighs.

He bent his head and kissed her throat, tasting her frantic pulse before trailing his tongue down over the lace, following the curves of her breasts to tease her nipples through the fabric. She shuddered, a soft gasp escaping her, and when he took one nipple into his mouth, she groaned, arching into him.

Her heat and her scent were intoxicating, and before he knew what he was doing, he'd gone to his knees in front of her, his hands spread out on her soft hips, holding her steady as he kissed his way down her stomach to the heat between her thighs, using the fabric of her nightgown to tease both her and himself.

'Orion.' His name was a gasp as he pressed his tongue

between her legs, dampening the white silk that veiled her, tasting her sweet feminine musk.

She was even more beautiful than he'd expected and suddenly he was tired of the nightgown. It had done its duty, but its role was over.

He gripped the delicate white silk in his hands and tore it open from hem to neck without a second's thought. Then he pulled away the fabric and rose to his feet once again, looking down at her nakedness.

His snow maiden was all white and pink and the most utterly delicious woman he'd ever seen.

She said nothing as he stared at her, only gave him a challenging look, as if daring him to do his worst, and of course he couldn't think of anything else he'd rather do. So he grabbed her by the hips and tossed her onto the bed, then followed her down onto it. He pinned her beneath him, covering her full mouth with his and kissing her hungrily.

She tasted hot and wild, her curvy little body shifting impatiently beneath his, and her hands were tearing at his tie and his suit jacket, trying to undo the buttons, trying to get to him.

He shifted astride her, rising to his knees and stripped away his tie, his jacket and his shirt, then he bent over her once again, kissing her deeply as her cool fingers touched his skin and he felt something shudder deep inside him.

He needed to slow down, get a handle on himself somehow, but then her hands were stroking his stomach and venturing further, getting bold as she traced the line of his erection through the material of his trousers.

Lights exploded in his head, electricity arcing down the length of his spine. He couldn't believe one touch would make him feel this way, but there was no denying he wanted her. He wanted her more than he wanted his next breath.

'So you do like to tease,' he growled against her mouth. 'Perhaps I'll repay you in kind.' Except he'd never felt less like teasing.

'No, please don't,' she whispered, arching against him. 'I just need… I need you.'

It felt good to be needed by her, so very good, and so he didn't wait.

Taking his mouth from hers, he found his wallet in the back pocket of his trousers and he extracted one of the condoms in there, because he never went anywhere without one. Then, after discarding the wallet, he pulled open his trousers and dealt with the protection before settling himself between her thighs.

He slipped one hand beneath the softness of her bottom and lifted her, tilting her hips and positioning himself. Then he thrust in hard, because he couldn't wait, not a second longer.

She gasped, stiffening beneath him and he knew a moment's shock, wondering if he'd hurt her. Then abruptly she curled one leg around his hip and lifted a hand, pushing her fingers into his hair and bringing his mouth down on hers, and the moment was gone.

There was only the wet heat of her sex gripping him so tight and the softness of her body beneath his. He moved deeper, harder, gathering her close and holding her against him, devouring her mouth before moving on to exploring her throat and the delicate structure of her collarbones.

She moaned beneath him, her hands clutching at his

shoulders before stroking down his back and then up again, as if she was lost in a storm and trying to find something to hold on to. So he took her hands and held them down on the pillows on either side of her head, threading his fingers through hers and holding on as he moved faster, deeper, driving them into insanity.

There was a time for watching prey and a time for taking the opportunity to attack. And then there was a devouring and that's what he wanted now. To devour her. To devour her utterly.

And as she tensed and cried his name, her inner muscles clenching tight around him, and he could feel the orgasm exploding along every nerve ending he had, he was exquisitely aware of one thing.

He was going to take her apart. Take her apart completely. Find out what made her tick, what made her so relentlessly fascinating to him, why it had to be her.

And he wasn't going to let her go until he did.

CHAPTER FIVE

ISLA CAME TO wakefulness slowly the next morning. She was full of a delicious lassitude, with aches in strange places, and a head full of memories from the night before that made her roll over and press her hot face into the pillow.

Orion...

Orion, and the way he'd looked at her with such ferocity. Orion, and how he'd touched her with such mastery. Of how he'd ripped apart that silly nightgown to get to her, then tossed her on the bed, unable to wait to be inside her.

She hadn't told him she was a virgin and maybe she should have, but she hadn't wanted him to stop. She hadn't wanted to get into any discussions about why and how either. She hadn't wanted anything that would interrupt the moment, especially when he'd been nothing but raw, unleashed passion. He'd been glorious and he'd made her feel glorious too. As if she'd thrown herself into the middle of a blazing fire and loved how intensely she'd burned.

He'd kept her there all night, stoking that fire over and over, making her rise like a phoenix from the ashes again and again. Exploring her body as if he was fascinated by it and wanted to discover all the ways it could bring her pleasure.

She hadn't known sex could be like that. She hadn't known she'd lose herself so completely.

You suspected, though. Which is why you can't allow it to happen again.

Something painful ached behind her breastbone, but she brushed it aside. It was true, she couldn't. One night, she'd promised herself. One night to take what she wanted and that's what she'd done. But she couldn't afford another. She couldn't let him get under her skin more than he had already, not when control over herself was already an issue for her.

And apart from anything else, they hadn't discussed what was going to happen now.

Perhaps it was simply about the sex, and now he's had you he'll put you on the first plane back to the UK.

Her stomach dropped away at the thought, which was disturbing, because why should she care? She didn't want to stay here with him. She needed to get back home and see her father. Ask him why he'd decided to agree to Orion's demand to marry her without even a word to her. It wasn't something she wanted to do, but she had to do it all the same.

You don't want to know why he thought so little of you that he sold you to one man, then when that didn't work out, he sold you to another.

But she didn't want that thought in her head, so she pushed it away, turning to look at the pillow next to her instead. But it was empty. She didn't know whether to feel disappointed about that or relieved.

Regardless, there was no point lying there with all

these questions. She had to get up and confront the man she'd married.

The bed was extraordinarily comfortable and she was warm, and she didn't particularly want to do any confronting right now, but there was nothing to be gained by delaying it. So she forced herself out of bed and into the ensuite bathroom.

There was a giant white-tiled shower with big windows that had views over the snowy landscape outside and Isla stood under the warm spray of water, staring out through the glass at the winter wonderland outside even as she relished the heat of the shower.

After she got out and towelled herself dry, she went over to the chest of drawers that stood near the windows and opened them. All the clothes she'd brought with her had been unpacked and folded neatly, so she grabbed some jeans and an oversized jersey in soft, light blue cashmere and got dressed.

Then she went out and down the stairs in search of Orion.

She could smell something delicious coming from the direction of what she assumed was the kitchen so she followed the scent, coming out into a large and very expensively fitted out open-plan kitchen, with lots of stainless steel and white tiles. Near the windows that had that same pretty snow-covered lake view was a dining table set for two with cutlery, plates and cups. There was a coffee pot and orange juice, and various different spreads.

Clearly Orion was expecting for them to have breakfast together, though he himself was nowhere to be seen.

Puzzled, she checked the lounge area, but he wasn't there either. So she went down the hall, passing another

bathroom, some more bedrooms and a cosy-looking library, and then, finally, a doorway that opened out into
an office.

It had the same floor-to-ceiling windows as the rest of
the lodge, but the view was out towards the mountains,
ridged and sharp and capped with snow. A huge rustic-
looking desk stood in front of the windows and behind
the desk sat Orion. His attention was on the flat screen
in front of him and he didn't look up as she entered.

She'd been subconsciously bracing herself for the reality of him after their night together, but it wasn't until
that moment that she realised that bracing herself for him
was impossible.

He was dressed casually, in worn jeans and a dark blue
T-shirt, and his feet were bare. His black hair was slightly
tousled and it was clear from the five o'clock shadow
lining his strong jaw that he hadn't shaved. He looked
thoroughly disreputable and so sexy her breath caught.

'Good,' he said, keeping his gaze on the screen. 'You're
up. I've made breakfast for us.'

She came slowly into the room, disturbed to find the
familiar fizz and crackle of electricity was prickling over
her skin again. Ridiculous. Why was she still feeling it?
Last night should have dealt with their physical chemistry and yet…apparently not.

Isla forced the feeling away as she approached his
desk.

'I've had my PR department handle the media,' he
went on before she could get a word out, 'since there was
apparently quite a fuss about our wedding. I've given
them a statement to send out that you and I had been
pining for each other all this time, and Gianni selflessly

stood aside at the last minute to allow me to marry you. Yes, it's a bit overly romantic, but the press love that kind of stuff.' He gave the mouse a decisive click. 'We'll be here for a couple of weeks and I have some excursions planned. Don't worry, you won't be bored.' He leaned back in his seat, his amber gaze meeting hers head-on. 'Any questions?'

Isla had many, *many* questions, yet the moment he looked at her, all of them went straight out of her head. He'd looked at her like this the night before, when she'd put on that nightgown and he'd stared at her, intent and utterly focused. Purposeful.

Yet she didn't want to stand there in silence. She had a plan and it didn't involve two weeks of 'excursions'.

'That sounds lovely,' she said, trying to sound cool and firm. 'But I can't stay, Orion. This isn't actually a honeymoon—I mean, our wedding wasn't even really a wedding—and I have to go home. I have to explain to the board what happened.'

Orion raised a brow. 'Explain? Explain what? Your father and I have handled it, and the board will be fine with me as Kendricks' new owner. And as far as our wedding not being a real wedding, I have the marriage certificate that proves otherwise.'

Irritation coiled inside her. '*You* and he might have handled it, but how do you think that looks to the board? I'm supposed to be the CEO at some point and yet there are already deals being done behind my back, without my knowledge.'

'As I said, I have that handled already,' Orion stated calmly. 'Besides, your father wanted you to marry someone, correct? Does it matter who?'

She wanted to tell him that of course it mattered who. Gianni had been chosen specifically because he was one of David's protégé's and well-respected by the Kendricks' board. Someone who would bolster confidence in her, not someone who might cause them to question her leadership potential. The worst thing was that Orion was probably aware of how little they thought of her already. It was why he'd targeted Kendricks'. She was a vulnerability and everyone knew it.

Tension crawled through her, acid gathering in the pit of her stomach. The lovely warmth she'd woken up with was dissipating and reality was asserting itself, the fallout of yesterday crashing down on her.

'I had to marry, Gianni,' she forced out. 'David was his mentor and he had standing with the board. It's a family company and being oriented around Christmas, that's what they require from their future CEO. A family. Me having to marry you at the last minute—'

'Was not ideal,' Orion interrupted with the same maddening calm. 'Which was why, if you'd given me a moment, I would have told you that I've also been on a video call with the board of Kendricks' this morning.'

Isla's stomach dropped away. 'What?'

'I met with them to discuss the sale of the company to me. I wanted to tell them personally. Also that I planned to keep the company intact for the next year at least, and to give them some explanation for our marriage and why it occurred in the manner it did. Be assured.'

Shock coursed through her as she stared at him. 'You couldn't have waited for me so we could have told them together?'

He only stared back, completely at his ease. 'I wanted

to spare you the awkwardness of lying about how in love with me you were.'

Isla opened her mouth then shut it again, not knowing at all what to say to that.

'I know that many of them don't have confidence in you,' he went on smoothly. 'That they're concerned you don't have the backbone they need in a CEO. You're too quiet and not authoritative enough. Too much your father's yes man. And I find that puzzling because the woman I married yesterday was *all* backbone. There was nothing quiet about her when she grabbed my tie and kissed me.'

Isla could feel colour creeping up her neck and flushing her cheeks. She'd never had her weaknesses catalogued so completely one moment, before being refuted the next.

She looked away, unable to deal with the directness of his gaze, staring down at her hands clasped in front of her instead. 'That's because I was angry with you. I have to lock that down in the boardroom.'

'Why? Anger can be a useful tool if you stay in command of it.'

But that was the problem, wasn't it? She couldn't stay in command of it. She had a problem with her temper and if she wasn't careful, it got away from her. It had lost her that one family years earlier, and earned her father's disapproval when she'd first started working at Kendricks'. She'd tried to bring up the subject of lifting wages for the lower-paid workers in the company, and had been roundly dismissed by the board. And she hadn't thought. She'd argued and had ended up shouting, before leaving the room in tears. David had been horrified, but not more horrified than she was at herself. She'd kept herself under strict control ever since. Not that she was going to explain that to him.

'Yes, well, be that as it may,' she said coolly, lifting her gaze to his once more. 'It was my responsibility to speak to the board, not yours.'

He shrugged, as if it was of no consequence. 'Perhaps, but it's done now. They were happy with my explanation so there's no need for you to contact them. And our marriage is also done now.'

She wanted to shout at him, but there was nothing to be gained from it, since he was right. 'So, what? I'm just your wife for ever?'

'No. I promised your father a year. A year for you to remain as my wife. A year for you to be CEO. And a year for me to keep Kendricks' intact.'

'So what happens now?'

'What happens now is our honeymoon. We can discuss the rest later. So, I'm sorry, Isla, but I'm afraid you're staying. I have a helicopter flight planned to see some of the major volcanic sites. Also some skating on the lake. You can use your bikinis for a dip in the hot pool near the lodge, since the water is heated by a natural hot spring related to the volcanic activity in the area. I should imagine you'd like to see the northern lights too. Oh, yes, and I was thinking that we could also do an overnight trip to Amsterdam. I'm told the Van Gogh Museum is a must-see.'

The tension inside her pulled tighter. He'd taken control of the situation and of her so easily, and now she was here, in his territory, and it seemed to her as if he wasn't going to let her leave.

'Let me get this straight,' she said, ignoring him. 'You're going to keep me here in this lodge, against my will, and we're just going to…what? Go on little trips?'

He lounged back in his chair, the dark gold of his eyes gleaning wolflike in the wan, snowy light coming through the windows. 'I'm not keeping you here against your will, Snow White. You can leave at any time. However, you'll need a pilot since the lodge is only accessible by helicopter. Also, the weather forecast isn't looking good for the next couple of days, so you'll probably end up staying anyway.' He smiled faintly. 'Why not enjoy yourself while you wait?'

A shiver went through her at that smile and the suggestion of heat in his voice. Oh, yes, she could enjoy herself. Especially if it involved—

But no. She couldn't get sucked into *that* and the way he made her feel. She wasn't sleeping with him, not again. And as for the 'excursions'…

Something pulsed inside her, an ache she hadn't realised was still there. She'd been the only child of a single mother who'd died of cancer when Isla was four. Her mother had had no family and so Isla had been placed in a children's home. It hadn't been awful but it hadn't been great, either, and to distract herself, she'd often dream of what her future would look like, the places she wanted to go, and the things she wanted to do. The experiences she wanted to have.

The girl she'd been would have loved visiting a volcano and seeing the northern lights. Going skating and lounging in a hot pool and seeing the Van Gogh Museum…

He's right. Why not enjoy yourself? Especially if you have to stay here a few days anyway.

She took a slow, silent breath. Arguing with him would only set her temper off and she couldn't afford that. So would it really be so bad to stay here with him? For a little while at least. She'd already planned for a week of honeymoon anyway so she wouldn't be losing anything. She was annoyed with how he'd taken charge, it was true, but she wasn't going to let him get his own way. She couldn't, not if she wanted to develop more of the CEO edge the board was hoping for.

Perhaps she could start that edge now. Perhaps, if he was going to demand some things of her, she'd demand something of him right back.

She eyed him. 'And what about our marriage after this so-called honeymoon is over?'

That faint smile was still playing around his mouth and she decided right there and then that she was going to knock it off his face as soon as she could. 'What about it?'

'Do I have to move in with you? Are we going to live together as husband and wife for the next year?'

'Maybe,' he said with infuriating calm. 'Or maybe we'll simply live separate lives. It depends on whether I've managed to explore our relationship to its fullest extent.'

'*You* don't get to decide that,' she snapped, losing patience and forgetting she was supposed to stay in control of her temper. 'In case you haven't noticed, I have a say in this, as well.'

'Oh, I haven't forgotten.' His cold voice was abruptly full of heat, and brilliant gold gleamed in his eyes. 'Believe me, I haven't forgotten.'

He was looking at her again that way, that fierce, intent way, and she could feel something throb deep inside her. An ache, a longing.

She liked the way he looked at her. She *wanted* it.

You can't want it too badly, and you really can't let him get under your skin.

That was true, that was a good reminder.

Isla swallowed. 'Fine. I guess since I have no choice in the matter then I'll stay. And I'll do your excursions. But I'm not sleeping with you again, Orion. And that's final.'

Orion sat behind his desk and stared at the self-contained little woman on the other side of it. Today she was in jeans and a soft-looking jersey in light blue cashmere, and her hair was hanging in the most glorious golden curls over her shoulders and down her back. The colour of her jersey highlighted the blue of her eyes and one shoulder had slipped down revealing her silky, pale skin.

He was already hard and she hadn't even got close to him.

He kept getting fixated by a couple of marks on her neck that he'd left on her during the previous night, and finding it oddly satisfying to see them there. He also kept thinking about how he wanted to leave more, and of course she'd let him, because how could she not? When their night together had been so intense?

He'd risen early that morning to speak to the board and to organise the rest of their honeymoon, already thinking of taking her back to bed after they'd had breakfast together.

He hadn't thought that first she'd tell him she needed to return to the UK as quickly as possible, before not only looking distinctly unimpressed by the trips he'd planned, but also coolly informing him that she wouldn't be sleeping with him again.

That wasn't what he wanted. What he wanted was to get to the bottom of his fixation with her, especially now that the fixation had a physical aspect to it, and so he hadn't been able to resist goading her. He wanted to see her lose that cool of hers, especially after last night.

Oh, yes, most especially after that. He'd underestimated their chemistry considerably, which had led to a loss of control he hadn't experienced since he'd been sixteen and Cleo had first come on the scene. That had *not* ended well to say the least and he'd been adamant with himself that it would *never* happen again.

Until Isla. Until those long, hot hours he'd spent exploring her, releasing her passion again and again. It had been addictive that passion and it had haunted him all morning. He'd been impatient in dealing with all the loose ends from their wedding and discussing the ins and outs of their marriage was the very last thing he wanted.

What he wanted was to take her to bed and explore their chemistry in greater depth, because now he'd had a taste, he couldn't wait to find out more.

Still, there was no point revealing how annoyed he was by her decision not to sleep with him again, so he only looked back at her calmly. 'Are you sure?'

'I think so.' She sounded cool and yet a deep red flush had stained her cheeks. 'It was a night to remember certainly, but I feel no need to revisit it.'

'Really?' He pushed his chair back. 'That must be why you refused to sleep until I made you come a third time. Because all your curiosity was satisfied and you feel no need to revisit it.'

Her blush deepened further and she carefully clasped

her hands in front of her. 'I'm sorry if that makes you un-happy. But we made no promises to each other.'

It shouldn't matter to him. This need to keep pushing for more from her shouldn't be so intense, and he certainly shouldn't be quite *so* disappointed by her refusal. And yet…

Hunger pulled at him, along with that nagging sense of fascination. As if she was a book he was desperate to read, written in a language he couldn't quite under-stand, and he knew that if he studied her long enough, everything would become clear. Every secret would be revealed.

He couldn't give that up. He wouldn't. His fascination hadn't become less for having slept with her. If anything, it had become more intense, as if the night they'd shared had created some kind of bond between them, a physical bond that deepened what was already there.

The intensity of his own need was slightly unsettling, but since the whole reason she was here was so they could explore that connection, he didn't see any need to be too concerned. No doubt his obsession, if given free rein, would soon pass.

'Wrong,' he said and got to his feet. 'We certainly did make promises to each other. To love, honour and cher-ish, if I remember correctly. Till death do us part, et ce-tera.' He moved around the desk, then leaned casually back against it. Getting closer to her, but not too close, observing what his nearness did to her.

She took a half step back, the pulse at the base of her throat beating faster, and he could feel satisfaction dig its claws in. She might not want to sleep with him again, but that didn't mean he didn't affect her.

'But you didn't mean them and neither did I,' she said.

Orion folded his arms. 'How do you know I didn't mean them?'

Her eyes narrowed into thin slits of sapphire. 'So you really are going to love me for as long as we both shall live?'

Little minx. He'd known for a few months about the board's doubts in her and while initially he'd agreed with them, he wasn't so sure now. Not with the way she was looking at him, all stubborn spirit and challenge, and not at all the quiet, self-effacing woman he'd seen in the boardroom.

Now he thought about it, that was another thing he was curious about. Why she was so quiet when she was definitely not quiet in the slightest? There were so many things he wanted to know.

'Love has nothing to do with our chemistry, Isla,' he said. 'And when you were calling my name last night, you certainly meant it.' He raised a brow. 'Or perhaps you didn't. Perhaps you were faking all those orgasms I gave you.'

Her mouth compressed with obvious irritation. 'I had no idea you were so invested in sex.'

'I'm a man, Snow White. Of course I'm invested in sex. And so are you, I think. Why else are you blushing so fiercely? Why else have you taken a step back from me?' He pushed himself away from the desk and closed the distance between them, looking down into her pink face. 'It's not because you're scared of me, is it?'

Anger glittered in her eyes and she held her ground, which pleased him immeasurably. 'No, of course not. But you're overestimating your abilities in the bedroom. Or rather, my interest in them.' Then she lifted her chin and if that wasn't a direct challenge, he didn't know what was. 'I don't need anything from you. Not a single thing.'

Oh, she might think that. She might even believe that. But she was wrong. He'd discovered that she was a passionate woman, that she was, indeed, a volcano, and last night she'd erupted all over him. It had been an incredible experience to release that in her, to stoke her passion so intensely she hadn't been able to keep it inside. Intoxicating almost. And while she might not admit to herself that she needed that release from him, she did.

And he was willing to give it to her wherever and whenever she wanted for the next twelve days at least.

'I suppose we'll see,' he murmured. 'I have an idea that I'd like to try. As a kind of getting-to-know-you thing.'

'I don't need to get to know you.'

'Indulge me, Snow White. You might like it.'

The look she gave him was suspicious, which amused him more than it should. But all he said was, 'It's twelve days until Christmas. So, I propose that for each of those twelve days, we give each other a gift.'

A small crease appeared between her brows. 'A gift? Such as?'

'Perhaps… I could help you overcome your shortcomings with the board. Give you some advice, something along those lines. And you will give me, say—'

'If it's sex,' she interrupted. 'Forget it. Don't be a cliché.'

She thought she knew him, didn't she? Well, she wasn't wrong about the sex, he did want that. But that wasn't all he wanted.

'I was thinking a kiss,' he said mildly. 'Or maybe a

secret. Your presence on one of these excursions I've organised.'

She frowned. 'A secret? My presence? Why?'

'I told you last night, Isla. You are interesting to me and I want to know why. Twelve days should be enough time to figure it out and then after that, we can go our separate ways, live separate lives until the year is up.'

'So, I can give you…anything?'

'It must be something you know I'd like.'

'What about if I don't want the gift you're going to give me?'

She was sharp, he'd give her that. 'A gift once presented cannot be refused.'

'That goes for you as well?'

'Of course.' He gave her another smile. 'Except the gift of your absence is not acceptable. Once you agree to this, we'll both be bound to remain here for the twelve days of Christmas.'

For a second she said nothing, studying him, clearly turning the idea over in her head. It was good she was thinking it through. He didn't want her to dismiss it out of hand, especially because now he'd thought of it, he wanted it. He wanted it badly, and that was a dangerous thing to allow. He couldn't let it mean anything. This was just a silly game he'd proposed, nothing more, and if she refused then he'd simply figure out something else.

'And if I say no?' she asked. 'If I want to go home in a couple of days?'

Orion ignored the way his gut tightened. 'You're not a prisoner here, Isla. You can leave whenever you like.'

'Twelve days,' she mused. 'That's a long time. It's Kendricks' busy period.'

'That didn't seem to bother you when you scheduled a December wedding,' he pointed out, trying to mask his impatience. 'And a honeymoon afterwards that you were going to go on.'

She didn't say anything to that, merely chewed on her bottom lip.

Had he given away how much he wanted this? Was she drawing this out deliberately?

He didn't like that idea, not at all, so he put out a finger and touched her lip gently. 'Make a decision, Snow White,' he murmured. 'I will not wait all day.'

Her eyes went wide and she stilled, her mouth opening a little. And this time the sparks in her eyes were flames.

Oh, she wanted him all right. She could deny it all she wanted, but they both knew the truth. For a second, he debated pushing her, because her mouth was very soft and he wanted to keep touching it, but then he decided against it, taking his finger away.

He wanted a present. A gift. Christmas had never meant anything to him because he'd had no family of his own, and the foster families he'd been placed with either hadn't cared about it or only in a minimal way. No one had ever thought of giving him a Christmas gift, for example.

But if she agreed to this then she would. She would give him little presents every day, things he didn't have to ask for, things he didn't have to take. Things he wanted.

He almost couldn't bear the thought of her refusal.

To cover his impatience, he turned and went back behind his desk and sat down. He didn't look at her, directing his attention back to his email instead and continuing to work as if she wasn't still standing there and he wasn't waiting for her to agree to his terms.

There was no point pressing her. Either she said yes or she didn't. It was up to her.

After a few moments, she finally let out a breath and said, 'Fine. Twelve days.'

Orion very carefully kept the triumph from his expression and ignored completely the relief that nearly made him catch his breath. 'Good. Why don't you go and have some breakfast and think about your first gift to me? I have to finish up some work.'

CHAPTER SIX

ISLA SPENT THE rest of the day wondering what she'd got herself into. Orion didn't emerge from his office all day, which was fine because quite frankly she needed a break from his overwhelming presence, not to mention some time to think.

Despite Orion's assurances that he'd 'dealt with it', she used her phone to email David to tell him that she was okay, though she couldn't quite bring herself to confront him about the deal he'd made with Orion and why he hadn't told her about it. After all, she was the one who'd agreed to marry for the sake of the company and for David. She could hardly complain about a change of groom when she didn't have any feelings for said groom either way.

She was annoyed however when she got his reply that the board were pleased about her marriage to Orion, regardless of the impulsive nature of the wedding. They had been unsure about her being kept on as CEO, but Orion's assurances that he'd keep the company intact for the next year at least had allayed some fears.

That did not help Isla's temper. Of course the addition of a man made her being CEO much more palatable and it rankled.

She wanted to do right by David, to prove that he'd made the right choice when he'd adopted her, but his lack of support only added to the feeling that what she was doing was making things worse not better.

One thing was clear to her though; she couldn't just leave. If the board thought her marriage to Orion was a good thing, then throwing a tantrum and flying home today wouldn't help her cause. That *would* be letting her anger get the better of her and she couldn't do that.

Also, she could hardly refuse the idea of Christmas presents, since that was what Kendricks' was all about. Except Christmas for her wasn't about family—David for all that he was the 'Christmas magnate' didn't celebrate it. Not when Christmas was the busiest time work wise for them. In fact, she couldn't remember a time where he had celebrated it with her. Usually, Christmas meant donating her time to work in a homeless shelter or something similar. She didn't mind that, having come from nothing herself, but she didn't much like the cynical way David always turned it into a media circus.

Yet that was the way he ran things and she couldn't argue. She wasn't any blood of his, only the girl he'd adopted because his wife before she died had wanted him to find a daughter to leave the company to.

Not a daughter to love.

Her heart ached at that thought, but it was an old pain and so she put aside. The most important thing was how she was going to handle Orion for the next twelve days, because she was going to have to keep him at a distance, not let him get too close.

She was also going to have to figure out what to get him as a 'gift'. Not something sexual since she'd already decided she wasn't going to sleep with him again, and anyway, she didn't want to give him something he'd expect. She also didn't want to give him something that would add to the power he already had, which meant it not only had to be unexpected, but also shake that supreme confidence of his in some way.

'It has to be something you think I would like.'

Except she didn't know what he would like. She didn't know anything about him, beyond him being a ruthless corporate raider. There were bios of him floating around on the internet, but she hadn't read any of them. She'd told herself she wasn't interested. She'd heard that he'd been an orphan like she was, but again, she hadn't wanted to find out any more because she hadn't wanted to feel sympathy or kinship towards him.

Besides, what did you get a man who had everything he could ever want?

He doesn't have you.

The thought refused to go away. And even though she spent the day in the little library she'd spotted, accumulating a nice stack of books to read and distracting herself now and then with stares out the window at the beauty of the snowy landscape beyond the glass, it was still there by the time night fell.

She was curled up in one of the chairs in the library when she heard the door to Orion's office open and then sometime later, shutting again. Half of her was relieved he hadn't bothered to come and find her, while the other half was annoyed. Not that she wanted him to. Of course, she didn't want him to.

Yet that left her alone with her thoughts and the fact

that if she wanted to give him something she knew he would like, it would have to be something to do with her.

It could be a secret...

She didn't have any secrets, though. There was nothing of interest about her, and why he was so fascinated with her she didn't understand. Still, she had to give him something.

That night she ate her dinner alone, then indulged in a bath in her ensuite before going to bed.

She slept like a log and when she woke up the next morning, she lay there going over what she was going to give Orion today.

Perhaps it would have to be a kiss. She didn't want to give him one, not when she knew she was too susceptible to it backfiring on her, and besides, she had to hold something back; it wouldn't do to give him everything he wanted straight away. Yet what else did she have?

When she went downstairs, breakfast was waiting for her and this time so was he, sitting at the table, casually sipping his coffee. His amber gaze was intent as it met hers and she found her heartbeat accelerating the way it always did when he was around.

He was just as gorgeous as he'd been yesterday, still dressed in jeans and a casual shirt of some soft-looking black textured fabric. The neck of the shirt was open, revealing the smooth olive skin of his throat, and she couldn't drag her gaze away from it.

She'd kissed him there that night they'd spent together and tasted the salt of his skin. The memory made her mouth go dry and her face feel hot.

As if he knew exactly what she was thinking, he gave her one of those slow-burning smiles that made her insides melt and something insistent throb between her legs. 'Good morning, Snow White.' His voice was on the edge of a purr. 'I trust you slept well.'

She pulled out the chair opposite and sat down, while he pushed a cup of coffee in her direction. 'Thank you,' she muttered, trying to calm her racing heart. 'Yes, I did.'

'I'm excited about my gift.' He took a sip of his own coffee, watching her, his dark golden eyes glinting in the cool winter sunlight coming through the windows. 'I'm assuming you've thought of something.'

Her heart was beating far too fast and she knew abruptly that she couldn't give him the kiss she'd been planning on. If he could make her this flustered simply by looking at her, she couldn't risk a kiss. It was a loss of control she couldn't allow herself.

'Yes.' She tried to make the word calm and cool. 'I'm going to give you a secret.'

It wasn't much of a secret, but she couldn't think of anything else.

He smiled, though, and the gleam that lit in his eyes was genuine interest. It was as if she'd offered him the rarest of jewels.

He put his coffee down and leaned his elbows on the table, expression expectant. 'A secret? I'm assuming it's a secret about you?'

She blushed helplessly. 'Yes, but it's silly. It's not even a secret.'

'I'll be the judge of that.'

She sighed and glanced away, cupping her coffee mug in her hands and pressing her fingertips against the hot ceramic. He was going to be disappointed. 'My favourite

artist is Vincent Van Gogh,' she said hesitantly. 'And…
I know everything about him.'

'Do you now?' He didn't sound…uninterested.

'Yes. I used to love going to art galleries and muse-
ums as a kid and looking at…beautiful things. And when
I found a piece I particularly loved, I liked reading all
about it and the person who made it.'

'Is that why you were able to explain Van Gogh's painting so eloquently?'

Bracing herself, Isla finally looked up from her mug
and met his gaze. He had that intent look on his face
again, focused on her as if he'd never heard anything as
fascinating as what she was telling him. It made something that had knotted tight and hard in her chest loosen
slightly.

*The most luminous thing in that gallery in that mo-
ment was you…*

He'd told her that on their wedding night and she'd
been so shocked by it. Because no one else had thought
she was luminous when she talked about art. In fact, she
never talked about it to anyone, because no one had ever
been interested.

'It's one of my favourite paintings of his,' she said, still
feeling shy. 'I love his use of colour.'

Orion's gaze didn't waver from hers. 'Tell me more.'

Her cheeks felt hot. 'You can't be interested.'

'Of course, I'm interested,' he said. 'I never say anything I don't mean.'

'It's nothing you won't already know.'

'But I don't,' he said gently. 'I know nothing about art
or artists. The creative impulse baffles me, but I'd like to
understand it. That's why I asked you to tell me about it.'

How could she say no to telling this supremely confident man something he didn't know? To help him understand something?

So she began to explain, hesitantly at first and then with more confidence, about Vincent Van Gogh's life and his early work. His mental health battles and his lack of acknowledgement from the art world. And Orion asked her more questions, about who else she liked, and so she told him about Millais and Rossetti, and the other Pre-Raphaelite artists, as well as Michelangelo and Titian, and then about some Greek sculptures she'd seen at the British Museum.

Orion listened the whole time, his attention never wandering, asking her questions and prompting her for more explanations. He appeared to be completely fascinated.

'And have you ever drawn anything?' he asked, after they'd both finished eating and were relaxing with the remainder of the coffee.

She shook her head. 'No. I don't think I have the talent.' And it wasn't that it hadn't occurred to her, it was just that drawing and art hadn't been appreciated by the foster families she'd been placed with. 'And it's not as if it's a viable career anyway.'

'How do you know if you haven't tried?' His mouth was curved in that half smile again, letting her know that it wasn't a challenge, more a question. And she realised with a sudden start that she hadn't felt unsettled or angry in his presence this time, not once. Only pleased to be talking with him about something she was passionate about.

'I wasn't adopted to be an artist.' She smiled back because she couldn't help herself. 'David wanted a CEO.'

And he didn't get one, did he?

The thought echoed uncomfortably in her head. Perhaps it was best if they changed the subject.

'Anyway,' she went on, 'that's my gift to you. Some boring art facts. If you want more, you'll have to wait for another day.'

Orion slowly sat back in his chair, giving her an enigmatic look. 'I suppose I can't argue with that. Though, for the record, I do want to know more and hearing you talk about it would definitely constitute a gift I would like to receive.'

The knot in her chest loosened further, something warm sitting there instead. She tried not to take any notice of it. 'Noted,' she said.

'Well,' he said. 'I liked my gift very much. Now it's time for yours.'

She tensed. If his gift was a kiss, she didn't know what she'd do. A gift couldn't be refused and she'd agreed to that. And if he kissed her, she'd... Well, she'd lose herself again, she just knew it. And that couldn't happen.

Orion smiled. 'How do you feel about a tour of an active volcano?'

He hadn't known what to expect when he'd given her his gift. He'd mentioned it as an activity he'd planned, but he hadn't known how she would take it. A gift couldn't be refused, yet if she'd really been afraid of the idea, he'd have thought of something else. Even her being afraid would have told him something about her.

But he suspected she wouldn't be. And he was pleased to find out he was right.

They started with an aerial tour in a helicopter flown

by a local pilot, along with a geologist who gave them a rundown of the particular volcanic field they were visiting.

Given how much she'd enjoyed the painting in the gallery, he'd wondered if she'd like the colours of the landscape, the violent glow of lava and the pristine white of the snow. The deep mineral blue of the volcanic lakes and the black rock that surrounded them.

Then, after she'd talked to him at breakfast, about Van Gogh and the other artists she liked, about their histories and their inspirations and their methods, he *knew* she'd like the colours. And she did.

As they sat in the helicopter, flying around one of Iceland's most recent eruptions and he watched her stare out the window, there was no mistaking the glow of wonder that lit her face. The same glow he'd observed in the gallery.

Steam rose in clouds, thick moving lava glowing from underneath the black rock, and she watched it all with rapt, open-mouthed attention.

It made desire twist hard in his gut, along with a satisfaction at his own efforts to recreate that moment of luminous delight he'd seen that night at the gallery.

He still didn't understand why it affected him so intensely, though. It might have been a simple response to her beauty, because she was lovely when she looked like this. Then again, he'd seen plenty of lovely women before and he'd not felt this same, almost…visceral punch whenever he looked at her.

It was puzzling.

She'd intrigued him still further, though. He knew her background, that she'd been a foster kid like he had, except she'd been adopted, while no one had ever wanted him. He'd been too volatile as a kid, too hungry, too intense, and people seemed to sense that in him and shy away from it. He didn't blame them.

He was different now, of course, and he could see why David had chosen Isla to be his successor. She had a hunger too, though she probably wouldn't have said so, and the way she'd pursued the things that interested her struck a chord with him also. She wanted to understand things the way he did, researching all about those artists of hers and their lives. Trying to understand the art they made.

He'd thought that discovering one of her secrets might have dissipated some part of his fascination, but it didn't. If anything, it only made him even more intrigued.

The helicopter landed on a flat bit of rock and the geologist took Orion and Isla across the sharp ground to get a close-up view of a lava flow. Her face was rapt under her helmet—they both had on protective gear—as the geologist guided them across the sharp volcanic rocks, Isla peppering him with questions.

Once, she stumbled on the uneven ground and Orion instinctively slid an arm around her waist to steady her. She was so caught up in the tour she didn't seem to notice, leaning into him briefly before giving his arm a little pat, as if he was a dog, before pulling away to continue walking. And he found himself amused and aggravated in equal measure that she was so involved in the tour that she hadn't seemed to notice his touch.

You're a fool to let it matter to you this much. You've slept with her. What more do you need to know?

He couldn't have said. Only that sex was merely a part of his interest and that interest hadn't been satisfied yet.

One thing he was sure of though, was that he couldn't move on from this obsession until he found the key, and so yes, it mattered. *She* mattered.

During the tour, he'd provided her with a camera since he thought she might want to take some better pictures than she could from her phone, and she hadn't protested. Not only had she asked the guide a million questions, but she'd spent just about every second taking photos of the rocks, the lava, the mountain and the snow, and once or twice, she'd even taken a couple of pictures of him.

He hadn't minded. If she wanted pictures of him, who was he to argue?

They spent a couple of hours exploring the mountain, and then a glacier, and in the helicopter afterwards, as they flew back to the lodge, she turned to him, her face alight, her blue eyes glowing. 'That was amazing! Honestly, I had no idea I'd enjoy getting that close to an active volcano. And all those colours... They were incredible!'

She wasn't self-contained now. The cork was out of that champagne bottle and she was fizzing everywhere, and not bothering to hide it. And he was seized by the almost uncontrollable urge to kiss her. He wanted to get a taste of her excitement and her joy, just a small taste, because it had been so long since he'd experienced anything like it, he couldn't remember what it felt like.

Have you ever *experienced anything like it?*

Possibly not. His life had had precious few moments of joy and wonder. Even his childhood had been lonely and isolated, the one bright spot being when he'd met Cleo. Except that had all gone to hell in a handcart and afterwards he'd decided he didn't need moments of joy. Satisfaction would do for him.

It would have satisfied him immensely to take a kiss from Isla, yet he held himself back. She'd been quite clear that she didn't want to sleep with him again, despite being still very attracted to him, and he found that for the second time in his life he didn't want to take something just because he could—and he could take that kiss. She wouldn't protest, he was sure of it.

Yet...he didn't want to. He wanted her to give a kiss to him of her own free will. Because she wanted to, because she wanted him, and not because he'd forced her into anything.

Especially after you forced her into marrying you.

Something uncomfortable shifted inside him. He'd told her that he hadn't regretted his threat to get her to marry him, but maybe he did. Maybe that hadn't been the correct course of action. Maybe that hadn't been the right opportunity to take.

He didn't like the feeling, just as he didn't like his own reluctance to take what he wanted from her. His ruthlessness, his edge, was what set him apart from others in the business world and he didn't want to lose it.

Except not enough to put his hand behind her head and draw her in for a kiss.

It was quite the conundrum.

'I thought you might like it,' he said instead, controlling himself firmly. 'From an artistic point of view.'

'Yes. I think I took about fifty million photos.' She grinned, her cheeks flushed with delight. 'Did you enjoy it too?'

It took him a moment to process the question, since he couldn't remember anyone ever asking him if he'd enjoyed anything. And it made the tight thing inside him shift yet again. Not only had she thought about him, she'd been interested enough to want to know if he'd shared her enjoyment. As if mattered to her.

For a second, he couldn't think. *Had* he enjoyed himself? Or had the entire day been more about his own satisfaction at putting that look on her face?

Yet deep in his frozen heart, like a small ray of midwinter sun rising on a cold dawn, came the realisation that, yes, he *had* enjoyed himself. He'd enjoyed watching her glitter and sparkle like sunlight on snow, and he'd enjoyed her company. Her questions and her smile, and how she'd taken photos of him as if she'd wanted to include him in her record of this day. He'd also enjoyed sharing with her something that he found beautiful himself and having her think so too.

Slowly he said, 'I did. Very much.'

She grinned. 'What was your favourite part?'

When you stumbled and I caught you, and you leaned against me. When you smiled and took my photo. When you asked the geologist a question he didn't know and he got a little irritated. When you watched the lava flow, your whole face alight.

The tight thing in his chest turned heavy, though he had no idea why, so he ignored it. 'Oh,' he murmured. 'I couldn't pick just one.'

Isla laughed, the sound surprisingly husky, whispering over his skin like velvet. 'Really? Come on. What do you like about volcanos?'

He thought about it for a moment and surprised himself with the honesty of his answer. 'I think it's very bracing to see nature's power close up. It's very easy to only think of the world as a collection of cities full of humans, yet we live on a planet. And that planet only allows us to be here on sufferance.'

Interest sharpened in her gaze. 'Yes, it's so easy to forget we're sitting on top of a living planet, isn't it? Is that why you chose to have a lodge here? For the landscape?'

Perhaps he should have bargained with her for the information, but he didn't even think about it. 'I have a few different houses in different places. But I come back to Iceland a lot. I like the isolation. The landscape is so wild and untamed and primal, and I like that too. Nature can't be tamed, all you can do is sit back and watch it with awe.' He smiled. 'It also has the gift of putting one's own problems into perspective.'

'Problems?' Amusement danced in her eyes. '*You* have problems? Please, what problems could the great and terrible Orion North have?'

The heaviness in his chest shifted again, gathering tighter. She was teasing him, with laughter in her blue eyes as she relaxed in the seat next to him, and she was just so…beautiful.

He almost couldn't look at her, the urge to grab her and pull her into his arms nearly overwhelming him. In fact, it shocked him how tenuous his control was. If he wasn't careful, the moment they landed, he really *would* grab her. He'd take her upstairs and rip her clothes off before she'd even had a chance to take a breath.

But he'd already decided he wasn't going to do that, and not just with a kiss either. When they slept together again, it would be because she wanted him, because she'd asked for it, because she'd given herself to him. It wouldn't be because he'd taken it.

So he forced away the tight feeling and gripped his

control. 'Why, none, of course,' he said. 'Men like me don't have problems.'

The words must have come out less casual and more bitter than he'd intended, because she gave him a worried look. 'I'm sorry. I didn't mean to imply that you didn't.'

He was being ridiculous. The only problem he had was her. Everything else had been relegated to a past he no longer thought of.

So he gave her what he hoped was a reassuring smile and said, 'No need to apologise. My problems are purely of the business kind and aren't very interesting I'm afraid.'

But the worried crease between her brows didn't disappear. She opened her mouth to say something, then, clearly thinking better of it, shut it again. And as he watched, the excitement and the amusement died slowly out of her eyes, the glow in her cheeks fading.

You did that. You ruined it.

It made him feel suddenly as if he was back in the hallway at Cleo's place, watching Luke's family sing 'Happy Birthday', his heart burning with the knowledge that if he wanted to be part of Luke's life, no matter what he did, it would involve throwing a bomb in the middle of Luke's happy little family and blowing it to smithereens.

He hadn't been able to do it. He hadn't been able to rip his son's life apart, purely to heal his own pain.

You never bring happiness to people, do you?

That didn't matter. He didn't need to bring happiness to people. Happiness didn't interest him. The satisfaction he got from his business, the thrill of the chase and then the intellectual stimulation involved in stripping away the broken parts of a company to find the productive core was all he needed. That's where he got his enjoyment. He pruned away the deadwood so the tree could grow, cut out the scar tissue so the patient could get better.

That was all he needed from life. That was what made him content.

Happiness required you to care and he was done with caring.

He decided he was better off not saying anything after that and so he stayed quiet for the rest of the flight back to the lodge.

Once they were back, he helped Isla out of the helicopter and into the lodge, then he took himself off to his office, needing some distance.

Or at least he tried to.

They were in the entrance way, having divested themselves of their protective gear, and he was just on the point of striding down the hall, when Isla put a tentative hand on his arm.

He stopped dead, her light touch holding him as surely as iron chains. He had a T-shirt on and unfortunately it meant her skin was against his, burning like the flow of lava they'd seen not a couple of hours earlier.

'Did I...? Did I say something?' she asked hesitantly. 'In the helicopter? If I did, I'm sorry—'

'No.' The word was sharp but he couldn't moderate his tone. 'You didn't. It was nothing.'

'But you—'

'Isla.' He turned around and looked down at her, letting her see the heat in his eyes. It granted her more power than she should have to reveal the extent of the effect she had on him, but she had to know. He wouldn't break his vow over something as meaningless as physical desire, however he wasn't in the mood to make it harder for himself than it already was. 'I wouldn't touch me if I were you. Not right now.'

Her gaze widened as it searched his, a flush of colour in her cheeks. 'Orion, I—'

'I don't want to take it,' he interrupted yet again, because he had to end this little scene right now and with the truth. He didn't want to hurt her if he could help it. 'I don't want to take you, do you understand? I want you, but if sex happens between us again, it will only be because you asked for it. I want it to be a gift you give me. But if you keep touching me like that, if you keep getting close to me, I might just change my mind and take it anyway.'

Her lush mouth opened, but he didn't want to stand here with her so close, discussing sex. He'd said his piece and his control was already hanging by a thread.

He needed to find it again.

So before she could say anything else, or worse, touch him again, he turned and strode off down the hallway.

CHAPTER SEVEN

ISLA DIDN'T SLEEP WELL that night and by the time dawn crept around, she was still tossing and turning in her bed.

She couldn't get the fierce gleam in Orion's eyes when he'd looked down at her in the hallway the night before out of her head. She'd only wanted to make sure that her teasing comment in the helicopter hadn't hurt him, which seemed ridiculous in retrospect since he seemed to be a man impervious to something as small as mere hurt.

The trip to the volcano had been a revelation, and she'd loved every second of it. The adrenaline rush of standing on the edge of a lava flow and listening to the geologist explain the workings of a volcano and how new rocks were made had been incredible. There had been so many things she'd wanted to know, so many colours to take in, the landscape around her in all its textures so fascinating.

It made such a change from the boardroom, and she'd got carried away in her excitement on the way back, thoughtlessly teasing Orion about his problems, because she'd never imagined a man like him would have any. Yet the sharpness of his response had brought her up short. She hadn't wanted to ruin the day by saying something careless, so in the hallway she'd only wanted to apologise.

Then he'd looked down at her and the heat in his eyes had locked the breath in her throat. As had the anger.

She hadn't realised he'd still wanted her, yet it was clear that he did. And badly. Except he wasn't going to take her. This time he wanted her to give herself to him.

Some part of her was thrilled at being such a test for his control, while another part was amazed that he was holding himself back from taking what he wanted.

She sighed and rolled onto her back, staring at the ceiling. The ferocious heat in his gaze, yet the rigid way he'd held himself in check had been an intoxicating combination. And far from making her not want to touch him, it made her want to keep touching him more. To push him, see how far she could take things before he broke...

'I want it to be a gift you give to me.'

Ah, but no, she couldn't push him. It wouldn't be right, not after he'd said that to her. Not now that he saw her as a gift to be given rather than a thing to take. It thrilled her down to the bone.

Twice she'd been chosen by people, and twice they'd regretted that choice. The first time she'd been returned like a pet no one had wanted and the second time, well... She hadn't been returned by David yet, but she was still under review. Her performance had been lacking, she knew it.

You were stupid to expect more from him. You weren't adopted, you were hired.

It was true. David had never acted as though he was her father. Right from the first day she'd come home with him, he'd been emotionally distant. All he'd ever wanted from her were excellent marks at school and then honours at university, which she'd given him. She hadn't known any other way to earn his approval and she still didn't.

Why do you even want his approval?

She wasn't sure. Maybe it was simply that his approval was better than his disappointment, and she had never been able to bear that.

Not that she wanted to think of David. It was Orion and how she was going to deal with him today that mattered.

You didn't want to sleep with him again. You were very clear.

It was true, yet she couldn't deny how her body reacted to the thought of being in his arms again. The dragging ache between her thighs and the excitement that crowded in her throat. The way every muscle tightened with anticipation whenever he got close.

Yesterday, on the tour, she'd stumbled and he'd slid an arm around her, anchoring her against his hard, powerful body. The shock of his warmth and the reassuring strength in his grip had unsettled her so much all she'd been able to do was pat his arm and step away as quickly as she could just to get her breath back.

Perhaps it was a reckless thing to contemplate, but would it be so very bad to offer herself to him? To give him the gift he wanted? Especially since she wanted him every bit as badly as he wanted her.

After all, she'd already had one night with him and nothing bad had happened afterwards. Her control over herself hadn't magically vanished just because she'd given in to passion. Was another night really such a risk?

Not finding any answers, eventually Isla hauled herself out of bed and got dressed. Then she found her camera from yesterday and went through the photos she'd taken, pleased with the shots. The stark, wild beauty of the Icelandic mountains and all that fire and ice set something vibrating deep inside her. And what had Orion told her in the helicopter on the way back? He'd spoken about nature's power and how it put things in perspective.

She'd liked his response. That he, a powerful man supremely in control of himself, could appreciate the untamed nature of the landscape. Not because he wanted to tame it, but because he wanted to get close to it, observe its majesty for himself.

Oh, he was interesting. She wanted to know more of his thoughts on nature and she also wanted to know very much what problems nature put into perspective.

A photo of Orion suddenly popped up on her screen. He was standing on the black rocks, looking at her, a half smile curving his hard, beautiful mouth. His eyes were gleaming in the light from the lava flow and the intensity in his face stole her breath.

He looked fierce, as hard and sharp as the rocks he stood on. As powerful as the volcano that towered over them.

Such a beautiful man, though his wasn't a conventional beauty. It was something untamed and wild, as primitive as the landscape around him.

He'd given her such an amazing experience, and abruptly she wanted to do something equally amazing for him. Make his gift today one that would surprise and delight him as much as she'd been surprised and delighted the day before.

You know already what you're going to give him.

Isla put the camera down, her heart thudding. Oh, yes, she knew.

Another night, she decided. He'd wanted her to give him the gift of herself, so she would.

Orion was seated at the table by the time she'd finished dressing and come downstairs in search of breakfast. And once again his presence brought her up short, making her catch her breath.

He didn't smile at her this morning and he wasn't sitting with his usual casual posture. He looked tense, his face set in hard lines. 'Sit,' he ordered, his deep voice rough sounding. 'I want to give you today's present.'

Instinctive irritation at the sharp command prickled over her, but since he didn't look like he'd slept well, she swallowed her annoyance and did as she was told. They'd had such a lovely day yesterday and she didn't want to ruin the morning with an argument.

'You look like you slept as well as I did,' she observed as she sat down.

He ignored her. It looked like he'd been there a while. An empty plate with a knife and fork arranged neatly on it had been pushed away, a half-drunk cup of coffee at his elbow. 'My present to you today will be skating on the lake,' he said shortly.

He'd mentioned that as one of the excursions he'd planned a day or so ago, and then it had sounded fun. Looking at his hard expression now, she wasn't so certain.

'Are you sure?' She kept her voice very neutral. 'You don't seem as if you want to go anywhere let alone skating on the lake.'

'I'm sure.' He sat back in his chair, his expression still hard. A muscle flicked in his strong jaw, the amber of his eyes darkening, all the bright gold in them gone. He looked as intimidating and ruthless as he ever had.

Was that all because of her? Because he wanted her? Or were there other things at play here? Yesterday, in the helicopter, she'd made that casual comment about his problems and his expression had shuttered in much the same way. Why? Was it because he did have problems and he'd resented her mentioning them? Or was it for another reason? And why did it matter to her?

'Is this about yesterday?' she asked carefully. 'About what you told me in the hallway last night?'

'No,' he said coldly. 'Not everything is about you, Isla.'

Heat crept into her cheeks, a flicker of hurt going through her. She ignored it. 'That's not what I meant. I just wanted to know why you're sitting at the breakfast table looking like you want to break rocks with your teeth.'

'It's nothing.'

'Like it was nothing up in the helicopter yesterday?'

'Are you really that interested in my moods? I thought you were more interested in your favourite artists.' There was a hint of bitterness in the words, the way there had been yesterday, and he was radiating frustrated anger. She could feel it pushing at her from across the table like the heat from the lava flow the day before.

'Are you sulking because I wouldn't sleep with you?' she couldn't help asking, even though she knew confronting him was hardly likely to improve his mood. 'Is that what this is about?'

For a second he looked so fierce she thought he was going to lose his temper, and it made her own anger rise, pulling at the chains she kept on it. She found herself staring at him almost hoping he would lose it, because she wanted to know what would happen if he did.

He was so controlled, so very in command of himself, and he would have seemed cold if not for that burning intensity in his eyes. There was fire at the heart of him, she realised suddenly. Fire that he couldn't let out for some reason.

Her heart raced and the strangest anticipation gripped her. And she was back on that volcanic field of yesterday once again, standing on the edge of a lava flow, looking up at the active volcano in terrified wonder as yet more lava flowed down its side.

Yet Orion didn't explode. Instead, he said. 'Give me my gift, Isla.'

It wasn't an answer, but it was most certainly a demand, and while it wasn't at all wise, Isla suddenly wanted very much to see what it would look like if Mt Orion North erupted.

'If you're going to sulk like a giant baby,' she said coolly. 'You'll have to wait for your gift. Skating first and then if you're very lucky I might give you something.'

Orion was in a foul temper. She was right, he hadn't slept well. He'd been up half the night, tortured by his desire for a woman he'd decided he wouldn't touch until she said he could. His vow infuriated him. The way it mattered to him infuriated him.

She infuriated him and he didn't know why.

Sex was nothing. He could deny himself till the cows came home and it had never bothered him before, and yet now he wanted her so badly it felt as if he couldn't breathe.

After hours of no sleep, he'd eventually had to get up and go into the lodge's gym to work out some of his frustration on the treadmill and then the rowing machine. A sauna had then eased the tension from his muscles, but of course, the moment she'd walked into the dining area, that tension had returned, even worse than it had the night before. And he was no closer to figuring out exactly why, hence the foul temper.

Then for her to stare at him coolly over the breakfast table and call him a giant baby… His temper roiled, pushing against his control.

She's not wrong. You are *sulking.*

He didn't appreciate that thought, not at all. Mainly because he knew it was correct. He also knew that if he didn't get hold of his temper, he'd end up ruining the skating on the lake that he'd planned for today and since he'd nearly ruined the volcano trip the day before, he didn't want to repeat his mistake.

Instead, he carefully and deliberately slid his chair back and slowly rose to his feet. 'Once you've had breakfast,' he said in the most neutral tones possible, 'come and meet me in the entrance hall and we can get geared up.'

Then without sparing her a glance, he left the dining area to prepare.

It was childish of him not to engage and definitely not to apologise, but he had to have some space to leash his hunger otherwise he was in danger of ruining this utterly.

A good half an hour later, Isla appeared, all cool and contained. Which of course made him want to crack her self-possession, put a dent in it somehow, ignite the fire that lit her up from within. But doing that when he was so on edge himself was a terrible idea, so he only handed her a thick white down jacket, a thick white scarf and hat and some gloves without a word.

Once they were both protected from the weather, he took both pairs of skates and led the way outside.

The morning was clear, the sky a deep, endless blue above them, the frigid air making white clouds of their warm breaths. There was a small wooden jetty that projected into the lake and they both sat down on it to put their skates on. He finished with his first and slid smoothly out onto the ice. He'd skated here many times and took pleasure in the solitude of the lake and the silence. He wondered if she too would appreciate that.

Turning, he watched as Isla gingerly put her skates onto the ice and slid out onto it, holding her hands out for balance. She looked adorable all wrapped up in the down jacket. Wisps of golden curls stuck out from under her hat, her scarf wrapped around her neck. She stayed where she was on the ice, still holding her hands out, as if she was afraid to move, and those deep blue eyes of hers were looking at him with trepidation.

'You haven't done this before, have you?' he asked.

She shook her head, and for some reason, the sharp edge of his mood eased.

He wanted her to enjoy this and she wouldn't if he stayed being angry. It was a gift, after all, and there should be pleasure in being given gifts. Or so he'd heard.

Orion skated over to her and took both her mittened hands in his. 'Just relax and keep your knees loose. I'm going to pull you along.' Keeping his grip firm, he began to slowly skate backwards, tugging her along with him.

She didn't fight him and soon the trepidation had gone from her eyes, and her cool self-possession along with it. She began to smile, her blue gaze sparkling as he went a little faster, giving her a few instructions on how to move, and he found himself smiling back, like a fool. But how could he not? She was irresistible. Glowing with that light he found so bewitching and again, he was the one who'd put it there.

He'd made her happy. Because that's what this was, wasn't it? It was happiness.

Don't worry, you'll ruin it soon. That's what you do. You destroy things.

His chest ached at the thought, but he pushed it away. He wanted to concentrate on this moment, not anything else.

'You're good at this,' she said, as they moved over the ice together.

'I've had a lot of practice.'

'What do you like about it?'

He moved in a slow gliding motion, drawing her along. 'It's very quiet and peaceful out on the ice. And sometimes it's as if you're the only person in creation.'

'You like being alone?'

'I'm always alone,' he heard himself say. Which was stupid. It revealed far too much about himself that he didn't want to share.

Yet a look of understanding shifted in her eyes. 'Me too,' she said. 'Since I was a kid.'

He slowed, the conversation more important than the skating all of a sudden. 'You were in the foster system, weren't you?'

'Yes. I was taken in by a family when I was around ten but…well, it didn't work out. And so I went into a home.'

He watched her face, drawn by the emotions shadowing her blue gaze. He too had been in a home, and he remembered the agony of wanting prospective adoptive parents to like him, to want him, to take him with them, to give him the family he'd always craved. Except they never had. But for her to have had a family only for it to be lost… He knew well what that agony was like.

'Why didn't it work out?' he asked and then, as a thought suddenly occurred to him, bringing with it a wave of protective anger so intense he could hardly breathe, he went on, 'Were they abusive?'

'No, nothing like that.' She glided forward as he moved back, managing to slide around a patch of rough ice. 'The couple already had a son and they wanted a girl. The son…didn't like me and would do things to get me into trouble. He was just a kid, like I was, but one day he scratched his dad's car and blamed it on me. And I'd taken the blame for months for various things, and that day I just…lost it.' She bit her lip, a shadow crossing her face. 'They didn't believe that it was their son, they just thought I was badly behaved and acting out, and so when I had a temper tantrum, that was the last straw. They decided that it would be best if they didn't adopt me after all.'

Orion was aware then of the strangest sensation in his chest. There was pain in her face and it was almost as if he could feel it too. Pain for her and what she'd experienced. Pain at the unfairness of it. Not to mention a violent anger at the carelessness of some people, who thought a child was a piece of furniture they could get rid of when it didn't fit their house.

He stopped on the ice and gently pulled her in close, his hands on her hips, holding her steady. 'And then what happened?'

She didn't pull away, only looked up at him. 'Then David adopted me. He liked my school marks and the reports from the people who ran the home. His late wife wanted him to adopt a girl and he needed an heir so he killed two birds with one stone.'

But this hurt her too and he could see that pain glittering in her eyes and he could feel it in his chest. He gripped her tighter. 'But that didn't work out either, did it?'

She took a small breath then glanced away. 'It wasn't… what I thought it was going to be.'

Orion put out a mittened hand to her jaw and gently urged her back to face him. 'Why not?' he asked, wanting to understand why this hurt her and perhaps why it also hurt him.

She sighed. 'I thought—hoped—that he might be a father to me. I thought he wanted a daughter, but…he didn't. He only wanted an heir, and he's been…disappointed in my performance.' She paused and then went on, 'He's been disappointed in his choice.'

A bright, fierce and protective anger turned over in Orion's gut. How dare David do that to her? How dare he find something as rare and precious as she was, and find it wanting?

He didn't question the intensity of the feeling, he only wanted to do something about the hurt in her eyes. 'David is a fool,' he said roughly. 'And if he regrets adopting you then he's even more of a fool than I thought he was.'

Isla's blue eyes turned dark. 'He's got reason, Orion. I thought he was going to be my father, but after he brought me home, it was clear that he didn't think he was. I knew that it was my school marks he wanted, my potential as a future CEO, nothing else. He didn't actually want…me.'

The last word sounded as if she'd forced it out, and

abruptly Orion was aware that he hated the thought of her thinking *she* was the problem. 'I stand corrected,' he growled. 'He *is* more of a fool than I thought he was.'

'It is me,' Isla said. 'I have a temper and I'm too volatile and I—'

'You're passionate,' Orion interrupted, not wanting to hear another word from her about all her shortcomings. Because they weren't shortcomings. None of them were. 'That's not a crime. You're smart, yes, but you're also interested, and you want to learn. You want to understand. In the boardroom all you need is more practice and better guidance. A mentor who will bolster your strengths not focus on your weaknesses.'

She stared at him and he was conscious that he was sounding far too vehement. But he didn't take any of it back. 'You really think so?' she asked, her voice husky. 'You really think there's hope for me?'

He couldn't stop himself then. He knew it was a bad idea, but he didn't want her hurt. He didn't want her believing she was somehow less because one man couldn't see the treasure that he'd found. He cupped her face in his hands, stared down into her eyes and let her see the belief in his. 'For months I've wondered what it is about you that has so fascinated me. Months, Isla. Ever since that night in the gallery. And I studied you, watched you, unable to think of anything but you. And I've decided it's not one thing. There are so many things about you that are interesting. Your fascinating mind and your passion. Your self-containment even when I can see there's a fire burning inside you. Your determination and your spine of steel. The way you matched wits with me and stood toe to toe with me, even as I was threatening your company.' Her eyes looking up into his were as bright as stars. 'The problem is *not* you. The problem was him. You wanted a father and that's what he should have been to you. A father, not a damn employer.'

She said nothing for a long moment. Then suddenly she reached up, took his face between her hands and pulled his mouth down on hers.

CHAPTER EIGHT

ORION'S LIPS WERE cool on hers, his body strong and powerful. It was stupid to kiss him on the ice when she could barely stand upright, but she couldn't help herself.

The fierce way he'd listed all her strengths, with the conviction gleaming in his wolf-gold gaze, as if he believed every single one of them had made her eyes prickle with tears.

No one had said those things to her before, not one person. No one had seen her temper as passion. Her father had only wanted her because of her school marks, but he hadn't told her she was smart or that she had a fascinating mind. Her determination had been detrimental to the board and her fire made her volatile, and her subsequent self-containment a blandness that was unacceptable.

They were all weaknesses not strengths.

No one had ever seen straight through to her heart and the secret fear that lay inside it that David had never wanted *her*, only her potential. That all the things that made her not CEO material, were also the reasons she'd never actually been his daughter.

Only Orion had seen those things. Only Orion, because he'd watched her, noticing things about her. Being interested in her. Months, he'd said. Months he'd been able to think of nothing but her. Ever since that night in the gallery.

She hadn't intended to tell him about her adoptive history, but when he'd said that he was always alone, she hadn't been able to stop herself. She knew what being alone felt like and she'd wanted him to know that too. Then he'd been so fierce when she'd told him about David, almost as if he was angry at David on her behalf and that's when her heart had felt painful. That's when she'd reached for him without thought.

He'd tensed and he didn't move, his mouth cool and smooth on hers.

He'd been so angry before and he wasn't now, but she could still taste the fire in him. The heat that only showed itself in his eyes. She wanted it to burn for her.

She put her arms around his neck, leaning into him and as she did so, she felt her skates begin to slide. But his hands were on her hips, steadying her. There were so many layers of clothes between them, the heat of his body tantalising her. She badly wanted all of those clothes gone.

Then his mouth lifted and she found herself looking up into eyes gone brilliant, flaming gold. 'What the hell was that for?' he demanded roughly.

A shiver worked its way down her spine and for some inane reason she felt like smiling. It was probably the taut look on his face, as if he was a junkie desperate for a fix and she was his drug of choice.

'That was my gift to you,' she said. 'I wanted to skate first and so we skated. And now I want to kiss you, if you'll let me.'

'If I'll let you?' he echoed, as if the words were foreign to him.

She loved the look on his face and the hunger in his eyes. 'You can't refuse a gift, Orion, remember? You have to take it.' She was teasing him and it was mean of her, but he'd threatened her into a marriage. He could stand a little teasing.

'Isla.' His hands tightened, bringing her hard up against his tall, powerful body.

'What?' She put her mittened palms flat to his chest, smiling up at him. 'I think I'm going to give you another gift too. That's allowed. We didn't say anything about not being able to give two gifts in one day.'

'Isla,' he said again, a warning this time.

She ignored it. 'I think I might want to give you another kiss. And this time in a place of my choosing.'

His gaze was nothing but gold now. *'Isla...'*

'You can't refuse.' Her knees felt unsteady, her heartbeat out of control. 'You have to take it.'

That muscle in the side of his jaw flexed, but he said nothing, the look in his eyes burning her to the ground.

'Where would you like it?' she murmured. 'Here or inside?'

'Is that all?' he demanded, rougher than the volcanic ground they'd walked over the day before. 'Is it just a kiss? Because you need to tell me.'

Isla decided to take pity on him. 'No,' she whispered. 'No, that's not all. You can have the rest of me too. If you want it.'

He went very still, searching her face as if to make sure that's what she was offering him. Then abruptly he picked her up in his arms.

Isla gave an undignified shriek. 'What are you doing?'

'Getting you back to the lodge.' He settled her against his chest. 'But we're doing this the fast way.'

Then they were gliding over the ice, the icy wind in her face, as he held her tight against his chest. He skated smoothly towards the jetty as if he'd been skating around with her in his arms for years, building up some speed. And when they reached it, he turned sharply on the edges of his skates, sending up a spray of ice as he stopped.

'Nice,' she murmured as he placed her on the side of the jetty and began undoing the laces of her skates himself. 'Are you trying to impress me?'

He looked up, his golden eyes brilliant. 'Perhaps. Is it working?'

'Perhaps,' she echoed, her heart now beating even faster, and smiled.

Orion dealt with their skates in record time, and then she was being pulled along the stone path back to the lodge, her mittened hands firmly in Orion's.

He got the front door open and once it had shut, he turned and pushed her up against it, holding her pressed to the wood by her hips, his head dipping to find her mouth.

'Kiss me,' he murmured against her lips. 'Give me your gift, Snow White.'

She could feel the tension in his body, the subtle vibration of a leashed predator desperate to be freed. It thrilled her to know how badly he wanted her and yet was holding back. And he must have wanted her *very* badly for him to shake like that.

He wanted his gift and so she gave it to him.

She tilted her head back and met his mouth, pressing her lips to his, gentle and soft. She felt the shudder that went through him and braced herself for the explosion, yet it didn't come. He remained still, as if waiting for more.

So she gave him more, tracing his mouth with her tongue, nipping at his bottom lip. And then when his lips parted, allowing her entry, she tasted him deeper, loving how he let her explore him, chasing his delicious flavour, because the more she had, the more she wanted.

Her hands were pressed to the hard plane of his chest and she arched into him, the throb between her thighs becoming demanding. Then the leash he had on himself snapped.

Orion lifted his head, his eyes gleaming with hunger. He pulled her mittens off, then her hat and her scarf. Then he proceeded to rip off the rest of her clothes, discarding them along with her boots in a heap on the floor.

He dealt with his own in seconds flat and then she was being taken down to the floor in the hallway, a soft rug beneath her, Orion's powerful body over her. She put her hands to his shoulders and stroked him, loving the feel of his hot skin, and the strong muscles that shifted and flexed beneath it. His mouth was on hers, the kiss getting deeper, hotter, and she returned it, as feverish and needy as he was.

He slid one hand between her thighs, finding the slick heat there and stroking her, making her gasp and shake, shifting beneath him because she wanted more, so much more. But he didn't give it to her.

Instead, he rolled over and she found herself sitting astride him. He had a condom in his hand. 'Put it on me,' he ordered, his voice gravelly and raw, his eyes blazing with demand. 'Now, Snow White.'

Her hands shook as she ripped open the packet and not because she was afraid. She was hungry too and the look in his eyes was making it difficult to think. He was desperate for her and she loved it. She wanted the explosion. She wanted the volcano he was to erupt.

She rolled on the condom and his hand came down over hers, holding her fingers tight around him, showing her how to stroke him. Her breath hitched as she followed his movements, watching as the gold in his eyes burned bright.

'Come here,' he growled at last. 'Put me inside you.'

So she did, lifting herself up and then sliding down onto him, his hands on her hips to guide her, feeling the delicious burn of her sex stretching around his, holding him tight.

He made a growling sound deep in his throat, and then he was showing her how to move and what rhythm gave them both the most pleasure. She fell into it naturally, easily, as if they'd been lovers for years and knew each other's bodies as well as their own.

She couldn't look away from his beautiful face, set in lines of taut hunger, gazing at her as if he wanted to eat her alive. And as the pleasure climbed higher, becoming more intense, more demanding, she didn't know what she'd been afraid of.

This was like skating, like flying. Like standing on the edge of a volcano with the wild glory of nature all around her. There was no stopping it. No controlling it. She wasn't ice and neither was he. They were both fire and they were letting that fire burn.

She moved faster, harder and then he rolled again, taking her beneath him and everything became hotter and more desperate. He grabbed her behind the knee and pulled her leg up around his waist, sliding deeper inside her and she couldn't breathe for the pleasure.

His mouth covered hers and he was inside her, around her. All she could taste was the delicious flavour of him and the dark spice of his scent surrounded her, and she couldn't think of anywhere she wanted to be right now but here, under him.

It was agony. It was ecstasy. And then suddenly it was a release that blinded her.

She screamed against his shoulder as the pleasure overwhelmed her, and dimly she heard him call her name as he followed her into the flames.

She was persuasive, his snow maiden. After the wild sex in the hallway, she tried to convince him that a soak in this fabled hot pool of his was just what she needed. But he'd been saving that gift and anyway, he wanted her somewhere warm and soft so he could have her whenever he wanted her. Which was all the time.

So he took her upstairs to the bedroom for a little while and when they were both satisfied for the moment, he ran a bath in the huge white marble tub in his bathroom. He got in with her and they both lay there in companionable silence, watching the snowy landscape out the window.

But of course, she was wet and slippery and one thing led to another which led them back to bed again.

He couldn't seem to get enough of her.

That night he explored her as thoroughly as he could and then it was her turn to explore him, which he liked a great deal. Yet the puzzling thing was that instead of his hunger getting less, it only seemed to deepen still further. She'd finally given him the gift of her body and he'd thought that once he'd had her again, he wouldn't be so hungry. But he was. He didn't understand it.

That might have concerned him if he hadn't known that he had another ten days of Christmas gift giving, which meant a lot of time to fully comprehend what was going on with her, and so he decided that holding back now wasn't an option. Clearly to get to the bottom of his fascination, he was going to have to go all in.

The next morning, he woke with her in his arms, nestled against him, her golden curls spread across his chest, and the pleasure that gave him was indescribable. He'd never felt anything like it. It was satisfaction and desire and a savage need to hold her close and never let her go in order to keep her safe.

The intensity of it set off some alarm bells, but since he wasn't holding back, he ignored the disquiet. Instead, he woke her with soft kisses that soon turned into hotter kisses and then a blazing desire that took at least an hour to fully satisfy.

Afterwards, she lay with her head on his chest, idly tracing circles on his skin, her lush mouth, still red from his kisses, curving in a self-satisfied smile that made him want to growl with pleasure.

'Your body is mine,' he said, feeling unaccountably possessive. 'You made it a gift to me and now I'm keeping it for the next ten days.'

She arched one golden brow, the blue of her eyes hot as a midsummer day. 'Is that a fact?'

'It is,' he said definitively. 'There will be no argument.'

'Bossy man.' She gave him a lazy smile. 'But I suppose I'll allow it.' She folded her hands on his chest. 'So, it's morning again and I don't have a gift.'

Idly, he took one of her curls between his fingers and tugged gently. 'Impatient woman. What about mine?'

Colour washed through her cheeks and her lashes lowered. 'I'm not sure I have anything else to give you. I already told you my secret.'

'That's not the only secret you have, I'm sure.'

She sighed. 'There really isn't that much to me, I'm afraid.'

'I don't believe that for a second.' He wound the soft silkiness of her curl around his finger. 'There's so much I don't know about you. For example, what's your favourite colour? And your favourite food? Your favourite book?'

She gave him a look from beneath her lashes. 'Those aren't secrets.'

'They're still gifts.' He held her gaze. 'Everything about you is a gift.'

The pink in her cheeks deepened. 'You're a shameless flatterer.'

'Come on.' He tugged insistently on her curl again. 'Tell me something about you that I don't know.'

'Well, okay.' She bit her lip, clearly thinking. Then she said, 'I actually hate Christmas.'

He couldn't help smiling at that. 'The Christmas CEO who hates Christmas? Sounds like the beginnings of a romantic comedy.'

'It's true,' she protested, smiling too. 'I hate it. But not because it's David's business. It's more because I don't think I've ever had a proper Christmas the way other people have it.'

He hadn't ever had a proper Christmas either. He'd never known his parents and the foster parents he'd been placed with had all been various shades of uninterested, distracted and/or outright abusive. There had never been Christmas trees in his childhood. Never been presents either. Not for Christmas and none at all for his birthday, if anyone bothered to remember it. In fact, his childhood had been nothing but a hard slog.

Until he'd met Cleo. He'd been working in a garage helping out as a mechanic's assistant when her father had brought his expensive Porsche in for repair. Cleo had been with him and she'd been beautiful, so soft and delicate; he'd never seen anything like her. They'd got talking and she'd been as taken with him as he with her and they'd swapped numbers. Then they'd meet up in secret, since Cleo wasn't allowed out at night. It had turned physical very quickly and then, because they were sixteen and hadn't been careful, she'd fallen pregnant. Then everything had gone to hell.

In her and their child he'd seen the family he'd never had and so he was desperate to hold on to them both. He was earning money in the garage. He was sure he could support them. But Cleo's parents had found out about the pregnancy and had forbidden him to see her, though that hadn't stopped him from trying. He'd turned up on their doorstep one night, insisting on seeing her and generally making a pest of himself. Even threats to call the police hadn't worked. So Cleo herself had at last come to the door and she'd looked him in the eye, telling him that he needed to leave. That there was no future for them. She didn't love him, she didn't want him and frankly it was best for their baby if he wasn't in their lives.

Back then he'd thought her father had turned her against him, so full of uncontrollable teenaged fury, he'd returned with a baseball bat and had taken it to her father's Porsche, smashing the headlights and the front panels, and the windscreen.

He'd been stupid. Her father had called the police, he'd been charged, and a non-molestation order had been issued, forbidding him from contacting Cleo or her family. And he'd lost his son. He probably would have lost him anyway, but that one moment of rage had guaranteed it.

So he'd decided to fight, to work hard, accumulate as much money and power as he could, since if you were rich and powerful you could do whatever you wanted. And then he'd get his son back.

It hadn't worked out that way, but he'd never regretted the decision he'd made to leave Luke where he was. He couldn't find happiness for himself, but he could give it to his son and so he had.

That had been the last time he'd ever given anyone anything. Until Isla.

'What made it different?' he asked, watching her pretty face.

'We didn't have a Christmas tree,' she said. 'Or presents. Instead we'd donate our time to various charities, so I did a lot of volunteering in homeless shelters or children's charities. I didn't mind that, and I didn't mind not receiving presents. It wasn't about getting "things". It was just… Christmas is about spending time with your family, but David never spent any time with me.' Her finger drew another small circle on his chest, her attention on it. 'That's what I always wanted for Christmas. Just some time with him where we felt like a family. But he never gave it. I kept thinking that maybe if I'd been different somehow, he might have treated me like a daughter, but…he never did.' She gave a faintly bitter laugh. 'I was never allowed to call him Dad, for example. He adopted me legally, but we weren't a family.'

Orion could hear the hurt in her voice and it made him want to growl. And in fact, the more he heard about David the more he wanted to fly all the way to the UK and give the man the sharp edge of his tongue. Or perhaps a punch in the face. He didn't know what David had been thinking to adopt a young girl and then deprive her of the one thing she wanted most. It was cruel and thoughtless.

He dropped her curl and touched her cheek instead, stroking her silky skin. 'Is that what you wanted?' he asked softly. 'A family?'

She leaned into his touch, the unconscious movement making his chest tighten. 'Yes. That's why I was going to marry Gianni. David said that it was important that the future CEO have a family since Kendricks' is a family company, and that it was time I started mine. He wanted me to marry someone within the company too, and he thought Gianni and I would be a good fit.'

The subject of Gianni made Orion want to growl yet again. 'You didn't want him,' he said, unable to keep the possessive note from his voice.

Isla's blue gaze looked up and met his. 'No. You were right, I didn't. I didn't love him either. But I…hoped that maybe one day I would.'

He could see the truth in her eyes. She *had* wanted that.

'A family is important to you?' He didn't know why the words felt as if they were echoing hollowly inside him.

She nodded. 'I never had one of my own, Orion. I was given the taste of one. In fact, I had the taste of one twice, but… The first one didn't work out and with David… Well, that wasn't even a family. I was an employee, not a daughter.'

She deserves one, too, especially after David essentially sold her to you. And you can't give it to her.

His chest felt unaccountably tight. He could see that now, how little Kendrick had cared for the daughter he'd adopted, for the person that she was. How he wanted an ideal to head his company, someone exactly like himself, not a living breathing woman with thoughts and feelings and desires of her own.

And you were complicit in that.

He didn't like that thought. He didn't like how regretful and vaguely ashamed of himself it made him feel. It didn't help knowing he'd never give anyone a family let alone her either. And not because he couldn't, but because he didn't want to. He'd had a partner and a child once, and he'd wanted to keep both of them more than he'd wanted his next breath.

But Cleo and his child had been taken from him. Cleo by her parents and then by her own choice, and his child along with her.

He'd had his taste of a family and when he'd lost it, it had nearly broken him. He didn't want to do it again, not for anyone.

'You'll find a family of your own one day, Snow White,' he said. 'Of that I have no doubt. In the meantime, I don't see why *we* can't have a proper Christmas.'

Emotions flickered in her blue gaze, so many and so fast he couldn't untangle them all. But then the sharp glitter of pain faded and her mouth softened. 'I'd like that. Did you ever have one? A proper Christmas, I mean?'

'No. I grew up in the foster system, like you did, and the homes I was placed in never seemed to celebrate it.'

Interest lit her eyes. 'Oh? What happened to your parents?'

There was no reason not to tell her. 'I never knew them. They were itinerant workers, traveling around Europe, and I think I was born somewhere in the Mediterranean, though no one quite knows for certain since I never had a birth certificate. They came to the UK eventually—don't ask me how—and were found one morning dead in a tent in a campsite. Overdose, I was told later. Anyway, someone heard me crying and so I was rescued and put into care.'

Her brow creased with sympathy. 'I was the child of a single mum. She died when I was four and she had no family so I was put into care too.' She stared at him as if he was the most interesting thing she'd ever seen in her life. 'I had no idea you had the same experience.'

He liked the way she looked at him. It was addictive as hell. 'My background isn't a secret. There are numerous bios floating around on the internet. It wasn't pleasant, but I got through it.'

'I want to hear all about it.' She pressed her mouth to his chest and gave him a kiss. 'But first I want my present.'

He smiled. 'Not only impatient but demanding too. Say please and I might tell you what it is.'

Excitement sparkled in her gaze. 'Please tell me it's the hot pool.'

'I couldn't possibly say.'

'Orion.' She shifted, sliding the rest of her body on top of his, pressing her delectable curves against him. 'Tell me.'

He was getting hard again, hunger turning his blood hot. He ran a hand down her back and squeezed the soft flesh of her bottom, making her gasp. 'Say please.'

'Please,' she murmured breathlessly. 'Tell me about my present, *please*.'

He laughed and told her. 'Yes, the hot pool. Tonight.'

CHAPTER NINE

THE HOT POOL turned out to be in a small hidden gorge just behind the lodge. The water was a bright mineral blue and steam rose from it in clouds. A wooden path led to the pool from the lodge, which then gave on to a flat area flagged in stone with some stone steps that led down into the water. A small wooden changing cabin stood nearby, well equipped with thick, fluffy towels, though they didn't need the cabin and Isla didn't need her bikini either since they were swimming naked.

Orion was already in the water by the time Isla had finished stripping off, and he stood in the middle of the pool, by the stone steps, his hand outstretched to help her down. She was freezing, the stone beneath her bare feet icy, and as she took his hand and went quickly down into the hot water, she gasped a little at the shock of it. It felt so warm and silky sliding over her skin after the frigid air, making her shiver.

The pool was wonderfully deep and she followed Orion into the deeper water, getting her shoulders under and sighing in pleasure as the heat stole away the remaining cold.

There was something magical about being submerged in warm water while snow drifted in the air.

The gorge itself was lit with small lights powered by solar batteries, the illumination enough to see the path and the edge of the pool, but not enough to obscure the glittering black bowl of the night sky upturned above them.

Orion was behind her, his powerful arms circling her as she leaned back against him, looking up at the stars. He'd promised her the northern lights tonight and she was excited to see them. In fact, she'd been excited about everything the past couple of days and she couldn't remember the last time she'd felt that.

She hadn't regretted her decision to sleep with him again, not for a single moment. And when he'd laid claim to her body that morning, she'd decided that well, he could have it. She hadn't thought what would happen the next day when she'd given herself to him in the hallway the day before, and that he wanted to keep her in his bed for the whole of the next ten days was okay by her. More than okay.

She still felt bad that her gifts to him weren't nearly as wonderful as his were. He'd said that he wanted to know more about her, but she was running out of interesting things to tell him. Were her favourite colour and food really all that interesting? He'd been amused by her Christmas confession, which had pleased her, and then he'd been so understanding when she'd told him why. And when he'd told her about his own childhood, and how similar it had been to hers, she'd felt…almost amazed. She'd met very few people who'd had similar experiences and to find that he'd been in the foster system too… Well, it had felt as if a bond had been created between them.

She felt vaguely ashamed of herself that she hadn't known. Then again, she hadn't liked him for a long time and had told herself she didn't want to know anything about him. Perhaps if she'd known about his childhood, she might have felt differently.

Not that it mattered. She felt differently about him now. In fact, she thought she might like him now. She definitely liked the way he touched her, the bonfire they created between them when they were in bed together. And she liked how he listened to her, looking at her as if every word that came out of her mouth was of intense interest to him. She liked how he teased her and how there was affection and warmth in his cold, deep voice whenever he did so. And she liked how he responded when she teased him, the amber of his eyes glinting with a wickedness that only made her want to tease him even more.

In fact, the only shadow on the day had been that morning when they were in bed together and he'd said, *'You'll find a family of your own one day, Snow White.'*

She didn't know why that made a kind of hollowness gather in her chest. Because she *would* find a family of her own one day. A family that was hers, that she got to keep. Who wouldn't send her away or be disappointed because she wasn't what they wanted.

It wouldn't be with Orion, naturally. It would be with someone who wanted the same things she did. Who would be good for the company, of course, and who would love to have children, because she wanted children.

She didn't have to be in love with him. Love had been a scarce commodity in her own life—in fact, she didn't know if anyone had ever loved her, apart from her mother—but she'd managed to survive without it so far.

And if it took time for love to develop between her and her chosen partner, then she was fine to wait for it.

You could fall in love with Orion.

The thought streaked through her brain like a comet streaking through the night sky, a brief burst of glowing light that she quickly shoved away. No, she wasn't going to fall in love with Orion. Absolutely not. He didn't love her and while that wasn't necessary, she did want someone who'd stick around for the duration. And he definitely wouldn't. He'd already told her that she was only here so he could get to the bottom of his fascination with her and then once he had, he'd move on.

Plus, he'd said that he hoped she'd find her family one day, obviously implying that it wouldn't be with him. Which was fine. Absolutely fine. She didn't want to be with someone who didn't want her and didn't want what she wanted.

Their marriage had to stand for a year, according to his promise, but after that she'd be free to find someone else. She didn't know why that thought made her throat close up.

Orion shifted her head so it rested on his shoulder and then pointed out a few of the major constellations, murmuring softly in her ear.

'Where's your belt?' she said, hoping to make him laugh.

And he did, a soft rumble in her ear. 'Very funny.'

'I bet you get that a lot.'

'Not as much as you might think.' His hands drifted over her beneath the water, undemanding and gentle.

The sky was black and deep above them, the stars glittering pinpricks of light.

Except she couldn't concentrate on the sky, not when

she was resting against his hot skin and his hands were on her, making her shiver and ache, making her long for something she couldn't name.

'Are you going to tell me any secrets?' she asked him idly. 'Or do I only get a fun itinerary of excursions?'

His hands stroked down her thighs. 'Do you want secrets from me?'

She wasn't sure why she was asking him about it. Probably because all her gifts to him seemed lame in comparison with volcano tours, skating and hot pools. Plus, he said he was fascinated with her and wanted to know her, but she wanted to know about him too. And he hadn't told her much about himself.

'I like what you've given me so far, don't get me wrong,' she said. 'I've loved the volcano and the skating, and this pool is magical, but... You know quite a lot about me, but I don't know anything about you apart from the fact that you were in the foster system.'

His hands slid up over her stomach and cupped her breasts. 'I wasn't aware you were interested in more than excursions.'

There was no heat in the words and yet she could sense a sudden tension in him. 'Perhaps I am.' She tried to sound as if she didn't care one way or the other. 'Perhaps I'd like to hear a couple of secrets. I can't be the only one to give up mine.'

He didn't say anything for a long moment. 'That would constitute an extra present.'

'I know, but I gave you an extra one yesterday,' she pointed out. 'A kiss *and* me.'

His thumbs circled her nipples lazily. 'Are you sure you wouldn't rather have something else?'

He was trying to distract her. Which meant that he didn't want to tell her. So, did that mean he did have secrets? And did that also mean that they were painful? If his childhood hadn't been easy then his life couldn't have been, so maybe they were.

'I might,' she allowed, since she was starting to feel hot and it wasn't just the water in the pool. 'But I'd rather have a secret first.'

For a long moment he was silent. Then his hands dropped from her breasts and he slid an arm around her waist, bringing her over to the side of the pool where there was a stone seat beneath the water.

He sat her down on it and then sat beside her, tilting his head back as he stared up at the sky. 'When I was sixteen I fell in love, and she fell pregnant unexpectedly. She came from a wealthy family, and I was just a sixteen-year-old foster kid working in a garage, and her family didn't approve. When they found out about the pregnancy, they stopped me from seeing her, and when our son was born, they stopped me from seeing him too.'

Isla went very still. His voice was smooth and even, betraying no hint of his feelings. He said the words as if they'd happened a long, long time ago and to someone else.

'I was furious, of course. When Cleo's father told me I couldn't see my son, that I wasn't even named on his birth certificate, I took a baseball bat from home and smashed up his car with it. That naturally enough earned me a police warning and a non-molestation order.'

The breath went out of her, a soundless sigh of shock. Again, his face betrayed nothing but casual interest as he stared at the sky. But the fact that he was searching it so intently told her everything she needed to know.

This was painful for him. Terribly, exquisitely painful.

'I swore that I'd get him back at some point,' Orion went on. 'When I had enough money and power, and about ten years ago, that's exactly what I did. Or at least that's what I intended to do.'

Isla realised she'd gone tense in the water, staring at him fascinated. 'What happened?' she asked, because something had. She hadn't heard anything about him having a child.

'Oh, I decided that I'd leave him with his family,' Orion said casually. 'I walked in during his birthday party and he was surrounded by his family, and he was so…happy.' For the first time Isla heard a hint of roughness in his voice. 'I couldn't take him away from that. He didn't know me. He didn't even know I existed. And I couldn't bring myself to take a ten-year-old boy away from the only family he'd ever known. So I turned around and walked out.'

There was a lump in Isla's throat, and it was painful. She swallowed, her heart aching. A few days ago she wouldn't have believed him. He was a man who took what he wanted, when he wanted it—that's what he'd told her. Yet he hadn't taken back his own child. He'd seen that his son was happy and he'd put his child's happiness before his own.

What must it have been like for him to come into that party and see his son surrounded by people who loved him? Seeing him happy? And knowingly giving that up for himself…

Isla stared at Orion's rough, handsome profile as he

looked up into the sky. At the hard lines of his face. 'I'm sorry,' she said thickly. 'That must have been—'

'Good,' he said, cutting her off. 'It was good. And satisfying to know he was loved and he was happy.' His hard mouth curved in a smile that had nothing of amusement in it. 'The gift of my absence was the only thing I could give him in that moment and so that's what I gave him.'

She could hear the roughness in his voice again, so very slight and not at all noticeable if she hadn't been listening for it. But she had been listening for it.

The gift of his absence…

God, how painful that must have been for him. He was an intense man, a passionate man, and there was fire in him deep down. She'd seen it burn. He must have wanted his child badly and to have to give that child up. To have that child never even know he existed…

Her heart twisted painfully and tears prickled behind her eyes. But it wasn't her sadness to bear, it was his, so she forced it away. 'Have you ever tried to meet him since?' she asked. 'Or has he ever tried to contact you?'

Orion shook his head. 'I decided it would be easier for all concerned if I just pretended he didn't exist for me the way I didn't exist for him. So no, I haven't contacted him nor has he contacted me. I don't know where he is or what he's doing and it's better that way.'

Isla looked away, blinking fiercely against the insistent tears. 'How could they take him away from you?' she couldn't help asking, her heart burning at the unfairness of it. 'How could they not even acknowledge you?'

He shrugged. 'I was just some poor kid who'd impregnated their daughter. And Cleo… She was so young and she was scared. I told her I'd look after her, but I wouldn't have been able to. I was sixteen. I had no qualifications and my job was part-time and paid a pittance. I couldn't have looked after a partner and a child, no matter how badly I wanted to at the time.'

'That wasn't fair,' she said, knowing she shouldn't keep pressing the issue, but unable to stop herself. 'They should have allowed you contact at least.'

Orion finally glanced at her, amber eyes dark. 'After I'd taken a baseball bat to the family car? I don't think so. And I don't blame them for it either. I was young and stupid and full of rage, and I wouldn't have allowed contact with me either.'

He's not angry, so why are you? It's not your trauma.

Except he was angry, she was sure of it. He was so rigidly controlled, keeping all the fire inside him locked down, and there had to be a reason for that. Was it to do with his son? Was it to do with the fury he must still feel and the pain that had to be there? Fury and pain that had nowhere to go and so he simply locked them both away?

She stared into his eyes and yes, she could see that wolf gold gleaming. He felt the pain of having a child he could never acknowledge, and the rage of having that child taken from him. Then the agony of knowing he could never see that child again, because that was what was best for the child.

I gave him the gift of my absence...

No one would ever know what he'd sacrificed. No one except her.

Isla didn't know what to say. She didn't have a child, but she knew what it was like to have the family she'd once longed for denied, and she knew how painful that was.

So she turned to him, shifting on the stone seat so she

was sitting in his lap, facing him. Then she took his face between her hands and kissed him.

Isla's mouth was soft and hot and he could taste salt on her lips. They were tears, tears for him.

He wanted to tell her that she didn't need to cry for him, that what had happened with Luke was all in the past. That he was done with it now and had come to terms with it. But there was something burning inside him, the rage and the pain that had never dissipated despite the years and all the assurances he'd made to himself. The love for a son he would never know and who would never know him.

It enraged him to feel any of those things. He'd thought he'd cut them out of his heart, but it seemed they were still there, and they ached, they burned.

He shouldn't have told her about Luke. He should never have said anything, but she'd wanted a secret from him and that was the only secret he had. He'd thought he should tell her anyway, after that conversation they'd had in bed that morning, and how she'd mentioned wanting a family. Whether she felt anything for him at all beyond desire or not, she should know at least that she couldn't look to him for that family, and here was the one reason why.

It should have been easy to tell her. It shouldn't have hurt. Yet when he'd turned to her and found her watching him, anger burning in her blue eyes, he could feel the pain ache inside him.

She's right. It wasn't fair.

Perhaps it wasn't, but there was nothing to be done about it now. He'd made his decision back in that Chelsea townhouse and if he had to make that decision again, he'd make the same one. But he didn't want her to hurt for it. That wasn't why he'd told her.

He lifted his hands and pulled hers away from him, raising his head. She was staring at him, the expression on her face fierce with sorrow and anger.

'Don't,' he said. 'Don't be sad for me. It was the only decision I could have made.'

'I know. Of course you wouldn't have wanted to take him away from his family. But *you're* his family too. You know that, don't you?'

Something shifted inside him, the ache a grief that never went away. He ignored it. 'I'm not his father, Isla,' he said. 'I didn't bring him up. I haven't been in his life. I'm nothing but a stranger to him.'

'You *are* his father. His biological father.' Her eyes glinted deep sapphire in the night. 'He'll want to know where he came from and what happened to you and I know that, because I never knew my biological father myself. He wasn't on my birth certificate. I've got nothing and I wish I could have had something.'

She was warm and slippery and silky in his lap and there were many other things they could be doing right now other than talking about a past that was dead and gone.

'Let it go.' He put his hands on her hips, holding her carefully. 'I have.'

'No, you haven't.' She was still staring fiercely at him. 'You're angry, Orion. I can see it in your eyes. And it hurts you, doesn't it?'

He could feel the heat of it in his chest, the sharp edges of a fire that had never burned itself out. She saw too much, his snow maiden.

'I made my choice,' he said flatly. 'I let him go. And it's easier if he stays gone.'

'Easier for who? For him or for you?'

Anger gathered in his gut and he couldn't help responding to it. 'This is none of your business, Isla, and I didn't ask for your input.'

Yet her jaw was tense and she didn't look away. 'He'll be twenty now. He'll be an adult. He'll be able to make decisions for himself about whether he finds out who is father is.'

'Yes, well, and he hasn't.' The words came out of him with such bitterness he could hardly believe he'd said them.

Isla's gaze flared, a deep sympathy in it that caught at the edges of his emotions as if they were still raw and new, making them hurt. 'Oh, Orion,' she said softly.

Abruptly he couldn't bear to be there with her any longer. He didn't want her looking at him like that, he didn't want her digging at the wound in his heart he'd thought long healed. He'd come to terms with the fact that he didn't have his son in his life and he'd chosen that himself. The fact that Luke hadn't contacted him was neither here nor there, and he wasn't upset about it. At all.

He tightened his grip on her hips, wanting to put her off his lap, but her arms were around his neck all of a sudden, and her cheek was against his shoulder, and he could feel the soft heat between her thighs pressing against him.

'I'm sorry,' she whispered. 'I don't mean to push you. I don't want to make it worse. It's just…not fair. You're a good man and you didn't deserve for him to be taken away from you.'

His throat was tight for a second and he couldn't move,

couldn't breathe. 'I was angry,' he heard himself say. 'I smashed up that car. No child deserves a violent, angry father.'

'You were a sixteen-year-old boy.' Isla turned her head and kissed his chest, her lips warm against his skin. 'A boy who'd been through the foster system. It's not as if you had the emotional maturity to know what you were doing. And they didn't give you a chance. That's on them, not you.'

Orion shut his eyes. He didn't know why he was still sitting there, listening to her, when he'd been about to get up and leave. He wanted distance, didn't he? He didn't want to keep talking, not about Luke. He'd made the right decision all those years ago, he had.

'I couldn't go back,' he said hoarsely. 'I knew I wouldn't be welcome and besides, I couldn't do anything. Cleo's father had money and contacts and I was... nothing. But I swore that one day, when I had money and power, I'd come back for him. Except I couldn't take him then either.'

Isla pressed another kiss to his chest. 'You put your child first. That's what a good father does.'

He wasn't gripping her now, his hands still on her thighs, the ache in his heart sharp and jagged. 'If I was a good father, I'd have fought for him more.' He shouldn't be telling her this and yet he couldn't seem to stop. 'If I was a good father, I wouldn't have let him go.'

'You *didn't* let him go.' Isla lifted her head, her blue gaze burning. 'You couldn't stop them, because you were too young. And by the time you were old enough to get him, you *couldn't*. Not without destroying his life.'

He knew that was only the truth and yet... Why did

it feel as if he could have done things differently? As if he'd let his son slip through his fingers. As if he hadn't fought for him at all.

And you're doing the same thing now.

The thought slid through him, sharp and insidious, and abruptly he was sick of talking.

He shifted one hand to her hip and gripped it, before sliding his fingers up her inner thigh. 'I'm tired of talking about this,' he said roughly. 'I'd prefer to do something else.'

But Isla ignored him. 'Why haven't you looked for him?'

The question felt like the edge of a knife against his skin. 'Didn't you hear me?' he snapped. 'This subject is closed.' It was a warning and he'd intended it to be.

Yet again, she just ignored him, her gaze searching. 'What are you afraid of?'

The knife slid into him, so sharp he barely felt the cut. But he certainly felt the pain, bright and hot.

You know what you're afraid of. That he'll blame you. That he'll tell you that you didn't fight hard enough. That you didn't want him enough. That he needed you and you weren't there for him.

The water was warm, but he felt the ice in his gut, sharp as a sliver of glass.

He needed distance. He needed to get away from Isla and her interrogation, prompting him to question things he hadn't questioned for years. To think about the boy he'd given up, the sacrifice he'd made because he'd thought it was the right thing.

It might have been, but then you cut him out of your life. How is that being a good father?

It wasn't; that was the issue. What man repudiated his own son?

You never build. You only destroy.

He shoved the thought away and gently, but firmly, put Isla from his lap and back onto the stone seat.

'Orion?'

He didn't look at her, pushing himself off the seat and moving over to the stairs.

'Orion.' There was a splash and when he glanced behind him, she was moving through the water after him. 'I'm sorry. I shouldn't have said anything.' She was upset, he could see that, her golden hair streaming down her back and floating like pretty golden kelp around her white shoulders. Her gaze had darkened. 'Please don't go.'

But the sliver of glass in the centre of his heart, the kernel of ice that had settled there the day he'd left his son for the final time, wouldn't go away. And everything she said only made him more aware of it. More aware of the pain and the rage that he'd thought had been vanquished and hadn't.

He shouldn't be around her when he was like this. It wasn't fair on either of them.

'I have some work to catch up on.' He tried to make his voice sound gentle and yet there was nothing of gentleness in him. 'You can stay here for as long as you like. The northern lights are—'

'I don't care about the northern lights.' The heat of the water had flushed her cheeks a deep pink and with her darkened eyes, she looked like a painting. A Venus in the water. 'I hurt you.'

He laughed because the idea that he'd let anyone hurt him was preposterous. Yet the sound wasn't quite as amused as it should have been. 'You didn't.' He turned away, because if he didn't get out now he was going to ruin her present with his mood and that was unacceptable. 'There are towels—'

Slender arms slid around his waist, holding him tight and a soft, warm body pressed up against his back. He stilled, his heart beating uncomfortably fast.

'Please don't go,' Isla whispered. 'It won't be the same if you're not here.'

It felt as if there was a large boulder sitting on his chest and he wasn't sure why. 'I'm not in the mood for swimming.' His voice was too rough. 'And I don't want to spoil it for you.'

'You won't spoil it for me. I was pushing and I shouldn't have, and I'll stop.'

The tightness in his chest shifted. 'Don't worry. I'll still see you in bed later.'

'I don't… It's not about sex.' Her arms closed tighter around him. 'I want you, your company. Please. Don't let me push you away.'

A cold shock went through him. Is that how she saw it? Did she think this was her fault? Her questions might have touched on some old wounds, but it was his baggage they were dealing with, not hers.

He could have pulled away then. Got out of the pool and headed back to the lodge. Left her there in the night to experience the beauty of the aurora on her own. But she didn't want that, he could hear the plea in her voice.

For some inexplicable reason, a completely baffling reason, she wanted him. And not just his body and the physical pleasure it could bring her, but she wanted *him*.

She wanted his company. He couldn't remember the last time someone had wanted that.

His life was all about business, about the hunt. He had colleagues, but he didn't cultivate friends. No one wanted to be friends with a pirate after all, and the ones who did were pirates themselves and he didn't trust them.

The women he slept with loved spending time with him, but only in bed. They didn't want to spend time with *him*. Then again, he'd never encouraged closeness, not with anyone.

He hadn't encouraged it with Isla either and yet somehow, here she was with her arms around him, wanting him to stay. Wanting his company.

Leaving was what he should do. But for some reason, around her, he never did what he should.

Orion turned and looked down. She still had her arms around him, her dark gaze staring up into his, and he knew in that moment he couldn't say no and he couldn't leave. His temper still raged and his heart still ached, and yet when she said 'please' like that and 'it won't be the same without you', he couldn't refuse. He didn't want to refuse. None of this was her fault after all.

'It's not you,' he said quietly. 'You didn't push me away. This is an old wound and your questions brought up some…issues that I thought I'd dealt with. But they're my issues, Isla, not yours. You have nothing to apologise for.'

'Whether they are or not, I'm still sorry. I just don't want you to go.'

He reached down and touched her cheek. 'I don't want to ruin your present.'

'You're not ruining anything.' She leaned into his touch

the way she had that morning in bed. 'Please, come and tell me about the aurora.'

The tightness in his chest eased. And he realised that there was nothing he wanted to do more than hold her in the water, in the warmth, watching that sky.

So he put away his pain and his rage, and he held her in his arms as the aurora borealis lit up the night sky and turned everything to glory.

CHAPTER TEN

THE NEXT FEW DAYS were amongst the happiest Isla had ever had. She put aside her worries about the company and the board. About David. About her and Orion's marriage. She put aside her worries about the future, full stop. It was the now that mattered and she'd decided to give herself to it wholeheartedly.

They continued the theme of gifts on the twelve days of Christmas and all Orion's gifts were magical. There was another flight to one of Iceland's gorgeous beaches and she saw blue-green icebergs sitting on the black sand like jewels. She took far too many photos of the icebergs and Orion and then made him take some photos of her.

There was an overnight trip to Amsterdam where they went to the Van Gogh Museum and she stayed there for hours, looking at the paintings with Orion patiently at her side. He didn't seem to mind as she waxed lyrical about each painting in great detail, or as he carried the umpteen dozen bags from her raid on the gift shop afterwards. Though that night in the luxury hotel in the middle of town, she made it up to him by letting him do whatever he wanted with her naked body before doing the same for him.

He gave her so many wonderful things and she couldn't

help feeling that she was failing by comparison. Her gifts to him were telling him more about her favourite artists and then her favourite foods. She told him about her silly fears and wildest dreams, and how she wished she had more memories of her mother.

She wished she had more to give him than these silly little pieces of herself, but she didn't know what. He didn't seem to need anything else.

Except that scene in the gorge in the hot pool wouldn't stop replaying in her head. Him telling her about the son he'd had taken from him, and then given up. There had been so much anger in his eyes, though he'd tried to dismiss it, and she hadn't made things any easier by pushing him on it.

She should have let it go, but the unfairness of the whole situation made her so angry. He didn't need her anger—it was clear he already had enough of his own—yet she hadn't been able to help it. She could see how it was hurting him and that felt like pain in her own heart too.

She'd only wanted to know why he hadn't contacted his son since, why he'd pretended that Luke didn't exist. The boy would be an adult now and surely if Orion wanted some contact, he could have reached out. He was a man who took what he wanted after all.

Yet he hadn't. And the only reason that made any sense to Isla was that he was afraid, though she didn't know what he'd be afraid of. He might be a corporate pirate but underneath that detachment and ruthlessness, Orion was a good man. Protective, and whether he knew it or not, kind. He might have used a threat to get her to marry him, yet he'd treated her with nothing but respect since they'd arrived. He'd given her choices. He hadn't forced her into anything.

She could understand that he might feel some trepidation about contacting his son, but to simply pretend that the boy didn't exist? She didn't understand that at all. And she might have dismissed it entirely if she hadn't sensed the pain that lay beneath his anger.

The loss of his son had created a wound inside him and it hadn't healed.

She hated that. He was a lion with a thorn in his paw and she wanted to be his Androcles. She wanted to take it out so he could heal.

As the days passed, she thought more about what she could do for him. She didn't stop to ask herself why his pain mattered to her so much, because she didn't want to delve too deeply into the reasons why. And when the idea of the perfect gift for him occurred to her as they flew back to Iceland from Amsterdam, she felt some trepidation. Because it was going to step over a line. Yet she couldn't get it out of her head.

When they returned to the lodge, she did some research, combing through social media to find what she was looking for. She didn't say anything to Orion—they hadn't spoken of anything personal since that night in the pool and she didn't want to rock the boat. Not when every moment she spent with him only made her want to spend more moments. Longer moments.

They discussed every subject under the sun, and she loved how he wasn't afraid to admit it when he didn't know something and how he always wanted to find out more. He told her a little more about his early life in the foster system and they traded stories with a black humour that most other people wouldn't have understood, but they did.

Sometimes he'd go into his office to handle a couple of work things and when he did, she'd go back to her search. Then a few days after they returned from Amsterdam, she finally found what she was looking for: Cleo's social media. Finding her son's after that was relatively easy.

There were pictures of Luke, a tall, handsome young man with coal-black hair and very familiar amber eyes. He looked so much like Orion that Isla's breath caught. And in a strange twist, she discovered that he was studying fine arts at university, and his social media pages were full of pictures of incredible sculptures he'd carved out of rock, and also of a lovely dark-haired girl who was clearly his girlfriend.

It felt wrong to look at pictures of him, to know more about him than his own father, but Isla couldn't stop herself. Besides, it wasn't as if Luke had been difficult to find. Orion could have looked for him at any time, yet he hadn't.

The next day, Orion unveiled his next present to her—a Christmas tree.

It was a living tree in an enormous pot and it was huge, the top almost brushing the ceiling of the lounge, filling the room with the crisp scent of pine. It had been decorated with tinsel and silver baubles and there was an angel on the top.

Isla loved it.

'You told me you'd never had a proper Christmas tree,' Orion said, watching her as she stared up in wonder at the tree. 'So I thought I'd provide you with your first.'

Her heart felt like he'd filled it up with light and now

it was pressing painfully against her ribs. A sweet pain. She hadn't thought he'd remember what she'd told him, but he had.

There were even a few carefully wrapped presents under the tree.

'This is amazing,' she said, reaching out to touch one of the delicate blue glass baubles. 'I actually did have a tree once. It was in that family that in the end didn't want me. They put up a little tree and there were decorations on it that their son had made and…and they put up one I had made too.' Her throat closed at the memory. 'It was the first time I felt like I was part of a family.'

There was warmth at her back and then Orion's arms slid around her, pulling her up against the hard heat of his body. 'I know it's not the same,' he murmured. 'But we can have a tree at least.'

Yet it was almost the same. She felt at peace here with him and if she squinted a little, she could imagine that the decorations on the tree had been made by their own children. And a sudden vision filled her head, of Christmas morning here, with the tree up and the fire going, and children unwrapping presents to the sounds of laughter and shrieks of delight.

Her heart clenched tightly in her chest, a shaft of longing piercing her.

She wanted that for herself.

What if this marriage was real? What if it was for ever?

That shaft of longing ached and ached, but she ignored it. Wanting their sham marriage to be real was ridiculous. And she hadn't known him long enough to start entertaining thoughts of a family with him, and apart from anything else, he'd basically implied that he wasn't looking to make a family with anyone. And why would he? When the one he'd had had caused him so much pain?

Which reminded her…

Are you sure this is a good idea?

Isla ignored that thought too. It was an opportunity, that's all it was, and he liked opportunities. He also didn't have to take it if he didn't want it, that was up to him. But he should still have the choice. He should know that there *was* a choice.

She stepped out of his arms and turned. 'I love it, Orion,' she said honestly. 'It's a beautiful gift.'

He smiled, his eyes full of warmth, and her heart caught. He was so gorgeous she sometimes didn't know what to do with herself. 'I hoped you'd like it,' he said. 'Now I'm feeling very smug.'

She wanted to tease him, tell him smugness wasn't a new feeling for him, but she was suddenly nervous. Perhaps this wasn't the right thing to do. But then… She hated the thought of this lion of a man going through the rest of his life with that thorn in his paw. With the constant nagging pain that wouldn't go away.

It wasn't fair. It wasn't right.

She swallowed and reached into her pocket for the piece of paper she'd put there that morning. 'Now it's time for my gift to you,' she said, her heart beating uncomfortably fast in her chest.

Orion frowned slightly. 'You look nervous,' he observed. 'Is it dangerous? An explosive of some kind?'

He was teasing her, which somehow made it worse. Perhaps this would ruin everything. He'd been upset before when she'd tried to push him in the pool about Luke, but… She had to do this. It was an opportunity, that's all.

Isla pulled the piece of paper out of her pocket and held it out. 'No. None of the above.'

Still frowning, Orion took the piece of paper and unfolded it, looking down at what she'd written. His frown deepened. 'What's this?'

Isla shoved her hands into the pockets of her jeans. 'It's an email address.'

'Whose email address?'

She took a breath and met his gaze. 'It's Luke's. Your son's.'

Orion went still, as if he'd been turned to stone, and yet something hot blazed suddenly in his gaze. 'Where did you get it?' He sounded so cool and calm, except she knew he was not. It was that blaze of gold in his eyes that gave it away.

You made a mistake.

A thread of ice wound through her, but she didn't look away. Perhaps this *was* a mistake, yet she'd made it now. There was no other option but to keep going.

'I found Cleo's social media profiles.' She tried to sound as calm as he did. 'And from there it was easy to find Luke's. He's studying fine arts at university, and he has a girlfriend. His email address is there and I thought...' She trailed off, her mouth dry.

Orion was standing so still, yet his golden eyes were blazing bright, fury rolling off him in waves. 'You thought what?' He sounded casual, as if he was asking her whether she preferred tea or coffee.

'I thought you might want to contact him,' she went on, because she'd given him the piece of paper now and there was no taking it back.

'And what makes you think I might want to do that?' His voice was dangerously soft.

Isla took a breath, her hands clenching in the pockets of her jeans. 'It's an opportunity, Orion. That's all it is. You don't have to take it if you don't want to. But I... I wanted to give it to you nonetheless.'

'Thank you,' Orion said. 'But this is one opportunity I think I'll pass on.' Then he moved over to the fire and casually threw the piece of paper into the flames, before turning around and walking straight out.

Anger moved in his blood like lava and once he was in his office with the door shut behind him, he had to stand in the middle of the room and take a couple of deep breaths just to stop himself from punching his fist through the nearest wall.

How dare she do that to him? How dare she bring up the subject of Luke again, after she'd told him that night in the gorge that she wouldn't? How dare she look for him and find him and *know* him?

It was none of her goddamn business.

'He's doing fine arts at university and he has a girl-friend.'

Orion stormed over to his desk and put his hands flat onto the desktop and leaned on them, staring down at the wood. He couldn't get a breath, rage and pain strangling him.

He didn't want to know. He'd cut Luke out of his life on purpose, because it was easier. Who the hell did she think she was bringing him back again?

'Easier for who? For him or for you?'

She'd said that to him the night in the pool, pushing

him, bringing up old doubts and old fears and old agonies. Old griefs he didn't want to deal with and didn't want to face. He wanted them to stay dead and buried where he'd put them.

Behind him he heard a sound, the door opening and slamming shut.

He pushed himself away from the desk and turned around sharply.

Isla had followed him, and stood there in the middle of his office, her golden hair in a cloud around her head, her blue eyes full of sympathy and yet also full of determination. 'I know you're angry with me,' she said. 'And I know I overstepped. I'm sorry. But you have to know that I did it for you. Because you're hurting.'

He bared his teeth at her, struggling to leash the anger that burned inside him. 'Perhaps I wouldn't be if you didn't keep bringing up things I didn't ask you to bring up.'

She didn't seem to be cowed by his anger. She even took a step closer, as if it didn't bother her in the slightest. 'I know that. And you don't have to do anything with the information. The choice is yours. But... Orion... He deserves to know you.' She took another step closer. 'He deserves to know what kind of father he has.'

Orion felt frozen even as the rage burned inside him. A fruitless, frustrated rage at the past. At all the chances that were taken from him. At the future he wanted so badly that had been denied him. He hadn't thought he'd still feel that, but he did. And it was pointless. The past was dead and gone, and he'd already chosen his future.

'The father he has is a man who destroys things,' he said through gritted teeth. 'A man who takes things apart.

He doesn't build anything. He doesn't create. He ruins everything he touches.'

Isla's eyes widened and a terrible compassion crossed her face. She moved, closing the distance between them. 'No,' she said softly, reaching for him 'No, that's not true.'

But before her hands could make contact, he grabbed her wrists, her skin warm against his fingers. He didn't want her to touch him. He couldn't bear the thought of it.

'It is true,' he said harshly, releasing her as quickly as he'd grabbed her. 'I ruined the wedding you planned. I ruined your hope for a family by paying off your fiancé. I threatened you with the destruction of your company to get you to marry me, and I'm still planning on taking it apart when the year is up. Tell me, Isla. What *haven't* I ruined?'

She blinked and he could see the sparkle of tears in her eyes. It tore something inside him. 'You didn't ruin *anything*,' she said passionately. 'Yes, you did those things, but you didn't force me into anything, Orion. You gave me choices and I made them. And you don't destroy things. You promised to keep the company intact and signed a legal agreement to do so. You created the most lovely Christmas here in the lodge, with a tree and presents. And you made me feel good about myself in a way no one ever has. You made me feel fascinating and precious and beautiful, as if I was worth something.' Her voice thickened, becoming husky. 'You made me feel wanted, Orion. And no one has ever made me feel that way, not one person.'

His chest tightened, but he shoved the feeling away. There was no room for anything but anger in his heart. 'Don't turn this into something it isn't, Isla,' he snapped harshly. 'I *bought* you, remember? Your father sold you to me for the price of Kendricks'. And I only wanted you because I was fascinated by you. It was about *my* fascination, not you.'

She went pale. 'So what are you saying? That everything we shared, everything we talked about, all those things you said to me… You didn't mean any of them? You were only pretending?'

He'd known that would hurt her, yet there wasn't any other way to make her see the truth of what he was. What he'd always been, even as a kid. Intense, desperate, wanting things he could never have. And what he couldn't have, he destroyed, like the bond he'd destroyed with his son. Cutting Luke out of his life as if he didn't exist.

He was selfish, that's what he was, and she needed to understand that.

'Of course, I was only pretending.' He had to force out the words, the rough edge in his voice turning them sharp and jagged. 'Did you truly think I meant any of it?'

She went white, her blue gaze darkening with hurt. 'But…you told me you never said anything you didn't mean.'

He had to end this. He had to bring this whole farce of a honeymoon to an end. He'd call a helicopter for her, send her back to the UK, get her out of his sight and out of his life, and then maybe once she was gone, everything would go back to normal.

'Well,' he said coldly. 'I lied.' He turned and went around the side of his desk, reaching into his pocket for his phone. He kept his gaze on the windows and the landscape outside. It was snowing, which wasn't ideal. 'I'm bringing this to a close, Isla,' he went on. 'It's been a nice week, but I believe I've come to the end of my fascination with you after all. It's time for you to go home.'

There was silence behind him, but he didn't turn around and he wondered if she'd leave him alone now, and felt something else tear inside him at the thought.

But he should have known she wouldn't go quietly. She had fire in her heart, the way he did, and abruptly she was coming around the desk and standing in front of him, small and curvy and as full of anger as he was.

'So you're just going to get rid of me like you did with Luke?' she demanded, apparently not caring that perhaps speaking his son's name wasn't a good idea. 'You're going to cut me out of your life? Pretend I don't exist either?' Hurt glittered in her blue eyes. 'What was it? Was it because I pushed? Because I got angry? Because I wanted too much?'

He held himself rigid, fought the need to reach for her and soothe her pain since that wouldn't make this any easier, not for him or for her. 'It's not you, Isla.'

'I don't believe that,' she flung back, her voice hoarse with pain. 'Not for a second. It's always me, Orion. Always. And no one ever tells me what I'm doing wrong, but it has to be something, otherwise why else would I always be the one who gets sent away?' A tear slid down the side of her nose. 'Why else would I always be the one no one wants?'

He'd wanted to push her away, to get her to storm out and away from him, but the pain in her eyes… Abruptly he hated himself and the lies he'd told her more than he'd thought possible.

He dropped his phone and reached for her, putting his hands on her hips and propelling her back against the windows and pinning her there with his body. She felt warm and soft against him and his rage began to change, to morph into something else, hotter and deeper and more demanding.

'It's nothing *you* did,' he said fiercely, staring down at her, wanting her to believe this if nothing else. 'I'm the destructive one. It's better if you're not anywhere near me.'

She was looking up at him, searching his gaze as if trying to find the truth there. 'I told you, you're not destructive,' she said huskily, somehow bypassing his rage and seeing the agony that still lived in his heart, the grief for the son he'd had to let go. 'Look, I know this is about Luke and I know you're afraid. But both of us understand what it's like to not have our parents in our lives. Wouldn't you want the chance to talk to your dad if you could? Wouldn't you want the chance to know him?'

She's right.

He couldn't remember his father or his mother, and part of him had been glad that he had no memories of them. Who'd want to remember parents who'd put an addiction to a drug over the needs of their own child? At least he hadn't put his son through that.

'Why would Luke want a father like me?' he heard himself say in a voice that didn't sound like his, so hoarse and raw. 'A father who gave him up?'

Isla lifted her hands to his face, her fingers cool on his hot skin. 'You didn't give him up, Orion,' she said softly. 'You gave him happiness. You gave him a place where he was safe and loved, and that's all a child really wants.' Her eyes were full of tears. 'And I know because that's all I ever wanted too.'

He wasn't sure when it changed, when the rage and the pain turned into heat and desperation. But it did. Perhaps it was the understanding in her eyes, the worry and the hurt that he knew was for him, and how she'd managed to tell him the one thing that made a difference. That walking away from his son had been the right thing to do. And of course she would know, she out of anyone would.

And you hurt her. You hurt her badly.

He'd only wanted to make this easier on both of them. A quick, clean ending. Yet by acting as though none of this past week had meant anything to him, that he'd been pretending all this time, he had hurt her in a place where she was exquisitely vulnerable: her own past and the rejections in it. It had been unconscionable of him and he regretted it with every part of him.

So he kissed her hard and deep, tasting her tears. Tasting her sweetness and the fire inside her. Tasting the understanding he'd never had from any other person. Wanting to give something back to her to make up for his cruelty, his selfishness. Especially when she was right. He'd been wrong to cut Luke out of his life. Wrong to let it go on so long, to pretend that his son didn't even exist. Because he couldn't. He'd never been able to.

'I loved him,' he whispered against her mouth. 'I loved him so much and it killed me to walk away from him.'

'I know.' Her hands were in his hair, smoothing it back. 'And Luke needs to know that too. He needs to know his father cared. You can't deny him, Orion. You can pretend he doesn't exist, but no matter what you do, you'll always be his father. No one can take *that* away from you.'

The truth of it settled down in him like a weight. She was right about that too. It didn't matter how much distance he put between himself and Luke, no matter how much he pretended he didn't have a son, that didn't change the fact that he did. And while life and circumstances had taken away his boy, the fact that he was Luke's father didn't change.

No one could take that away from him.

Need flooded through him, for her and for the gift she'd given him. Because she had given him a gift. The acknowledgement of his son. That he was Luke's father, that his blood ran in Luke's veins and that couldn't be ripped from him. That he was as much a part of his son as his son was part of him.

Orion deepened the kiss, sweeping his tongue inside her mouth, wanting to give her back something as precious as what she'd just given him. Except he didn't have anything except himself and his hunger and that's what he gave her.

Her arms went around his neck and when he picked her up and held her against the glass, she twined her legs around his waist, arching into him. Pressing the soft heat between her thighs against his achingly hard groin, raising his desire to fever pitch.

Orion forgot everything. Everything but the need to be inside her. He held her pinned to the glass as he undid the zip of her jeans, tugging them down and her knickers too until she was open to him. Then he got his own jeans undone and after adjusting their positions slightly, seconds later he was pushing inside her, making them both gasp aloud.

Her blue eyes were dark with desire and he couldn't look away, transfixed by all that burning sapphire. And as he moved inside her, he was conscious of something unfurling inside him, an awareness. Of her. Of the tight wet heat of her sex gripping him. Of her arms around his neck. Of her soft gasps of pleasure. Of her intoxicating scent.

Of her heart of fire.

And he knew.

He'd never get to the bottom of his fascination with her. There would be no end. She would continue to occupy his thoughts for the next week, the next month, the next year. She would continue to occupy his thoughts for ever.

Because his heart burned too and it always had. It burned with love for his son, a love he'd been trying to deny and yet in the end, hadn't been able to. It was too powerful. And now it burned with love for her too.

She'd set it alight that day in the gallery and that fire had never gone out; he just hadn't recognised it. Until now.

He moved harder, deeper, wanting to cover himself with her, inhale her sweetness and take it inside himself, because he knew too how this was going to end. He was going to have to give her up the way he'd given up Luke.

She wanted things he couldn't give her. Things he was done with. She wanted a family and he didn't. He'd had a family and it was gone, and he wasn't going to do it again.

It would hurt her. It would hurt her badly, and yet there was no other way this could go. But before that moment, he could at least give her some pleasure to take with her, so he did, slipping his fingers between her thighs and stroking her as moved. Making her moan and cry out and twist against him.

The orgasm came before he was ready and he wanted to resist it, to draw out the ecstasy for as long as possible, but it was too intense. It swept over both of them, relentless as a king tide, leaving them both gasping, and he held her for a long time against the glass, neither of them speaking.

Finally, he eased away and let her down gently so she was standing once again, then dealt with their clothing, taking his time because this was the last time he would touch her. The last time he'd kiss her, stroke her hair, touch her skin.

It was agony when he finally stepped away, but he did it.

Perhaps she had a sense of what was coming because her face was pale once again, all the pretty colour from her orgasm leached away from her skin. 'You're still going to send me away, aren't you?'

His heart ached at the hurt in her eyes. He hadn't thought she'd feel so strongly about all of this and that had been careless of him. He should have kept her at a distance. He should have made it all about sex and nothing more. He shouldn't have let her in.

But he had and now there was no help for it. He'd made his choice.

'I'm sorry, Isla.' He had to work to keep the rough edge from his voice. 'But yes, it's time for our honeymoon to end.'

She just stood there staring at him as if he'd made the ground she walked on suddenly disappear under her feet. 'Why? I thought it wasn't me?'

It hurt to look at the bewilderment on her face, but what could he say? Telling her how he felt would only make this even worse for her. Because how could he explain why love was always sacrifice? Why love was always pain? Better to spare her that while he could. She'd have plenty of time to figure that out for herself.

'It's not,' he said. 'But I never wanted a wife, Isla. I never wanted a family. I had one and then I lost it and I'm not doing it again.'

'So it's a choice,' Isla said flatly and it wasn't a question. 'This is something you're actively choosing.'

He didn't understand what she was getting at. 'Yes, didn't I just say that?'

'And what about for someone you loved? Would you do it for them?'

The question caught him off guard and for a second all he could do was stare at her, while his heart shouted, *Yes, I'd do it for you. I love you. And the family you want, I want too, and we could have one together.*

But he swallowed down the words. Because somewhere, somehow, at some point in time, he would destroy that family. He would ruin it, because that's what he did. Or maybe something else would happen and it would be ripped from him once again anyway. Either way, he couldn't risk it happening again. The first time it had just about destroyed him. The next time it would kill him.

'No,' he said quietly. 'Not even then.'

She didn't say anything for the longest time. Then finally all the fight seemed to drain right out of her, and she turned and left his office without a word.

CHAPTER ELEVEN

ISLA DIDN'T KNOW what to do. He'd told her it wasn't her, yet he was sending her away all the same and it didn't make any sense. The way it felt as if he'd ripped her heart out of her chest didn't make any sense either.

She'd only known him a week. What did it matter if he didn't want a family? She'd had that brief, wonderful vision of being here at Christmas time with a family of her own, one with children. Orion's children. And while that vision had made her long for it deeply, she could have that wonderful family Christmas with another man, couldn't she? It didn't have to be with Orion.

She didn't understand why that thought left her so desolate.

He spent the rest of the day in his office, only coming out to tell her that due to the weather, the helicopter wouldn't be able to take her back to the UK until tomorrow.

Getting rid of you the way that family got rid of you. Like David got rid of you.

She couldn't stop thinking about that, or about how Orion had told her that David had sold her to him. Because he had. She hadn't really taken it in when Orion had arrived at the church that day and told her about the deal he'd done with David, because she'd had too many other things to worry about.

But she was thinking about it now. How her happiness or what she wanted had never mattered to him. He hadn't considered those things at all; only the company had ever been important. Never her.

And it was clear she wasn't important to Orion either, if he could get rid of her the way everyone else had, with absolutely no difficulty whatsoever.

It hurt. It hurt so much.

That night he didn't join her in bed the way he normally did, so she lay awake, tossing and turning and aching. Until eventually, sometime before midnight, she got up and went downstairs.

The Christmas tree glowed in the room, the lights turned on and twinkling in the dimness.

She went over to it and sat down, staring up at the lights, her throat feeling sore and her eyes dry and gritty, her thoughts returning to Orion and the desolation she felt at being sent away. The agony seemed disproportionate to what was simply the end of a perfectly lovely affair and she had no idea why.

The end of that scene in his office earlier had been so painful, especially because she'd thought she was getting through to him. She shouldn't have followed him in there after he'd burned the gift of Luke's email address, but she couldn't stand leaving him alone with such pain. She'd wanted him to know that he didn't need to be afraid, that Luke would love him because—

Because you *love him. That's why it hurts so much. That's why you feel so desolate.*

The lights in the tree blurred, the whole world falling away.

She couldn't breathe. Was that true? Had she fallen in love with Orion? Was this why him sending her away left her feeling as though her heart had been ripped out? Why the thought of his pain made her hurt too? And why all she'd been able to see when he'd shown her the Christmas tree, had been children? Their children?

Her eyes closed and it felt as if the weight of an entire mountain was sitting on her chest.

He didn't want a family; he'd been very clear, and it was only now that she understood why. He must have felt this way, standing in the hallway of that house, watching his son. He must have felt this same tearing pain, and it was pain. The pain of wanting something with your whole heart and having to give it up.

No wonder he didn't want to revisit this feeling again. She'd asked him that in his office, if he'd change his mind about having a family with someone he loved, and he'd said no. Yet she hadn't understood the reality of her own question. She understood now, though. She understood completely.

Isla stared up at the lights, feeling tears slide slowly down her cheeks, her heart in agony, not knowing what to do.

You do *know what to do. You know deep down inside.*

Her throat closed. He didn't want her, the way that family hadn't wanted her. The way David didn't want her. Oh, they all thought they did. They'd all liked the idea of her, but when it came to the reality of her in their lives, they'd changed their minds.

And you let them. You never fight to stay.

It was true. That family that sent her back, she'd never told them not to. She'd never told them she wanted to stay. She'd never done that with David either. She'd done what he wanted, because she hadn't felt as if she could rock the boat.

You have so much fight, but you never fight for what you actually want.

A shiver went through her. It was true, she hadn't, and she hadn't because she was afraid. Afraid that even fighting wouldn't be enough. That *she* wouldn't be enough. Just like she hadn't been enough for David or that family. Or Orion.

So, what? You're just going to leave? Like a good little dog?

Isla closed her eyes, her throat aching. But what else could she do? She could fight for what she wanted, fight for more, fight for this marriage they'd entered into, but Orion didn't want that. He'd been very clear. And who was she to change his mind?

He sacrificed having his son in his life in order to make Luke happy. But does that mean he has to sacrifice his own happiness too? Doesn't he deserve some himself? A chance for it at least?

A shiver went through her like a small electric shock. Yes, he *did* deserve more. He deserved a *lot* more. He'd sacrificed everything for his son, leaving precious little for himself except a view of himself as selfish and destructive, which was the opposite of the man he truly was. The man she'd fallen utterly and completely in love with.

That man deserved happiness. That man deserved everything.

And you think you're the one to give it to him? After he told you he didn't want you?

She didn't have much to recommend her. She had a temper and she cared too much about things. She was too stubborn and she pushed when she shouldn't. She wasn't CEO material at all, and she clearly hadn't been daughter material for anyone.

But as he'd shown her, that temper, that passion was a strength, not a weakness. It came from love and he needed to know that. He needed to know that she loved him, that his happiness mattered to her and she was prepared to fight for it.

Her last gift to him would be her heart, and while it might still not be enough for him, it was worth the risk to offer it. Because he was more important than her own fear. Because he was worth it, full stop.

She wiped her eyes and finally got to her feet, and then she turned around.

To find Orion standing behind her, tall and gorgeous and dressed only in a pair of jeans.

She hurriedly wiped her eyes again. 'Sorry. Was I making a noise?'

He stared down at her, his beautiful face enigmatic. 'No. What are you doing up?'

'I couldn't sleep.' She swallowed and straightened. 'I... I've been thinking.'

'Isla—'

'No, let me finish.' She took a breath and squared her shoulders. 'I never fought when that family sent me away. I never told them I wanted to stay. And I never told David that I wanted to be his daughter either. I just did what I was told, because I thought not making a fuss, not rocking the boat, would make me more acceptable. But it didn't.' She swallowed and met his gaze head-on. 'And now I'm tired of not making a fuss. I'm tired of trying to be more acceptable. I'm tired of letting myself be sent away and not fighting for what I want. And what I want is you, Orion. What I want is your happiness. You think you're this terrible, selfish destructive person, but you're not. You think your happiness isn't important, but it is. It is to me.' She gripped tight to her courage and looked into his dark amber gaze, letting her conviction burn in hers. 'I know you don't want a family again. I know you don't want a wife. But you loved your son so much, and I think that no matter what you tell yourself, you *do* want that. And I can give it to you. I *want* to give it to you.'

She glanced at the clock on the mantelpiece and saw that it had just turned twelve, so she glanced back. 'So today's gift to you is my heart, Orion. Because I love you.'

Orion didn't understand the words at first. He'd got up because he hadn't been able to sleep either, and had seen her sitting under the tree. There had been tears on her cheeks and his heart had twisted and ached. He shouldn't have gone to her. He'd made the right decision yesterday to give her up, for her own good, and he thought he wouldn't regret that decision.

Yet all he felt was regret. Especially now, because apparently, she loved him and he had no idea, no idea at all what to do with that. It didn't make any sense after yesterday, when he'd been so cruel to her.

'Why?' he said, unable to think of a single reason why she should.

'Because you're kind and patient, and caring and

strong. Because you took me to Amsterdam and listened to me witter on about Van Gogh, and asked me questions and were interested. And you took me to a volcano and you showed me how to skate, and you showed me the northern lights.' She took a step forward, her blue gaze fierce. 'You showed me pleasure and you showed me your pain. You showed me your heart and you showed me your love. And I… I will never be the same, Orion. How could I? I didn't know what love was until you told me about Luke and what you did for him, and then I couldn't understand how he wouldn't love you. Because I loved you.' She took another step. 'All I want is happiness for you—I don't care about anything else. So please let me try. Please let me try to make you happy.'

She was so beautiful standing under the tree, her dark blue eyes glittering like the lights of the tree itself. Like the aurora.

The gift of her heart. She had already given him so much, how could he say no? He loved her already and what she was offering him…he wanted it so badly. He *wanted* it.

She deserves happiness, too, and hers is just as important as yours.

He didn't want another family. He couldn't bear the thought. But he also couldn't bear the thought of her giving up her own happiness for him. He didn't want her doing what he'd done all those years ago, sacrificing a future for love.

So give it to her. You want it too. Don't deny it.

'You shouldn't love me, Isla,' he heard himself say. 'All I'll do is hurt you.'

She lifted a shoulder, seeming casual, yet there were

more tears in her eyes. 'It's too late for that, I love you already.'

You want this. You want more. You want it all. You always have.

He did—he could feel it, burning there in his heart. A bone-deep longing for love, family, a home, a place where he belonged. For children that were his, that he didn't have to give up and a woman at his side whom he loved and who loved him. No more breaking. No more destroying. Only building. Only creating.

You can't send her away. You can't reject her like everyone else. She deserves more than that.

He felt as if he was on the edge of a cliff and the wild wind was trying to pull him off. 'Isla...' He couldn't sound detached now and he didn't even try. 'If you were smart, you'd leave me. You'd get on that helicopter and you'd never come back.'

There was something hot in her blue eyes, something fierce. The love she'd offered him, her burning heart. 'Do you want me to? Do you really want me to?'

He should have said yes. He should have turned and walked away. But he couldn't, not this time. The thought of her pain if he sent her away was too much, because no, she *didn't* deserve that. She didn't deserve to bear the brunt of his fear. And that's what it was, wasn't it? Fear of the pain that love was, fear of risking his heart again. Fear that he didn't deserve this second chance somehow.

But she thought he did, and she thought his happiness was important, and what was important to her, was also important to him, so...how could he refuse her? How could he let his pain and fear be more important than her love? He couldn't.

Something burst free in him in that moment and it came to him, in a sudden rush of insight, that loving her wasn't a sacrifice. Loving her didn't mean having to give her up. Loving her meant joy. Loving her meant happiness, because that's what he'd had with her here in this little lodge.

For the first time in his life, he'd been happy. And he could keep that happiness if he wanted it. He could keep it for ever.

Orion North was a man who took what he wanted and so he took what she offered him. Because he wanted it more than he wanted his next breath.

'No,' he said roughly. 'No, I don't.' And somehow the distance between them was gone and she was in his arms, warm and soft against him, her face pressed to his chest.

'I want this,' she said, her voice muffled. 'I want you. I want everything, Orion. If you truly don't want a family, that's okay. We don't have to have one. I can—'

He took her face between his palms and kissed her before she could go on, and then he lifted his mouth and looked down into her eyes. And he let the wind pull him off the cliff and he was flying. 'No,' he said. 'I don't want you giving up what you want for me. What you want is important, because *you're* important. I told you the truth yesterday, when I said you weren't a fascination to me any more. You aren't. Because you're more than a fascination, more than an interest.' He bent and brushed his mouth over hers. 'The truth is that I love you. And I have loved you since that moment I saw you in the gallery, luminous and beautiful and everything I ever wanted.'

Something lit in her face then, an incandescence that ignited something in him. 'Can we stay married then? Please. I don't want anyone else to be my husband but you.'

'Yes.' He brushed another kiss over her mouth. 'We'll stay married for a year. For five. For ten. For ever, Snow White, and that's a promise.'

She put her arms around his neck, arching into him. 'We don't have to have many children. Just one if that's all you want.'

He tightened his hold on her, because she was where she'd always been meant to be. Where he'd always wanted her to be right from the first moment he saw her. Here in his arms. 'We will have as many children as you want.'

'And Christmas. I want a proper Christmas.'

'Always. Every Christmas will be a proper one.' Then, because he'd had enough of talking, he covered her mouth and kissed her hard and deep and long.

Orion had always thought love was pain, an agonising sacrifice. He'd never known that love could also be joy, a foundation of happiness on which to build a life.

And together they built that life,

And it was glorious.

EPILOGUE

CHRISTMAS MORNING AT the lodge was always chaos, but Isla didn't mind.

She sat on the couch next to Orion, while their twins, Ava and Molly, squealed with delight as they opened their presents.

Orion had their new son in the crook of his arm, rocking him absently as he talked to Luke, who had joined them for Christmas this year.

It had taken Orion at least a few months to get in contact with Luke, but after Isla had fallen pregnant with the twins, Orion had finally taken that step and emailed him. Isla had been worried, desperately hoping that Luke would in fact want to get in contact and afraid that for all her confidence, he wouldn't.

Yet she needn't have worried. Luke was ecstatic to meet his father and the two had hit it off immediately, getting on like a house on fire. The relationship they'd built together over the past few years had healed the wound in Orion's heart, as had the birth of his children.

It had healed Isla too.

David would never be a father to her, but after she'd returned from Iceland with Orion, she'd realised she didn't want him to be. She had the acceptance and love she'd craved from her husband, and she didn't need it from him or from the board of Kendricks'.

Certainly she didn't need it after Orion bought Kendricks' and Isla became CEO. Orion had decided he was done with corporate raiding and wanted to try growing a company instead of taking it apart, and so he'd become her CFO instead, the two of them deciding to channel much of Kendricks' profits into charitable enterprises. Luke had even offered to design some special Christmas ornaments they could use as fundraising items.

Molly was kneeling in a sea of wrapping paper and demanding Luke's help with building the plastic brick spaceship that he'd given her for Christmas, and when he got off the couch to help her, Isla glanced up at her husband. Only to find him looking back, his wolf-gold eyes gleaming.

'You look happy, Snow White,' he said, the special smile he saved just for her playing around his mouth.

'Yes,' she said simply. 'I'm the happiest I've ever been.'

Orion's smile deepened into something so hot it could have melted all the ice in Iceland. 'That sounds like a challenge to me.'

Then he set about proving that, while she might be the happiest she'd ever been in that moment, there could be moments when she was even happier.

And as it turned out he was right.

* * * * *

COMING SOON!

We really hope you enjoyed reading this book.
If you're looking for more romance
be sure to head to the shops when
new books are available on

Thursday 21st December

To see which titles are coming soon, please visit

millsandboon.co.uk/nextmonth

MILLS & BOON

MILLS & BOON®

Coming next month

AN HEIR MADE IN HAWAII
Emmy Grayson

A dull roaring drowned out the sounds around her. Each beat of her heart felt magnified, thundering inside her body as Anika stared at him.

'What?' she finally managed to gasp.

'You want me. I want you.'

'I never said I wanted you,' she sputtered.

Nicholas watched her, his fingers pressing more firmly against her back, his eyes glowing with that same predatory light she'd glimpsed on the catamaran.

'You also never said you didn't. So tell me now, Anika. Tell me you haven't thought about me kissing you. Tell me,' he continued, his husky voice washing over her and sending sinful shivers racing over her body, 'you didn't think about how we'd be together when you were in my arms on the boat. That you didn't imagine me tracing my fingers, my lips, over every inch of your incredible body.'

Say something!

But she couldn't. Not when her imagination was conjuring up carnal images of her and Nicholas entwined, arms wrapped around each other as he trailed his lips over her neck, her breasts, his hips pressing against hers without any barriers between them.

'Ah.' His smile deepened. 'So you have thought about it.'

Continue reading
AN HEIR MADE IN HAWAII
Emmy Grayson

Available next month
www.millsandboon.co.uk

Copyright ©2023 by Emmy Grayson

OUT NOW!

Barbara
DUNLOP

Karen
BOOTH

Yvonne
LINDSAY

3
BOOKS
IN ONE

A CHRISTMAS
Seduction

Available at
millsandboon.co.uk

MILLS & BOON

OUT NOW!

3
BOOKS
IN ONE

Ami
WEAVER

Janice
MAYNARD

Yvonne
LINDSAY

CHRISTMAS
NIGHTS
with the Ex

Available at
millsandboon.co.uk

MILLS & BOON

OUT NOW!

3 BOOKS IN ONE

THE ITALIAN'S CHRISTMAS PASSION

SHARON KENDRICK   KATE HEWITT   CAROL MARINELLI

Available at
millsandboon.co.uk

MILLS & BOON

LET'S TALK

Romance

For exclusive extracts, competitions and special offers, find us online:

- **MillsandBoon**
- **@MillsandBoon**
- **@MillsandBoonUK**
- **@MillsandBoonUK**

Get in touch on 01413 063 232

For all the latest titles coming soon, visit
millsandboon.co.uk/nextmonth

MILLS & BOON

THE HEART OF ROMANCE

A ROMANCE FOR EVERY READER

MODERN

Prepare to be swept off your feet by sophisticated, sexy and seductive heroes, in some of the world's most glamourous and romantic locations, where power and passion collide.

HISTORICAL

Escape with historical heroes from time gone by. Whether your passion is for wicked Regency Rakes, muscled Vikings or rugged Highlanders, awaken the romance of the past.

MEDICAL

Set your pulse racing with dedicated, delectable doctors in the high-pressure world of medicine, where emotions run high and passion, comfort and love are the best medicine.

True Love

Celebrate true love with tender stories of heartfelt romance, from the rush of falling in love to the joy a new baby can bring, and a focus on the emotional heart of a relationship.

Desire

Indulge in secrets and scandal, intense drama and sizzling hot action with heroes who have it all: wealth, status, good looks... everything but the right woman.

HEROES

The excitement of a gripping thriller, with intense romance at its heart. Resourceful, true-to-life women and strong, fearless men face danger and desire - a killer combination!

To see which titles are coming soon, please visit

millsandboon.co.uk/nextmonth

MILLS & BOON
A ROMANCE FOR EVERY READER

- FREE delivery direct to your door
- EXCLUSIVE offers every month
- SAVE up to 30% on pre-paid subscriptions

SUBSCRIBE AND SAVE

millsandboon.co.uk/Subscribe